THE BEST
HORROR OF THE YEAR

VOLUME EIGHT

Also Edited by Ellen Datlow

THE BEST
HORROR OF THE YEAR

VOLUME EIGHT

EDITED BY ELLEN DATLOW

NIGHT SHADE BOOKS
NEW YORK

The Best Horror of the Year Volume Eight © 2016 by Ellen Datlow
The Best Horror of the Year Volume Eight © 2016 by Night Shade Books, an
imprint of Skyhorse Publishing, Inc.

Night Shade books may be purchased in bulk at special discounts for sales
promotion, corporate gifts, fund-raising, or educational purposes. Special
editions can also be created to specifications. For details, contact the Special Sales
Department, Night Shade Books, 307 West 36th Street, 11th Floor, New York,
NY 10018 or info@skyhorsepublishing.com.

Night Shade Books™ is a trademark of Skyhorse Publishing, Inc.®, a Delaware
corporation.

Visit our website at www.nightshadebooks.com.

10 9 8 7 6 5 4 3 2

Library of Congress Cataloging-in-Publication Data is available on file.

Interior layout and design by Amy Popovich
Cover art by Blake Malcerta

Print ISBN: 978–1-59780–853-8

Printed in the United States of America

ACKNOWLEDGMENTS

Thanks to Nathan Ballingrud, for your recommendation.

Thanks to all the publishers and editors who sent me material from 2015.

And thanks especially to Kristine Dikeman, my stalwart reader, and to my patient editor Jason Katzman.

TABLE OF CONTENTS

SUMMATION 2015

First, here are some numbers: There are twenty stories and novelettes in this year's volume. They were chosen from anthologies, print magazines, webzines, and single-author collections. Eleven of the contributors live in the United States, one lives in Canada, one in New Zealand, and seven in the United Kingdom.

Seven stories are written by women and thirteen by men. The authors of six stories have never appeared in previous volumes of my year's best. The longest story is 14,500 words, with the shortest being 500 words.

AWARDS

The Horror Writers Association announced the winners of the 2014 Bram Stoker Awards® on May 9, 2015, at the Marriott Marquis Hotel in Atlanta, Georgia. The presentations were made at a banquet held as the highlight of the combined Bram Stoker Awards Weekend with the 2014 World Horror Convention. The winners:

Superior Achievement in a Novel: *Blood Kin* by Steve Rasnic Tem (Solaris Books); Superior Achievement in a First Novel: *Mr. Wicker* by Maria Alexander (Raw Dog Screaming Press); Superior Achievement in a Young Adult Novel: *Phoenix Island* by John Dixon (Simon & Schuster/ Gallery Books); Superior Achievement in a Graphic Novel: *Bad Blood* by Jonathan Maberry (Dark Horse Books); Superior Achievement in Long Fiction: "Fishing for Dinosaurs" by Joe R. Lansdale *(Limbus, Inc., Book II,*

JournalStone); Superior Achievement in Short Fiction: "The Vaporization Enthalpy of a Peculiar Pakistani Family" by Usman T. Malik (*Qualia Nous*, Written Backwards) and "Ruminations" by Rena Mason (*Qualia Nous*, Written Backwards), tie; Superior Achievement in a Screenplay: *The Babadook* by Jennifer Kent (Causeway Films); Superior Achievement in an Anthology: *Fearful Symmetries* edited by Ellen Datlow (ChiZine Publications); Superior Achievement in a Fiction Collection: *Soft Apocalypses* by Lucy A. Snyder (Raw Dog Screaming Press); Superior Achievement in Non-Fiction: *Shooting Yourself in the Head for Fun and Profit: A Writer's Survival Guide* (Post Mortem Press); Superior Achievement in a Poetry Collection: *Forgiving Judas* by Tom Piccirilli (Crossroad Press).

The Specialty Press Award: ChiZine Publications, Canada.

The Richard Layman President's Award: Tom Calen, Brock Cooper, and Doug Murano.

The Silver Hammer Award: Rena Mason.

HWA introduced the Mentor Award "honoring writers who, through the Mentoring Program, provide excellent support to their mentees." Mentor of the Year went to Kathy Ptacek.

Life Achievement Awards: Jack Ketchum and Tanith Lee.

—◇—

The 2014 Shirley Jackson Awards were given out at Readercon on July 12, 2015, in Burlington, Massachusetts. Jurors were Andy Duncan, Nancy Holder, Livia Llewellyn, Simon Kurt Unsworth, and Kaaron Warren.

The winners were: Novel: *Annihilation* by Jeff VanderMeer (FSG Originals); Novella: *We Are All Completely Fine* by Daryl Gregory (Tachyon); Novelette: "The End of the End of Everything" by Dale Bailey (*Tor.com*, April 2014); Short Fiction: "The Dogs Home" by Alison Littlewood (*The Spectral Book of Horror Stories*, Spectral Press); Single-Author Collection: *Gifts for the One who Comes After* by Helen Marshall (ChiZine Publications); Edited Anthology: *Fearful Symmetries* edited by Ellen Datlow (ChiZine Publications).

The World Fantasy Awards were presented November 8, 2015, at a banquet held during the World Fantasy Convention in Saratoga Springs, New York. The Lifetime Achievement recipients, Sheri S. Tepper and Ramsey Campbell, were previously announced. The judges were Gemma Files, Nina Kiriki Hoffman, Bénédicte Lombardo, Bruce McAllister, and Robert Shearman.

Winners for the best work in 2014: Novel: *The Bone Clocks* by David Mitchell (Random House/Sceptre, UK); Novella: *We Are All Completely Fine* by Daryl Gregory (Tachyon Publications); Short Fiction: "Do You Like to Look at Monsters" by Scott Nicolay (Fedogan & Bremer chapbook); Anthology: *Monstrous Affections: An Anthology of Beastly Tales* edited by Kelly Link and Gavin J. Grant (Candlewick Press); Collection: *Gifts for the Ones That Come After* by Helen Marshall (ChiZine Publications) and *The Bitterwood Bible and Other Recountings* by Angela Slatter (Tartarus Press); Artist: Samuel Araya; Special Award, Professional: Sandra Kasturi and Brett Alexander Savory, for ChiZine Publications; Special Award, Non-Professional: Ray B. Russell and Rosalie Parker, for Tartarus Press.

NOTABLE NOVELS OF 2015

A Head Full of Ghosts by Paul Tremblay (William Morrow) is a terrific novel about a teenager who manifests symptoms of schizophrenia. Doctors are no help. Her desperate father consults a Catholic priest who, feeding the father's religious mania, believes the girl demonically possessed and pushes for an exorcism. A reality show is produced about the family and their troubles. The story is told mostly from the point of view of the eight-year-old younger sister who adores her sister but has some mental/emotional problems of her own, and because of this and her youth may not be the most reliable narrator. It's no coincidence that the younger of the two sisters is named Meredith, shortened to Merry (pace Merricat from *We Have Always Lived in the Castle*).

Dreams of Shreds and Tatters by Amanda Downum (Solaris) is about a woman who intuits through her nightmares that her best friend is in trouble, thousands of miles away. And she's correct. Her friend, a talented gay artist who finally found love in Vancouver, currently lies in a coma after his dabbling in sorcery brings forth something deadly pushing through to our world. The book effectively uses Lovecraftian and Robert Chambers Carcosian motifs to create a disturbing, dark urban fantasy.

Disintegration: A Windy City Dark Mystery by Richard Thomas (Alibi) is a gritty modern noir about a very broken hired killer determined to bring down the rest of the world with him. Dark, vicious, and fast-moving.

The Dead Lands by Benjamin Percy (Grand Central)—in which the author takes on the dystopian science fiction subgenre, with all its attendant horrors—is better than his earlier, pedantic take on the werewolf novel, but not good enough to stand out from the crowd.

Finders Keepers by Stephen King (Scribner) is terrific. I haven't been keeping up with King's novel output for a while so hadn't realized this book is a sequel to 2014's *Mr. Mercedes*, which I've not read. But that matters not. A novelist retires after writing a bestselling literary trilogy. The final book ends unsatisfactorily for at least one reader—a psychopath. There are rumors of a sequel and the unhinged reader wants to read that manuscript—at any cost, setting off a tense, terrifying series of events. This is a great novel about obsession and a writer's responsibility to his readers.

A Song of Shadows by John Connolly (Atria Books/Emily Bestler Books) is a strong entry in the author's Charlie Parker novel series. Parker is in a small Maine town, recuperating from serious wounds sustained at the climax of the previous book. But even so, he can't help but get involved when a man's body is washed up on the beach in front of his rental house. What ensues is a twisted plot originating in a Nazi concentration camp during WWII. The series is not only exceedingly dark, but there's always a whiff of the supernatural surrounding each book.

The Library at Mount Char by Scott Hawkins (Crown) is an utterly refreshing debut about gods as monsters. A young woman who, along with several other neighborhood children, was plucked from a normal life when they were all orphaned in one destructive event is raised by a mysterious man who becomes their demanding "father." Whenever the reader is certain of what comes next, the plot veers wildly into a different, perfectly controlled direction. This is especially evident about three quarters of the way in, when the story seems to be over. It's not. A fabulous, exceedingly dark fantasy about the monstrosity of gods. By turns funny and horrifying, it hits every mark. While I don't want to oversell it, this is the finest, most satisfying dark novel I've read in 2015.

Crooked by Austin Grossman (Mullholland) is about a public figure I thought I'd never willingly read about: Richard Nixon. What else but occult interference could possibly explain Tricky Dick's political career? In this brilliant alternate history, Nixon's still a jerk, but is almost heroic in his confusion and paranoia, as he's caught up in a terrifying web of occult conspiracy far worse than the "Red Scare." This is an entertaining tour-de-force of Lovecraftian horror mixed with Cold War politics.

Carter and Lovecraft by Jonathan L. Howard (Thomas Dunne Books) is a clever Lovecraftian novel about a former detective traumatized by his last case. He inherits a bookstore in Providence from a total stranger but that bookstore is run by the last known descendant of H. P. Lovecraft—a young African American woman who chafes at suddenly acquiring a new boss. But when people start dying horribly, Daniel Carter and Emily Lovecraft are pulled into a terrible vortex of evil.

Experimental Film by Gemma Files (CZP) is a great example of one of my favorite types of weird dark fiction: secrets behind movies and movie-making. A former film teacher, suffering from depression and anxiety as a result of dealing with an autistic child, is pulled into a mystery that becomes more and more dangerous to her and those around her. The novel's about so much: gods and what they require in their worship, the difference between looking and seeing—and knowing when to look away. The danger of obsession. Wonderfully creepy. One of the best of the year.

The Devil's Detective by Simon Kurt Unsworth (Doubleday) is an intriguing first novel about an "Information Man" of Hell, assigned the task of investigating a murder more brutal than the usual crimes taking place in the underworld. But as he maneuvers among demons, Hell's bureaucrats, humans, and the Angels who regularly deliver redemption to Hell's denizens, Thomas Fool comes to discover that he's being used, but by whom/what? A good read, despite a conclusion that doesn't really satisfy.

ALSO NOTED

Killing Pretty by Richard Kadrey (HarperVoyager) is Sandman Slim's seventh outing, at the start of which Stark, a Nephilim who's been in and out of Hell several times—now living in Los Angeles—is persuaded to hunt the murderer of Death, who showed up in human form at the end of *The Getaway God* with his heart torn out. *The Damned* by Andrew Pyper (Simon & Schuster) about a man haunted by his psychopathic twin. *Within These Walls* by Ania Ahlborn (Gallery) is about a true crime writer seduced by an imprisoned cult leader into writing of a murder, about which the killer promises to reveal all after remaining silent for thirty years. *Brother*, also by Ahlborn (Gallery) is about a young man trying to escape the murderous habits of his family. *Dawn of the Dead* by George A. Romero and Susanna Sparrow (Gallery Books) is a reissue of the novel originally published in 1974, with an introduction by Simon Pegg. *The Scarlet Gospels* by Clive Barker (St. Martin's Press) features supernatural detective Harry L'Amour, who, when hired to clean out a dead man's secret rooms in New Orleans, finds a lot more than he bargained for. If you want to know what happens to Pinhead, you might like this a lot. If you haven't read many of Barker's novels, this likely isn't the one with which to start. *The Fifth House of the Heart* by Ben Tripp (Gallery) is a vampire novel with enough additions and variations on the trope to raise it above the usual. Sax, a cowardly antiques dealer, has acquired great wealth in his youth by stealing hoards owned by vampires. Now his past is catching up with him as those he's stolen from are hunting him down. Sax's repeated insistence upon his cowardice gets tired quickly, but still overall a very readable book. *Damage Done* by Amanda Panitch (Random House) is a psychological suspense novel about a twin desperately trying to escape the stigma of her mass-murdering brother. The book tried a bit too hard to be a *Gone Girl* for teens. *Point Hollow* by Rio Youers (CZP) is about a man returning to his supposedly idyllic hometown after his marriage fails, in an attempt to jog old memories loose. *The Night Clock* by Paul Meloy (Solaris) is an inventive and intriguing dark fantasy about a time and place that exists just beyond the one we know. However, this first novel doesn't quite come off because of a muddle of too many characters, some introduced for the first time in the last pages. *Lord Byron's Prophecy* by Sean Eads (Lethe Press) is a dark fantasy that shifts between the past of Lord Byron and his circle of friends and the present of a professor and his son—all three plagued by psychological demons and linked by their disturbing visions. *The Consultant* by Bentley Little (Cemetery Dance) is a dark satire about an awful guy brought in to streamline a troubled company's operations. *Mr. Suicide* by Nicole Cushing (Word Horde) is about an abused and disaffected child evolving into a lunatic. *The Subterranean Season* by Dale Bailey (Underland Press)—When an ominous hole appears in a ne'er-do-well PhD student's office on a college campus obsessed with football, what could possibly go wrong? *The Glittering World* by Robert Levy (Gallery Books) is about the dangerous supernatural mysteries lurking in the past of a man returning with friends to sell his childhood home in Nova Scotia. *The Darkest Part of the Forest* by Holly Black (Little, Brown) is a dark young adult fairy tale. *The Deep* by Nick Cutter (Gallery) is about attempts to discover a cure for a plague decimating humankind. *Werewolf Cop* by Andrew Klavan (Pegasus) is about a cop cursed during his hunt for gangsters. *Submerged* by Thomas F. Monteleone (CD Publications) is a horror thriller about contemporary amateur divers who find a sunken Nazi submarine that carried a secret weapon. Christopher Golden has two new novels out: *Tin Men* (Ballantine), about a plot to take down the US by sabotaging the mechanical units on which an elite group of soldiers rely, and *Dead Ringers* (St. Martin's Press), about doppelgangers appearing out of nowhere. *Positive* (HarperVoyager) has David Wellington returning to zombies. *Vermilion: The Adventures of Lou Merriwether, Psychopomp* by Molly Tanzer (Word Horde) is a dark fantasy western about a young female gunslinger, whose job as Psychopomp is to keep San Francisco safe from ghosts, shades, and geung si (hopping vampires or zombies). *Necronomicon: The Manuscript of the Dead* by Antonis Antoniades (Hippocampus Press) is a fictionalized history of the ancient book so central to H. P. Lovecraft's mythos. *Last Night at the Blue Alice* by Mehitobel Wilson (Bedlam Press) is about a woman who must pass a test to get the job she wants: Psychopomp.

MAGAZINES, JOURNALS, AND WEBZINES

I believe it's important to recognize the work of the talented artists working in the field of fantastic fiction, both dark and light. The following artists created dark art that I thought especially noteworthy in 2015: Galen Dara, Nick Stathopoulos, George Cotronis, Ben Baldwin, Richard Wagner, Steve Gilberts, John Coulthart, Vincent Sammy, Jill Bauman, Neil Williams, Lynette Watters, Paul Lowe, Martin Hanford, Joachim Luetke, Steve Santiago, David Palumbo, Gary Nurrish, Kat Weaver, Gregory St. John, Stephen Mackey, Stacy Nguyen, John Jude Palencar, Elizabeth Leggett, Polly Rose Morris, Daniele Serra, Paul Lowe, Anna O'Brien, John Stanton, and Tara Bush.

Video Watchdog edited by Tim Lucas is a gem. It's erudite and entertaining, and with issue 179, the magazine celebrated its twenty-fifth anniversary. In addition to movie reviews and articles, the magazine runs a regular audio column by Douglas E. Winter, a book review column, and a regular column by Ramsey Campbell. There were three issues published during 2015, one of which had a major piece about "*Dr. Strangelove* at 50."

Rue Morgue edited by David Alexander is a Canadian nonfiction magazine for the horror movie aficionado. It's superficial but entertaining and has up-to-date information on most of the horror films being produced. The magazine includes interviews, articles, and lots of gory photographs, along with regular columns on books, horror music, and graphic novels.

BFS Horizons, all fiction, and *BFS Journal*, all nonfiction, are magazines given to members of the British Fantasy Society, and in 2015 they were edited by Sarah Newton and Ian Hunter.

The Green Book: Writings on Irish Gothic, Supernatural and Fantastic Literature edited by Brian J. Showers brought out two issues in 2015. There's a "lost tale" by Bram Stoker that hadn't been reprinted in almost 150 years, plus commentary on the story by David J. Skal; an article about early influences on Lafcadio Hearn, one about a letter praising Sheridan Le Fanu written by Robert Louis Stevenson; a reminiscence by Lord Dunsany on WWI; and other fascinating articles, interviews, and reviews.

Thinking Horror: A Journal of Horror Philosophy Volume 1 edited by S. J. Bagley debuted in 2015 and plans to focus on interviews and critical analyses of horror. The first issue had interviews with Michael Kelly, Nathan Ballingrud, Molly Tanzer, Simon Strantzas, Silvia Moreno-Garcia, and Nate Southard. Jeremy R. Smith works on creating "A General Theory of Horror" and Helen Marshall seeks the "Medieval in Twenty-first Century Literature." There are other interesting-looking articles in the first issue and although some of the pieces might be a bit too academic for general readers, it's a very promising enterprise.

Lovecraft Annual edited by S. T. Joshi (Hippocampus Press) is an invaluable resource for Lovecraftian scholarship accessible to the layperson. The 2015 edition is almost 230 pages and features papers, letters to and from Lovecraft, essays, and reviews.

Lovecraft eZine edited by Mike Davis specializes in new Lovecraftian fiction and poetry in print and online. During 2015 there were two issues, with notable fiction by Josh Wagner, Jon Padgett, Josh Reynolds, K. C. Grifant, and J. T Glover.

The Horror Zine edited by Jeani Rector is a long-running webzine regularly running horror fiction and poetry by established and new names. The site also has a news column, as well as book and film reviews.

Cemetery Dance edited by Richard Chizmar has been running behind schedule for awhile now, so some of the reviews and columns seem a bit dated (I have a regular book column) and two of the stories in the first 2015 issue were actually published first in *Cemetery Dance's* twenty-fifth anniversary anthology, *Turn Down the Lights.* That said, among the originals was a notable story by Stephen Bacon.

Black Static edited by Andy Cox has long been one of the best horror magazines in the field. In addition to fiction, the bi-monthly regularly includes interviews, book and movie reviews, and commentary by Lynda E. Rucker. In 2015 there were notable stories by Ralph Robert Moore, Simon Avery, Emily B. Cataneo, Tyler Keevil, Stephen Hargadon, Danny Rhodes, Priya Sharma, Steve Rasnic Tem, E. Catherine Tobler, Neil Williamson, Damien Angelica Walters, Kate Jonez, John Connelly, Sarah Read, James Van Pelt, Stephen Bacon, Andrew Hook, Thana Niveau, and Gary McMahon. The Jonez story ("All the Day You'll Have Good Luck") is reprinted herein.

Supernatural Tales edited by David Longhorn is an excellent digest-sized magazine that runs consistently good fiction and also includes reviews. Two issues were published in 2015 and featured notably creepy stories by Steve Duffy, Adam Golaski, Lynda E. Rucker, Mark Valentine, Jane Read, Jeremy Schliewe, Tom Johnstone, Rosalie Parker, and Helen Grant.

The Dark edited by Jack Fisher and Sean Wallace is a quarterly fiction webzine devoted to dark fantasy, although there are occasionally stories that flow into horror. In 2015 there were strong dark stories by Lisa L. Hannett, Kevin McNeil, Cassandra Khaw, Kristy Logan, Megan Arkenberg, Angela Slatter, and Michael Wehunt.

Nightmare Magazine edited by John Joseph Adams publishes online monthly and by email subscription. Each issue includes two original and two reprinted stories plus nonfiction. Following their successful special Kickstarter-funded *Women Destroy Horror* published in 2014, with fiction edited by Ellen Datlow, there was a special *Queers Destroy Horror* October issue with fiction edited by Wendy N. Wagner. During the year there were notable stories by Megan Arkenberg, Maria Dahvana Headley, Kat Howard, Matthew Kressel, Alison Littlewood, Carmen Maria Machado, Karen Munro, Nate

Southard, and Dale Bailey. The Bailey ("Snow") and Machado ("Descent") stories are reprinted herein.

Cyäegha edited by Graeme Phillips is a horror and weird zine. There were two issues out in 2015. The first was #13, co-edited by D. H. Tyrer, which took the King in Yellow as its theme. The second was #14, which was dedicated to work in translation and co-edited by Jaap Boekestein and Marcel Orie.

Dark Discoveries edited by Aaron J. French published two issues in 2015. The magazine includes fiction, interviews, and reviews. The nonfiction is always good but the fiction is uneven.

Mixed-genre Magazines

Not One of Us edited by John Benson is one of the longest-running small press magazines. It's published twice a year and contains weird and dark fiction and poetry. In addition, Benson puts out an annual "one-off" on a specific theme. The theme for 2015 was "The Long and the Short and the Tall." There was notable fiction and poetry by Patricia Russo, Sonya Taaffe, and J. C. Runofson. *The Magazine of Fantasy and Science Fiction* edited by Charles Coleman Finlay mostly publishes science fiction and fantasy but occasionally has terrific horror stories. In 2015 there was notable horror by Bud Webster, Albert E. Cowdrey, Dale Bailey, Bo Balder, Sadie Bruce, Dennis Etchison, David Gerrold, Maria Dahvana Headley, Kat Howard, Alice Sola Kim, Bruce McAllister, and Tamsyn Muir. *Lady Churchill's Rosebud Wristlet* edited by Gavin J. Grant and Kelly Link (with Michael J. DeLuca guest editing #33) is an irregularly published small press zine. In 2015, it published notable dark tales by Carmen Maria Machado, Alyc Helms, and J. M. McDermott. *SQ Magazine* edited by Sophie Yorkston and Gerry Huntsman is a webzine from Australia. It published notable dark fiction by Eric Guignard, Michelle Jager, S. G. Larner, Gary McMahon, and Jason Nahrung. *Uncanny Magazine* edited by Lynne M. Thomas is a webzine that refers to what it publishes as science fiction and fantasy, but contains a generous helping of dark, sometimes horrific stories. The site has notable dark fiction by Sofia Samatar, Mary Robinette Kowal, Ursula Vernon, Emily Devenport, and Samuel J. Miller. *Tor.com* (for which I acquire short fiction) publishes science fiction, fantasy, and horror. In 2015, there were notable dark stories on the site by Bruce McAllister, Lucy Taylor, Jeffrey Ford, and Priya Sharma. The Sharma story ("Fabulous Beasts") is reprinted herein. There are a host of magazines that only rarely publish stories dark enough to consider horror, but I recommend you check them out if you're open to reading other types of fiction in addition to horror. *Mythic Delirium* edited by Mike Allen, which published notable dark work by Beth Cato and Sunny Moraine. *Bourbon Penn* edited by Erik Secker published a notable dark story by H. Andrew Lynch. *On Spec*, Canada's best known genre magazine, is published quarterly by a revolving committee of volunteers since 1989. The most recent issue included notable darker stories by Tyler Keevil and Aliya Whitley. *Phobos* is a magazine of weird fiction edited by Robert M. Corry and Luke St. Germaine. Issue Three had good dark stories by A. C. Wise, Andrea Bradley, and Adam Halterman. *Conjunctions* edited by Bradford Morrow had good dark fiction by Sequoia Nagamatsu, China Miéville, and Matthew Baker. Others are *Clarkesworld* edited by Neil Clarke, *Strange Horizons* edited by Niall Harrison, *Space & Time* edited by Hildy Silverman, *Tin House* edited by Rob Spillman, *Granta* edited by Sigrid Rausing, *Interfictions* published online twice yearly and edited by a revolving group of editors, and *McSweeney's* edited by Timothy McSweeney.

ANTHOLOGIES

The Library of the Dead edited by Michael Bailey (Written Backwards) has a framing story about a library within a mausoleum in Oakland, California. Each story is about someone whose ashes are interred there. There are fifteen original stories by a variety of horror writers—each illustrated by GAK—with notable stories by Norman Partridge, Roberta Lannes, and Michael McBride.

Seize the Night edited by Christopher Golden (Gallery Books) is a strong vampire anthology of twenty-three stories. The stories that most impressed me were by Laird Barron, Kelley Armstrong, Rio Youers, John Langan, Dana Cameron, Robert Shearman, Lucy A. Snyder, Gary A. Braunbeck, Michael Koryata, Seanan McGuire, and a collaboration by Dan Chaon and Lynda Barry. The Armstrong ("We Are All Monsters Here") and Barron ("In a Cavern, In a Canyon") stories are reprinted herein.

October Dreams II: A Celebration of Halloween edited by Richard Chizmar and Robert Morrish (Cemetery Dance Publications) is a hefty volume of stories (some new, some reprinted), personal memories of Halloween, and essays about the history of Halloween. There was notable original fiction by Gemma Files, Ian McDowell, Stephen Graham Jones, Roberta Lannes, Alison Littlewood, Bev Vincent, and Tina Callaghan. The Jones story ("Universal Horror") is reprinted herein.

The 2nd Spectral Book of Horror Stories edited by Mark Morris (Spectral Press) is a solid, non-theme horror anthology of nineteen original stories. Most of the stories were very good.

Creeping Crawlers edited by Allen Ashley (Shadow Publishing) has nineteen stories (all but one being originals) about weird and horrific insects, arachnids, arthropods, crustaceans, and other crawling creatures that we fear. There are notable stories by Adrian Cole, Mark Howard Jones, David Birch, Ralph Robert Moore, and David Turnbull.

Horrorology: A Lexicon of Fear edited by Stephen Jones (Jo Fletcher Books) features twelve stories and novellas, the strongest by Kim Newman, Lisa Tuttle, Robert Shearman, Angela Slatter, Michael Marshall Smith, and Pat Cadigan. The cover art and illustrations were all created by Clive Barker.

Edge of Sundown: Tales of Horror in the Wild West edited by Kevin Ross and Brian M. Sammons (Chaosium) is an original anthology of nineteen stories. Notable stories by Silvia Moreno-Garcia, Eric Red, and John Shirley.

Mark of the Beast: A Collection of Werewolf Stories edited by Scott David Aniolowski (Chaosium, Inc.) features twenty-nine stories (all but one being originals). There are notable stories by Lois Gresh, T. E. Grau, Eric J. Guignard, and Rebecca L. Brown.

Cassilda's Song: Tales Inspired by Robert W. Chambers' King in Yellow Mythos edited by Joseph S. Pulver Sr. (Chaosium Inc.) follows up on Pulver's 2012 anthology, *A Season in Carcosa*. This time around there are eighteen new stories, all by women. There are notable stories by Mercedes M. Yardley, Molly Tanzer, Selena Chambers, Anya Martin, Helen Marshall, Lucy A. Snyder, and Maura McHugh.

Midian Unmade edited by Joseph Nassise and Del Howison (Tor) contains twenty-three stories set in the world of Clive Barker's *Nightbreed*. Unfortunately, few of the stories work without some knowledge of Barker's novella *Cabal*, or the movie made from it, *Nightbreed*. Some stories stand out from the pack: Weston Ochse, Ian Rogers, Christopher Monfette, and Brian Craddock.

The Eleventh Book of Black Horror edited by Charles Black (Mortbury Press) is, with fourteen original stories, a strong entry in this long-running horror series. There are notable stories by Stephen Bacon, John Forth, Tom Johnstone, Sam Dawson, and David Williamson. The Johnstone ("Slaughtered Lamb") and Bacon ("Lord of the Sand") stories are reprinted herein.

Inhuman edited by Allen Koszowski debuted in 2004 with the intention of being a regularly published magazine, but has never able to keep to a schedule. Issue #6, published in 2015, was the first appearance of the publication since 2011, so I'm treating it more like an anthology than a periodical. If you're into old-fashioned pulp and tentacles, this is the magazine for you. It's profusely illustrated by its artist-editor and contains mostly original fiction with a few reprints.

Snowbound with Zombies: Tales of the Supernatural Inspired by the Life & Work of John Greenleaf Whittier edited by David Goudsward (Post Mortem Press) is an anthology whose intent is to benefit the Whittier Birthplace Museum. The volume includes twenty-two stories, with eight reprints (including one by Whittier himself). It also includes an afterword by Faye Ringel discussing Whittier as a collector of supernatural folk tales.

Shrieks and Shivers from the Horror Zine edited by Jeani Rector (Post Mortem Press) features thirty-one tales of horror fiction by a variety of writers including Elizabeth Massie, P. D. Cacek, Lisa Morton, William F. Nolan, Ray Garton, and Tom Piccirilli. The best story is a western horror tale by newcomer Gary Robbe. Although the volume is non-thematic, for some reason John Russo has been roped into providing a brief introduction about the zombie movies he's written, almost as if it's intended for a different book.

Expiration Date edited by Nancy Kilpatrick (Edge) includes twenty-five all-new stories about death and dying. The strongest is by Tobin Elliott, and two collaborations, one by Judith and Garfield Reeves-Stevens and the second by Steve Rasnic Tem and Melanie Tem.

Nightmares Unhinged: Twenty Tales of Terror edited by Joshua Viola (Hex Publishers) features nineteen unthemed original stories and one reprint, with the publisher/co-editor including three of his own stories and two others co-written by him. Despite this, there are notable stories by Keith Ferrell, Steve Rasnic Tem, Stephen Graham Jones, Dustin Carpenter, and Edward Bryant.

Sharkpunk edited by Jonathan Green (Snowbooks) is—despite the wretched title (can anthologists please stop with the "punk" suffix?)—pretty good, featuring twenty new stories about killer sharks. The best stories are by Den Patrick, Ian Whates, Amy and Andy Taylor, Richard Salter, Jenni Hill, Steven Savile, and Gary McMahon.

Eulogies III edited by Christopher Jones, Nanci Kalanta, and Tony Tremblay (HW Press) is a non-theme horror anthology with thirteen stories, all but one being originals. Each story has an interior illustration by Keith Minnion and includes an introduction by Robert Dunbar. The best stories are by Bracken MacLeod, Matt Moore, Elizabeth Massie, Chet Williamson, Paula D. Ashe, and Brian Hodge.

Aickman's Heirs edited by Simon Strantzas (Undertow Publications) is a varied tribute volume to the late great creator of eerie, quiet horror: Robert Aickman. In the book are fifteen stories stories of the weird. All the stories are good, but for me the strongest are by John Langan, Malcolm Devlin, and Nadia Bulkin. The Langan story ("Underground Economy") is reprinted herein.

Dark Screams Volume Three edited by Brian James Freeman and Richard Chizmar (Hydra) is a mini eBook-only anthology of five short horror stories, one a reprint. The best are by Brian Hodge and Jack Ketchum.

Terror Tales of the Scottish Highlands edited by Paul Finch (Gray Friar Press) is a weaker entry than usual in the series, with more than its fair share of mopy pairs of siblings or couples going off the meet bad ends during unwise explorations. Of the fifteen new stories (one being a reprint), the strongest were by Barbara Roden, Carole Johnstone, Ian Hunter, Craig Herbertson, Tom Johnstone, and D. P. Watt. The editor provides interstitial material between each tale.

Terror Tales of the Ocean edited by Paul Finch (Gray Friar Press) has thirteen stories, four reprints, and interstitial material between each story. The strongest of the new stories are those by Adam Nevill, Robert Shearman, Conrad Williams, Stephen Laws, and Lynda E. Rucker. The Nevill story ("Hippocampus") is reprinted herein.

The Blumhouse Book of Nightmares: The Haunted City presented by Jason Blum (Blumhouse Books/Doubleday) is an all-original anthology of sixteen dark stories about cities, edited by a producer of horror movies and written mostly by Hollywood types. Despite the lack of variety, there are notable stories by Sarah Langan, Nissar Modi, Dana Stevens, and Eli Roth.

Death's Realm edited by Anthony Rivera and Sharon Lawson (Grey Matter Press) features sixteen original stories about death and dying. There are notable stories by Rhoads Brazos, John C. Foster, and Aaron Polson.

The Big Bad II edited by John G. Hartness and Emily Lavin Leverett (Dark Oak Press) contains twenty-four original stories about bad guys. Included are notable stories by Gail Z. Martin, Jason Corner, and Edmund R. Schubert.

Flesh Like Smoke edited by Brian M. Sammons (April Moon) is an anthology of sixteen stories about transformation, mostly into werewolves. Good stories by Darrell Schweitzer, Scott R. Jones, and Cody Goodfellow.

Giallo Fantastique edited by Ross E. Lockhart (Word Horde) is an all-original anthology of twelve stories inspired by the stylized, violent, often grisly Italian crime/horror movies by Dario Argenti, Mario Bava, and Lucio Fulci. All the stories are worth reading, but my favorites were by Ennis Drake, E. Catherine Tobler, and Orrin Grey.

Blood Sisters edited by Paula Guran (Night Shade) is a reprint anthology of twenty-five vampire stories by women. Included are writers such as Nalo Hopkinson, Pat Cadigan, Tanith Lee, Storm Constantine, Laurell K. Hamilton, and Chelsea Quinn Yarbro.

The Monstrous edited by Ellen Datlow (Tachyon Publications) is a reprint anthology (with one original by John Langan) of twenty stories about what makes a monster, human or otherwise. It includes stories by Peter Straub, Kim Newman, Jeffrey Ford, Sofia Samatar, Christopher Fowler, Gemma Files, and others, with illustrations throughout.

The Humanity of Monsters edited by Michael Morrison (ChiZine) contains twenty-six reprints, with no stories overlapping with *The Monstrous*. There are stories by Catherynne M. Valente, Neil Gaiman, Kij Johnson, Nathan Ballingrud, and others.

Better Weird: A Tribute to David B. Silva edited by Richard Chizmar, Brian James Freeman, and Paul F. Olson (Cemetery Dance) is a lovingly produced anthology of original and reprinted stories in honor of the writer, editor, and publisher. Each story is graced by a remembrance of Silva. The best of the originals is by Bentley Little.

The Doll Collection edited by Ellen Datlow (Tor) contains seventeen original horror and dark fantasy stories about dolls of all types. Illustrated throughout with photos taken by Datlow, Ellen Klages, and Richard Bowes.

Darkest Minds edited by Ross Warren and Anthony Watson (Dark Minds Press) features twelve stories (all but one being originals) about crossing borders. I'm not convinced the theme works, but there are strong stories by Stephen Bacon, Tracy Fahey, Robert Mammone, Tom Johnstone, and David Surface.

Wild Things: Thirteen Tales of Therianthropy edited by Steve J. Shaw (Black Shuck Books) has mostly original stories of shape shifting. There's one excellent new story by Rachel Halsell.

In the Shadow of Edgar Allan Poe: Classic Tales of Horror 1816–1914 edited by Leslie S. Klinger (Pegasus Books) begins with E. T. A. Hoffman's "The Sandman," but moves into a more gothic selection of twenty stories.

Dark City: A Novella Collection by Brian Hodge and Gerard Houarner (Necro Publications) is a beautiful trade paperback with three original novellas, two by Houarner and one by Hodge.

Daughters of Inanna edited by Brian Keene (Thunderstorm Books) features horror novellas by Livia Llewellyn, Chesya Burke, Amber Fallon, and Rachel Deering, with an introduction by Brian Keene.

⬥

There were a plethora of original and reprint anthologies full of stories influenced by the works of H. P. Lovecraft that were released in 2015.

Whispers in the Dark edited by Scott Harrison (Snowbooks) contains novellas by Thana Niveau, Johnny Mains, and Alison Littlewood, each influenced by Lovecraft and taking place during a different period in time.

Whispers from the Abyss: The Horrors That Are and Shall Be edited by Kat Rocha (01 Publishing) has twenty-five stories inspired by Lovecraft. The best are by Laird Barron, John Palisano, Cody Goodfellow, and Jonathan Sharp.

That Is Not Dead: Tales of the Cthulhu Mythos through the Centuries edited by Darrell Schweitzer (PS Publishing) has fourteen new historical takes of

Lovecraftian lore. There are notable stories by S. T. Joshi, John R. Fultz, W. H. Pugmire, and Lois H. Gresh.

She Walks in Shadows edited by Silvia Moreno-Garcia and Paula R. Stiles (Innsmouth Free Press) features twenty-five original Lovecraftian stories by women, interspersed with ten black and white illustrations by different artists. The strongest stories were by Gemma Files, Amelia Gorman, Arnaud de Vallois, E. Catherine Tobler, Pandora Hope, Sharon Mock, Rodopi Sisamis, Nadia Bulkin, Angela Slatter, and Jilly Dreadful.

Dreams from the Witch House: Female Voices of Lovecraftian Horror edited by Lynne Jamneck (Dark Regions Press) consists of twenty stories, three being previously published, with strong work by Gemma Files, Storm Constantine, R. A. Kaelin, Amanda Downum, Marly Youmans, Karen Heuler, Molly Tanzer, Sonya Taaffe, and Tamsyn Muir. The Muir story ("The Woman in the Hill") is reprinted herein.

Resonator: New Lovecraftian Tales from Beyond edited by Scott R. Jones (Martian Migraine Press) has seventeen stories inspired by H. P. Lovecraft's story "From Beyond," about the Tillinghast Resonator, a machine that stimulates dormant senses to bad effect. The theme's somewhat narrow in inspiration, preventing the contributors from really taking off on it, but there are notable stories by Scott Nicolay, Christopher Slatsky, and Orrin Grey.

Beyond the Mountains of Madness edited by Robert M. Price (Celaeno Press) has fourteen stories (all but two being originals), all intended to be sequels to H. P. Lovecraft's *At the Mountains of Madness*. One reprint, written in 1927 by John Martin Leahy, is thought to be the inspiration for Lovecraft's classic novella. There are notable stories by Stephen Mark Rainey, Edward Morris, Pierre V. Comtois, Laurence J. Cornford, Cody Goodfellow, C. J. Henderson, and Brian M. Sammons.

The Outsiders edited by Joe Mynhardt (Crystal Lake Publishing) is a shared-world anthology with a Lovecraftian cult at its center. The five British writers do an okay job with what they're given—the best stories are by V. K. Leslie and Rosanne Rabinowitz.

Cthulhu Fhtagn! edited by Ross E. Lockhart (Word Horde) features nineteen original stories inspired by H. P. Lovecraft. The strongest are by Ann K. Schwader, Laird Barron, Cody Goodfellow, and a collaboration by Molly Tanzer and Jesse Bullington.

The Madness of Cthulhu, Volume Two edited by S. T. Joshi (Titan) is an all-original anthology of fourteen varied new stories inspired by Lovecraft. The strongest are by Laird Barron, Jonathan Maberry, Donald Tyson, Jason C. Eckhardt, Karen Haber, and Steve Rasnic Tem.

Black Wings IV: New Tales of Lovecraftian Horror edited by S. T. Joshi (PS) is disappointing compared to the earlier volumes. The seventeen stories and one poem are mostly pastiches, something I admittedly dislike, but there's notable fiction by Caitlín R. Kiernan and Simon Strantzas.

Shadows over Main Street edited by Doug Murano and D. Alexander Ward (Hazardous Press) features twenty-two stories on the theme of Lovecraftian horror taking place in small towns (one story is a reprint). Although a few stories border on the silly, there's notable work by Lisa Morton, Josh Malerman, Richard Thomas, Nick Mamatas, Lucy A. Snyder, Stephanie Wytovich, and Brian Hodge, with a foreword by Ramsey Campbell. The book is nicely illustrated by Galen Dara, Vincent Chong, John Coulthart, Paul Carrick, and HagCult. The Hodge ("This Stagnant Breath of Change") and Wytovich (The 21st Century Shadow") stories are reprinted here.

The Gods of H. P. Lovecraft edited by Aaron J. French (JournalStone) has twelve new stories, each featuring a deity created by Lovecraft. With interior illustrations by Paul Carrick, John Coulthart, and Steve Santiago, plus commentary on each god by Donald Tyson. The strongest stories are by Joe R. Lansdale, Seanan McGuire, Jonathan Maberry, and Laird Barron.

Innsmouth Nightmares edited by Lois H. Gresh (PS Publishing) is a handsome hardcover with great cover art by Ben Baldwin. It has twenty-one stories (all but one being originals), and while forcing contributors to stick with the Innsmouth theme is a bit narrow, there are strong stories by Donald Tyson, Nancy Holder, Laird Barron, Nancy Kilpatrick, John Langan, Lisa Morton, and Steve Rasnic Tem. The Tem story ("Between the Pilings") is reprinted herein.

Cthulhu: Deep Down Under edited by Christopher Sequeira and Bryce Stevens (Horror Australis) is an Australian anthology of twenty-four stories (six reprints) written in Lovecraft's mythos. Each story features a colored plate illustrated by a different Australian artist. There are notable stories by Jason Franks, Bill Congreve, Jason Fischer, and Aaron Sterns, with an introduction by Ramsey Campbell.

MIXED-GENRE ANTHOLOGIES

Exigencies edited by Richard Thomas (Dark House Press) is billed as neo-noir. While there are some very good stories here (all are original), a few lack the *juice*: the necessary hard-boiled aspect of the subgenre. Also, a couple of the stories don't fit into the mix, one of them science fiction (which isn't to say science fiction noir is impossible—this story just isn't it). The most impressive stories are by Letitia Trent, Jason Metz, and S. P. Johnson. The Trent story ("Wilderness") is reprinted herein. *Professor Challenger: New Worlds, Lost Places* edited by J. R. Campbell and Charles Prepolec (Edge) is an engaging, all-original anthology of ten new adventures about Sir Arthur Conan Doyle's scientist Professor George Edward Challenger. The best of the darker stories are by J. R. Campbell, Simon Kurt Unsworth, and Stephen Volk. *nEvermore: Tales of Murder, Mystery, and the Macabre* edited by Nancy Kilpatrick and Caro Soles (Edge) includes twenty-two original stories written in homage to Edgar Allan Poe. The strongest darker stories are by Michael Jecks, Richard Christian Matheson, Tanith Lee, and a collaboration by Carol Weekes and Michael Kelly. *Insert Title Here* edited by Tehani Wessely (Fablecroft Publishing) presents twenty-one original science fiction, fantasy, and dark fantasy stories. The best, darkest ones are by Joanne Anderton, Marianne de Pierres, Matthew J. Morrison, and Daniel Simpson. *XIII* edited by Mark Teppo (Underland Press) has twenty-eight stories and poems concerning transformation, a few of them dark. The best of those is by George Cotronis. Also quite good, but not all that dark, are stories by Richard Bowes and Rebecca Kuder. *Breakout PS #34/35* edited by Nick Gevers (PS Publishing) is an unthemed anthology of science fiction, fantasy, and horror with twenty-eight stories, all but one being new. The strongest horror stories are by Adrian Tchaikovsky, James Cooper, Emma Coleman, Simon Strantzas, and Kelly Barnhill. *Hanzai Japan* edited by Nick Mamatas and Masumi Washington (Haika Sora) is a mixed reprint and original anthology of science fiction, fantasy, and crime fiction, with a few of the stories quite dark. The strongest dark originals are by Chet Williamson, Violet LeVoit, and Naomi Hirahara. *Strange Tales V* edited by Rosalie Parker (Tartarus Press) is an unthemed anthology of seventeen weird and dark stories. The best of the darker ones are by David McGroarty, Andrew

Hook, L. S. Johnson, Elise Fornier Edie, Nathan Alling Long, Andrew Apter, Steve Rasnic Tem, and Tara Isabella Burton. *Gods, Memes and Monsters: A 21st Century Bestiary* edited by Heather J. Wood (Stone Skin Press) is an entertaining mix of over sixty entries, some of them horror. The best of the darker ones are by Erinn Dembo, Malcolm Devlin, and Dave Gross. *The Uncanny Reader: Stories from the Shadows* edited by Marjorie Sandor (St. Martin's Press/Griffin) includes thirty-one stories from around the world, including those from Egypt, Uruguay, Sweden, and Zambia. The stories were originally published between 1817 and 2013. *The Haunted Tropics: Caribbean Ghost Stories* edited by Martin Munro (The University of West Indies Press) contains fifteen mostly new stories about ghosts, but there's no horror in the book. *Nightscript I: An Anthology of Strange and Darksome Tales* edited by C. M. Muller (Chthonic Matter) is a very promising anthology debut of what's intended to be an annual, with content along the lines of *New Genre* and *Supernatural Tales* magazines. The first volume has twenty stories. There are notable ones by Patricia Lillie, Daniel Mills, David Surface, Charles Wilkinson, Clint Smith, Damien Angelica Walters, Ralph Robert Moore, and Jean Claude Smith. *Canada Noir* edited by Jean Lalamière and David Nickle (Exile) has twenty-two stories of crime, only a few actually fitting within the noir sub-genre. There are notable dark stories by Ada Hoffman, Patrick Fleming, and Keith Cadieux. *African Monsters* edited by Margrét Helgadóttir and Jo Thomas (Fox Spirit Books) is the second in a series of anthologies about monsters from around the world. This volume has sixteen dark fantasy and horror stories, two of them reprints, plus numerous illustrations. There are strong new stories by S. Lotz, Joe Vaz, Toby Bennett, David-Brenan de Burgh, Chikodili Emelumadu, and Vianne Ventor. *Soliloquy for Pan* edited by Mark Beech (Egaeus Press) brings together classic reprints and original stories, plus poems and essays about Pan. Although more weird and uncanny than horrific, there is some excellent dark fiction and poetry by D. P. Watt, Rosanne Rabinowitz, Martin Jones, Bethany Van Rijswijk, Lynda E. Rucker, and Stephen Clark. *Blurring the Line* edited by Marty Young (Cohesion Press) is an interesting mix of fiction and non-fiction, but I don't really get the theme. In any case, there are good horror stories by Lisa Morton, Kaaron Warren, Lisa L. Hannett, and Stephen Lloyd Wilson. *Legacy of the Reanimator: Chronicles of Dr. Herbert West* edited by Peter Rawlik and Brian M. Sammons (Chaosium

Press) presents eight stories and two round-robins about Lovecraft's mad scientist, resurrected and still up to the same mischief. *Romances of the White Day* (Sarob Press) is a mini-anthology of three weird tales by John Howard, Mark Valentine, and Ron Weighell. None of the three are very dark, but all are engagingly mysterious. *Ghostly* edited by Audrey Niffenegger (Simon & Schuster/Scribner) has sixteen reprinted ghost stories ranging in publication date from Poe to Gaiman, with illustrations by the editor. *Congregation of Innocents: Five Curious Tales* is a limited edition mini-anthology created in England upon the fiftieth anniversary of the death of Shirley Jackson. Two of the five stories—by Tom Fletcher and Richard Hirst—are notably dark. An introduction is included, written by Patrick McGrath. *The Burning Maiden 2: Where Literature Meets the Supernatural* edited by Greg Kisbaugh (Evileye Books) is a strong original anthology of sixteen stories and poems. However, not all the stories have supernatural elements, and one is science fiction. The editor also includes a story of his own in the book. The best of the horror stories are by Richard Chizmar, Ramsey Campbell, Orrin Grey, Molly Tanzer, and Paul Tremblay. *X-Files: Trust No One* edited by Jonathan Maberry (IDW Publishing) has fifteen new stories inspired by the classic (and now revived) television show. There were several best of the year anthologies published in 2015 that included horror, dark fantasy, and darkly weird material: *Best New Horror #26* edited by Stephen Jones (PS) overlapped with my own *Best of the Year* with one story; *Year's Best Weird Fiction Volume Two* edited by Kathe Koja and Michael Kelly (Undertow Books) overlapped my best of the year with one story; and *The Year's Best Dark Fantasy and Horror: 2015 Edition* edited by Paula Guran (Prime) overlapped on one story with my own and one story with *Year's Best Weird Fiction*.

COLLECTIONS

Night Music: Nocturnes Volume 2 by John Connolly (Atria Books/Emily Bestler Books) is an excellent second collection of thirteen supernatural tales by the Irish author of crime novels that are often imbued with the uncanny. There are five new stories, and one, "Razorshins," originally published in *Black Static* several months before the collection's publication, is especially good.

The Strangers by Robert Aickman (Tartarus Press) features five previously unpublished stories and one novella by the master of ghostly and weird stories. The volume also includes previously unpublished or uncollected nonfiction and poetry. The nonfiction ranges from movie and book reviews to an unpublished introduction to a ghost story anthology Aickman proposed, and an essay on the river Avon. This is a boon for Aickman aficionados.

Friends of the Dead by James Doig (Sarob Press) is a very good first collection featuring eight stories, originally published between 1998 and 2007. Included are two original stories.

Blood 20: Tales of Vampire Horror by Tanith Lee (Telos) is one of several collections that came out after her death. There are fifteen reprints and five previously unpublished stories in this volume. The other collections were *Dancing through the Fire: A Collection of Stories in Five Moves* (Fantastic Books) with seventeen stories and a poem and *Legenda Maris* (Immanion Press) with eleven stories.

Probably Monsters by Ray Cluley (ChiZine Publications) is a terrific debut by a writer who has been getting increasing and well-deserved attention in Great Britain (one story won the British Fantasy Award). These twenty stories showcase his broad range, including three new stories, one of which ("Indian Giver") is reprinted herein.

The Night Listener and Others by Chet Williamson (PS Publishing) is the author's second collection, with twenty-two short stories published between 1984 and 2015, two appearing for the first time. Several of the stories were nominated for awards, and a couple were reprinted in my *Best of the Year* anthologies. Richard Christian Matheson provides an introduction.

Awaiting Strange Gods by Darrell Schweitzer (Fedogan & Bremer) contains twenty-two Lovecraftian stories, one of them being an original. The stories were published mostly in anthologies and in a few journals and magazines.

Painted Monsters & Other Strange Beasts by Orrin Grey (Word Horde) is the author's entertaining second collection, with thirteen stories—most about monsters—three seeing their first publication. Includes an introduction by John Langan.

The Bazaar of Bad Dreams by Stephen King (Scribner) contains twenty stories and poems (a few new), with brief introductions to each by the author. Most but not all have supernatural elements.

The Sea of Blood by Reggie Oliver (Dark Renaissance Books) is a generous selection of twenty-one stories and novelettes from Oliver's six previous collections, with two original stories. It is a hefty trade paperback of almost four hundred pages of excellent weirdly dark horror fiction. A few of the stories appeared in *The Year's Best Fantasy and Horror* and in previous volumes of my *Best Horror of the Year* anthologies. One of the two new stories ("The Rooms Are High") is reprinted herein.

Hungry Celluloid by Frank Duffy (Dark Minds Press) is the author's third collection and has thirteen stories, more than half being originals.

The Annotated Poe by Edgar Allan Poe, edited by Kevin J. Hayes (Harvard/Belknap) contains in-depth notes alongside the tales and poems to elucidate Poe's sources, obscure words and passages, and literary, biographical, and historical allusions. Poe's various works are illustrated by a variety of artists.

A House of Hollow Wounds by Joseph S. Pulver Sr. (Hippocampus Press) is this weird and horror fiction stylist's fourth collection and includes over forty (mostly original) prose poems, vignettes, and stories filled with poetry. Oblique and often visionary, Pulver's work is not for everyone, but if you're interested in decadent, dark experimentation, check this out.

Sing Me Your Scars by Damien Angelica Walters (Apex Publications) is the first collection of this promising writer, with twenty stories, eight of them being originals. The title story is particularly good.

The Nameless Dark by T. E. Grau (Lethe Press) is the debut by another fresh voice. These fourteen stories, all published since 2011 (three of them new), show off the author's range. Includes an introduction by Nathan Ballingrud.

Cult of the Dead and Other Weird and Lovecraftian Tales by Lois Gresh (Hippocampus Press) features twenty stories published between 1994 and 2014 in various magazines and anthologies.

Halfway Down the Stairs by Gary A. Braunbeck (JournalStone) is a 600-plus page omnibus of this fine short story writer's work for the past twenty years.

Peripheral Visions: The Collected Ghost Stories by Robert Hood (Dark Phases) is a hefty overview of this Australian fantasist's forty-year career, containing forty-four stories covering 1986 to 2015, including three originals. The collection includes illustrations by Nick Stathopoulos.

In the City of Ghosts by Michael Chislett (Sarob Press) is a gorgeous looking collection of thirteen ghost stories set in a fictional London suburb. Two of the stories are originals.

Give Me These Moments Back by Mike Chinn (The Alchemy Press) contains eighteen very dark stories published since 2001 (two original to the collection) in various British anthologies and magazines.

Dancing Tuatara Press plans to publish several collections of British writer John S. Glasby's short fiction. *The Brooding City and Other Tales of the Cthulhu Mythos* is the first in the series by the prolific writer, who died in 2011. He was a fan of Lovecraft and wrote often within the mythos, but he also wrote weird fiction. Includes an introduction by John Pelan. *Beyond the Rim and Other Tales of Cosmic Horror*, also by Glasby, collects eight Lovecraftian pastiches (two never previously published). The press also published *The Broken Fang and Other Experiences of a Specialist in Spooks* by Uel Key, stories about a supernatural sleuth—bringing these stories back into print for the first time in eighty-five years. Edited and introduced by John Pelan.

A Confederacy of Horrors by James Robert Smith (Hippocampus) is a debut collection of twenty-five stories, nine original, with an afterword by Stephen Mark Rainey.

Dark Renaissance Books, run by Joe Morey, has been publishing weird and dark fantasy in limited as well as trade editions. *Carnacki: The Watcher at the Gate and Other Stories* by William Meikle is an entertaining volume of twelve pastiches, seven original, using the ghost finder character created by William Hope Hodgson. Includes illustrations by M. Wayne Miller. *Tales of Alhazred* by Donald Tyson features ten new stories about the "mad Arab" who supposedly wrote the infamous grimoires of the *Necronomicon*, used in so many Lovecraftian tales.

Hippocampus Press brought out a three-volume hardcover set of the *Collected Fiction of H. P. Lovecraft: A Variorum Edition* edited by S. T. Joshi. All three volumes contain text revised by Joshi as a result of thirty years of research. The first volume covers 1905–25, with the stories printed in chronological order. The second, 1926–30, presents stories published after Lovecraft's return to Providence after returning from New York City. The third covers 1931–36 and the stories and novellas he wrote during the last years of his life.

Black Ceremonies by Charles Black (Parallel Universe Publications) is the first collection by a writer better known for the editing of his horror anthology series, *The Black Books of Horror*. The volume contains thirteen stories, four of them originals.

The Mirrors by Nicole Cushing (Hippocampus Press) is the author's first full-length collection and has twenty stories, two of them originals.

Dark Tales from the Den by Dona Fox (James Ward Kirk Publishing) features eighteen stories in this debut collection.

Goat Mother and Others by Pierre V. Comtois (Chaosium) contains all of the author's Mythos fiction, with an introduction by Robert M. Price.

Southpaw Nights by Benjamin Blake (James Ward Kirk Fiction) presents almost seventy previously unpublished micro poems and prose pieces.

Sacrificing Virgins by John Everson (Samhain) features twenty-five stories (two original) originally published in magazines and anthologies since 1999.

Voices of the Damned by Barbie Wilde (SST Publications) is an illustrated volume of eleven stories (one original) of body horror. The illustrations are by several luminaries in the field of horror art, including Clive Barker, Ben Baldwin, Vincent Sammy, Daniele Serra, and others.

Mixed-genre Collections

The End of the End of Everything: Stories by Dale Bailey (Arche Press) features nine fantasy, dark fantasy, and horror stories that are as beautifully written as they are startling, with some of them reminiscent of Bradbury at his best. Even his apocalypses bring joy to the reader. *Apocalypse Girl Dreaming* by Jennifer Brozek (Evil Girlfriend Media) has eighteen reprints and two original tales that range from retold fairy tales and military fiction to the Lovecraftian. The reprints were mostly published in anthologies and a few magazines, and the book includes an introduction by Jody Lynn Nye. *Skein and Bone* by V. K. Leslie (Undertow Press) is an impressive debut collection of fourteen weird, often dark stories. Four of the stories are published for the first time. *The Finest Ass in the Universe* by Anna Tambour (Ticonderoga Publications) is the author's second collection, showcasing twenty-six weird and quirky science fiction, fantasy, and sometimes very dark stories. *Ghost Summer: Stories* by Tananarive Due (Prime Books) is the author's first short fiction collection. The fifteen science fiction, fantasy, and horror stories and a novella were originally published between 2000 and 2015, with one story appearing for the first time. *Dark Equinox and Other Tales of Lovecraftian Horror* by Ann K. Schwader (Hippocampus Press) is a collection of sixteen dark fantasy tales—four published for the first time—by a writer better known as a poet. *The Anniversary of Forever* by Joel Lane (The Swan River Press) is a posthumous collection of thirteen stories, three published for the first time. Melancholy and bleak, the weird, often dark stories in this slim, beautiful volume are a fitting coda to Lane's life's work. *Dominoes in Time* by Matthew Warner (Thunderstorm Books) is a collection of eighteen science fiction and horror stories published between 1998 and 2014. *Human Pieces* by James Cooper (PS Publishing) is this British author's third collection of dark crime fiction and horror. Cooper writes well about the underbelly of society, whether dealing with psychological or supernatural horror. The book includes thirteen stories and novelettes, five published for the first time. *Led Astray: The Best of Kelley Armstrong* (Tachyon) is a large overview of the author's work, most of which is supernatural fiction, with twenty-three stories, two of them originals. *Walkers with the Dawn* by Maurice Broaddus (BlackWyrm Publishing) features sixteen science fiction, fantasy, and horror stories, four of which are originals. Includes brief notes by the author on each story. *Dead Water and Other Weird Tales* by David A. Sutton (The Alchemy Press) is the second collection of the author, and is a wonderful mix of his work in science fiction, fantasy, horror, and the weird from 1976 through 2015 (with two original stories). *Bobby Owen, Black Magic, Bloodshed & Burglary: Selected Short Stories of E. R. Punshon* (Ramble House) is a collection of twenty-one stories published between 1898 and 1954 by an English horror and crime writer. Includes an introduction by Gavin O'Keefe. *Out Stack and Other Places* by Gary Couzens (Midnight Street Press) features eighteen fantasy and dark fantasy/horror stories (several published for the first time). Occasionally an idea trails off, never quite coming together as a story, leaving the reader unsatisfied, but at his best, Couzens's work is powerful. Includes an introduction by Andrew Hook. *Trigger Warning: Short Fiction and Disturbances* by Neil Gaiman (William Morrow/HarperCollins) has five poems and nineteen stories, including one original ("Black Dog"), which is reprinted herein. *Dreams of Ys and Other Invisible Worlds* by Jonathan Thomas (Hippocampus Press) is the fourth collection of stories by this writer, which are more weird than horrific. It includes nine stories (several original) and a "suite" of interconnected tales. *Darkling Incidence: Obscure Reflections* by K. M. Tonso (Nightscape Press) contains sixteen stories (four reprints), some of which are horrific. *Cherry Crow Children* by Deborah Kalin (Twelve Planets) is a collection of four powerful stories of dark fantasy and/or horror. *Let Me Tell You* by Shirley Jackson, edited by Laurence Jackson Hyman and Sarah Hyman DeWitt (Random House) contains previously unpublished and uncollected stories, essays, and other writings. A must-have for enthusiasts. *Gutshot* by Amelia Gray (Farrar, Straus and Giroux) is an intriguing collection of very brief, dark and strange tales. Only a few drift into horror territory, but the author is definitely one to watch. *Get in Trouble* by Kelly Link (Random House) is this brilliant writer's fourth collection. Only nine stories here, but each is a gem, and at least a few have horrific over- or undertones. *The Satyr and Other Tales* by Stephen J. Clark (The Swan River Press) reprints four novellas of the occult, with illustrations by the author. The title novella has been expanded and developed since its original publication in 2010. *November Night Tales* by Henry C. Mercer (The Swan River Press) reprints six weird tales from the original collection, published in 1928, plus one story published after the author's death in 1930. Includes an introduction by Peter Bell. *In the Gulfs of Dream and Other Lovecraftian Tales* by David Barker and W. H. Pugmire (Dark Renaissance Books) is a generous helping of twenty-six solo and collaborative Lovecraftian tales (mostly pastiches) written in the brazenly decadent style of the authors. Four of the stories (one a novella) are originals. Cover art, end papers, and frontispiece are by Erin Wells. *Tell No Lies* by John Grant (The Alchemy Press) was out in late 2014, and I missed it then. Includes twelve stories of science fiction, fantasy, and horror, all well-written and worth reading. The author doesn't write short fiction as much as he should. *Striking Fire* by Dirk Flinthart (Fablecroft Publishing) features twenty-one science fiction, fantasy, dark fantasy, and horror stories by this Tasmanian writer. Eight were published in 2015 for the first time and six of those first appear in this collection. *Falling in Love with Hominids* by Nalo Hopkinson (Tachyon) has eighteen stories published between 2002 and 2015, some of them quite dark, including the one original. *Make Something Up: Stories You Can't Unread* by Chuck Palahniuk (Doubleday) collects twenty-two stories and a novella by the infamous author of in-your-face fiction (but surprisingly, neither "Guts" nor "Hotpotting," two of his most horrific stories—reprinted in *The Year's Best Fantasy and Horror #18* and *19*, respectively). *The Bloody Tugboat and other Witcheries* by Robert H. Waugh (Hippocampus Press) includes twenty-five stories of weird and/or dark stories. All but three are originals. *You Have Never Been Here: New and Selected Stories* by Mary Rickert (Small Beer Press) is the second collection by this celebrated writer of fantasy and horror. It contains eleven stories and novellas, several of which won the Shirley Jackson and World Fantasy Award. One story is an original. *Three Moments of an Explosion* by China Miéville (Del Rey) contains twenty-eight science fiction, fantasy, and horror stories and vignettes by a writer best known for his weird novels mixing science fiction, fantasy, and horror. All of the included pieces are beautifully written and intriguing, even those that are lightweight. Several or the stories are originals. *New Avalon: Love and Loss in the City of Steam* by Neal F. Litherland (James Ward Kirk Publishing) is an interesting collection of ten stories of fantasy and dark fantasy about an imaginary city. *Monstrous Aftermath* by W. H. Pugmire (Hippocampus Press) features sixteen stories influenced by Lovecraft, Wilde, and Chambers but all in Pugmire's distinctive style. A treat for Pugmire's fans. *The Faster Redder Road: The Best Unamerican Stories of Stephen Graham Jones* by Stephen Graham Jones (University of New Mexico Press) does the author a disservice. Jones is a terrific writer of dark crime and horror fiction, but this volume is filled with novel excerpts and stories that can be found in other collections by the author. There are a few more mainstream stories from literary magazines not previously reprinted, but I'd wait for them to appear in a better retrospective than this one. Edited and with an introduction by Theodore C. Van Alst Jr. *Orpheus on the Underground and Other Stories* by Rhys Hughes (Tartarus Press) is another good-looking book from Tartarus Press. A terrific showcase for this quirky writer's weird fiction. Occasionally horrific, but more often . . . strange. All but one of the sixteen stories is an original, and the book includes illustrations by Chris Harrendence. *Music in the Bone and Other Stories* by Marian Pitman (The Alchemy Press) has twenty mixed-genre stories that originally appeared in magazines and anthologies. One original story is included. *Ghost Signs* by Sonya Taaffe (Aqueduct Press) is part of the Conversation Pieces series. Taaffe is better known as a poet than a prose writer, but she's proficient in both forms, as demonstrated in these thirty-six poems (two original) and one original story. *Insect Literature* by Lafcadio Hearn (The Swan River Press) is a gorgeous little illustrated hardcover reprinting twenty essays and stories about insects by the Irish-Greek writer who made his name in Japan, where he lived and died. An introductory essay by Anne-Sylvie Homassel is included. It's definitely a wonderful book to dip into. *Death's Sweet Echo* by Maynard Sims (Tickety Boo Press) collects thirteen ghost stories and strange tales. *Bastards of the Absolute* by Adam Cantwell (Egaeus Press) consists of eleven stories and novellas, illustrated by Charles Schneider and with an introduction by George Berguño. *Leinster Gardens and Other Subtleties* by Jan Edwards (The Alchemy Press) has fourteen stories, several of them about ghosts, with one original. Includes an introduction by David A. Sutton. *The Massacre of the Mermaids* by Alessandro Manzetti (Kipple) has six extremely dark stories of sf and horror, all translated into English for the first time. *American Nocturne* by Hank Schwaeble (Cohesion Press) has ten stories of dark fantasy, noir, and horror, with several of them being originals. Includes an introduction by Jonathan Maberry.

POETRY JOURNALS, WEBZINES, ANTHOLOGIES, AND COLLECTIONS

The 2015 Rhysling Anthology *The Best Science Fiction, Fantasy, and Horror Poetry of 2014*, selected by the Science Fiction Poetry Association and edited by Rich Rostow (Science Fiction Poetry Association/Hadrosaur Productions), is used by members to vote for the best short poem and the best long poem of the year. *Spectral Realms* edited by S. T. Joshi (Hippocampus Press) is a fine new showcase for weird and dark poetry. Two issues came out in 2015. In addition to original poems, there's a section with classic reprints and a review column. There were notable poems by Ann K. Schwader, Wade German, Gemma Files, K. A. Opperman, Michael Kelly, Jonathan Thomas, Ian Futter, Chad Hensley, Reiss McGuinness, and Stephanie M. Wytovich. *Star*Line* is the official quarterly newsletter of the Science Fiction Poetry Association. The journals regularly publish members' poetry. During 2015, there was notable dark work by Bruce Boston and Weronika Łaszkiewicz. *Resonance Dark and Light* by Bruce Boston (Eldritch Press) presents fifty-two poems of all genres. Four are published for the first time. *The Robot Scientist's Daughter* by Jeannine Hall Gailey (Mayapple Press), who writes gorgeous, impressive dark science fiction and fantasy poems about Oak Ridge, Tennessee (Atomic City), where she grew up and other places touched by nuclear activity. *Eden Underground* by Alessandro Manzetti (Crystal Lake Publishing) is an excellent collection of mostly new dark poetry by an Italian author of prose in addition to poetry. *The Crimson Tome* by K. A. Opperman (Hippocampus Press) is full of the dark gothic and cosmic weird, and most of the poems are previously unpublished. *The Book of Jade: A New Critical Edition* by Park Barnitz, compiled by David E. Schultz and Michael J. Abolafia (Hippocampus Press) contains the complete text of *The Book of Jade*, plus biographical and critical material about the decadent poet who killed himself at twenty-three in 1901. *The Acolyte* by Nancy Hightower (Port Yonder Press) is a volume of dark, modern takes on the Old and New Testaments, several published for the first time. *Dark Parchments: Midnight Curses and Verses* by Michael H. Hanson (MoonDream Press) is a haunting and lyrical collection of over eighty short poems, with a foreword by Janet Morris. *Dark Energies* by Ann Schwader (P'rea Press) is a welcome new collection by an excellent and consistent poet of the dark. Includes a preface by S. T. Joshi and an interview by Charles Lovecraft, with illustrations by David Schembri Studios. *An Exorcism of Angels* by Stephanie M. Wytovich (Raw Dog Screaming Press) presents almost 150 mostly tiny dark poems about love, loss, men, and women. *They* by Michael Tugendhat (James Ward Kirk Publishing) features about one hundred dark poems.

CHAPBOOKS

The Visible Filth by Nathan Ballingrud (This is Horror!) is a slowly building novella about an unambitious bartender who finds a cell phone left in the bar after a brawl. His decision to keep it sends him into a deadly tailspin. *The Home* by Tom Fletcher (Nightjar Press) is a vignette that reminds one of the existential weirdness of Samuel Beckett and is quite creepy despite its brevity. A man views his wife on TV walking on a deserted plain. *The Rolling Darkness Revue 2015: The Voyage of the Dead* (Earthling) is the ninth chapbook created by Glen Hirshberg and Peter Atkins for their live performance of readings, taking place in October since 2005 (missing only 2011 and 2014). This volume includes a reprint by Atkins and two originals, one by Hirshberg and the other by Thomas St. John Bartlett, with interstitial material by Atkins and Hirshberg. *There's a Bluebird in My Heart* by Gary McMahon (White Noise Press) is a beautifully produced chapbook about a broken man, barely surviving in an ugly future in which murderous monsters are said to be hunted down by the government and put on prison ships. But oddly no one ever sees these monsters. *Witches of Lychford* by Paul Cornell (Tor.com) is a novella about the danger of building a supermarket on a haunted site in England. *In the Lovecraft Museum* by Steve Rasnic Tem (PS) is about the return to England of a man whose child disappeared there many years earlier. Dunhams Manor Press publishes paperback chapbooks of weird fiction, with writers such Nicole Cushing, Scott Nicolay, W. H. Pugmire, T. E. Grau, Joseph Pulver Sr., D. P. Watt, Mark McLaughlin, and others. Borderlands Press continues its adorable hardcover series of chapbooks in 2015, with volumes by Laird Barron, Jack Ketchum, Poppy Z. Brite, Ray Gardon, Edward Lee, and Rick Hautala. Each different colored book collects obscure stories, bits of nonfiction, excerpts from autobiographies, and all sorts of other odds and ends

NONFICTION

Body Gothic: Corporeal Transgression in Contemporary Literature and Horror Film by Xavier Aldana Reyes (University of Chicago Press) celebrates the transgressive qualities of the horror genre. Reyes considers relevant popular literary and filmic movements of the past three decades and reads them as updates in a long gothic tradition that goes back to the eighteenth century. *Body Gothic* contains case studies of key texts in splatterpunk, body horror, the new avant-pulp, the slaughterhouse novel, torture porn, and surgical horror. *The Literary Haunted House: Lovecraft, Matheson, King and the Horror in Between* by Rebecca Janicker (McFarland Books) focuses on the work of H. P. Lovecraft, Richard Matheson, and Stephen King, while offering a fresh perspective on one of the most popular motifs in American fiction. Case studies demonstrate how these authors have kept the past alive while highlighting the complexities of modern society, using their ghostly tales to celebrate and challenge twentieth-century American history and culture. *Wrapped in Plastic: Twin Peaks* by Andy Burns (ECW Press) is an in-depth guide to the classic David Lynch television series that's getting a reboot this year. *Horrors of War: The Undead on the Battlefield* by Cynthia J. Miller and A. Bowdoin Van Riper (Rowman and Littlefield Publishing) contains four sections of essays about supernatural war stories in literature, gaming, comics, graphic novels, film, and television. Includes fifty illustrations. *Something in the Blood: The Untold Story of Bram Stoker, the Man Who Wrote Dracula* by David J. Skal (Liveright) is a psychological and cultural portrait of the man who created one of the western world's most enduring icons. *Such a Dark Thing: Theology of the Vampire Narrative in Popular Culture* by M. Jess Peacock (Resource Publications) examines how the figure of the vampire is able to traverse and interconnect theology and academia within popular culture. *Monster Mash: The Creepy, Kooky Monster Craze in America 1957–1972* by Mark Voger (Twomorrows) is an illustrated appreciation of a unique period in US history. *Zombies: A Cultural History* by Roger Luckhurst (Reaktion Books) traces the history of the zombie through anthropology, folklore, travel writings, colonial histories, popular literature and cinema, medical history, and cultural theory. *The Stephen King Companion: Four Decades of Fear from the Master of Horror* by George Beahm, illustrated by Michael Whelan and Glenn Chadbourne (Thomas Dunne Books/St Martin's Press) is the book's third edition, updated from the second edition, first published in 1995. *Monsters and Monstrosity from the Fin de Siècle to the Millennium: New Essays* edited by Sharla Hutchison and Rebecca A. Brown (McFarland) is an academic look at the monster as metaphors for specific societal anxieties of its age. *Ghosts: A Haunted History* by Lisa Morton (Reaktion Books) is illustrated and more skeptical than not of historical hauntings. *Italian Gothic Films: 1957–1969* by Roberto Curti (McFarland) examines the sub-genre, including previously unpublished production information drawn from official papers and original scripts. Each entry includes a complete cast and crew list, home video releases, plot summary, and the author's analysis. Excerpts from interviews with filmmakers, scriptwriters, and actors are also included. *Zombie Talk: Culture, History, Politics* by David R. Castillo, David Schmid, David A. Reilly, and John Edgar Browning (Palgrave) is an academic book containing essays examining the zombie through an array of cultural products from different periods and geographical locations. In addition to the explosion of Lovecraftian horror anthologies published in 2015, there were also several tomes of scholarship published about him and his work. Hippocampus Press, especially, is notable for its focus on H. P. Lovecraft. In 2015 they brought out *The Rise, Fall, and Rise of the Cthulhu Mythos*, a revised and retitled edition of S. T. Joshi's 2008 volume on Lovecraft-inspired work. *Lovecraft: An American Allegory* by Donald R. Burleson is a very readable volume of "selected essays on H. P. Lovecraft" ranging from thematic studies to analyses of some of Lovecraft's poetry. *Letters to Bloch and Others* edited by David E. Schultz and S. T. Joshi collects H. P. Lovecraft's correspondence with a host of young writers, editors, and fans including Robert Bloch, Donald A. Wollheim, and Natalie H. Wooley, among others. *Lovecraftian Proceedings No 1* edited by John Michael Sefel and Niels-Viggo S. Hobbs (Hippocampus Press) is the official organ of the Dr. Henry Armitage Memorial Symposium, established in 2013 as a component of NecronomiCon Providence. In this volume, there are fourteen papers gathered from the Symposium. *H. P. Lovecraft and The Black Magickal Tradition* by John L. Steadman (Weiser Books) studies and analyzes claims by some devotees of Lovecraft's work that the author was himself a practicing occultist and his mythos a deliberate work system of magick. Centipede Press continued its impressive series Studies of the Horror Film with *Stanley Kubrick's The Shining* edited by Danel Olson. The hefty 750-page volume is filled with color photographs taken from the movie, and the text includes cast and crew interviews in addition to eleven essays about the movie. *Horror Guide to Florida* by David Goudsward and Scott T. Goudsward (Post Mortem Press) is a map to geographical locations, real and fictional, utilized in horror tales and films set in Florida. Includes an introduction by Jeff Strand. *The Art and Making of Hannibal: The Television Series* by Jesse McLean (Titan Books) describes the means used by the show's creators to pass the censors on network television. More gore, fewer butt cracks, apparently. Also included are interviews with creator Bryan Singer and some of the cast members, as well as discussion of the color palette used throughout the show and the special effects. Includes color photos throughout. From the Devil's Advocate series of Auteur Publishing, *Black Sunday* by Martyn Conterio is a short book placing Mario Bava's movie in the historical context of being one of the first sound Italian horror films and explaining how its success kick-started the Italian horror boom; *The Blair Witch Project* by Peter Turner helps explain the influence of the movie on horror and non-horror films. *The Supernatural Cinema of Guillermo Del Toro* edited by John W. Morehead (McFarland & Company) discusses cultural, religious, and literary influences on del Toro's work and explores key themes of his films, including the child's experience of humanity through encounters with the monstrous. *Scream: Chilling Adventures in the Science of Fear* by Margee Kerr (PublicAffairs) is written by a sociologist who researches haunted places, goes on scary adventures, and attempts to analyze why humans like to be scared.

ODDS AND ENDS

Illustro Obscurum Book of One Thousand Forms I (Seventh Church Of the Illuminator Press) is a compilation of twenty-four illustrations of avatars of Nyarlathotep by Michael Bukowski based on the writings of H. P. Lovecraft. This book also contains collaborations with contemporary authors Laird Barron, Victoria Dalpe, Gemma Files, Philip Gelatt, Orrin Grey, John Langan, Livia Llewellyn, Silvia Moreno-Garcia, W. H. Pugmire, and Molly Tanzer. Each author wrote an original description of Nyarlathotep for Michael Bukowski to illustrate. *Unclean Spirits* by Jeanne D'Angelo (Seventh Church Of the Illuminator Press) is an homage to Nikolai Gogol's horror stories, with reproductions of the fifteen paintings she created that were inspired by those stories.

The Art of Horror: An Illustrated History edited by Stephen Jones (Applause Theatre and Cinema Books) is a coffee-table book focusing on images ranging from the nineteenth century up to modern times. Arranged by monster, each section has an essay by writers such as David J. Skal, Kim Newman, and Richard Dalby on ghosts, as well as S.T. Joshi, Lisa Morton, and Robert Weinberg, among others. Includes more than 400 images. *Harry O. Morris: A Portfolio* (Centipede) is a large retrospective of Morris's art with autobiographical information. He was one of the 1970s generation of horror artists experimenting with photo collage as a primary component of their work. Includes a preface by Richard Christian Matheson. *Fearsome Creatures of the Lumberwoods* by Hal Johnson and illustrated by Tom Mead (Workman) is a fun book of weird and creepy creatures and their stories, best enjoyed with kids around a campfire. *Sirenia Digest* is a subscription-based monthly newsletter consisting of original or hard-to-find stories and vignettes by Caitlín R. Kiernan, accompanied by art, news, and occasionally commentary. She reached 114 by the end of the 2015.

WE ARE ALL MONSTERS HERE

KELLEY ARMSTRONG

S o disappointing. After decades of movies and TV shows and books filled with creatures by turns terrifying and tempting, it was a guarantee that the real thing could never live up to the hype. We knew that. Yet we were still disappointed.

When the first stories hit the news—always from some distant place we'd never visited or planned to visit—the jokes followed. Late-night comedy routines, YouTube videos, Internet memes . . . people had a blast mocking the reality of vampires. The most popular costume that Halloween? Showing up dressed as yourself and saying, "Look, I'm a vampire." Ha-ha.

Then cases emerged in the US, and people stopped laughing.

While vampirism was no longer comedy fodder, people were still disillusioned. They just found new ways to express it. Some started petitions claiming the term "vampire" made a mockery of a serious medical condition. Others started petitions claiming it made a mockery of long-standing folklore. There was actually a bill before Congress to legislate a change of terminology.

Then the initial mass outbreak erupted, and no one cared what they called it anymore.

◄◦►

I first heard about the vampires in a college lecture hall. I couldn't tell you which course it was—the news made too little of an impression for me to retain the surrounding circumstances. I know only that I was in class, listening to a professor, when the guy beside me said, "Hey, did you see this?" and passed me his iPhone. I was going to ignore him. I'd been doing that all term—he kept sitting beside me and making comments and expecting me to be impressed, when all I wanted to say was, "How about trying to talk to me *outside* of class?" But that might be an invitation I'd regret. So I usually ignored him, but this time, he'd shoved his phone in front of me and before I could turn away, I see the headline.

The headline read, *Real-Life Vampires in Venezuela.* The article went on to say that there had been five incidents in which people had woken to find themselves covered in blood . . . and everyone else in the house dead and bloodless.

"Vampires," the guy whispered. "Can you believe it? I'd have thought they'd have been scarier."

"Slaughtering your entire family isn't scary enough for you?"

He shifted in his seat. "You know what I mean."

"It's not vampires," I said. "It's drugs. Like those bath salts."

I shoved the phone back at him and turned my attention back to the professor.

◄◦►

Two years later, I was still living in a college dorm, despite having been due to graduate the year before. No one had graduated that term, because that's when the outbreak struck our campus. Classes were suspended and students were quarantined. The lockdown stretched for days. Then weeks. Then months. The protests started peacefully enough, but soon we realized we were being held prisoner and fought back. The military fought back harder. The scene played out across the nation, not just in schools, but every community where people had been "asked" not to leave for months on end. Martial law was declared across the country. The outbreaks continued to spread.

Given what was happening in the rest of the world, soon even the college's staunchest believers in democracy and free will realized we had it good. We were safe, living in separate quarters equipped with alarms and deadbolts so we could sleep securely. Otherwise, we were free to mingle, all our food and entertainment supplied as we waited for the government to find a cure.

One morning I awoke to the sound of my best friend Katie banging on my door, shouting that the answer was finally here. I dressed as quickly as I could and joined her in the hall.

"A cure?" I said.

Her face fell. "No," she said, and I regretted asking. I'd known Katie since my sophomore year, and she bore little resemblance to the girl she'd been. I used to envy her, with her amazing family and amazing boyfriend back home. It'd been a year since she'd seen them. Three months since she'd heard from them, as the authorities cut off communications with her quarantined hometown. She'd lost thirty pounds, her sweet nature reduced to little more than anxiety and nerves, unable to grieve, not daring to hope.

"Not a cure," she said. "But the next best thing. A method of detection. We can be tested. And then we can leave."

◄◦►

A method of detection. Wonderful news for an optimist. I am not an optimist. I heard that and all I could think was, *What if we test positive?* At the assembly, I was the annoying one in the front row badgering the presenters with exactly that question. "What would happen if we had the marker?"

That's what it was—a genetic marker. Which didn't answer the question of transmission. Two years since the first outbreak, and no one knew what actually caused vampirism. It seemed to be something inside us that just "activated." Of course, people blamed the government. It was in the vaccinations or in the water or the genetically-modified food. What was the trigger? No one knew and, frankly, it seemed like no one cared.

Those who had the marker would be subjected to continued quarantine while scientists searched for a cure. The rest of us would be free to go. Well, free to go someplace that wasn't quarantined.

The next day, the military lined us up outside the cafeteria. There were still people who worried that the second they got a positive result, the nearest guy in fatigues would pull out his semi-automatic. Bullshit, of course. The semi-automatic would make noise. If they planned to kill us, they'd do it much more discreetly.

To allay concerns, the testing would be communal. As open as they could make it. I had to give them props for that.

They took a DNA sample and analyzed it on the spot. That instant analysis wouldn't have been possible a couple of years ago, but when you're facing a vampire plague, all the best minds work day and night to develop the tools to fight it, whether they want to or not.

My results took eight seconds. I counted. Then they handed me a blue slip of paper. I looked down the line at everyone who'd been tested before me. Green papers, red, yellow, purple, white and black. They didn't dare use a binary system here. So we got our papers and we sat and we waited.

When Katie came over clutching a green slip of paper, she looked at mine and said, "Oh," and looked around, mentally tabulating colors.

"They say the rate is fifteen percent," I said. "There are seven colors. That means an equal number for each so we don't panic."

Once everyone was tested, they divided us into our color groups. Then we were laser-tattooed on the back of our hands.

I got a small yellow circle. When I craned my neck to look at the group beside us—the reds—they were getting the same. So were the blacks to my left. I exhaled in relief and looked around for Katie.

A woman announced, "If you have a yellow circle, you are clear and you may—"

That's when the screaming started. From the green group. I caught sight of Katie, standing there, staring in horror at the black star on her wrist. I raced over. A soldier tried to stop me, but I pushed past him, saying, "I'm with her."

A woman in uniform stepped into my path. "She's—"

"I know," I said. "I'm staying with her."

◄◦►

It wasn't a particularly noble sacrifice. That circle on my wrist meant I could leave at any time. She could not. I had nowhere to go anyway. My family . . . well, let's just say that when I got accepted to college, I walked out and never looked back and don't regret it. I won't explain further. I don't think I need to.

I would stay with Katie because she needed me and because I could and because—let me be frank—because it was the smart thing to do. I'd heard what the world was like beyond our campus. I was staying where there was food and shelter and safety and a friend.

Assemblies and a parade of officials and psychologists followed, all reassuring the others that their black star was not a death sentence. Not everyone who had the marker "turned." Those who did were now being transported to a secure facility, where they'd continue to await a cure.

There were private sessions that day, too, with counselors. During those, I sat in one of the common rooms with the other yellow suns. Yes, I wasn't the only one. We all had our reasons for staying, and most were like mine, part loyalty, part survival. We sat and we played cards, and we enjoyed the break from being hugged and told how wonderful and empathetic and strong we were, when we felt like none of those things.

Night came. Before today, the locks had been internal, meant to protect us while reassuring us that in the event of an emergency, we *could* leave. Now the doors had been fitted with an overriding electronic system. Perhaps it's a testament to how far things had gone that not a single person complained. We were just happy for the locks, especially now, in a building filled with dormant monsters.

I woke to the first shot at midnight. I bolted up in bed, thinking I'd dreamed it. Then the second shot came. No screams. Just gunshots. I yanked on my jeans and ran to the door, in my confusion forgetting about the new locks. I twisted the knob and . . .

The door opened.

I yanked it shut fast and stood there, gripping the knob.

Was I really awake? Was I really me? How could I be sure?

People who "turned" were not usually killed on sight, not unless they were caught mid-rampage and had to be put down. Studies said that when vampires woke in the night, they later had no memory of it. People took comfort in that—at least if you turned, you'd be spared the horror of remembering you'd slaughtered your loved ones. I took no comfort because it also meant there was no way of knowing what it felt like to turn. Would you be conscious in that moment? Did it seem real at the time?

I looked at the unlocked door. My gaze swung down to the yellow sun on the back of my wrist.

Another shot, this one so close that I ducked, the echo ringing in my ears. The shot had come from the other side of the wall. Katie's room.

I threw open my door and raced to hers, and finding it open, I ran through and . . .

Katie lay crumpled on the floor. In her outstretched hand was a gun.

I ran to her and then stopped short, staring. She lay on her stomach, and the side of her chest . . . there was a hole there. No, not a hole—that implies something neat and harmless. It was bloody and raw, a crater into her chest, just below her heart. I dropped to my knees, a sob catching in my throat.

She whimpered.

There was a moment when I didn't move, when all I could think was that she'd come back to life, like a vampire from the old stories and Hollywood movies. Except that wasn't how real vampires worked. They weren't dead. They weren't invulnerable. I grabbed her shoulders and turned her over.

Blood gushed from her mouth as I eased her onto her back. I tried not to think of that, tried not to let my brain assess that damage. It still did. I was pre-med. I'd spent enough hours volunteering in emergency wards to process the damage reflexively. She'd tried to shoot herself in the heart, not the head, because she didn't know better, because she was the kind of person who couldn't even watch action movies. So she'd aimed for her heart and missed, but not missed by enough. Not nearly enough.

I shouted for help. As I did, I heard other shouts. Other shots, too, and screams from deep in the dormitory and I tried to lay Katie down, to run out for help, but she gripped my hand and said "No" and "Stay" and I looked at her, and as much as I wanted to believe she'd survive, that she'd be fine, I knew better. So I shouted, as loud as I could, for help, but I stayed where I was, and I held her hand, and I told her everything would be fine, just fine.

"I couldn't do it," she whispered. "I couldn't wait to turn. I couldn't make you wait."

"I would have," I said, squeezing her hand as tears trickled down my face. "I'd have stayed for as long as you needed me."

A faint smile. "Just a few more minutes. That's all I'll need. Then you can go."

I told her I didn't want to go, just hold on, stay strong and hold on and everything would be fine. Of course it wasn't and we both knew that, but it gave us something to say in those final minutes, for me to tell her how brave and wonderful she was, and for her to tell me what a good friend I'd been.

"There," she whispered, her voice barely audible as her eyelids fluttered. "You can go now. Be free. Both of us. Free and . . ."

And she went. One last exhalation, and she joined her family and her boyfriend and everyone she'd loved and known was dead, even if she'd told herself they weren't.

I sat there, still holding her hand. Then as I lifted my head, I realized I could still hear shouts and shots and screams. I laid Katie on the floor, picked up the gun, and headed into the hall.

-o-

How many times had I sat in front of the TV, rolling my eyes at the brain-dead characters running *toward* obvious danger. Now I did exactly that and understood why. I heard those shots and those screams and I had to know.

I got near a hall intersection when the guy who'd showed me the news of the first reported deaths two years ago came barreling around the corner. He skidded to a halt so fast his sneakers squeaked. He stared at me, and there was no sign of recognition because all he saw was the gun. He dropped to his knees and looked up at me, and even then, staring me full in the face, his eyes were so panic-filled that he didn't recognize me. He just knelt there, his hands raised like a sinner at a revival.

"Please, please, please," he said. "I won't hurt you. I won't hurt anyone. I couldn't do it. I just couldn't. I need to say good-bye. My mom, my sister, my nephew . . . please just let me say good-bye. That's all I'll do, and then I'll do it, and if I can't, I'll go away. I'll go far, *far* away."

I lowered the gun, and he fell forward, convulsing in a sob of relief, his whole body quaking, sweat streaming from his face, the hall filling with the stink of it.

"Thank you," he said. "Oh God, thank you. I know I should do it—"

"Where did the guns come from?"

He looked up, his eyes finally focusing. "I know you. You—"

"My friend had this gun. I hear more. Where did they come from?"

He blinked hard, as if shifting his brain out of animal panic mode. Then his gaze went to my yellow sun. "You aren't . . . So you don't know. Okay." He nodded, then finally stood. "When the black stars had their private counseling session, they gave us guns. Access to them, that is. They told us where we could find them, if we decided we couldn't go on. Except . . ." He looked back the way he came. "Not everyone is using theirs to kill themselves first."

"They're killing the other black stars?"

He nodded. "They think we should all die. To be safe. They're killing those who didn't take the guns."

Footsteps sounded in the side hall.

"I need to go," he said quickly. "You should, too."

I lifted my hand to show my tattoo. "I'm not a threat."

He shook his head but didn't argue, just took off. I waited until the footsteps approached the junction.

"I'm armed," I called. "But I'm not a threat. I've got the yellow sun—"

"And I don't really give a shit," said a voice, and a guy my age wheeled around the corner, blood spattered on his shirt, his gun raised. "Kill them all and let God sort them out."

I dove as he fired. He shot twice, wildly, as if he'd never held a gun before tonight. When he tried for a third shot, the gun only clicked. I ran at him, but didn't shoot. I couldn't do that. I smashed the pistol into his temple and he went down. Then I heard running footsteps and more shouts, and I raced down the hall, taking every turn and running as fast as I could, until I saw the security station ahead. I fell against the door, banging my fists on it. When no one answered, I held my wrist up to the camera.

"Yellow sun!" I shouted. "Let me in!"

A guy opened the door. His gray hair had probably been cut military short a couple of years ago, but no one enforced those rules now and it stood on end like porcupine quills.

"Get in," he said.

I fell through. When I got my balance, I saw a half-dozen military guards watching the monitors. Watching students killing each other.

"You need to get out there," I said. "You need to stop this."

The gray-haired guy shrugged. "We didn't give them the guns."

"But you need to—"

"We don't need to do anything." He lowered himself into a chair. "You want to, girlie? You go right ahead. Otherwise? Wait it out with us."

I hesitated. Then I turned away from the monitors and slumped to the floor.

⤙⚬⤚

I was released the next day. That was their term for it: *released.* Cast out from my sanctuary. They escorted me back to my room to get my belongings and gave me a bag to pack them in. Then they walked me to the college gates, and for the first time in over a year, I set foot into the world beyond my campus.

It was fine in the beginning. Better than I dared to hope for. The entire college town had been tested, the black stars already rounded up and taken away, and while families grieved and mourned their loved ones, there was a sense of relief, too. Was it not better that their loved ones be taken somewhere safe . . . so the remaining family members would be safe *from* them, if they turned? That's what it came down to in the end. What left us safe.

I boarded with an elderly couple who'd lost their live-in nurse and declared that my years of pre-med were good enough for them.

It was four months later when we heard the first report of a yellow sun turning vampire.

No one panicked. The story came from California, which might only be across the country, but was now as foreign to us as Venezuela had been. The reports kept coming though. Yellow suns waking in the night and murdering their families. Then rumors from those who worked in the nearest black star facility that they'd had only a few occurrences of the dormant vampires turning. Finally, the horrible admission that the testing had failed, that the stars seemed to indicate only a slightly higher likelihood of turning.

That's when the world exploded, like a powder keg that'd been kept tamped down by reassurances and faith. People had been willing to trust the government, because it seemed they were honestly trying their best. And you know what? I think they were. As much as my early life had taught me to trust no one, to question every motive, I look back and I think the authorities really did try. They simply failed, and then everyone turned on them.

I lived with the elderly couple for almost a year before their daughter came and kicked me out. She said I was taking advantage of them, pretending to be a nurse without credentials. The fact that her town had been taken over by militants had nothing to do with her decision to move home. No, her parents—whom she'd not contacted in years—needed her, so she'd be their nurse now.

The old couple argued. They cried. They begged me to stay. Their daughter put a gun in my face and told me to leave.

A month later, after living with some former classmates in a bombed-out building, I went back to try and check up on the old couple. I heard the daughter had turned. She'd killed her parents. Killed their neighbors too because these days, no one was watching. Unless someone reported them, the vampires just kept killing, night after night. Some committed suicide. Some surrendered. Some ran off into the wilderness, hoping to survive where they'd be a danger to no one. The old couple's daughter just kept living in their house while her parents' bodies rotted and a growing swath of neighbors died.

I thought about that a lot. The choices we made. What it said about us. What I'd do if I woke covered in blood. I decided if that happened I'd head for the wilderness. Try to survive and wait for a cure. Or just survive, because by that point, no one really expected a cure. No one even knew if the government was still trying. Or if there still was a government.

I spent the next year on the streets, sometimes with others, but increasingly alone. I was lucky—none of my companions turned on me in the night. I hadn't even seen a vampire. That wasn't unusual. Unless you spotted one being dragged from a house to be murdered in the streets, you didn't see them. And even those who were hauled into the street? Well, sometimes they weren't vampires at all. No one asked for proof. If you wanted shelter, you could cut yourself, smear the blood on some poor soul, drag him out, let the mob take care of him and move into his house. Two of the groups I was with discussed doing exactly that. I left both before that thought turned into action.

◄o►

I'd been walking for six months. That was really all there was left to do: walk. Wander from place to place, seeking shelter where you could find it. The cities and towns weren't safe, as people reverted to their most basic animal selves, concerned only with finding a place to spend the night and food to get them through the day.

It was better in the countryside. No one could be trusted for long, but that was the curse of the vampirism. That kindly old woman who offered you a warm bed might rise in the night, kill you, and go right on being sweet and gentle when she woke up. Until she saw the blood.

In the country, there were plenty of empty homes to sleep in and flora and fauna to eat. I met a guy who taught me to trap and dress game. I returned the favor with sex. It wasn't a hardship. He didn't demand it, and in another life, it might even have turned into something more. It lasted six weeks. We would meet at our designated place to spend the day together, walking and hunting, and talking and having sex. Then we'd separate to our secret spots for the night, for safety. One morning, he didn't show up. I went back twice before I accepted he was gone. Maybe he turned, or he met someone who had. Or maybe someone had fancied his bow and his knife and his combat boots and murdered him for them. He was gone, and I grieved for him more than I'd done so for anyone since Katie. Then I picked up and moved on. It was all you could do.

I found a house a few days after that. Not just any house—there were plenty of those. The trick was to find exactly the right one, hidden from the road, so you wouldn't need to worry about vampires or fellow squatters. Even better if it was a nice house. "Nice" meant something different these days, as in not ransacked, not vandalized, not bloodied. The last was the hardest criteria to fill. There'd been so many deaths that after a point, no one bothered cleaning up the mess. You'd find drained bodies left in beds, lumps of desiccated flesh, and tattered cloth. But other times, you'd just find smears of old blood on the sheets and on the floor, where some squatter before you had been too tired to find other lodgings and simply dragged the rotting corpses to the basement and settled in.

But that house? It was damned near perfect. Out in the middle of nowhere, hidden by trees, so clean it seemed the family had left voluntarily and no one had found it since. The pantry was stuffed with canned and dry goods, as if they'd stocked up when things started going bad.

I lived there for three weeks. Read half the books in the house. Even taught myself to use the loom in the sitting room. Damned near paradise. But one day I must have been sloppy, let someone see me returning from hunting. I woke with a knife at my throat and a man on top of me. There was a moment, looking up at that filthy, bearded face, when I thought, *Just don't fight.* Let him have what he wanted and let him leave. Just lie still and take it and he'd go and I'd have my house back.

That's when I saw the others. Three of them, surrounding the bed, waiting their turn. And it was as if a pair of scales in my head tipped. I fought then. It didn't do any good, and deep inside, I knew it wouldn't. I don't even think I was fighting to escape. I was just fighting to say, *I object,* and in the end, lying there, bloodied and beaten, I took comfort in that, when every part of me screamed in pain. *I fought back.* No matter what had ultimately happened, I'd fought back.

It was a week before the leader—Ray—decided he'd broken me and I could be allowed out of that room. It took another week to build their confidence to the point where they left me alone long enough to escape that place, because of course they hadn't broken me. As a child, I'd been inoculated against far more than mumps and measles. They did what they would do, and I acted my part: the cowed victim who comes to love the hand raised against her. An old role that I reprised easily.

Which is not to say that those two weeks didn't leave their mark, and not simply physical ones. But I survived, and not for one moment did I consider *not* surviving, consider taking Katie's way out. I respected her choice, but it was not mine. It never would be.

◄O►

As I walked along a deserted country road a day after my escape, I remembered an old TV show about a zombie apocalypse. I'd been too young to watch it, but since those hours in front of the TV were the best times I had with my family, I took them, even if it meant watching something that gave me nightmares.

That show had endless scenes just like this one, a lost soul trudging along an empty road. While I didn't need to worry about the undead lurching from the ditches, at least in that world you knew who the monsters were. In ours, the existence of vampires was almost inconsequential. In the last year, I'd had a gun to my head twice, a knife to my throat three times, and been beaten and raped repeatedly. And I had yet to meet an actual vampire.

When I heard the little girl singing, I thought I was imagining it. Any parent worth the title had taken their children and run long ago. There were fortified communities of families run by the last vestiges of the military, sanctuaries you couldn't enter unless you had a kid. That's another reason parents kept them hidden—so no one stole their children to gain entry.

But this really was a girl. No more than eight or nine, she sang as she picked wild strawberries along the road. When the woman with her took off her wide-brimmed straw hat and waved it, calling, "Hello!" I cautiously approached.

"You're alone," the woman said. She was about thirty. Not much older than me, I reflected.

I shook my head. "I have friends. They're—"

"If you're not alone, you should be," she said, waving at my black eye and split lip.

I said nothing.

"Do you need a place to stay?" she asked. "Somewhere safe?"

"No, I—"

"I can offer you a room and a properly cooked meal." The woman managed a tired smile. "I was an apprentice chef once upon a time, and I haven't quite lost the touch."

"Why?" I asked.

She frowned. "Why do I still cook?"

"Why give me a bed and a meal?"

She shrugged. "Because I can. I have beds and I have food, and as much as I'd love to share them with whoever comes along this road, most times I grab my daughter and hide in the ditch until they pass."

"And I'm different?"

"Aren't you?"

The little girl ran over and held out a handful of strawberries. I took one and she grinned up at me. "We have Scrabble."

"Do you?" I said.

"And Monopoly. But I like Scrabble better."

"So do I," I said, and followed her to the strawberry patch to continue picking.

⟶⟵

If I thought the last house was heaven, that only proves how low my standards had fallen. With this one, even before the vampires, I'd have been both charmed and impressed. And maybe a little envious of the girl who got to grow up in this cozy sanctuary, like something from an old-timey English novel; the ones where children lived charmed lives in the English countryside, spending their days with bosom friends and loyal dogs and kindly grownups, getting into trouble that really wasn't trouble at all.

The house itself was as hidden by trees as the one I'd left. The woman had seeded the lane with weeds and rubble, so it looked as if nothing lay at the other end. There was a greenhouse filled with vegetables, fruit trees in the yard, a chicken coop, even goats for milk. The pantry was overflowing with home-canned goods.

"Keeps me busy," the woman said as she took out a jar of peaches for afternoon tea.

For dinner, we had a meal beyond any I'd dare dreamed of in years. Then we played board games until the little girl was too tired to continue. After that, her mother and I read for an hour or so. Finally, we headed off to bed, and I was shown how to lock myself in. There were two deadbolts, one fastened on either side of the door. As to be expected these days.

I said good-night. Then I went inside, turned my lock, and climbed into bed.

I lay there, in that unbelievably comfortable bed, with sheets that smelled of lemons and fresh air. I lay, and I waited. Hours later, when I heard footsteps in the hall, I closed my eyes.

The woman rapped softly on my door and whispered, "Are you awake?"

I didn't answer. She carefully unbolted the lock on her side. Then came a rattle, as she used something to pop mine. The door opened. Eyes shut, I waited until I heard breathing beside my bed. When I pinpointed the sound, I leaped.

I caught the woman by the throat, both of us flying to the floor. I saw a blur of motion and heard a muffled snarl and turned to see the little girl with a canvas sack over her head. Her mother swung at me. I ducked the blow and slammed her against the wall. The girl was snarling and fighting against the sack. As I pinned her mother, the girl got free of the bag.

The child's eyes didn't glow red. Her fingers weren't twisted into talons. Her canines weren't an inch long and sharpened. She looked exactly like the girl I'd just played Scrabble with for two hours. But the look in her eyes told me I'd guessed right. Yes, I'd hoped it was still possible for a stranger to be kind to me, to take me in and feed me and give me shelter because we were all in this hell together. I'd taken the chance, because I still dared to hope. But I'd known better.

If I was surprised at all, it was because I presumed the mother was the vampire. But this made sense.

"She's my daughter," the woman said. "All I have left."

I nodded. I understood. I really did. In her place, maybe I'd have done the same, as much as I'd like to think I wouldn't.

I looked at the little girl. Then I threw her mother at her. The woman screamed and tried to scramble away. The girl pounced.

It was not over quickly. I'd heard stories of how the vampires kill. The rumor was they paralyzed their victims with a bite. But the girl kept biting and her mother kept struggling, at first only saying the girl's name and fighting to control her. Then came the panic, the kicking and screaming and punching, any thought of harming her child consumed by her own survival instinct. The girl bit her mother, over and over, blood spurting and spraying, until finally the woman's struggles faded, and the girl began to gorge on the blood while her mother lay there, still alive, still jerking, eyes wide, life slowly draining from them.

I walked out of the guest room and locked the door behind me.

The next morning, I hit the road, back the way I'd come. I walked all morning with the little girl skipping beside me, then racing off to pick wildflowers and strawberries. She'd woken in her own room, her nightgown and face clean.

I'd woken her at dawn, seemingly panicked because I couldn't find her mother. Something must have happened, and we had to go find her.

The girl followed without question. Now she walked without question. I'd told her that her mother had vanished, and she still skipped and sang and gathered flowers. Proving maybe a little part of her *was* still that monster after all.

At nightfall we reached my old sanctuary, the horror I'd escaped two days ago. I led her right up to the porch and rang the bell.

One of the guys answered. Seeing me, he stumbled back, as if a vengeful spirit stood on the porch.

"I want to see Ray," I said.

He looked at the little girl. "Wha . . . ?"

"I want to see—"

"Hey, girlie." Ray appeared from the depths of the dark hall.

"I want to come back," I said.

He threw back his head and laughed. "Realized it's not so bad, compared to what's out there, huh?"

"I brought a gift," I said. "My apology for leaving."

That's when he saw the girl. He blinked.

"You can use her to get into a refugee camp," I said. "We'll say we're her parents, and the guys are your brothers."

"Huh." He thought for a moment, but it didn't take long before he smiled. "Not bad, girlie. Not bad at all."

"I just want one thing," I said.

He chuckled. "Of course you do. Gotta be a catch."

"I'm with you," I said. "Just you. None of the others."

The smile broadened to a grin. "You like me the best, huh? Sure, okay. I accept your condition and your apology . . . and your gift. Come on in."

◄◦►

After midnight, I slipped from under Ray's arm and crept out. I tiptoed down the hall, unlocking doors as I went. It was an old house, the interior locks easily picked. The last one I opened was the little girl's. Then I continued along the hall, down the stairs, and out the front door to begin the long walk back to the other house, my new home.

I got as far as the road before I heard the first scream. I smiled and kept walking.

UNIVERSAL HORROR

STEPHEN GRAHAM JONES

The game was the same as every year. Rachel could have called it in July, if she'd wanted. For every age-inappropriate costume that knocked on the door of their no-kids party—six-year-old sexy nurses, second-grade saloon girls—Bill had to do a shot. For every comic book or television character, Nalene had to do a shot. Usually David got drunk off ethnic-insults-on-parade—kids in headdresses, kids-as-pimps—but three months ago his girlfriend 'Carrie' had given birth to a bouncing baby boy, so he wasn't even *at* the party this year. David's ex Jen always called animal-costumes, but, like David, she was starting over somewhere else.

Last Halloween, Rachel had had pirates and soldiers, a category she'd come up with herself, that had got her thoroughly sloshed by eight o'clock, in need of a restorative bump from Bill's famous stash. This year she'd gone Russian roulette, just pulled a strip of paper from the salad bowl in the kitchen.

Universal Horror.

"But that's everything?" she'd said, holding it up like she wasn't going to fall for this.

Bill, their expert, groaned.

"Think thirties, forties," he said, gesturing with his tumbler. "Frankenstein, Dracula, Mummy, Wolf Man. Phantom of the Opera." He sung the last part, and gestured his arm wide and grand, to encompass the whole neighborhood.

"Kids don't listen to opera anymore," Nalene said.

"*Anymore?*" Rachel said.

"Black Lagoon, Invisible Man, Bride of Frankenstein . . ." Bill was still reeling off.

And so the night began.

⟿

The No-Kids Pre-November Drunkfest had started right out of college. Now Bill and Nalene and Rachel were the last hold-outs, the 'loyalists' as David had called them when he was one: the diehards still sticking to their ideals of ten years ago, when they were never going to sell out, never going to buy in.

There'd been eight of them, then. Four couples against the world.

The only couple left standing now was Bill and Nalene.

"Our ranks are thinning," Bill had been noting out loud since Rachel had walked over at five, and then he'd lift his tumbler to who they used to be.

Aside from David stepping out on Jen with Carrie the house-sitter, a development so ripped-from-the-sitcoms that Rachel could hardly even muster an ironic smile, Ali and Bethany had packed up and moved away (the farewell party had been epic, a throwback), were rumored to be pregnant-at-a-distance as well, having their progeny in shame. In a *not*-so-generic move, Ted had left Rachel in August for a willowy bag boy he'd found at the neighborhood grocery store.

Ted claimed not to be gay, to just be in love, but Rachel wasn't stupid. He was being Ted was what it was: polite to a fault, careful of her feelings, trying to pull all the blame onto himself.

Instead of having the balls to just tell her it was over, that he'd never expected it to last this long, he was feigning infatuation, trying to make himself out to be a victim of love, caught in sudden headlights out on the highway of life.

It *was* pretty cliché, Rachel guessed. Except for the groping in the dark with a younger version of himself part. Really, it was pathetic—though Rachel did get a rush from trying to imagine how he had to hold his eyes when pointing his fingers to shove his left hand down into the hip-hugging pants of his bag boy. And it was delicious, too, how they probably had to be fast—breaks are fifteen minutes—and quiet, because the Coke machine they were pressed up against was high traffic, and the assistant manager of produce had already warned them once, about love.

So, for the first time in better than a decade, she was alone for Halloween.

And now the doorbell was ringing with the first trick 'r treater of the night.

Bill popped his plastic fangs in, said to Nalene and Rachel, "Bottoms up, ladies?"

Some things you don't even dignify.

◄◦►

It was a little mummy, all alone.

Rachel, at the door, looked back to Bill like he'd set all this up, hadn't he?

"Like you came here to be sober?" Nalene said, nudging into the doorway with Rachel.

The rule was you take your shot *after* you shut the door. Because there were always parents watchdogging it at the curb, their flashlights forming yellow puddles of fear at their feet.

"A scary *mummy*," Rachel said, holding the plastic bowl of candy out.

"That's real gauze," Nalene said, rubbing a trailing piece between the pads of her fingers. "Hospital grade."

"Trick 'r treat," the kid said, or something with that singsong lilt. There was no mouth hole, just too many layers of grimy white.

"Oh, yeah," Rachel said. "Um, trick?"

She couldn't remember the exact protocol. Did this mean she was asking for a trick, or promising one?

"Hey now . . ." Nalene was saying now.

Rachel refocused.

The little mummy had produced a foil-wrapped square skewered on a toothpick.

"Did you *make* this?" Rachel said, playing impressed (she had nieces and nephews), and took it, rattled the candy bowl like shaking up the *secret* candy from the bottom.

The little mummy's gauze fingers went in, shoved around, came out with a single piece, and then he coughed under all that gauze, his mouth-fabric staining red.

"There's your trick," Nalene said, impressed. She called back to Bill, "Have you still got some of those?"

Bill looked around, said, "Blood capsules?"

The ritual over, the little mummy stepped off the porch.

Rachel looked around for the mummy's mom, saw the dad instead in a una-bomber hoodie—costume? no? He stabbed a cigarette into the deep shadow his face was, was already casing the next house, holding his smoke in for longer than Rachel could have, like savoring every last gray swirl.

Not a neighborhood dad, Rachel figured. A weekend dad, bringing his kid to where the good candy was.

"Next?" Nalene said, leaning out.

It was early yet, hardly even dusk.

"Think he made it himself?" Rachel said, peeling the foil from the bite of brownie, letting it bloom at the top of the toothpick like a husk just opened.

"*Special* brownie . . ." Bill said, balancing Rachel's first shot over.

"It's *us* who poisons *them*, right?" Rachel said, popping the brownie in, "not the other way around."

"There's probably crayola in it," Nalene said. "And cooties."

Rachel chased the brownie with the shot.

It made her eyes water.

↦◦↤

Twenty minutes later—an astronaut they'd *all* had to drink for, as he filled no category, and a band of miniature pirates Nalene graciously claimed—Bill came back from the kitchen with the the video camera.

"Liver Chronicles time . . ." he announced, as if there were more of them than there were.

"We still doing that?" Nalene said.

She was digging through the candy bowl for butterscotch. This was the one night of the year she allowed herself to indulge.

"Do you ever watch them?" Rachel called to Bill over the back of the couch.

"Every day," he said, and plopped down. "I call them the Blackmail Tapes, actually."

"There's not enough of us to make it fun," Rachel said.

"What the—?" Nalene said.

Rachel and Bill looked over.

She was extracting something from the candy bowl.

A bloody fingernail.

"Trick," Bill said, and spit his fangs out into his palm, delivered them to a coaster on the coffee table.

"It's fake, isn't it?" Rachel said about the scabby fingernail.

Nalene was holding it up, inspecting it against the lamp.

"I don't think I'm hungry anymore," she said, and deposited the fingernail in the leather trashcan they used for umbrellas.

The doorbell rang again. Witches.

"That'd be David's shot, for ethnic insult," Bill said, getting the camera cued past last year's confessions. "Witches have gypsy noses. Like in Oz. Tell me I'm wrong."

"Magical creatures," Rachel corrected. "That's Ted."

She took the shot, had to close her eyes to swallow it down.

"You all right?" Nalene said.

"Good," Rachel coughed out.

"Who's first?" Bill asked.

The Liver Chronicles were campfire stories, minus the campfire. Secrets you tell when you're drunk.

"I don't have any left," Nalene said. "I didn't last year either, remember? I just told that one about pouring nail polish remover on that cop car."

"That wasn't even you," Rachel said.

"I was there," Nalene said.

The rule was it had to be something punishable by law.

Bill turned the camera on himself.

"When I was sixteen," he said, taking a long drink to let the tension build, "we used a sandwich bag for a rubber once."

"Mixed *company*?" Nalene said, playing offended. "As in, there's *wives* here?"

"Wives singular," Rachel corrected, swirling her finger around to exclude herself.

This time when the doorbell rang, they looked that direction like it was already becoming a chore.

"Okay, okay," Rachel finally said, and poured herself off the couch, collected the candy, swung the door back.

"Another mummy," she said loud enough for Bill and Nalene.

That wasn't exactly right, though.

"Have I seen you before?" she said down to the little mummy.

"Ask if he has another brownie!" Bill called.

"Here," Rachel said, and offered the bowl.

The mummy hauled his arm up, sifted through. Rachel didn't watch his fingers, but his one eye. He either had a filmy contact in—you can buy something like that for a kid?—or this was a real live mummy.

"Good gauze," she said, just for herself, letting the back of her index finger brush the little mummy's mummied cheek.

"*Dirty* gauze," Nalene said, suddenly there again, rubbing a trailing strip between her fingers, careful to avoid the stained parts that were supposed to be old blood. Or embalming fluid? She leaned down to look into the mummy's face. "You're not going to leave us any surprises in with the candy again, are you?"

"Leave him be," Rachel said, and pulled the bowl away, her eyes trying to see the whole sidewalk at once. Trying to see the hoodie-dad, so she could tell from his stance whether he knew this was the same house or not. So she could tell if he was in on this or not.

"Good trick . . ." Nalene was saying to the little mummy.

Rachel backtracked, saw: the little mummy had three pieces of candy in his wrapped fingers, but his trailing gauze was still sticky on back, it seemed. It had collected a butterscotch.

"That was mine," Nalene said, reaching for it.

The little mummy twitched the candy away.

"Where's your dad?" Rachel said to the little mummy, looking past him again.

"Why?" Nalene said, tiptoeing to look. "Is he a candidate?"

Rachel shut the door.

◄○►

Because the little mummy's costume had been so good, Rachel did the one shot she had to, since he was a monster from the thirties, but then she poured another, carried it with her the way Bill always held his cut-glass tumbler.

He lifted it to her, drank a sip, and raised the camera to her.

"Do we have to?" she said.

"Tradition," Bill said, tracking her face.

Rachel crossed to the couch, sat all the way back into it and shook her head like she wasn't going to do this.

But she already was.

"There was one I never told," she said. "Because, you know. Ted."

"Is he *in* it?" Nalene asked, thrilled, her bare feet tucked under her on the couch beside Rachel.

"I couldn't tell it because it wasn't *him*," Rachel said.

"Now we're getting somewhere . . ." Bill said, and the way he put his fangs back in, Rachel could see him at seventy, with dentures.

"Don't record this one, though," she said.

"Just with this," Bill said, tapping his temple with his middle finger.

"That means turn the camera off," Nalene prompted.

Bill hissed a vampire hiss at her and clapped the camera in his lap shut.

"Thanks," Rachel said to Nalene, then looked at the door like it was the only thing that could save her now. When it didn't, she came back, chewed her cheeks in like she hated, and said, "Remember Craig D?"

"Which one was he?" Bill asked.

"Davidson," Nalene filled in. "The other was Morrison."

"Moris*sey*," Rachel corrected. "We never dated, really. We just went out twice, I guess."

"And you couldn't tell Ted about this?" Bill asked.

"I could *now*," Rachel said. "Let's just say we were driving. And only one of us was watching the road."

"Oh," Nalene said, her lower lip sucked in, eyes hot.

"Second date?" Bill said. "What, were you a prude back then?"

Rachel flipped him off, kept going. "We were out in that industrial park place, just kind of taking random rights."

"The road to heaven is paved with—" Bill started, but Nalene saw his hand-mouth motion coming, was already tossing a pillow at him.

"Go on," she said.

"That's it, really," Rachel said. "Remember how there were all those rabbits out there, though?"

"You killed Thumper?" Bill said, impressed.

Rachel drank a sip, then just shot the rest.

She wasn't going to make eight o'clock this year either, she knew. Not without help.

"We hit something. I felt it, like, in the floor. When we got back to my apartment, there was blood and hair on the front of that Camaro he had? The red one?"

"He had a name for it," Bill said, looking past Rachel, at the door.

"I'm sure he did," Rachel said. "Like I said, it was just that once. But then—do you remember that week? Right before finals, junior year?"

Nalene let her eyes scan all the internal headlines she always had on instant. "No," she said, when she got to that week.

"I—I don't know," Rachel said.

"What?" Bill said, leaning forward, picking up on the seriousness in Nalene's tone.

"That kid, the hit and run," Nalene said, staring at Rachel, waiting for Rachel to smile, waiting for this all to be a joke. "We went to the vigil, remember?"

Bill looked up to the right corner of the room, nodded, came back with, "That thing at the flagpoles, where we all had candles but nobody lit them, yeah."

"Because he was burned by the time they found him," Rachel said, shrugging like it didn't matter. "Whoever hit him, they went back. To hide the evidence. Right there in the road."

"You can't burn a whole body with gasoline," Nalene said.

"You can burn paint off that body, though," Rachel said.

"Returning to the scene of the crime," Bill said, shaking his head at the stupidity.

"And so—" Nalene said, getting her words right, "and so you've, ever since then, you've been thinking it was *you*? That it was *because* of you?"

Rachel shrugged again.

"Even if it was Craig, then it was *Craig*," Nalene said. "You were just an innocent bystander. You wouldn't even count as a witness."

"I'd probably count as something," Rachel said, watching Bill's fangs, on the coffee table again.

"I don't think you're in any real danger of him ratting you out," Bill said. They both turned to him.

"Craig Davidson," he said, and when they both still just stared, waiting, he said, "Do y'all, like, live in this city?"

"What?" Nalene said.

Bill cocked a hanging hand around an invisible noose and kicked his head over sideways, tongue lolling. "Last Halloween . . ." he croaked, trying to roll his eyes back. "Best trick ever . . ."

And then the doorbell rang again.

◄○►

Rachel flinched hard enough that her drink would have spilled if it wasn't already gone.

"Your turn," she said, and climbed up from the suddenly-deep couch.

She was talking to Nalene, but it was Bill who rose, leading with his glass.

"Oh shit," he said.

It was a squad of zombie cheerleaders. *Sexy* zombie cheerleaders, none of them past fourth grade yet.

On her way past, for the guest bathroom, Rachel picked the cheerleader's den mom out at the curb, the side of her face lit with a cellphone, her skirt just as short as the cheerleaders'.

In the bathroom, Rachel just had to get her face close to the toilet to start vomiting. She splashed all her shots into the toilet, along with the crumbled, soggy bite of brownie.

And—what the hell?

Squirming blind in the puke water, trying to live, were four or five blind maggots.

Rachel threw up again, from deeper, and flushed before opening her eyes this time.

"*It's for you!*" Nalene was calling through the door with fake cheer. "You all right in there?"

Rachel wiped her face, pulled herself up with the brass doorknob.

No doorbell, but when there was a line off the porch like rush hour, you just stood there, waited for the next little monster.

"C'mon already . . ." Nalene said, hooking her arm through Rachel's, dragging her to the front door.

The little mummy.

"Told you," Bill said, and clapped his sixth consecutive shot down onto the coffee table. Because there'd been six zombie cheerleaders.

"How long was I in there?" Rachel said, looking back to the bathroom.

"Here," Nalene said, thrusting the candy bowl into Rachel's gut, pushing her at the little mummy.

"We know what you're doing," Rachel said to the little mummy. "It's called cheating."

The little mummy guided its trembly hand into the candy.

"And stickies don't count," Nalene said over Rachel's shoulder.

The little mummy creaked something and Rachel nodded like she understood, was already dreading the next shot, then, as the door was closing, she keyed on the hoodie-dad out at the curb. A line of smoke seeped up from the shadow his face was, then dissipated up into the night

"Wait—" she said, trying to catch the door.

It opened again, onto a pair of teenage Wonder Women, their star-spangled bustiers dangerously loose.

"A twofer," Rachel said, or, heard herself saying.

Because of the comic book origins, Nalene had to drink. Because of the skin-on-display, Bill had two more shots coming.

"And one for me," Rachel said.

Because of the mummy.

◄•►

For the first time Rachel knew about since college, Bill passed out before the party was over. Before it really even started.

"He started at lunch," Nalene said, positioning a couch pillow under his head. "Guess we're getting old, right?"

Rachel didn't answer.

"Not that you look it," Nalene said, lifting Rachel's hair on one side. "That brownie was good for you, girl. Ted doesn't know what he's missing."

"I don't have the right parts for Ted anymore," Rachel said.

"World's full of Teds," Nalene said, and opened the liquor cabinet like the door to another world.

"Think I need a little boost," Rachel said, touching the side of her nose Santa-style so Nalene would hear the snow in her words.

"You and me both," Nalene said. "But sleepyhead over there—you know how paranoid he can get? He keeps his stash somewhere in the garage. Says it's better if I don't know."

Rachel was too out of it to even be amused.

"We are getting old," she said.

"You ever think about it?" Nalene said, pouring herself something opaque. "The biological clock, I mean? Tick-tick-tick?"

"I'm not a bomb," Rachel said, and took Nalene's drink from her, took a deep swig. "I'd be a terrible mom, though."

"You seen some of the costumes out there?" Nalene said. "I don't think there's exactly a lot of adult supervision going on."

Rachel took another bitter drink.

"I should buy some more water," she said.

Nalene studied her, didn't follow. Rachel didn't explain. Her garage had some thirty five-gallon jugs of water stacked all across it. It was because she liked to watch Ted's bag boy carry them out, try to fit them in the trunk.

Initially, her thought had been to tip him, not have enough money, then invite him back to her place for some real gratuity.

He was so pretty, though. So young. So unaware.

Let Ted keep him, she told herself. Ted deserves someone nice, someone good.

This time when the doorbell rang, she didn't even flinch.

"I already know," she said to Nalene, and killed whatever her vile drink was.

Instead of the mummy, it was a werewolf. Or, an adult werewolf mask on a kid who could maybe spell his name, if given three tries and a running start.

"I like you," Rachel said, and squatted down, shifted through the candy bowl, finally came up with the swirly lollipop that somehow hadn't been grabbed yet.

"You just want him to mess up his costume," Nalene said, the two of them watching the werewolf cub waddle away.

"I don't want one, no," Rachel said. "I don't deserve it."

Nalene looked over to her, her eyes holding Rachel's.

"Nobody deserves that," Nalene said.

Rachel closed her eyes, the house spinning around her.

Next up was the Legion of Doom, or some superhero team.

Nalene curled her shoulders forward like she'd just been punched in the gut.

Rachel opened another bottle, started pouring.

⊸⊶

It was a ghost who found what was hiding in the candy bowl.

The reason it was a ghost was that he didn't have gloves, just had little-kid fingers to reach out from under his sheet.

It wasn't quite a maggot, but it wasn't quite a fly yet either.

Worse, it seemed to be looking up at Rachel and Nalene. Like it was well aware what a vulnerable state it was in. Like it expected whatever they had to do, here.

Nalene opened her hands, the bowl falling for minutes, it felt like.

The next group of kids—soldiers, which would have been deadly last year—fell to their knees, stuffing their cargo pockets and cartridge belts with candy.

"What's happening?" Rachel said to Nalene, clutching her forearm hard.

Nalene shut the door, twisted the deadbolt and smeared her hand across the bank of switches, turning the porch light off the same way people in movies close the eyes of dead people.

"We *need* that bump . . ." she said, which is how her and Rachel ended up in the garage, neck-deep in Bill-land.

Thirty minutes later, Nalene caught the back of her ankle on some hidden blade in what felt like the lawn maintenance corner, and it bled and bled, and then bled some more.

In the bathroom, on the sink, she collapsed in laughter.

Rachel had jammed cottonballs between Nalene's toes like this was a pedicure.

Rachel caught the laugh, couldn't stop. By the end of it, she was crying.

"I think I miss him," she said, looking up to Nalene. "How stupid is that?"

Nalene, never mind her ankle, stood, hugged Rachel close and patted the back of her head.

"We'll kill him," she said. "You didn't deserve this, girl."

Rachel's breath hitched and then she was really crying, Nalene stroking the back of her hair flat.

"There there," she was saying.

In the mirror, Rachel caught her face. She pushed away, looked harder at her reflection.

"I'm breaking out," she said, turning her face sideways for the cloud of red at the corner of her mouth.

"Stress," Nalene said.

"There was something in that brownie," Rachel said.

"Like a reaction?"

"Like I don't know. They're not from this block."

"Damn foreigners," Nalene said, sure to use her family's accent.

Rachel closed her eyes, tried to *think*.

Somewhere in the swirly center of that moment, the doorbell rang.

⬦

"But it's him!" Rachel said, Nalene holding her by the wrist, keeping her from the door.

"We don't have any more candy," Nalene said.

"I don't think he wants candy," Rachel said, and jerked away, cracked the complicated mechanics of the deadbolt—it was the kind with a key to turn it—and swung the door back fast enough that her hair sucked forward.

She was looking down at denim knees. At jeans.

She tracked up, up.

"*David*," Nalene said.

"And David, Jr.," Rachel added, already looking past them, to the sidewalk.

"Is he—is he—?" Nalene was trying to get out.

David finished it for her: "Spider-Man."

Rachel felt Nalene deflate beside her.

"You knew, didn't you?" Nalene said. "Did Bill call, tell you?"

"Bill?" David said, craning around then saying it: "Oh, man. Party foul. Early ejection."

It was what they'd all used to say.

David was holding a baby now, though. One he'd made. One he'd dressed up as a superhero. One too young to even gum any of this candy.

Rachel pushed past him, onto the lawn.

"Have you seen a mummy?" she asked.

"You mean Carrie?" David said.

"She thinks this cute little mummy has it in her for," Nalene said, out on the porch with David now. "He stole all our candy."

"Seriously?" David was saying behind Rachel. Like in another world.

Rachel was to the sidewalk now. Looking one way then the other.

There were enough shots out here to drown a whale.

Walk far enough one way, and the parking lot of the grocery store would open up. Back the other way there were just houses forever, cul-de-sacs and dead-ends and streets named after trees and presidents.

"Here, mummy mummy mummy," Rachel said.

As if in answer, a pale piece of trash in the street flopped over in the breeze.

A strip of gauze.

Rachel stepped out, was squatted down to peel it up from the hot asphalt when her world went white and loud.

The car had stopped six inches from her face.

She stood holding the fluttering gauze, like that would explain it, and then Nalene was there, limping to the rescue, making things worse by yelling at the driver, who'd spilled his beer into his lap, was yelling too.

Finally David, his baby on his hip, was able to calm the driver, get him to move on past.

"Nothing to see here," Rachel said to herself.

When Nalene guided her back to the porch, Rachel having to help Nalene stand, David didn't follow.

This is how goodbyes work, she knew.

⟶

"How did you not know about Craig D?" Rachel said.

They were on the couch again.

"I don't, like, stalk everyone I used to know," Nalene said, holding her hair away from the coffee table so she could inhale a generous second line.

She offered the ceremonial straw to Rachel but the back of Rachel's throat was already that hot kind of drippy, her thoughts already that grainy kind of cold.

"But you've got that memory," Rachel said, doing her fingers to indicate Nalene's big brain.

Nalene sighed back into the couch, either had no answer or no interest in answering.

The way they'd found the stash was by waking Bill. With the old trick of ice cubes on his closed eyes. He'd staggered up, fell halfway down, and for his few moments of groggy awareness Nalene asked him where the stash was, the stash the stash the stash.

Bill mumbled something about fishing, and tried to do his hands around an imaginary rod and reel but couldn't seem to remember if he was right- or left-handed. It was enough.

Now they were here, deeper into the night.

"Think that's the one they used?" Nalene said, pointing her finger in the general direction of the sandwich bag the stash had been sleeping in.

It took Rachel an instant to make the connection from this to Bill's confession about the condom that wasn't.

"He had to be lying," she said. "No girl would ever let—" but lost the tail of the thought, once the words turned into an image.

"Girls he knew in high school . . ." Nalene said, and wowed her eyes out like not much would surprise her, here.

"Girls he knew in college . . ." Rachel said back, meaning the two of them.

Nalene threw a balled-up napkin at her.

This time when the doorbell rang, neither of them looked back to the door.

"Ali and Bethygirl," Nalene finally said, her voice slurring. "Big reunion tour."

Rachel did her hands around the idea of a pregnant belly.

They collapsed into spasms of laughter.

Nalene rose, did Rachel's line, then wiped her nose on the back of her hand and looked at it, pressed it to her right nostril.

"I'm not letting you walk home like that," she said to Rachel.

"You're the one with the ankle," Rachel said.

"I mean," Nalene said, doing her fingers by her head to show, "your state of *mind*."

Rachel shrugged, looked back to the door just when it chimed again.

"This is it," she said, and vaulted over the back of the couch.

"No, don't—" Nalene said, reaching across Bill, but it was too late.

Rachel opened the door hard, let its knob clap into the wall, shake all the pictures.

"Oh," she said.

A fourth-grader in a white t-shirt, something clever written on the front in marker. Something saying what this lo-fi costume was.

Instead of staring until her eyes could rearrange the letters, she reached back for the candy bowl that wasn't there.

"Oh, shit," she said, and the fourth-grader snapped his eyes up to her about her slip then out to the huddle of parents at the sidewalk, watching. Lip-reading.

"No, no, here," Rachel said, dropping to her knees.

Wedged against the sun-bleached stone frog guarding the top of the stairs was some chocolate doodad in wax paper.

Rachel held it up to the fourth-grader.

When he didn't understand, she grabbed his hand, forced the candy into it, and folded his fingers back.

Now one of the dads was walking across the grass, to stop this.

Rachel straightened her left arm to lean against it better—what she'd always considered a Scarlett O'Hara pose for some reason—and waited for whatever was next.

◄०►

When Nalene couldn't find the shot glass for the shot she owed the world—the marker on the fourth-grader's chest had been T-SHIRT MAN—she just curled up around the bottle.

"This isn't a good sign," Rachel said, afraid to sit down now. She might not be able to haul herself back up.

"We're getting old, girl," Nalene said, and took a swig.

"Speak for yourself," Rachel said, pushing away from the back of the couch. "I'm going to bed."

When the deadbolt didn't work anymore, she looked back to Nalene for help.

Nalene held up the deadbolt key, then slid it neatly down the front of Bill's pants.

"You don't think I'll do it?" Rachel said.

"Let me," Nalene said, and rolled over on top of Bill, her hand back down the front of his pants, her body trying hard to writhe him awake.

Rachel watched until she didn't want to see anymore, then zeroed in on the banister, let it deliver her upstairs, to the guest room.

Piled on the bed and avalanching off it were the bags of yarn Nalene always had.

They were in plastic shopping bags.

Rachel lifted one, smelled the handle-part for bag-boy scent. For Ted. And then she had to balance her face up to keep her eyes from spilling.

She turned around, fell backwards into the pile like a tea commercial.

The yarn was soft, the plastic crinkly and loud.

She blinked once, blinked again, and there was already crust in the corners of her eyes.

◄०►

It wasn't morning yet, she professionally surmised. The window was still black.

Her mouth was tacky, tasted bad.

She'd left the hall light on, too. Now that she could see it, it was too bright.

"Stupid, stupid," she said, and rolled out of the pile of bags, her hair and fingers trailing yarn. One red strand even hooked to the back of her earring.

When the light switch sucked the brightness back into itself, it brought a different kind of quiet with it.

Something was dripping downstairs.

Rachel reeled back through the evening, decided the sound had to be Nalene dry-humping Bill, the bottle a casualty of love behind her.

But this was thicker. The sound. Slower, more deliberate.

Rachel cocked her head over, swallowed, and for a bad instant flashed on Nalene and Bill tangled on the couch, each of their throats smiling, those bright red smiles arranged against each other for a last kiss.

She threw up, right onto the brand new carpet.

"Sorry, sorry," she said, trying to wipe it away with her hands, and then a car honked once out in the street, like a date.

When it honked again, Rachel slung her face up, crossed fast to the window of the guest bedroom, pulled the miniblinds open hard enough that they stayed.

Stopped in the street, its parking lights orangey-yellow at all four corners, its headlights glowed down, was a cherry red Camaro.

The driver door was open, the driver leaned back against the hood, his legs crossed at the ankle.

A breath of smoke seeped up from his hoodie and he lifted his cigarette hand to Rachel, saluted her seeing him.

Rachel fell back, into the bags and the yarn.

"Nalene!" she said, her voice rising to a scream. "*Nalene!*"

Nalene was dead, though. She knew that now.

Rachel grubbed back for a shopping bag, poured its yarn out, breathed into the bag four times, five.

And then she realized her hands were on the handles of the bag. That she could put it on like a hat, snug it down tight at the neck. That it would be so easy. Just like it had been for Craig D.

"No, no," she said, standing, shaking the bag away.

There was something else sticking to her hand, though.

The gauze.

When she pulled it away, it took a patch of skin with it.

Rachel fell to her knees, her mouth open in shock and pain, her left hand clapped over the torn spot on her right wrist, and then became sure something was about to stand from the pile of bags. Something draped in yarn. Something rotten under all that color.

She kicked back, away from the bed. Pressed her back against the wall.

"Nalene," she said, quieter now, because Nalene couldn't hear.

Would Nalene even know that was Craig D out there in the street? That he'd stepped over, become something else?

He was asking Rachel to come with.

Just for a quick ride.

That had been his name for the Camaro: *Quick Ride*.

Rachel felt a laugh burble from her lips and held her hand over it, and in that moment there was a distinct knock, one-two-three.

From the door beside her. The closet.

When Rachel didn't answer, it knocked again, harder. More insistent.

Shaking her head no about it the whole time, she stood, faced the door, and twisted the knob.

Because it was a dream, she was telling herself. Because at the instant in her dreams that a scary thing showed itself, she always shook herself awake.

It was time to wake up.

She pulled the door back, ready to fall into the next day's morning—into November—but, instead of waking, she saw the scary thing.

The little mummy.

"Trick 'r treat," he said, through the gauze.

Because that's what they do for burn victims. That's what they do for kids who weren't really dead when they were burned alive.

The little mummy held his hand up to Rachel.

"I'm—I'm so sorry," Rachel said.

The little mummy nodded, knew, its one eye even holding a teaspoon of pity for her, it seemed.

His hand was sticky. From the gauze.

"Oh," Rachel said, when he turned, led her back into the vast blackness of the closet.

Rachel's breath when she breathed, it was delicate and white, but just for a moment.

Then it was gone altogether.

SLAUGHTERED LAMB

TOM JOHNSTONE

"What was *your* first job then, Bob?"

A fog of pungent, sweet-smelling smoke veiled the room, as Robert Benton considered his reply.

Troy Sharp had asked the five members of the Sacred Order of the Followers of Dionysus about their first experience of gainful employment, not counting paper rounds.

Sackville had mentioned a spell at Smith's Crisps; Greenock, a season or two grape picking. Merrick had confessed to working in the St. Ivel margarine factory in Hemyock, Devon. Sharp himself had started his working life with British Rail, when that entity still existed.

The Sacred Order of the Followers of Dionysus was the mock-reverential title for this loose affiliation of gentle-, and not-so-gentlemen, who met every Wednesday to break up the tedium of the working week by indulging their taste for mild narcotics, booze, salty or sugary snacks, and agreeable discourse.

When it came to Benton, his usual diffidence delayed his reply, but as the joint circulated and he refilled his glass, he warmed to his subject.

⬦

This also answers your earlier question about my first trip abroad, Troy: This was it, if you can call Southern Ireland abroad, though it did seem a strange land to an English provincial boy. The first thing I remember from my coach journey from Rosslare was the shrines to the Holy Virgin that appeared from time to time in little gaps in the hedge beside the winding road, pale and ghostly amid the green leaves.

It's also the story of why I became a vegetarian. I often ask myself why, and when people ask me why, I can't answer in any thought-out way. I don't really buy into all the conventional ethical or ecological wisdom that's supposed to motivate me, though I might have believed it at one time. Now my continued attachment to this diet seems a hollowed-out shell of what it was—until I remember some of the events I'm about to tell you, that is. Usually I try to forget it, but not tonight.

In fact, it was my *not* being a vegetarian that got me the job in the first place. I was working for a theatre company I had met at the Edinburgh Festival. Their agitprop show about the Birmingham pub bombings and their aftermath had been playing at the Richard Demarco Gallery Theatre, where I had a summer job as Assistant Stage Manager. One of my duties as part of getting out the previous show and getting in their one was to help them hang their main prop from the rafters: the actual torso of a lamb, with meat hooks inserted into the flesh attached to chains secured to the ceiling. The actors dramatised the carnage of the pub bombings by driving nails into the pale meat of the dead animal, amid pyrotechnics and furiously strobing lights.

By no means the least of my duties was dealing with the increasingly manky carcass. You see, they couldn't afford to replace it with a fresh one. So for three weeks, during a very hot August, I carried the thing up and down the stairs to and from its resting place in the cellar, as it grew progressively more ragged from its puncture wounds, and more rancid from exposure to the hot lights of the theatre space. Its flesh turned from pale pink to a sickly yellow shot through with green, rather like Stilton. And did it stink! Perhaps more so when I discovered it was alive with maggots and threw it in a tin bath full of bleach, the sharp tang of the detergent masking but also highlighting the pungent, nauseating reek of putrefaction.

Chris Mulligan's eyes laughed behind the NHS spectacles that added an air of studiousness to his butch masculinity, as he helped me stow the carcass in the bath. Chris was one of the Birmingham-Irish brothers who'd founded the Dole Players, as the company was called, funded as it then was entirely by its members' social security cheques. Watching me trying not to gag, he said he was used to the smell, having grown up in a household surviving on knocked-off meat but without a fridge or freezer. There was something pointed about his reminiscence, which gave me the impression that he could smell my bourgeois background, rather as Hoederer in Sartre's *Les Mains Sales* could smell that of his secretary and would-be assassin Hugo, saying class is "*une question de peau*," a matter of skin, or perhaps flesh.

But the Dole Players weren't staging Sartre, and there was nothing metaphysical or philosophical about the vile odour that assailed the nostrils of the audience. Existential maybe: It existed all right, and certainly inspired nausea. On the other hand, it seemed to add to the play's confrontational impact. One critic wrote in *The Scotsman*, much to Kev's derision as he read the review aloud to general hilarity from the rest of the cast:

"As the story of the Birmingham Six unfolds on stage, the sacrificial lamb hangs there as a metaphor, not just for the innocent victims of the bombing, but also for the scapegoating of the hapless Irishmen with vaguely Republican sympathies, fitted up for being in the wrong place at the wrong time; its putrefying flesh symbolises the corruption of the judicial system that cynically framed them to appease a public thirst for vengeance. The festering wounds from the nails and meat hooks appear like stigmata, expressing sympathy for the suffering of these contemporary martyrs."

Well, it seemed as if someone liked it.

As the festival drew to a close, Kev Mulligan, the writer-director, told me they'd landed a fully funded tour of Ireland with their play, and invited me to ASM for the tour. The stage manager they'd taken on was a vegetarian, so couldn't be expected to handle the prop, so would I like to do it? I asked if we'd be taking the same carcass.

"Not likely," he said. "Tour don't start 'til late September!"

Not only that: Their funding allowed them to budget for a fresh carcass for each performance!

So that's how I came to be sitting on a coach, trundling through Wexford and Waterford on my way to Limerick, the first date on the Dole Players' tour.

The initial problem for me was sourcing the meat. The budget hadn't taken account of the prices charged by the local butchers. Running a hand through his dirty blonde hair, scraped back from his doughy-white face into a ponytail, Kev Mulligan offered a solution:

"Just go round the local pubs, Bob. In every pub there's always some bloke who can sort you out some knock-off meat, mate, at very reasonable prices . . ."

He dug in his leather jacket pocket, produced a wad of cash. His eyes stared outwards in different directions, a feature that together with his thick West Midlands accent gave him the air of a rougher, stockier version of Kevin Turvey, as he grinned amiably at his own largesse.

"Off you go then, Bob," he shooed me away.

Despite some initial misgivings, I soon found many a sympathetic ear among the drinkers in the Rising of the Moon Tavern, when I told them what the carcass was for. One man I spoke to remembered being in England at the time of the bombings, and having to avoid speaking for fear of reprisals if someone heard his brogue. With that fabled Irish *failte* hospitality, compounded by my assumed sympathy for the Republican cause, he plied me with stout before introducing me to a guy he knew who could help me out. The only trouble was, I'd drunk too much to drive, so I had to do the whole thing on foot, leaving the hired car parked near the pub. My memory of the long walk to the lock-up is a little hazy. My memory of the walk back with the carcass slung over my shoulder is even hazier. I hadn't eaten and I'd never really drunk much before. The thick black ooze roiled in my gut as the ripe smell of raw meat in late summer heat filtered through my nostrils to my queasy insides. I must have vomited a couple of times on the way, and only arrived back just in time for the get-in, to a bollocking from Kev, his powerfully built brother looming behind him, while Charlotte, the vegetarian stage manager, looked on through her piercing blue eyes. As I recall, she always had an amused look on her face. Her diet hadn't improved her health, for her skin was pale, almost translucent, under her ash-blonde, eighties-bouffant hair.

Thus it was, every day, through Limerick, Sligo, and Dublin, though the further north we went, and with an Indian summer cooling into autumn, it no longer seemed necessary to fetch a fresh carcass every day. In fact, Kev Mulligan seemed inclined to keep the lamb longer in Dublin, where the response of the Abbey Theatre audience seemed decidedly lukewarm. Maybe theatre-goers used to more refined dramatic fare found the play's angry invective, shouted by six burly blokes in rhyming couplets, more than they could stomach. Maybe its message, which had seemed so urgent and impossible to ignore in the more claustrophobic Demarco theatre, was lost on the Dublin intelligentsia, swallowed up by the larger auditorium. Mind you, it hadn't seemed to set the other provincial repertory theatres alight either, despite all the pyrotechnics.

For Kev, the answer was simple: Hang onto the carcass for longer. If he couldn't shout them into submission, maybe the stench of putrefaction would make the chattering classes of Dublin sit up and take notice, a measure that would also save cash. So my daily visits to various pubs and lock-ups became less frequent. In Sligo, I even found I had enough leisure time between shows to chat up a girl named Sinead, who worked in the local art gallery. She had chestnut hair and skin like buttermilk. I say "chat up": I was too awkward to say much, and we weren't in town that long. I left without even saying goodbye, miserably assuming I'd never see her again.

Things changed as we drew closer to the border. After a week off in Donegal, we hit Clones, County Monaghan, home town of Barry McGuigan. All the local shops sold tea towels, beer tankards, coasters, and other souvenirs depicting the "Clones Cyclone" in a typically pugilistic pose.

The show that night played to rapturous applause, nothing like the polite clapping of the audiences in Limerick and Dublin. Or for that matter, Sligo. Now, I was looking at a map of Ireland the other day, and I realised that Sligo's as far north as Monaghan, indeed further north than Clones, both about the same distance from the border between the Irish Republic and Northern Ireland.

And yet in my recollections of this time, I've always come to think of it as further south. This may have something to do with the more muted response the Dole Players' show received in Sligo, compared with the whooping, floor-stamping standing ovation it inspired in Clones. But I'm getting sidetracked by the vagaries of my memory, although it does throw light on some aspects of later events and my perception of them in retrospect.

As the applause died down, Kev said:

"Must be the Provos in tonight, lads!"

There was a nervousness to the jest, and the laughter it provoked from the rest of the cast, derived from the knowledge that tomorrow we were to play Belfast.

This is where my cheerful little travelogue takes a more macabre turn.

Our gig at Queen's University was the final leg of our tour, and the only one in Northern Ireland. Possibly one date too many. It's easy to forget now that these were the days before the Good Friday Agreement, before the successful appeals by the Birmingham Six and the Guildford Four, before *In the Name of the Father*, before power-sharing at Stormont. The injustices the play was exposing weren't the *cause celebre* they later became. I'd go so far as to say that Kev Mulligan was something of a pioneer.

But pioneering comes at a price. We were now venturing into territory where the Catholics who made up our potential audience were the minority, a land of army checkpoints and steel-shuttered, barbed wire-clad RUC stations that looked like above-ground fall-out shelters, of vast, dour murals commemorating past victories and past atrocities. We were no longer in the Land of a Thousand Welcomes.

Hanging onto the slaughtered lamb for this final date was out of the question, I suppose, though why I went on my own to fetch the carcass for that night's show, I'll never know. Maybe I wanted to prove myself to the Mulligan brothers, though why they let me is beyond me. They can't have realised quite how clueless I was about the whole situation over there. I've read up on it since, but back then, I had no idea.

And of course, you think you're invincible at that age, don't you? That's what people say anyway.

I look back on my eighteen-year-old self with a sense of wonder at my complete obliviousness to the changes in the murals as I drove through town, as well as to the implications of the tailback at the army checkpoint. Perhaps it doesn't seem so totally stupid, I suppose: After all, one large painting of armed men wearing balaclavas looks much the same as another to the uninitiated! In hindsight, of course, it's obvious: I should have noticed when the flags the painted paramilitaries were standing under changed from the Irish tricolour to the Red Hand of Ulster, when Shamrocks gave way to Orange Order regalia.

I should have noticed that the pub I'd entered was called the Battle of the Boyne.

It might as well have been the Slaughtered Lamb.

I think I sensed something was wrong as soon as I walked in there. Maybe it was the portrait of the Queen hanging in pride of place behind the bar. Maybe it was the dead-eyed stares of the three men sitting in front of it. But before the penny had a chance to drop, I'd gone into my spiel about the play and its need for a fresh lamb carcass before I knew what I was doing.

The oldest of the three men looked at me for a moment.

Something about that look made me stop in mid-sentence.

The older man took a sip of his pint. My throat suddenly felt terribly, terribly dry.

Somehow I knew I wouldn't be offered a drink here though.

At last, he spoke.

"So you're English right enough." His voice was a low burr with a Belfast twang.

I nodded, wanting to leave, but transfixed, rooted to the spot.

"D'you love your Queen and Country then?"

I moved my head again, not so much a nod, more a tremble.

He peered at me, his eyes squinting. There were angry mutterings from the two younger men. There was a Union flag tattooed on the thick, pink roll of flesh around his neck.

"Well do ya or don't ya? Maybe you prefer Reds and Provos, is that it?"

"I—" I began.

"Aye?" he repeated.

"No."

"Uh?" His face was close to mine now. I could see pink rims around his yellow eyes. I could smell his sweat and tobacco.

"Wee cunt," I heard one of the others spit.

His meaty hand reached out and cupped the side of my face.

"I'm gonna show you something," he whispered. "What's your name, son?"

"Robert."

"Well, Robert. Bob? Can I call you Bob? You all right with that? Good. Come with us . . ."

Refusal was not an option, though none of the men offered me any actual violence. They didn't need to. Several more men suddenly appeared as if from nowhere, surrounding me in that smoky, sawdust-wreathed room.

"You're looking for some meat, are you, wee man? Well, me and the lads here happen to know a butcher works round the corner from here, don't we, boys?"

There were grunts of assent, some low, mean chuckles. The men corralled me and escorted me out onto the street.

"Where are you taking me?" My voice squeaked shamefully. There was an awful lump in my throat, and tears were prickling. Hot urine trickled down my trouser leg. No one seemed to notice this. It was as if it was all in a day's work.

"Just for a little walk," he replied, his voice curt. "Not far."

One of the younger men who'd been there when I first walked in the pub said something about "Murphy's." At first, I hung onto this word, persuading myself it was all a joke and they were going to take me for a pint of stout or something.

I soon realised that what he actually said was:

"We taking him to Murphy's place, Da'?"

It wasn't a long walk, shorter than others I'd taken between pubs and meat lockers, but it seemed longer, either because of the piss-soaked trousers chafing against my legs or because of the dreadful prospect that this was strictly a one-way journey. Somehow the worst thing was the way the men exchanged small talk as if I wasn't there, some of it I guessed about what was in store for me, such as discussions about the price of a jerry can of petrol, or about where the Lagan Canal was deepest.

They led me to a rusting garage door, warped so that it wouldn't shut properly. The older man, the one who'd done most of the talking, told me to kneel, and don't move or he'd make me choke on my own piss-stained, Fenian cock. This he said in the same low, soft voice, as he stood behind me with the others sniggering at his side. He told me to shut my eyes, keep them tight shut or he'd stab the fuckers out, to shut my fucking mouth and keep still until the Butcher came.

I stayed like that for a while, just listening to the broken door flapping in the wind.

At some point, I realized they'd just gone and left me there. The loose stones from the concrete surface near the garage dug into my knees. Though I was alone, I still found it hard to bring myself to open my tightly screwed shut eyes. It was like when you wake from a nightmare yet still don't dare open your eyes until your heart has stopped hammering in your chest.

I say I was alone. At least, that's what I thought.

When my eyes finally opened, there was someone there. I hadn't heard his footsteps, but out of the corner of my eye I could see his right hand holding something, a long something that glinted in the sunlight. There was a livid scar on his left palm. There was a red hand tattooed on the forearm, not much redder than the figure's actual hands, which were ingrained with dark, rust-coloured stains, similar to how a motor mechanic's hands are permanently grimed with engine grease. I was still kneeling, so I didn't see his face. I didn't dare look up. I heard his voice though, a kind of rusty drawl so close it seemed to echo inside my head:

"Poor Tommy . . . Begged me to kill him in the end. I did, mind, but only after I'd peeled him like a banana. Know what I'd like more than anything right now, Bobby-boy?"

I realised he was addressing me, but I still couldn't bring myself to look up into his face.

"A nice, wee Catholic girl . . . Toasted chestnuts . . . Nice bit of buttermilk . . ."

I shut my eyes again, screwed them tight for a long time, but it didn't stop the scalding hot tears from rolling down my sorry, young cheeks.

When I came to myself, he was gone.

Somehow I found my way back to the hired car, and to the sanctuary of the university, expecting a bollocking from Kev for my failure to bring back a carcass for the show. He seemed surprisingly indifferent to my empty-handed abjectness. In fact, he hardly seemed to notice that I'd come in. I stood there for a while, saying nothing. I was in shock, I suppose.

Eventually, his nostrils wrinkled. One of his beady eyes regarded me with amusement.

"You wanna change those strides, mate. You had an accident or summat?"

I might have been embarrassed, had it not been for my numbness. But apart from Kev, there was no one else to be embarrassed in front of: Where were the rest of the cast and crew? Even Chris wasn't around to right-hand-man his brother. Kev explained they'd all gone back to their digs.

"Vice-chancellor only went and pulled the show . . . Death threats, he said. Fookin' lackey of British imperialism!"

So that was the end of the Dole Players' tour of Ireland. And that was the last I saw of them until the following summer, when they revived the play in Edinburgh. They went back to England the following day. I had unfinished business.

I took the next bus back to Sligo, my heart pounding with the memory of Sinead's smile and her buttermilk skin, but also with the memory of the words of the man with the nine-inch blade. To my intense relief and joy, she was there, though I've since inflated the romance of my return to Sligo in my memory, thinking it was further south than Monaghan.

"You're alive," I said.

"Of course I am," she laughed. "Why shouldn't I be? What a thing to say!"

And I'm alive too, I thought to myself as I took her hand in mine.

And before anyone says anything, yes, she was *that* Sinead, the same one you all know, the girl I married!

I later read up on some Irish history, found out about Lenny Murphy, the chief Shankill Butcher, the Red Right Hand of Ulster with a scar on his left hand and a nine-inch, double-bladed knife in his right; the one he used to carve strips of skin off Tom Madden as he dangled from the ceiling of a lock-up garage. It said in the book that there were 147 stab wounds on Madden's body, though the cause of death was slow strangulation with a ligature. Reading about the tattoos on his arms and the scar on his left palm, I realised he must have been the man I met at the garage, the one who seemed to see Sinead in my mind.

And yet after reading on, I knew my memory must be playing some kind of trick on me about this too, for the book said that Murphy got killed in 1982, about five years before the Dole Players toured Ireland with their play. That didn't stop me having nightmares about a flayed human torso suspended on chains and meat hooks, rotting but still moving, squirming with agony or maggots.

It wasn't until quite some time after I became a vegetarian that the nightmares stopped.

IN A CAVERN, IN A CANYON

LAIRD BARRON

Husband number one fondly referred to me as the Good Samaritan. Anything from a kid lost in the neighborhood to a countywide search-and-rescue effort, I got involved. If we drove past a fender-bender, I had to stop and lend a hand or snap a few pictures, maybe do a walk-around of the scene. A major crash? Forget about it—I'd haunt the site until the cows came home or the cops shooed me away. Took the better part of a decade for the light bulb to flash over my hubby's bald head. He realized I wasn't a Samaritan so much as a fetishist. Wore him down in the end and he bailed. I'm still melancholy over that one.

Lucky for him he didn't suffer through my stint with the Park Service in Alaska. After college and the first kid, I finagled my way onto the government payroll and volunteered for every missing person, lost climber, downed plane, or wrecked boat scenario. I hiked and camped on the side. Left my compass and maps at home. I wanted to disappear. Longest I managed was four days. The feds were suspicious enough to send me to a shrink who knew his business. The boys upstairs gave me a generous severance check and said to not let the door hit me in the ass on the way out. Basically the beginning of a long downward slide in my life.

Husband number three divorced me for my fifty-fourth birthday. I pawned everything that wouldn't fit into a van and drove from Ohio back home to

Alaska. I rented a doublewide at the Cottonwood Point Trailer Park near Moose Pass, two miles along the bucolic and winding Seward Highway from Cassie, my youngest daughter.

A spruce forest crowds the back door. Moose nibble the rhododendron hedging the yard. Most folks tuck in for the night by the time Colbert is delivering his monologue.

Cassie drops off my infant granddaughter, Vera, two or three times a week or whenever she can't find a sitter. Single and working two jobs (hardware cashier by day, graveyard security at the Port of Seward Wednesday and Friday), Cassie avoided the inevitability of divorce by not getting married in the first place. She kept the dumb, virile fisherman who knocked her up as baby-daddy and strictly part time squeeze. Wish I'd thought of that. Once I realized that my nanny gig was a regular thing, I ordered a crib and inveigled the handsome (and generally drunken, alas) fellow at 213 to set it up in my bedroom.

On the nanny evenings, I feed Vera her bottle and watch westerns on cable. "Get you started right," I say to her as Bronson ventilates Fonda beneath a glaring sun, or when a cowboy rides into the red-and-gold distance as the credits roll. She'll be a tomboy like her gram if I have any influence. The classic stars were my heroes once upon a time—Stewart, Van Cleef, Wayne, and Marvin. During my youth, I utterly revered Eastwood. I crushed big time on The Man with No Name and Dirty Harry. Kept a poster from *The Good, the Bad and the Ugly* on my bedroom wall. So young, both of us. So innocent. Except for the shooting and murdering, and my lustful thoughts, but you know.

Around midnight, I wake from a nap on the couch to Vera's plaintive cry. She's in the bedroom crib, awake and pissed for her bottle. The last act of *High Plains Drifter* plays in scratchy 1970s Technicolor. It's the part where the Stranger finally gets around to exacting righteous vengeance. Doesn't matter that I've missed two rapes, a horsewhipping, Lago painted red and renamed HELL . . . all those images are imprinted upon my hindbrain. I get the impression the scenes are *always* rolling down there against the screen of my subconscious.

I am depressed to recognize a cold fact in this instant. The love affair with bad boy Clint ended years and years ago, even if I haven't fully accepted the reality. Eyes gummed with sleep, I sit for a few seconds, mesmerized by the stricken faces of the townspeople who are caught between a vicious outlaw gang and a stranger hell-bent on retribution. The Stranger's whip slithers through the saloon window and garrotes an outlaw. I've watched that scene on a dozen occasions. My hands shake and I can't zap it with the remote fast enough.

That solves one problem. I take the formula from the fridge and pop it into the fancy warmer Cassie obtained during a clearance sale. The LED numerals are counting down to nothing when it occurs to me that I don't watch the baby on Sundays.

⟶

The night in 1977 that my father disappeared, he, Uncle Ned, and I drove north along Midnight Road, searching for Tony Orlando. Dad crept the Fleetwood at a walking pace. My younger siblings, Doug, Shauna, and Artemis, remained at home. Doug was ostensibly keeping an eye on our invalid grandmother, but I figured he was probably glued to the television with the others. That autumn sticks in my memory like mud to a Wellington. We were sixteen, fourteen, eleven, and ten. Babes in the wilderness.

Uncle Ned and I took turns yelling out the window. Whenever Orlando pulled this stunt, Dad swore it would be the last expedition he mounted to retrieve the "damned mutt." I guess he really meant it.

Middle-school classmate Nancy Albrecht once asked me what the hell kind of name was that for a dog, and I said Mom and Dad screwed on the second date to "Halfway to Paradise," and if you laugh I'll smack your teeth down your throat. I have a few scars on my knuckles, for damn sure.

Way back then, we lived in Eagle Talon, Alaska, an isolated port about seventy miles southwest of Anchorage. Cruise ships bloated the town with tourists during spring, and it dried up to around three hundred resident souls come autumn.

Eastern settlers had carved a hamlet from wilderness during the 1920s; plunked it down in a forgotten vale populated by eagles, bears, drunk Teamsters and drunker fishermen. Mountains and dense forest on three sides formed a deep-water harbor. The channel curved around the flank of Eagle Mountain and eventually let into Prince William Sound. Roads were gravel or dirt. We had the cruise ships and barges. We also had the railroad. You couldn't make a move without stepping in seagull shit. Most of us townies lived in a fourteen-story apartment complex called the Frazier Estate. We kids shortened it to Fate. Terra incognita began where the sodium lamplight grew fuzzy. At night, wolves howled in the nearby hills. Definitely not the dream hometown of a sixteen-year-old girl. As a grown woman, I recall it with a bittersweet fondness.

Upon commencing the hunt for Orlando, whom my little brother Doug had stupidly set free from the leash only to watch in mortification as the dog trotted into the sunset, tail furled with rebellious intent, Dad faced a choice—head west along the road, or troll the beach where the family pet sometimes mined for rotten salmon carcasses. We picked the road because it wound into the woods and our shepherd-husky mix hankered after the red squirrels that swarmed during the fall. Dad didn't want to walk if he could avoid it. "Marched goddamned plenty in the Crotch," he said. It had required a major effort for him to descend to the parking garage and get the wagon started and pointed in the general direction of our search route. Two bad knees, pain pills for said knees, and a half-pack-a-day habit had all but done him in.

Too bad for Uncle Ned and me, Midnight Road petered out in the foothills. Moose trails went every which way from the little clearing where we'd parked next to an abandoned Winnebago with a raggedy tarp covering the front end and black garbage bags over the windows. Hobos and druggies occasionally used the Winnebago as a fort until Sheriff Lockhart came along to roust them. "Goddamned railroad," Dad would say, despite the fact that if not for the railroad (for which he performed part-time labor to supplement his military checks) and the cruise ships and barges, there wouldn't be any call for Eagle Talon whatsoever.

Uncle Ned lifted himself from the back seat and accompanied me as I shined the flashlight and hollered for Orlando. Dad remained in the station wagon with the engine running and the lights on. He honked the horn every couple of minutes.

"He's gonna keep doing that, huh?" Uncle Ned wasn't exactly addressing me, more like an actor musing to himself on the stage. "Just gonna keep leanin' on that horn every ten seconds—"

The horn blared again. Farther off and dim—we'd come a ways already. Birch and alder were broken by stands of furry black spruce that muffled sounds from the outside world. The black, green, and gray webbing is basically the

Spanish moss of the Arctic. Uncle Ned chuckled and shook his head. Two years Dad's junior and a major league stoner, *he'd* managed to keep it together when it counted. He taught me how to tie a knot, paddle a canoe, and gave me a lifetime supply of dirty jokes. He'd also explained that contrary to Dad's Cro-Magnon take on teenage dating, boys were okay to fool around with so long as I ducked the bad ones and avoided getting knocked up. *Which ones were bad?* I wondered. Most of them, according to the Book of Ned, but keep it to fooling around and all would be well. He also clued me in to the fact that Dad's vow to blast any would-be suitor's pecker off with his twelve-gauge was an idle threat. My old man couldn't shoot worth spit even when sober.

The trail forked. One path climbed into the hills where the undergrowth thinned. The other path curved deeper into the creepy spruce where somebody had strung blue reflective tape among the branches—a haphazard mess like the time Dad got lit up and tried to decorate the Christmas tree.

"Let's not go in there," Uncle Ned said. Ominous, although not entirely unusual as he often said that kind of thing with a similar, laconic dryness. *That bar looks rough, let's try the next one over. That woman looks like my ex-wife, I'm not gonna dance with her, uh-uh. That box has got to be heavy. Let's get a beer and think on it.*

"Maybe he's at the beach rolling in crap," I said. Orlando loved bear turds and rotten salmon guts with a true passion. There'd be plenty of both near the big water, and as I squinted into the forbidding shadows, I increasingly wished we'd driven there instead.

Uncle Ned pulled his coat tighter and lit a cigarette. The air had dampened. I yelled "Orlando!" a few more times. Then we stood there for a while in the silence. It was like listening through the lid of a coffin. Dad had stopped leaning on the horn. The woodland critters weren't making their usual fuss. Clouds drifted in and the darkness was so complete it wrapped us in a cocoon. "Think Orlando's at the beach?" I said.

"Well, I dunno. He ain't here."

"Orlando, you stupid jerk!" I shouted to the night in general.

"Let's boogie," Uncle Ned said. The cherry of his cigarette floated in mid-air and gave his narrowed eyes a feral glint. Like Dad, he was middling tall and rangy. Sharp-featured and often wry. He turned and moved the way we'd come, head lowered, trailing a streamer of Pall Mall smoke. Typical of my uncle. Once he made a decision, he acted.

"Damn it, Orlando." I gave up and followed, sick to my gut with worry. Fool dog would be the death of me, or so I suspected. He'd tangled with a porcupine the summer before and I'd spent hours picking quills from his swollen snout because Dad refused to take him in to see Doc Green. There were worse things than porcupines in these woods—black bears, angry moose, wolves—and I feared my precious idiot would run into one of them.

Halfway back to the car, I glimpsed a patch of white to my left amidst the heavy brush. I took it for a birch stump with holes rotted into the heartwood. No, it was a man lying on his side, matted black hair framing his pale face. By pale, I mean bone-white and bloodless. The face you see on the corpse of an outlaw in those old-timey Wild West photographs.

"Help me," he whispered.

I trained my light on the injured man; he had to be hurt because of the limp, contorted angle of his body, his shocking paleness. He seemed familiar. The lamp beam broke around his body like a stream splits around a large stone. The shadows turned slowly, fracturing and changing him. He might've been weirdo Floyd who swept the Caribou after last call, or that degenerate trapper, Bob-something, who lived in a shack in the hills with a bunch of stuffed moose heads and mangy beaver hides. Or it might've been as I first thought—a tree stump lent a man's shape by my lying eyes. The more I stared, the less certain I became that it was a person at all.

Except I'd heard him speak, raspy and high-pitched from pain; almost a falsetto.

Twenty-five feet, give or take, between me and the stranger. I didn't see his arm move. Move it did, however. The shadows shifted again and his hand grasped futilely, thin and gnarled as a tree branch. His misery radiated into me, caused my eyes to well with tears of empathy. I felt terrible, just terrible, I wanted to mother him, and took a step toward him.

"Hortense. Come here." Uncle Ned said my name the way Dad described talking to his wounded buddies in 'Nam. The ones who'd gotten hit by a grenade or a stray bullet. Quiet, calm, and reassuring was the ticket—and I bet his tone would've worked its magic if my insides had happened to be splashed on the ground and the angels were singing me home. In this case, Uncle Ned's unnatural calmness scared me, woke me from a dream where I heroically tended a hapless stranger, got a parade and a key to the village, my father's grudging approval.

"Hortense, please."

"There's a guy in the bushes," I said. "I think he's hurt."

Uncle Ned grabbed my hand like he used to when I was a little girl, and towed me along at a brisk pace. "Naw, kid. That's a tree stump. I saw it when we went past earlier. Keep movin'."

I didn't ask why we were in such a hurry. It worried me how easy it seemed for him and Dad to slip into warrior mode at the drop of a hat. He muttered something about branches snapping and that black bears roamed the area as they fattened up for winter and he regretted leaving his guns at his house. *House* is sort of a grand term; Uncle Ned lived in a mobile home on the edge of the village. The Estate didn't appeal to his loner sensibilities.

We got to walking so fast along that narrow trail that I twisted my ankle on a root and nearly went for a header. Uncle Ned didn't miss a beat. He took most of my weight upon his shoulder. Pretty much dragged me back to the Fleetwood. The engine ran and the driver side door was ajar. I assumed Dad had gone behind a tree to take a leak. As the minutes passed and we called for him, I began to understand that he'd left. Those were the days when men abandoned their families by saying they needed to grab a pack of cigarettes and beating it for the high timber. He'd threatened to do it during his frequent arguments with Mom. She'd beaten him to the punch and jumped ship with a traveling salesman, leaving us to fend for ourselves. Maybe, just maybe, it was Dad's turn to bail on us kids.

Meanwhile, Orlando had jumped in through the open door and curled into a ball in the passenger seat. Leaves, twigs, and dirt plastered him. A pig digging for China wouldn't have been any filthier. Damned old dog pretended to sleep. His thumping tail gave away the show, though.

Uncle Ned rousted him and tried to put him on Dad's trail. Nothing doing. Orlando whined and hung his head. He refused to budge despite Uncle Ned's exhortations. Finally, the dog yelped and scrambled back into the car, trailing a stream of piss. That was our cue to depart.

◄◦►

Uncle Ned drove back to the Frazier Estate. He called Deputy Clausen (everybody called him Claws) and explained the situation. Claws agreed to gather a few men and do a walkthrough of the area. He theorized that Dad had gotten drunk and wandered into the hills and collapsed somewhere. Such events weren't rare.

Meanwhile, I checked in on Grandma, who'd occupied the master bedroom since she'd suffered the aneurysm. Next, I herded Orlando into the bathroom and soaked him in the tub. I was really hurting by then.

When I thanked Uncle Ned, he nodded curtly and avoided meeting my eye. "Lock the door," he said.

"Why? The JWs aren't allowed out of the compound after dark." Whenever I got scared, I cracked wise.

"Don't be a smartass. Lock the fuckin' door."

"Something fishy in Denmark," I said to Orlando, who leaned against my leg as I threw the deadbolt. Mrs. Wells had assigned *Hamlet*, *Julius Caesar*, and *Titus Andronicus* for summer reading. "And it's the Ides of August, too."

My brother and sisters sprawled in the living room front of the TV, watching a vampire flick. Christopher Lee wordlessly seduced a buxom chick who was practically falling out of her peasant blouse. Lee angled for a bite. Then he saw, nestled in the woman's cleavage, the teeny elegant crucifix her archaeologist boyfriend had given her for luck. Lee's eyes went buggy with rage and fear. The vampire equivalent to blue balls, I guess. I took over Dad's La-Z-Boy and kicked back with a bottle of Coke (the last one, as noted by the venomous glares of my siblings) and a bag of ice on my puffy ankle.

The movie ended and I clapped my hands and sent the kids packing. At three bedrooms, our apartment qualified as an imperial suite. Poor Dad sacked out on the couch. Doug and Artemis shared the smallest, crappiest room. I bunked with Shauna, the princess of jibber-jabber. She loved and feared me and that made tight quarters a bit easier because she knew I'd sock her in the arm if she sassed me too much or pestered me with one too many goober questions. Often, she'd natter on while I piped Fleetwood Mac and Led Zeppelin through a set of gigantic yellow earphones. That self-isolation spared us a few violent and teary scenes, I'm sure.

Amid the grumbles and the rush for the toilet, I almost confessed the weird events of the evening to Doug. My kid brother had an open mind when it came to the unknown. He wouldn't necessarily laugh me out of the room without giving the matter some real thought. Instead, I smacked the back of his head and told him not to be such a dumbass with Orlando. Nobody remarked on Dad's absence. I'm sure they figured he'd pitched camp at the

Caribou like he did so many nights. Later, I lay awake and listened to my siblings snore. Orlando whined as he dreamed of the chase, or of being chased.

From the bedroom, Gram said in a fragile, sing-song tone, "In a cavern, in a canyon, excavatin' for a mine, dwelt a miner forty-niner and his daughter Clementine. In a cavern in a canyon. In a cavern, in a canyon. In a cavern, in a canyon. Clementine, Clementine. Clementine? Clementine?"

⏤⟨⟩⏤

Of the four Shaw siblings I'm the eldest, tallest, and surliest.

According to Mom, Dad had desperately wanted a boy for his firstborn. He descended from a lineage that adhered to a pseudo-medieval mindset. The noble chauvinist, the virtuous warrior, the honorable fighter of rearguard actions. Quaint when viewed through a historical lens; a real pain in the ass in the modern world.

I was a disappointment. As a daughter, what else could I be? He got used to it. The Shaws have a long, long history of losing. We own that shit. *Go down fighting* would've been our family motto, with a snake biting the heel that crushed its skull as our crest. As some consolation, I was always a tomboy and tougher than either of my brothers—a heap tougher than most of the boys in our hick town, and tougher than at least a few of the grown men. Toughness isn't always measured by how hard you punch. Sometimes, most of the time, it's simply the set of a girl's jaw. I shot my mouth off with the best of them. If nothing else, I dutifully struck at the heels of my oppressors. Know where I got this grit? Sure as hell not from Dad. Oh, yeah, he threw a nasty left hook, and he'd scragged a few guys in the wars. But until Mom had flown the coop she ruled our roost with an iron fist that would've made Khrushchev think twice before crossing her. Yep, the meanness in my soul is pure-D Mom.

Dad had all the homespun apothegms.

He often said, *Never try to beat a man at what he does.* What Dad did best was drink. He treated it as a competitive event. In addition to chugging Molson Export, Wild Turkey, and Absolut, Dad also smoked the hell out of cannabis whenever he could get his hands on some. He preferred the heavy-hitting bud from Mexico courtesy of Uncle Ned. I got my hands on a bag those old boys stashed in a rolled-up sock in a number-ten coffee can. That stuff sent you, all right. Although, judging by the wildness of Dad's eyes, the way they started and stared at the corners of the room after he'd had a few hits, his destination was way different than mine.

Even so, the Acapulco Gold gave me a peek through the keyhole into Dad's soul in a way booze couldn't. Some blood memory got activated. It might've been our sole point of commonality. He would've beaten me to a pulp if he'd known. For my own good, natch.

Main thing I took from growing up the daughter of an alcoholic? Lots of notions compete for the top spot—the easiest way to get vomit and blood out of fabric, the best apologies, the precise amount of heed to pay a drunken diatribe, when to duck flung bottles, how to balance a checkbook and cook a family meal between homework, dog-walking, and giving sponge baths to Gram. But above all, my essential takeaway was that I'd never go down the rabbit hole to an eternal happy hour. I indulged in a beer here and there, toked some Mary Jane to reward myself for serving as Mom, Dad, Chief Cook and Bottle Washer pro-tem. Nothing heavy, though. I resolved to leave the heavy lifting to Dad, Uncle Ned, and their buddies at the Caribou Tavern.

Randal Shaw retired from the USMC in 1974 after twenty years of active service. Retirement didn't agree with him. To wit: the beer, bourbon, and weed, and the sullen hurling of empties. It didn't agree with Mom either, obviously. My grandmother, Harriet Shaw, suffered a brain aneurysm that very autumn. Granddad passed away the previous winter and Gram moved into our apartment. By day, she slumped in a special medical recliner we bought from the Eagle Talon Emergency Trauma Center. Vivian from upstairs sat with her while I was at school. Gram's awareness came and went like a bad radio signal. Sometimes she'd make a feeble attempt to play cards with Vivian. Occasionally, she asked about my grades and what cute boys I'd met, or she'd watch TV and chuckle at the soaps in that rueful way she laughed at so many ridiculous things. The clarity became rare. Usually she stared out the window at the harbor or at the framed Georgia O'Keeffe knockoff print of a sunflower above the dresser. Hours passed and we'd shoo away the mosquitos while she tunelessly hummed "In a cavern, in a canyon, excavatin' for a mine" on a loop. There may as well have been a VACANCY sign blinking above her head.

After school, and twice daily on weekends, Doug helped bundle Gram into the crappy fold-up chair and I pushed her around the village; took her down to the wharf to watch the seagulls, or parked her in front of the general store while I bought Dad a pack of smokes (and another for myself). By night, Dad or I pushed the button and let the air out and she lay with her eyes fixed on the dented ceiling of the bedroom. She'd sigh heavily and say, "Nighty-night, nighty-night," like a parrot. It shames me to remember her that way. But then, most of my childhood is a black hole.

◄◦►

The search party found neither hide nor hair of Dad. Deputy Clausen liked Uncle Ned well enough and agreed to do a bigger sweep in the afternoon. The deputy wasn't enthused. Old Harmon Snodgrass, a trapper from Kobuk, isolated footprints in the soft dirt along the edge of the road. The tracks matched Dad's boots and were headed toward town. Snodgrass lost them after a couple hundred yards.

In Deputy Clausen's professional opinion, Randal Shaw had doubled back and flown the coop to parts unknown, as a certain kind of man is wont to do when the going gets tough. Uncle Ned socked him (the Shaw answer to critics) and Claws would've had his ass in a cell for a good long time, except Stu Herring, the mayor of our tiny burg, and Kyle Lomax were on hand to break up the festivities and soothe bruised egos. Herring sent Uncle Ned home with a *go and sin no more* scowl.

"How's Mom?" Uncle Ned stared at Gram staring at a spot on the wall. He sipped the vilest black coffee on the face of the earth. My specialty. I'd almost tripped over him in the hallway on my way to take Orlando for his morning stroll. He'd spent the latter portion of the night curled near our door, a combat knife in his fist. Normally, one might consider that loony behavior. You had to know Uncle Ned.

"She's groovy, as ever. Why are you lurking?" The others were still zonked, thank God. I hadn't an inkling of how to break the news of Dad's defection to them. I packed more ice onto my ankle. My foot had swollen to the point where it wouldn't fit into my sneaker. It really and truly hurt. "Ow."

"Let's go. Hospital time." He stood abruptly and went in and woke Doug, told him, "Drop your cock and grab your socks. You're man of the house for an hour. Orlando needs a walk—for the love of God, keep him on a leash, will ya?" Then he nabbed Dad's keys and took me straightaway to the Eagle Clinic. Mrs. Cooper, a geriatric hypochondriac, saw the RN, Sally Mackey, ahead of us and we knew from experience that it would be a hell of a wait.

So Uncle Ned and I settled into hard plastic waiting room chairs. He lit a cigarette, and another for me, and said, "Okay, I got a story. Don't tell your old man I told you, or he'll kick my ass and then I'll kick yours. Yeah?"

I figured it would be a story of his hippie escapades or some raunchy bullshit Dad got up to in Vietnam. A tale to cheer me up and take my mind off my troubles. Uh-uh. He surprised me by talking about the Good Friday Earthquake of '64. "You were, what? Two, three? You guys lived in that trailer park in Anchorage. The quake hits and your Dad's been shipped to 'Nam. My job was to look over you and your mom. Meanwhile, I'm visiting a little honey out in the Valley. Girl had a cabin on a lake. We just came in off the ice for a mug of hot cocoa and BOOM! Looked like dynamite churned up the bottom muck. Shit flew off the shelves, the earth moved in waves like the sea. Spruce trees bent all the way over and slapped their tops on the ground. Sounded like a train runnin' through the living room. Tried callin' your mom, but the phone lines were down.

"I jumped in my truck and headed for Anchorage. Got part way there and had to stop. Highway was too fucked up to drive on. Pavement cracked open, bridges collapsed. I got stuck in a traffic jam on the Flats. Some cars were squashed under a collapsed overpass and a half-dozen more kind a piled on. It was nine or ten at night and pitch black. Accidents everywhere. The temperature dropped into the twenties and mist rolled in from the water. Road flares and headlights and flashing hazards made the scene extra spooky. I could taste hysteria in the air. Me and a couple of Hells Angels from Wasilla got together and made sure people weren't trapped or hurt too bad. Then we started pushing cars off the road to get ready for the emergency crews.

"We were taking a smoke break when one of the bikers said to shut up a minute. A big, pot-bellied Viking, at least twice the size of me and his younger pal. Fuckin' enormous. He cocked his head and asked us if we'd heard it too—somebody moaning for help down on the flats. He didn't hang around for an answer. Hopped over the guardrail and was gone. Man on a mission. Guy didn't come back after a few minutes. Me and the younger biker climbed down the embankment and went into the pucker-brush. Shouted ourselves hoarse and not a damned reply. Mist was oozin' off the water and this weird, low tide reek hit me. A cross between green gas from inside a blown moose carcass and somethin' sweet, like fireweed. I heard a noise, reminded me of water and air bubbles gurglin' through a hose. Grace a God I happened to shine my light on a boot stickin' out a the scrub. The skinny biker yelled his buddy's name and ran over there."

Uncle Ned had gotten worked up during the narration of his story. He lit another cigarette and paced to the coffee machine and back. Bernice Monson, the receptionist, glared over her glasses. She didn't say anything. In '77 most folks kept their mouths shut when confronted by foamy Vietnam vets. Bernice, like everybody else, assumed Uncle Ned did a jungle tour as a government employee. He certainly resembled the part with his haggard expression, brooding demeanor, and a partialness for camouflage pants. Truth was, while many young men were blasting away at each other in Southeast Asia, he'd backpacked across Canada, Europe, and Mexico. Or, *went humping foreign broads and scrawling doggerel,* as my dad put it.

Uncle Ned's eyes were red as a cockscomb. He slapped the coffee machine. "I didn't have a perfect position and my light was weak, but I saw plenty. The Viking laid on top of somebody. This somebody was super skinny and super pale. Lots of wild hair. Their arms and legs were tangled so's you couldn't make sense of what was goin' on. I thought he had him a woman there in the weeds and they was fuckin'. Their faces were stuck together. The young biker leaned over his buddy and then yelped and stumbled backward. The skinny, pale one shot out from under the Viking and into the darkness. Didn't stand, didn't crouch, didn't even flip over—know how a mechanic rolls from under a car on his board? Kinda that way, except jittery. Moved like an insect scuttling for cover, best I can describe it. A couple seconds later, the huge biker shuddered and went belly-crawling after the skinny fellow. What I thought I was seeing him do, anyhow. His arms and legs flopped, although his head never lifted, not completely. He just skidded away, Superman style, his face planted in the dirt.

"Meanwhile, the young biker hauled ass toward the road, shriekin' the whole way. My flashlight died. I stood there, in the dark, heart poundin', scared shitless, tryin' to get my brain out a neutral. I wanted to split, hell yeah. No fuckin' way I was gonna tramp around on those flats by myself. I'm a hunter, though. Those instincts kicked in and I decided to play it cool. Your dad always pegged me for a peacenik hippie because I didn't do 'Nam. I'm smarter, is the thing. Got a knife in my pocket and half the time I'm packin' heat too. Had me skinning knife, and lemme say, I kept it handy as I felt my way through the bushes and the brambles. Got most of the way to where

I could see the lights of the cars on the road. Somebody whispered, "Help me." Real close and on my flank. Scared me, sure. I probably jumped three feet straight up. And yet, it was the saddest voice I can remember. Woeful, like a lost child, or a wounded woman, or a fawn, or some combination of those cries.

"I might a turned around and walked into the night, except a state trooper hit me with a light. He'd come over the hill lookin' after the biker went bugshit. I think the cop thought the three of us were involved in a drug deal. He sure as hell didn't give a lick about a missing Hells Angel. He led me back to the clusterfuck on the highway and I spent the rest of the night shivering in my car while the bulldozers and dump trucks did their work." He punched the coffee machine.

"Easy, killer!" I said and gave an apologetic smile to the increasingly agitated Bernice. I patted the seat next to me until he came over and sat. "What happened to the biker? The big guy."

Uncle Ned had sliced his knuckles. He clenched his fist and watched the blood drip onto the tiles. "Cops found him that summer in the water. Not enough left for an autopsy. The current and the fish had taken him apart. Accidental death, they decided. I saw the younger biker at the Gold Digger. Must a been five or six years after the Good Friday Quake. He acted like he'd forgotten what happened to his partner until I bought him the fifth or sixth tequila. *He* got a real close look at what happened. Said that to him, the gurglin' was more of a slurpin'. An animal lappin' up a gory supper. Then he looked me in the eye and said his buddy got snatched into the darkness by his own guts. They were comin' out a his mouth and whatever it was out there gathered' em up and reeled him in."

"Holy shit, Uncle Ned." Goose pimples covered my arms. "That's nuts. Who do you think was out there?"

"The boogeyman. Whatever it is that kids think is hidin' under their bed."

"You tell Dad? Probably not, huh? He's a stick in the mud. He'd never buy it."

"Well, you don't either. Guess that makes you a stick in the mud too."

"The apple, the tree, gravity . . ."

"Maybe you'd be surprised what your old man knows." Uncle Ned's expression was shrewd. "I been all over this planet. Between '66 and '74, I roamed. Passed the peace pipe with the Lakota; ate peyote with the Mexicans;

drank wine with the Italians; and smoked excellent bud with a whole lot of other folks. I get bombed enough, or stoned enough, I ask if anybody else has heard of the Help Me Monster. What I call it. The Help Me Monster."

The description evoked images of Sesame Street and plush toys dancing on wires. "Grover the Psycho Killer!" I said, hoping he'd at least crack a smile. I also hoped my uncle hadn't gone around the bend.

He didn't smile. We sat there in one of those long, awkward silences while Bernice coughed her annoyance and shuffled papers. I was relieved when Sally Mackey finally stuck her head into the room and called my name.

The nurse wanted to send me to Anchorage for X-rays. No way would Dad authorize that expense. No veterinarians and no doctors; those were ironclad rules. When he discovered Uncle Ned took me to the clinic, he'd surely blow his top. I wheedled a bottle of prescription-strength aspirin, and a set of cheapo crutches on the house, and called it square. A mild ankle sprain meant I'd be on the crutches for days. I added it to the tab of Shaw family dues.

Dad never came home. I cried, the kids cried. Bit by bit, we moved on. Some of us more than others.

❦

I won't bore you with the nightmares that got worse and worse with time. You can draw your own conclusions. That strange figure in the woods, Dad's vanishing act, and Uncle Ned's horrifying tale coalesced into a witch's brew that beguiled me and became a serious obsession.

Life is messy and it's mysterious. Had my father walked away from his family or had he been taken? If the latter, then why Dad and not me or Uncle Ned? I didn't crack the case, didn't get any sense of closure. No medicine man or antiquarian popped up to give me the scoop on some ancient enemy that dwells in the shadows and dines upon the blood and innards of good Samaritans and hapless passersby.

Closest I came to solving the enigma was during my courtship with husband number two. He said a friend of a friend was a student biologist on a research expedition in Canada. His team and local authorities responded to a massive train derailment near a small town. Rescuers spent three days clearing out the survivors. On day four, they swept the scattered wreckage for bodies.

This student, who happened to be Spanish, and three fellow countrymen were way out in a field after dark, poking around with sticks. One of them heard a voice moaning for help. Of course, they scrambled to find this wretched soul. Late to the scene, a military search-and-rescue helicopter flew overhead, very low, its searchlight blazing. When the chopper had gone, all fell silent. The cries didn't repeat. Weird part, according to the Spaniard, was that in the few minutes they'd frantically tried to locate the injured person, his voice kept moving around in some bizarre acoustical illusion. The survivor switched from French, to English, and finally to Spanish. The biologist claimed he had nightmares of the incident for years afterward. He dreamed of his buddies separated in a dark field, each crying for help, and he'd stumble across their desiccated corpses, one by one. He attributed it to the guilt of leaving someone to die on the tundra.

My husband-to-be told me that story while high on coke and didn't mention it again. I wonder if that's why I married the sorry sonofabitch. Just for that single moment of connectedness, a tiny and inconstant flicker of light in the wilderness.

◄○►

High noon on a Sunday night.

Going on thirty-eight haunted years, I've expected this, or something like this, even though the entity represents, with its very jack-in-the-box manifestation, a deep, dark mystery of the universe. What has drawn it to me is equally inexplicable. I've considered the fanciful notion that the Shaws are cursed and Mr. Help Me is the instrument of vengeance. Doesn't feel right. I've also prayed to Mr. Help Me as if he, or it, is a death god watching over us cattle. Perhaps it is. The old gods wanted blood, didn't they? Blood and offerings of flesh. That feels more on the mark. Or, it could be the simplest answer of them all—Mr. Help Me is an exotic animal whose biology and behavior defy scientific classification. The need for sustenance is the least of all possible mysteries. I can fathom *that* need, at least.

A window must be open in my bedroom. Cool night air dries the sweat on my cheeks as I stand in the darkened hall. The air smells vaguely of spoiled meat and perfume. A black, emaciated shape lies prone on the floor, halfway across the bedroom threshold. Long, skinny arms are extended in a swimmer's pose. Its face is a smudge of white and tilted slightly upward to regard me. It is possible that these impressions aren't accurate, that my eyes are interpreting as best they can.

I slap a switch. The light flickers on, but doesn't illuminate the hall or the figure sprawled almost directly beneath the fixture. Instead, the glow bends at a right angle and gathers on the paneled wall in a diffuse cone.

"Help me," the figure says. The murmur is so soft it might've originated in my own head.

I'm made of sterner stuff than my sixteen-year-old self. I resist the powerful compulsion to approach, to lend maternal comfort. My legs go numb. I stagger and slide down the wall into a seated position. Everybody has had the nightmare. The one where you are perfectly aware and paralyzed and an unseen enemy looms over your shoulder. Difference is, I can see my nemesis, or at least its outline, at the opposite end of the hall. I can see it coming for me. It doesn't visibly move except when I blink, and then it's magically two or three feet closer. My mind is in overdrive. What keeps going through my mind is that predator insects seldom stir until the killing strike.

"Oh my darlin', oh my darling, oh my darlin' Clementine. You are lost and gone forever, dreadful sorry Clementine." I hum tunelessly, like Gram used to after her brain softened into mush. I'm reverting to childhood, to a time when Dad or Uncle Ned might burst through the door and save the day with a blast of double-aught buckshot.

It finally dawns upon me that I'm bleeding, am sitting in a puddle of blood. Where the blood is leaking from, I've not the foggiest notion. Silly me, *that's* why I'm dead from the waist down. My immobility isn't a function of terror, pheromones, or the occult powers of an evil spirit. I've been pricked and envenomed. Nature's predators carry barbs and stings. Those stings deliver anesthetics and anticoagulants. Have venom, will travel. I chuckle. My lips are cold.

"Help me," it whispers as it plucks my toes, testing my resistance. Even this close, it's an indistinct blob of shadowy appendages.

"I have one question." I enunciate carefully, the way I do after one too many shots of Jager. "Did you take my dad on August 15th, 1977? Or did that bastard skip out? Me and my brother got a steak dinner riding on this."

"Help me." The pleading tone descends into a lower timbre. A satisfied purr.

One final trick up my sleeve, or in my pocket. Recently, while browsing a hardware store for a few odds and ends, I'd come across a relic of my youth—a black light. Cost a ten spot, on special in a clearance bin. First it made me smile as I recalled how all my childhood friends illuminated their funkadelic posters, kids as gleeful as if we'd rediscovered alchemy. Later, in college, black light made a comeback on campus and at the parties we attended. It struck a chord, got me thinking, wondering . . .

Any creature adapted to distort common light sources might be susceptible to *uncommon* sources. Say infrared or black light. I hazard a guess that my untutored intuition is on the money and that thousands of years of evolution hasn't accounted for a twenty-dollar device used to find cat piss stains in the carpet.

I raise the box with the black light filter in my left hand and thumb the toggle. For an instant, I behold the intruder in all its malevolent glory. It recoils from my flashlight, a segmented hunter of soft prey retreating into its burrow. A dresser crashes in the bedroom, glass shatters, and the trailer rocks slightly, and then it's quiet again. The moment has passed, except for the fresh hell slowly blooming in my head.

The black light surprised it and nothing more. Surprised and amused it. The creature's impossibly broad grin imparted a universe of corrupt wisdom that will scar my mind for whatever time I have left. Mr. Help Me's susurrating chuckle lingers like a psychic stain. Sometimes the spider cuts the fly from its web. Sometimes nature doesn't sink in those red fangs; sometimes it chooses not to rend with its red claws. A reprieve isn't necessarily the same weight as a pardon. Inscrutability isn't mercy.

We Shaws are tough as shoe leather. Doubtless, I've enough juice left in me to crawl for the phone and signal the cavalry. A quart or two of type-O and I'll be fighting fit with a story to curl your toes. The conundrum is whether I really want to make that crawl, or whether I should close my eyes and fall asleep. *Did you take my father?* I've spent most of my life waiting to ask that question. Is Dad out there in the dark? What about those hunters and hikers and kids who walk through the door and onto the crime pages every year?

I don't want to die, truly I don't. I'm also afraid to go on living. I've seen the true, unspeakable face of the universe; a face that reflects my lowly place in its scheme. And the answer is yes. Yes, there are hells, and in some you are burned or boiled or digested in the belly of a monster for eternity. Yes, what's left of Dad abides with a hideous mystery. He's far from alone.

What would Clint Eastwood do? Well, he would've plugged the fucker with a .44 Magnum, for starters. I shake myself. Mid-fifties is too late to turn into a mope. I roll onto my belly, suck in a breath, and begin the agonizing journey toward the coffee table where I left my purse and salvation. Hand over hand, I drag my scrawny self. It isn't lost on me what I resemble as I slather a red trail across the floor.

Laughing hurts. Hard not to, though. I begin to sing the refrain from "Help." Over and over and over.

BETWEEN THE PILINGS

STEVE RASNIC TEM

The dark blue neon scribble was so faint he had to stare awhile to determine if it said VACANCY or not. Finally Whitcomb decided to take a chance. He went up to the battered screen door beneath the water-damaged sign: BETWEEN THE PILINGS, and in smaller letters INNSMOUTH BEACH, and in even smaller letters, an afterthought, worn almost to illegibility, ACCOMMODATIONS.

A light was on inside over a small counter, no brighter than a nightlight, really, and he couldn't tell if the hunched shape beneath it was a person or the back of a chair. But the door was unlocked, so he went inside.

He didn't see the clerk. Indeed it was just a counter with a battered surface and the rounded top of a chair behind. He gazed around the shabby, antiqued room. The lichen green wallpaper appeared to be dotted with tiny pale flowers, but they were so faded they might have been random stains. The armchairs and the couch might have originally been of high quality, but were now so scraped and worn it was hard to believe a business would countenance their use. The rug sparkled, but he determined it was from the grains of sand worked into its fibers. There might have been a central pattern, but the design was thoroughly obscured in grime.

Because of the numerous faded rectangles on the walls, he decided a number of pictures had been taken down. He had vague memories that it had been a fairly full gallery of past patrons displayed here. He didn't remember this room being so dilapidated. But he'd been barely eight years old when last he'd been here, so how could he know? He'd had no standards. He'd been happy just to be alive, to swim and play and watch television. And to eat cake. Oh, how he'd loved his cakes, the strawberry ones his mother used to make, the slices delivered to him on sparkling white plates, with a kiss on the cheek.

"Room?"

The word was so low-pitched and faint it might have come from the floor. Whitcomb looked more closely at the counter, the door behind it. The bluish glow coming from somewhere below the counter's edge. Had someone just come through the door? But he still didn't see them. He moved closer, peering over the edge.

He didn't believe in staring at people with disabilities—people all had differences, and we were all better off for it, in his opinion. But because he couldn't quite grasp the young man's malady, Whitcomb's gaze was fully engaged in staring.

The body on the wide chair was relatively short, fat and lopsided and, he thought, collapsed as if the spine or a portion of the spine had been removed, allowing the rest of the young man to fall down in a clump because now there was too much flesh for the available height. The head was pushed forward by the swollen neck so that it was easier for the young man to look at the small computer screen in front of him than to look at Whitcomb above him. His too-fleshy fingers flapped against the keys. His skin was pale and oily, and poorly washed. Whitcomb thought of a giant frog that had once frightened him as a boy.

"Yes. I would like to rent a room. For three days, perhaps four."

"That'll be two days in advance then," the young man said, still without looking up. "Forty-five dollars on the counter please."

Whitcomb put his money down. The clerk used a pole with a hook on it to transfer keys from a pegboard to the counter, all without taking his eyes off the screen. "Number eight. You been here before?"

"A long time ago. I was a child."

"Won't have changed much, 'cept the beach is a tad closer. You have to leave your car parked up here on the street. Nobody'll bother it—Innsmouth isn't like other places. There's some steps at the end of the building. You take those down under the boardwalk and out to the beach. The rooms are built around the timber pilings."

"I remember that part. It's unusual."

"It's why we have the name. Number eight is near the middle. But you'll have to wait up here a bit while the maid sweeps it out."

"Sweeps it out?"

"We have a sand problem."

Whitcomb didn't remember a sand problem, nor was he exactly sure what that phrase meant. But children often didn't notice the things adults classified as disastrous. The opposite, Whitcomb thought, was also true.

He looked for a place to sit. The couch looked like it might sink and fold itself around him, and the seats of all the chairs were thoroughly, darkly stained. He picked the least objectionable one, closed his eyes, and sat down. It made a squishing sound, as of rotting fruit.

The room was silent for a time except for the flap-clicking of the keys on the other side of the counter and the occasional sigh or struggle of breath from the clerk. Whitcomb could see out the dingy front window and down the street: spare of street lamps or even the usual illuminations leaked from windows or car headlights. Still, a bit of parchment glow made the shadows deeper and fuzzy-edged and sometimes runny, as darkness flowed from door to door, from one side of the street to the other. Feet and fingers and faces turned away. It was probably just him and his softly dying memories, but they might have been real. Had it been this way when he was a child? But everything was some bright adventure in a child's eyes, especially on vacation. His mother had hated it, he remembered that much, right up until the end.

That summer, his mother had wanted to return to the Southern seacoast where she'd been raised, to the extensive sands of Myrtle Beach or at least Virginia Beach so that their son could have "a proper beach experience," but his father insisted they had to stay in New England—they couldn't afford to travel farther than that. His father had won—as he did all arguments in which money was involved. At that point Mother wanted nothing more to do with the planning.

He hated those old men who babbled all the time, who had to fill up every silence with their voices, but there was so much to talk about, and no one to talk to.

"The billboards on the highway going in? I remember them as being so much brighter. That first one, VISIT HISTORIC INNSMOUTH, with a collage of quaint Victorian buildings. You can barely make out the details now."

The clerk said nothing. But even when Whitcomb had been a child and saw that billboard for the first time, the colors had seemed off, shaded into dirty greys. Far more bothersome had been the cartoon character who was supposedly speaking those words. Whitcomb had guessed it was meant to be a fish. But the eyes were wrong, the pupils appearing fixed and dilated. Perhaps he was editing it in the remembering, but he recalled them as the eyes of a dead human being. On this trip that figure was missing completely, that side of the billboard scratched out.

"The second billboard, well, there's not much of an image left at all, is there? I remember this lovely picture of the Innsmouth pier with a wide shot of the ocean. Now everything is so heavily graffitied—loops and swirls and all kinds of nastiness emerging from the waves."

"I've never been to the highway," the clerk murmured. "I've never seen them."

"Oh, sorry." Whitcomb thought perhaps he'd been rude to the young man, insensitive to his disability, whatever its specifics. He would not ask him, then, about the final billboard, now completely blank. Worse than blank, actually—scoured down to grey, flaking wood. He couldn't imagine how the damage had occurred—even a hurricane wouldn't have created such complete erasure.

He tried to remember what it had looked like before, but he had never understood what it had been intended to depict. It had been in the process of being changed at the time, he thought, newer strips pasted over older ones, or perhaps the newer bits torn off to reveal what lay underneath: the legs of a sun-bathing beauty married to a beached sea lion or something similar, a chaos of torn and frayed buildings collapsing over them.

He felt a cold draft and glanced at the front door. He saw no obvious gap at the bottom, but there was sand there, fingers of it flowing his way as if blown. Suddenly the door banged open, and a squat grey woman stood there holding the largest broom he had ever seen, the thick shaft of it filling her hand. "The Mister's room is ready!" she proclaimed, and glared at him. He came quickly off the chair and squeezed past her, dashing to his car to retrieve a small suitcase.

The trip down the stairs was long, and Whitcomb was glad not to have a steamer trunk to drag. It was also dark and the railing minimal, so he took the steps slowly. In fact, it was so deeply in shadow in places that the only illumination was a sliver of moonlight reflected off the damp edges of scattered timbers.

He remembered negotiating these steps as a child. Of course it had been daylight and mid-summer then. He remembered alternating areas of sunlight so bright it glazed the grey boards a brilliant white between shadows so dark he disappeared stepping into them. His mother behind him had been hysterical, sure he would kill himself flying down those rickety stairs.

Now at the bottom Whitcomb was confused. He remembered how it had been when he was eight: a broad strip of grass with a fountain and a bordering walk that shimmered from all the sea shells embedded in the concrete, and beyond that the gleaming white beach. It would never look as good as it had on that first glimpse, and over the years he would wonder if his imagination had simply embellished it, because every day after that while they were there it had appeared a bit greyer, a bit shabbier.

Now there was no grass at all—he had stepped off into sand. And a few feet away were the piles of rubble, broken concrete, and other rubbish. And looking around him, he didn't see the rooms. Certainly the few closest to the staircase were gone, leaving only hollow dark cavities filled with more sand.

He started walking parallel to the pilings, peering into the darkness for some sign of the old motel and finding none. It was hard to fathom how the young man up in that office at street level could believe he could get away with such a blatant con, taking money for rooms which no longer existed, but Whitcomb had his own eyes and the memory of what had once been here. He even ventured into the deeper shadows beneath the boardwalk thinking the rooms might have been set back further into the seaside structure than he remembered, but the area was wiped clean.

Then he passed one of the thicker pilings and there was what was left of the old motel: a short stretch of rooms with battered screen doors and a single window each. He remembered the walls as a bright coral red, but these were a pale salmon color, repaired here and there with grey cement like disease spots or patches of dead skin.

A small light glowed above each door along with a number. The first he saw was number six. He paused in front of eight before trying the key.

He remembered following his father into the room all those years ago. He had no idea which number it had been—it hadn't been important to him and they had all looked the same. There had been a bright multicolored oval rug inside, some blonde furniture, and one large bed. He'd gazed at that bed in dismay until he'd seen the rollaway they'd rented just for him. He'd sat on that bed and bounced, declaring it perfect.

His mother had come in slowly, her face drawn. She was rubbing her arms. "This sand, the wind blows it everywhere. It's burning my arms."

"It's just ordinary sand, dear," Whitcomb's father had said. "You probably just have a sunburn."

"We've barely arrived, how could I—"

"The drive in, all those miles. You had your window rolled down, remember? And your arm resting on the frame? I told you you should have put on sunblock when the trip began."

"I'm wearing long sleeves." She'd said it crossly. She hadn't wanted to come here at all.

"Lightweight fabric. You can practically see your arms through the cloth. It doesn't take much, a hot day like this."

His father had never thought his mother intelligent. That was why he'd always been explaining things to her, trying to explain why she shouldn't feel upset, why she shouldn't be disappointed or angry. Everything was always fine, the way his father had explained things, even when Whitcomb didn't understand the explanations.

Obviously his mother didn't understand them either, because as far as Whitcomb could remember, they had never helped. He'd resented that sometimes. She could have at least pretended to be happy. She could have been a good sport. Part of being happy, as he remembered from his childhood, was being able to pretend.

Whitcomb felt strangely hesitant to enter number eight. He was afraid to be disappointed in what he found inside. Sand as white, as pure-looking as snow, had drifted out of the shadowland fronting the ocean and up to the concrete step in front of each door. It required only the dim light above each number to bring out the sand's unusual brilliance, its eerie luminescence. He looked down at his feet—of course, he was standing in it. There was no grass or sidewalk anymore. From above it looked oddly liquid, milk-like, rising and falling around his shoes—nothing like sand at all.

But he was tired, and he was drunk with memory. He fixed his eyes on the door and stepped forward. It was late, and the world was always a different place in the morning.

The key made a scraping sound as it went into the keyhole. It felt like there might be debris inside. He turned the key and tiny particles drifted out of the hole and down to the threshold, joining the fingers of sand that had already blown onto the recently-swept step. He pushed the door open.

It was dark and chilly in the room, as if instead of going inside he'd actually gone out. He reached for a light switch and found it, coated in grit, so was not optimistic about the maid's cleaning job. But when the lights came on he was pleasantly surprised.

The room brought back vividly the one from decades before. The furniture was the same or of a similar style, blonde wood with clean lines, typical of the fifties. There was even a rollaway, although the mattress was greyish, the frame spotted with rust. But the floor was clean, and the rug, although it wasn't the colorful one from years before. The colors were more muted, as were the colors throughout, he realized, shaded toward greying pastels. The blonde wood duller. The ceiling white less white. But there was a comfort in all that. After all, if it had been exactly the same he might have been terrified.

But that was all quite enough. Whitcomb thought he could not bear to be awake any longer. He dressed into his pajamas quickly, turned off the light, and slipped into bed. The sheets didn't feel crisp, but at least they weren't sandy. He didn't bother to set the alarm clock—he hadn't even noticed if there was one. He was content with awakening whenever.

He had no idea how long he had slept when he first awakened. It was still dark out, according to his window, but he hadn't slept through the night in years, so that wasn't surprising. Wind scratched and occasionally beat on the door. He thought it might be raining because he could hear the spray against the glass. Surely the ocean was too far away for it to be the advance spray of a wave, but he could not bring himself to check. Better not to know if he was about to drown.

He leaned over the side of the bed to get a good view of the door—white had eased through the bottom, a few threads of it. Sand. But perhaps he'd just tracked that in when he first came inside.

His mother had complained of the sand, the way it burned, the whole time they had been here. Whitcomb hadn't understood—he'd loved it, couldn't get enough of it, the way it squeezed between the toes. It frightened him that she should have such a strong reaction. For years afterward he would think of her when he met anyone with allergies or peculiar sensitivities. Some people lived in an unfriendly world. Certainly, no one lived in his world, and he was uncomfortable whenever he ventured out of it.

"You're supposed to drive your life, not let your life drive you." Jane had shared that bit of insight the last time she'd consented to see him. "Do something spontaneous for once!" It was goodbye advice, but at least she had been sincere. She might have liked him more if he'd managed to be someone else.

He might have pretended to her that his return visit to Innsmouth was a spontaneous act, but of course it was not—it had been coming for years. He'd just been gathering his nerve.

Over the years, he'd tried to remember every detail of that vacation when he'd been eight, and although he'd recreated much of it, a great many moments were still missing. It angered him, the way the bits wore off, and he could not decide if it was the mind's normal decay or the old realities themselves which were going away. Something about the process seemed deliberate, as if the universe didn't want him to remember everything.

He did not feel sorry for himself—he'd made his choices, but he realized not everyone had a choice. Eventually all the bits of a life wore off, and for some even the memories went away. His father had gone on with his life, using drink to wipe the memory. But Whitcomb would remember his mother until the end.

He must have dozed off, because when he opened his eyes again the window was burning up with sun. He dressed himself in the sweats he'd bought for the occasion—he'd never owned a pair before. The door refused to open. He supposed the dampness had made it swell. He kept pulling until it came loose with a pop sound. A rain of grit poured from the jamb.

He stepped out into an intense scouring of sky and sand, so much blue and white he had to close his eyes, opening them slowly again using his hand as a shield. The beach looked ravaged, a churning of tiny white dunes and pitted places, black timbers and rocks showing ragged edges as if chewed. Streamers of rotting seaweed laced the beach, gulls landing to snatch tidbits, swiftly leaving as if the sand were too hot or corrosive to touch. Large amounts of fish flesh lay in partially digested chunks, the reek of it so foul his nose refused to process the smell. He gagged and turned to go back inside, but deciding he would not be so easily defeated, struck off down the line of pilings again, thinking he would see what remained here from his memories.

There appeared to be no one else about, and given the unpleasant state of the shore here, he supposed that should come as no surprise. In bright daylight, he had a good look at what was left of the motel—eight units, with the last two missing numbers and doors. He couldn't imagine who might rent such lodgings, unless they were beyond desperate or ignorant like himself. Perhaps they did all their renting after dark, when the extent of the damage could not be seen. He was curious if he had neighbors, but wouldn't go out of his way to meet them.

The place hadn't been that busy when he'd been here before, when things were painted, in good repair, and at the height of summer. At best there had been five or six other family groupings, and a few isolated stragglers, tall figures in rain gear with large hats pulled down over their features, strolling the beach. And not all the family members made use of the beach—some, like his mother, made only rare forays past their motel doors or the grassy areas in front.

But vacations weren't for everyone, or so he had heard. There were always some who felt safer, if not happier, at home.

He gazed down the beach to where it narrowed, eventually disappearing into a tumble of stone. There was the main part of Innsmouth, the old docks, the church towers and the sprawling meeting halls. Several buildings near the edge had actually tumbled into the sea, leaving a slope of woody debris soaking up the ocean salt and a splay of broken uprights. Surely he was mistaken, but he had a vague memory of the same ruins, the same collapse, present when he'd been here as a child.

A broken chorus of voices rose with a sudden flight of black birds as if riding their backs into the air. The voices dissipated with the scattering paths of wings. Whitcomb had no desire to venture into that part of town, thinking it a far more dangerous place than this poor strip of sand.

He caught sight of a familiar sign and, walking closer, caught himself in a tease of a smile. BY THE SANDS: MINIATURE GOLF. His family had discovered the place their second day there, and even his mother had seemed to enjoy herself. It appeared to still be in business. He found himself passing through the gate without considering.

At first he thought the fellow taking money was the motel clerk from the night before. They might have been twins. Then he saw that this one was a little taller, not as fat, and he hid one arm inside a voluminous sleeve. He handed the fellow a dollar and was pointed to a rack of balls and clubs beside Hole #1.

It was the usual layout of obstacles, ramps, windmills, passages through miniature buildings, and wide metal curves the ball could cling to for a left or right-hand turn. But there were local touches as well: a giant brass frog with a wide mouth—a ball entered the mouth and shot out the anus in some random direction. A water obstacle with leaping mechanical fish—periodically a fish would alter its trajectory by some mysterious means and snag the ball. An array of dilapidated buildings—he couldn't really tell if the destruction was cosmetic and faked, or actual damage incurred by the miniature buildings because of exposure and lack of care. He didn't remember many specifics about this miniature golf course from his previous visits decades ago, but it seemed that some of these features might be new to him—except for the frog. Now that he thought about it, the brass frog had been here before.

The last few holes had been invaded by sand. But that fit the golfing theme, did it not? Sand traps designed to defeat even the most professional of golfers. At hole fifteen the sand trap moved, and the ball dissolved amidst a swirl of greedy silvery grit, ending his game.

As he left the golf course, he found himself staring at the ocean, the endless repeating waves, the long curving edges of foam, that meandering line where dark grey sea met an only slightly softer sky. As a boy, he'd thought that line dividing the air and water impossibly high, an instability that threatened everything he held dear. Now it seemed worse, and he thought he could detect structures inside it, only vaguely covered by the water—long reticulating lines, horizontal and vertical edges, the boxy shapes of some lost city drowned beneath the waves.

It made him feel empty, void of substance, and he realized he hadn't yet eaten and had gone to bed without dinner the night before. There had been a few small cafes, he remembered, accessible only from the beach, and he continued walking in the direction of that denser part of Innsmouth, hoping one might still be in business.

He closed his eyes at one point, having walked far longer than he had hoped, and near to exhaustion. He did not remember finding the restaurant, or sitting down, or ordering. But the next thing he knew he was blinking rapidly, and he was holding a large spoon, and warm and slippery things were washing down his throat. He almost choked when he realized it, and had to down a large glass of water which tasted a bit too salty and whose color was less than assuring. His teeth felt unstable, his tongue sore, the inside of his mouth scraped.

He only vaguely remembered the meals he'd had when his parents brought him here as a child. He remembered feeling ravenous the whole time, and devouring hotdogs and something else—some sort of pita-like concoction—from beach-side stands. His parents ate hardly anything at all. His father had been drinking, not as committedly as he would after that vacation, but enough that it made him quiet, grumpy, and without appetite. His mother—he was never sure if his mother ate anything during that trip. He vaguely remembered sitting with them in a small restaurant like this one, only cleaner, brighter, and watching her dab at her mouth with a cloth napkin, always dabbing, touching her lips with it, her teeth, and a redness coming away on the cloth.

He looked down into his soup, or stew. Very little was left, a small bit of tail sticking out of a thick, grey broth. He pushed the bowl away, looked around him. There were other patrons in the small café. This shouldn't have surprised him, except that he had seen no one except the motel clerk and his near-doppelganger, the golf attendant, since his arrival the night before.

There were five, no, six others, huddled over their food. Thickly dressed in layers, high collars, some with weedy mats of hair slapped on top their heads. Some with stocking caps, despite the warm day. All looked vaguely ill or hung over, here to recover, perhaps, from the night before. The fellow closest to Whitcomb had a similar soup bowl in front of him, filled with grey. Periodically he jabbed his fork into the liquid as if attacking.

The walls looked greasy, with large spots by the tables along the perimeter, as if people had rested their heads there, soiling the dingy green paint. He saw a tall man in a muscle shirt asleep at one of those tables, perhaps a sailor given the theme of his tattoos—fish and whales and frogs and waves and some things tendrilled, perhaps vegetation, perhaps not. His torso leaned against the wall, one arm pressed beneath his chest, his head lolling, cheek smeared flat.

The sailor suddenly woke up, startled, glared at Whitcomb, and pulled his head and arm away from the wall. Sticky pale threads ran from his flesh to where bits of him still clung to the wall, including part of a bluish anchor design.

Whitcomb stumbled out of his chair and went through the door. Had he paid? No one shouted, no one chased him. But he stopped himself out on the beach, thinking that if he hadn't paid, the proprietor would catch up to him and he could apologize, explain that it was a mistake, and pay what he owed, pay double what he owed. But no one came.

He looked back down the beach searching for his motel. He had no idea how far he had come. He also hadn't realized that he'd been walking up a slope, this part of the beach being noticeably higher than from where he'd come. From here he could see the entire stretch of it, hundreds of yards, and the way the waves came in, taking greedy nibbles. And all that had been ruined. And how the sand moved, minutely, but seeing it all together like this, multiplied, so that for the first time he could be sure, all that sand, everywhere, was moving.

He must have fallen quite hard, because he was suddenly on the ground, eyes and mouth gaping. The sand edged around him. He shut his eyes, trying to force it out.

He'd awakened that night, all those years ago, because of a noise or a dream of a noise. Someone crying, someone lost. Bits of his memory from that time had wandered off, but this memory, at least, he had found.

His father lay passed out on the bed. Whitcomb was on the rollaway, shivering—he'd always been so skinny as a boy, and easy to chill. As he sat up he'd realized it was because the motel room door was open, and the ocean breeze was coming in, and the sand. He'd looked around for his mother then, but she was nowhere to be seen.

He'd wandered out. His feet must have been damp, because he could remember the sand sticking to them. He remembered looking down, all that clinging sand making his feet look frosted, sparkling in the moonlight.

Out on the beach there was a tall, thin form. He'd recognized his mother's pale yellow gown. She was swaying, and the wind was lifting her gown, and he'd thought he should turn away because he shouldn't be seeing this.

She'd turned her head then, and her mouth was so red, and he'd thought she was looking at him, but it quickly became clear she was gazing at the ground behind her, the sandy beach, which was moving.

She'd tried to get away from it. She never would have left him if she could have helped it. She'd always been devoted to him, despite her flaws.

He didn't know where she was running. He'd only been eight, but even then he'd understood that the ocean wouldn't have helped her.

The sand trailed up and her gown began to fall away. He was embarrassed and closed his eyes, but forced them open again as the hazy softness of her went dark. Later his father would hold the empty gown and ask him if he had seen anything. And he would say he had not, because he had not.

Whitcomb opened his eyes and saw the drift of tiny particles on the beach in front of him; felt them float in and out of his mouth, in and out of his ears. Red bits and soft bits, and an endless streaming of sand.

A lifetime later he sat out in front of his room, taking in the ocean, taking in all the sand. He was missing pieces. He could not remember why he had come here, just that it had been a compulsion, beyond important, but that memory was useless to him now. As were all other memories, scoured and taken and blown away by the wind. But it was almost a relief to see them go.

He gazed down at his sweatpants, which were almost empty now. He began to smile, but could feel that even bits of his smile were gone.

SNOW

DALE BAILEY

They took shelter outside of Boulder, in a cookie-cutter subdivision that had seen better days. Five or six floor plans, Dave Kerans figured, brick façades and tan siding, crumbling streets and blank cul-de-sacs, no place you'd want to live. By then, Felicia had passed out from the pain, and the snow beyond the windshield of Lanyan's black Yukon had thickened into an impenetrable white blur.

It had been a spectacular run of bad luck, starting with the first news of the virus via the satellite radio in the Yukon: three days of disease vectors and infection rates, symptoms and speculation. Calm voices gave way to anxious ones; anxious ones succumbed to panic. The last they heard was the sound of a commentator retching. Then flat silence, nothing at all the length of the band, NPR, CNN, the Outlaw Country Station, and suddenly no one was anxious to go home, none of them, not Kerans and Felicia, not Lanyan or his new girlfriend, Natalie, lithe and blonde and empty-headed as the last player in his rotating cast of female companions.

On the third day of the catastrophe—when it became clear that humanity just might be toast—they'd powwowed around a fire between the tents, passing hand-to-hand the last of the primo dope Lanyan had procured for the trip. Lanyan always insisted on the best: tents and sleeping bags that could weather a winter on the Ross Ice Shelf, a high-end water-filtration system, a portable gas stove with more bells and whistles than the full-size one Kerans and Felicia used at home, even a Benelli R1 semi-automatic hunting rifle (*just in case*, Lanyan had said). The most remote location, as well: somewhere two thousand feet above Boulder, where the early November deciduous trees began to give way to Pinyon pine and Rocky Mountain juniper. Zero cell-phone reception, but by that time there was nobody left to call, or anyway none of them cared to make the descent and see. The broadcasts had started calling it the red death by then. Kerans appreciated the allusion: airborne, an incubation period of less than twenty-four hours, blood leaking from your eyes, your nostrils, your pores and, toward the end—twelve hours if you were lucky, another twenty-four if you weren't—gushing from your mouth with every cough. No-thank-yous all around. Safe enough at seventy-five-hundred feet, at least for the time being—the time being, Lanyan insisted, lasting at least through the winter and maybe longer.

"We have maybe two weeks' worth of food," Kerans protested.

"We'll scout out a cabin and hunker down for the duration," Lanyan said. "If we have to, we'll hunt."

There was that at least. Lanyan was a master with the Benelli. They wouldn't starve—and Kerans didn't have any more desire to contract the red death than the rest of them.

All had been going according to plan. Inside a week they'd located a summer cabin, complete with a larder of canned goods, and had started gathering wood for the stove. Then Felicia had fallen. A single bad step on a bed of loose scree, and that had been it for the plan. When Kerans cut her jeans away, he saw that the leg had broken at the shin. Yellow bone jutted through the flesh. Blood was everywhere. Felicia screamed when Lanyan set the bone, yanking it back into true, or something close to true, splinting it with a couple of backpack poles, and binding the entire bloody mess with a bandage they found in a first-aid kit under the sink. The bandage had soaked through almost immediately. Kerans, holding her hand, thought for the first time in half a dozen years of their wedding, the way she'd looked in her dress and the way he'd felt inside, like the luckiest man on the planet.

Luck.

It had all turned sour on them.

"I'm taking her down, first thing in the morning," he told Lanyan.

"What for? You heard the radio."

"You want to die, too?" Natalie asked.

"I don't want *her* to die," Kerans said. That was the point. Without help, she was doomed, anybody could see that. There wasn't a hell of a lot any of them could do on their own. A venture capitalist and a college English professor and something else, a Broncos cheerleader maybe, who knew what Natalie did? "Even if it's as bad as we think it is down there," he added, "we can still find a pharmacy, antibiotics, whatever. You think there's any chance her leg isn't going to get infected?"

Grim-faced, Lanyan had turned away. "I think it's a bad idea."

"You have a better one?"

"How are you going to get down, Dave? You planning to use the Yukon?" Kerans laughed in disbelief. "I can't believe you'd even say that."

"What?" Lanyan said, as if he didn't know.

"You were the best man at my wedding. Hell, you introduced me to Felicia."

"We have to think of ourselves now," Natalie said.

"Fuck you, Natalie," Kerans said, and that had been the end of the conversation.

He was wakeful most of the night that followed. Felicia was feverish. "Am I going to die, Dave?" she'd asked in one of her lucid moments. "Of course not," he'd responded, the lie cleaving his heart.

Lanyan woke him at dawn. They stood shivering on the porch of the cabin and watched clouds mass among the peaks. The temperature had plunged overnight. The air smelled like snow.

"You win," Lanyan said. "We'll go down to Boulder."

-◦-

The snow caught them when they were winding down the rutted track from the cabin, big lazy flakes sifting through the barren trees to deliquesce on the Yukon's acres of windshield. Nothing to worry about, Kerans thought in the backseat, cradling Felicia's head in his lap. But the temperature—visible in digital blue on the dash—continued to plummet, twenty-five, fifteen, ten; by the time they hit paved road, a good hour and a half from the cabin, and itself a narrow, serpentine stretch of crumbling asphalt, the weather had gotten serious. The wipers carved slanting parabolas in the snow. Beyond the windows, the world had receded into a white haze.

Lanyan hunched closer to the wheel.

They crept along, pausing now and again to inch around an abandoned vehicle.

"We should have stayed where we were," Natalie said, and the silence that followed seemed like assent.

But it was too late to turn back now.

Finally the road widened into a four-lane highway, clogged with vehicles. They plowed onward anyway, weaving drunkenly among the cars. By the time they reached the outskirts of Boulder, the headlights stabbed maybe fifteen feet into the swirling snow.

"I can't see a thing," Lanyan said. They turned aside into surface streets, finding their way at last into the decaying subdivision. They picked a house at random, a rancher with a brick façade in an empty cul-de-sac. The conventions of civilization held. Lanyan and Kerans scouted it out, while the women waited in the Yukon. They knocked, shouting, but no one came. Finally, they tested the door. It had been left unlocked; the owners had departed in a hurry, Kerans figured, fleeing the contagion. He wondered if they'd passed them dead somewhere on the highway, or if they'd made it into the higher altitudes in time. The house itself was empty. Maybe they'd gotten lucky. Maybe the frigid air would kill the virus before it could kill them. Maybe, Kerans thought. Maybe.

They settled Felicia on the sectional sofa in the great room, before the unblinking eye of the oversized flatscreen. Afterward, they searched the place more thoroughly, dosing Felicia with the amoxicillin and oxycodone they found in the medicine cabinet. Then the food in the pantry, tools neatly racked in the empty garage, a loaded pistol in a bedside table. Natalie tucked it in the belt of her jeans. Kerans flipped light switches, adjusted the thermostat, flicked on the television. Nothing. How quickly it all fell apart. They hunched around a portable radio instead: white noise all across the dial.

Welcome to the end of the world, it said.

Not with a bang, but a whimper.

-◦-

The snow kept coming, gusts of it, obscuring everything a dozen feet beyond the windows, then unveiling it in quick flashes: the blurred limb of a naked tree, the shadow of the Yukon at the curb. Kerans stood at the window as night fell, wondering what he'd expected to find. A hospital? A doctor? The hospitals must have been overwhelmed from the start, the doctors first to go.

The streetlights snapped alight—solar-charged batteries, the death throes of the world he'd grown up in. They illuminated clouds of billowing white that in other circumstances Kerans would have found beautiful. Cold groped at the window. He turned away.

Lanyan and Natalie had scrounged a handful of tealight candles. By their flickering luminescence, the great room took on a cathedral air. Darkness encroached from the corners and gathered in shrouds at the ceiling. They ate pork and beans warmed over the camp stove, spread their sleeping bags on the carpet, and talked. The same goddamn conversation they'd had for days now: *surely we're not the only ones* and *how many?* and *where?* and *what if?*

"We're probably already dying," Natalie said, turning a baleful eye on Kerans. "Well, we're down here now," she said. "What's your plan, Einstein?"

"I don't have a plan. I didn't figure on the snow."

"You didn't figure on a lot of things."

"Cut it out," Lanyan said.

"We didn't have to do this, Cliff," Natalie said.

"What did you expect me to do? I've known Felicia for years. I've known Dave longer. It's not like we had access to weather reports."

No, Kerans thought, that was another thing gone with the old world. Just like that. Everything evaporated.

By then the cold had become black, physical.

Kerans got to his feet. He tucked Felicia's sleeping bag into the crevices of the sofa. She moaned. Her eyes fluttered. She reached for his hand.

Kerans shook two oxycodone out of the bottle.

"These'll help you sleep."

"Will you stay with me, Dave?"

All the way to the end, he thought, and he knew then that at some level, if only half-consciously, he had accepted what he had known in his heart back at the cabin. She was gone. She'd been gone the moment she'd slipped on that bed of scree. And he'd laughed, he remembered that, too. *Whoops*, he'd said, and she'd said, *I'm hurt, Dave*, her voice plaintive, frightened, tight with agony. He'd never heard her use that voice in seventeen years of marriage, and he knew then that she was beyond help. There was no help to be had. Yet Lanyan had surrendered the Yukon all the same, and they had knocked on the door before barging into this house, just as they had knocked on the door of the summer cabin in the mountains before that. How long, he wondered, before they reverted to savagery?

"Will you stay with me, Dave?" she said.

"Of course."

He slid into his sleeping bag. They held hands by candlelight until the oxycodone hit her and her fingers went limp. He tucked her arm under her sleeping bag—he could smell the wound, already suppurating with infection—and lay back.

The last of the tealights burned out.

Kerans glanced at the luminescent dial of his watch. Nine-thirty.

The streetlight's spectral blue glow suffused the air.

He closed his eyes, but sleep eluded him. An endless loop unspooled against the dark screens of his eyelids: Felicia's expression as the earth slipped out from under her feet. His helpless whoop of laughter. *I'm hurt, Dave.*

He opened his eyes.

"You awake, Cliff?" he said.

"Yeah."

"You think Natalie's right? We're all going to wind up coughing up blood in twenty-four hours or so?"

"I don't know."

"Maybe the snow," Kerans said. "Maybe the cold has killed the virus."

"Maybe."

They were silent.

"One way or the other, we'll find out, I guess," Lanyan said.

Snow ticked at the windows like fingernails. Let me in. Let me in.

"About the Yukon—" Kerans said.

"It doesn't matter, Dave. You'd have done the same for me."

Would he? Kerans wondered. He liked to think so.

"I'm sorry I was an asshole," Lanyan said.

"It doesn't matter."

"Felicia's going to be okay."

"Sure she is. I know."

Kerans gazed across the room at the shadowy mound of the other man in his sleeping bag.

"What do you figure happened?"

"Hell, I don't know. You heard the radio as well as I did. Something got loose from a military lab. Terrorists. Maybe just a mutation. Ebola, something like that."

Another conversation they'd had a dozen times. It was like picking a scab.

A long time passed. Kerans didn't know how long it was.

"It doesn't matter, I guess," he said, adrift between sleep and waking.

"Not anymore," Lanyan said, and the words chased Kerans down a dark hole into sleep.

-o-

Lanyan woke him into that same unearthly blue light, and for a moment Kerans didn't know where he was. Only that strange undersea radiance, his sense of time and place out of joint, a chill undertow of anxiety. Then it all came flooding back, the plague, Felicia's fall, the blizzard.

Lanyan's expression echoed his unease.

"Get up," he said.

"What's going on?"

"Just get up."

Kerans followed him to the window. Natalie crouched there, gazing out into the sheets of blowing snow. She held the pistol in one hand.

"What is it?" he whispered.

"There's something in the snow," she said.

"What?"

"I heard it. It woke me up."

"You hear anything, Cliff?"

Lanyan shrugged.

Wind tore at the house, rattling gutters. Kerans peered into the snow, but if there was anything out there, he couldn't see it. He couldn't see anything but a world gone white. The streetlamp loomed above them, a bulb of fuzzy blue light untethered from the earth.

"Heard what?" he asked.

"I don't know. It woke me. Something in the snow."

"The wind," Kerans said.

"It sounded like it was alive."

"Listen to it blow out there. You could hear anything in that. The brain, it"—he hesitated—

"What?" Natalie said.

"All I'm saying is, it's easy enough to imagine something like that. Voices in the wind. Shapes in the snow."

Natalie's breath fogged the window. "I didn't imagine anything."

"Look," he said. "It's late. We're all tired. You could have imagined something, that's all I'm saying."

"I said I didn't imagine it."

And then, as though the very words had summoned it into being, a thin shriek carved the wind—alien, predatory, unearthly as the cry of a hunting raptor. The snow muffled it, made it hard to track how far away it was, but it was closer than Kerans wanted it be. It held for a moment, wavering, and dropped away. A heartbeat passed, then two, and then came an answering cry, farther away. Kerans swallowed hard, put his back to the wall, and slid to the floor. He pulled his knees up, dropped his head between them. He could feel the cold radiating from the window, shivering erect the tiny hairs on his neck. He looked up. His breath unfurled in the gloom. They were both watching him, Lanyan and Natalie.

"It's the wind," he said. Hating himself as he said it, hating this new weakness he'd discovered in himself, this inability to face what in his heart he knew to be true.

Came a third cry then, still farther away.

"Jesus," Lanyan said.

"They're surrounding us," Natalie said.

"They're?" Kerans said. "They're? Who the hell do you think could be out there in that?"

Natalie turned and met his gaze. "I don't know," she said.

-◦-

They checked the house, throwing deadbolts, locking interior doors and windows. Kerans didn't get the windows. You wanted to get inside bad enough, you just broke the glass. Yet there was something comforting in sliding the little tongue into its groove all the same. Symbolic barriers. Like cavemen, drawing circles of fire against the night.

As for sleep, forget it.

He leaned against the sofa, draped in his sleeping bag, envying Felicia the oblivion of the oxycodone. Her skin was hot to the touch, greasy with perspiration. He could smell, or imagined he could smell, the putrescent wound, the inadequate dressing soaked with gore.

Across the room sat Lanyan, the Benelli flat across his legs. At the window, her back propped against the wall, Natalie, cradling the pistol in her lap. Kerans felt naked with just the hunting knife at his belt.

The snow kept coming, slanting down past the streetlamp, painting the room with that strange, swimming light. Lanyan's face looked blue and cold, like the face of a dead man. Natalie's, too. And he didn't even want to think about Felicia, burning up under the covers, sweating out the fever of the infection.

"We should look at her leg," he said.

"And do what?" Natalie responded, and what could he say to that because there *was* nothing to do, Kerans knew that as well as anyone, yet he felt compelled in his impotence to do something, anything, even if it was just stripping back the sleeping bag and staring at the wound, stinking and inflamed, imperfectly splinted, oozing blood and yellow pus.

"Just keep doling out those drugs," Lanyan said, and Kerans knew he meant the oxycodone, not the amoxicillin, which couldn't touch an infection of this magnitude, however much he prayed—and he was not a praying man. He couldn't help recalling his mother, dying in agony from bone cancer: the narrow hospital room, stinking of antiseptic, with its single forlorn window; the doctor, a hulking Greek, quick to anger, who spoke in heavily accented English. *We're into pain management now*, he'd said.

"How much is left?" Natalie said, and Kerans realized that he'd been turning the prescription bottle in his hands.

"Ten, maybe fifteen pills."

"Not enough," she said. "I don't think it's enough," and a bright fuse of hatred for her burned through him for giving voice to thoughts he could barely acknowledge as his own.

After that, silence.

Kerans's eyes were grainy with exhaustion, yet he could not sleep.

None of them could sleep.

Unspeaking, they listened for voices in the storm.

◄●►

At two, they came: one, two, three metallic screeches in the wind.

Lanyan took one window, Natalie the other, lifting her pistol.

Kerans stayed with Felicia. She was stirring now, coming out of her oxycodone haze. "What is it?" she said.

"Nothing. It's nothing."

But it was something.

"There," Natalie said, but she needn't have said it at all.

Even from his place by the sofa, Kerans saw it: a blue shadow darting past the window, little more than a blur, seven feet long or longer, horizontal to the earth, tail lashing, faster than anything that size had any right to be, faster than anything human. There and gone again, obscured by a veil of blowing snow.

Kerans's own words mocked him. Imagination. Shapes in the snow.

He thought of that icy tapping, like fingernails at the window.

Let me in.

Felicia said, "Dave? What is it, Dave?"

"It's nothing," he said.

Silence prevailed. Shifting veils of snow.

"What the hell was that thing?" Lanyan said.

And Natalie from her window. "Let's play a game."

Nobody said a word.

"The game is called 'What if?'" she said.

"What are you talking about?" Kerans said.

"What if you were an alien species?"

"Oh, come on," Kerans said, but Lanyan was grim and silent.

"Way ahead of us technologically, capable of travel between stars."

"This is crazy, Dave," Felicia said. "What is she talking about?"

"Nothing. It's nothing."

"And what if you wanted to clear a planet for colonization?"

"You read too much science fiction."

"Shut the hell up, Dave," Lanyan said.

"We're intelligent. They would try to—"

"We're vermin," Natalie said. "And what I would do, I would engineer some kind of virus and wipe out 99 percent of the vermin. Like fumigating a fucking house."

"And then?" Lanyan said.

"Then I'd send in the ground troops to mop up."

Kerans snorted.

"Dave—"

"It's craziness, that's all," he said. He said, "Here, these'll help you sleep."

Nothing then. Nothing but wind and snow and the sound of silence in the room.

After a time, they resumed their posts on the floor.

Felicia, weeping, lapsed back into drugged sleep.

"We're going to have to get to the Yukon," Natalie said.

"We can't see a fucking thing out there," Kerans said.

"At first light. Maybe the snow will stop by then."

"And if it doesn't?" Lanyan said.

"We make a run for it."

"What about Felicia?" Kerans said.

"What about her?"

Kerans looked at his watch. It was almost three o'clock.

⊸⊙⊸

He must have dozed, for he came awake abruptly, jarred from sleep by a distant thud. A dream, he thought, his pulse hammering. It must have been a dream—a nightmare inside this nightmare of dark and endless snow, of a plague-ravished world and Felicia dying in agony. But it was no dream. Lanyan and Natalie had heard it, too. They were already up, their weapons raised, and even as he stumbled to his feet, shedding like water the sleeping bag across his shoulders, it came again: a thump against the back of the house, muffled by snow and the intervening rooms.

"What is it?" Felicia said, her voice drowsy with oxycodone.

"Nothing," he said. "It was nothing. A branch must have fallen."

"That was no branch," Natalie said. "Not unless it fell twice."

And twice more after that, two quick blows, and a third, and then silence, a submarine hush so deep and pervasive that Kerans could hear the boom of his heart.

"Maybe a tree came down."

"You know better," Lanyan said.

"Dave, I'm scared," Felicia whispered.

"We're all scared," Natalie said.

Felicia began softly to weep.

"Shut her the fuck up," Natalie said.

"Natalie—"

"I said shut her up."

"It hurts," Felicia said. "I'm afraid." Kerans knelt by the sectional and kissed her chill lips. Her breath bloomed in the cold air, sweet with the stink of infection, and he didn't think he'd ever loved her more in his life than he did at that moment. "There's nothing to be afraid of," he whispered, wiping away her tears with the ball of his thumb. "It's just the wind." But even she was past believing him, for the wind had died. The snow fell soft and straight through the air. The streetlamp was a blue halo against the infinite blackness of space. Natalie's game came back to Kerans—what if—and a dark surf broke and receded across the shingles of his heart. Felicia took his hand and squeezed his fingers weakly. "Just don't leave me here," she said. "Don't leave me here to die."

"Never."

The glitter of shattering glass splintered the air. Felicia screamed, a short, sharp bark of terror—

"Shut her up," Natalie snapped.

—and in the silence that followed, in the shifting purple shadow of the great room with its sectional sofa and the gray rectangle of the flatscreen and their sleeping bags like the shucked skins of enormous snakes upon the floor, Kerans heard someone—something—

—let's play a game the game is called what if—

—test the privacy lock of a back bedroom: a slow turn to either side. *Click. Click.*

Silence.

Felicia whimpered. Kerans blew a cloud of vapor into the still air. He clutched Felicia's fingers. He remembered a time when they had made hasty love in the bathroom at a friend's cocktail party, half-drunk, mad with passion for each other. The memory came to him with pristine clarity. He felt tears upon his cheeks.

And still the silence held.

Lanyan snapped off the safety of the Benelli.

Natalie put her back to the foyer wall, reached out, and flipped the deadbolt of the front door. She pushed it a few inches ajar. Snow dusted the threshold.

"The Yukon locked?" she whispered.

"No."

Once again, the thing tested the lock.

"Dave, don't leave me—"

"Natalie—"

She froze him with a glance. God help him, he didn't want to die. He choked back a sob. They had wanted children. They had tried for them. In vitro, the whole nine yards.

"I won't leave you," he whispered.

Then the privacy lock snapped, popping like a firecracker. The door banged back. Something came, hurtling down the hallway: something big, hunched over the floor, and God, God, shedding pieces of itself, one, two, three as it burst into the room. Guns spat bright tongues of fire, a barrage of deafening explosions. The impact flung the thing backward, but the pieces, two- or three-foot lengths of leg-pumping fury, kept coming. Snapping the Benelli from target to target, Lanyan took two of them down. Natalie stopped the third one not three feet from Kerans's throat. It rolled on the floor, curving needle-teeth snapping, leathery hide gleaming in the snow-blown light, and was still.

Those alien cries echoed in the darkness.

"Time to go," Natalie said.

Lanyan moved to the door.

Felicia clutched at Kerans's hand, seizing him with a tensile strength he did not know she still possessed. The cocktail party flashed through his mind. They had wanted children—

"Felicia—" Kerans said. "Help me—"

"No time," Natalie said.

And Lanyan: "I'm sorry, Dave—"

The moment hung in equipoise. Kerans wrenched his hand away.

"Time to go," Natalie said again. "We can't wait. You have to decide."

She ducked into the night. A moment later, Lanyan followed.

Glass shattered at the back of the house, one window, two windows, three.

"Don't leave me, Dave," Felicia sobbed. "Don't leave me."

Outside the Yukon roared to life.

"Dave," Felicia said, "I'm scared."

"Shhh," he said, brushing closed her eyelids with his fingers. "Never. I'll never leave you. I love you."

He bent to press his lips to hers. His fingers fumbled at his belt. They closed around the blade.

A moment later, he was running for the Yukon.

INDIAN GIVER

RAY CLULEY

Every man carries his share of ghosts, but there are those who listen to them more than others. That was Grady's opinion, anyways. And most of those listenin' didn't much like what they heard; that was his opinion, too. So he wasn't surprised to see Tom stumblin' across the darkening yard towards him. If he was surprised at all it was only that it had taken the man so long.

The taming of the wild west was something Grady never saw—he was a proper lieutenant, not a glorified book-keep or ledger-maker (though there were plenty of those)—but even so, all he saw of the west was tired and worn down. Land *and* people. Native people, mostly, but Tom carried the same look himself right now. He had something in his hand that was supposed to be Tennessee whiskey but probably wasn't. It would taste right, though. And they'd drink it down just fine. A tale of woe was best punctuated with whiskey.

Seeing Tom made him think of that Philly boy, of course. Stick a city man out here and it gets to him sometimes, that was true, but Grady wasn't so sure that was the thinking this time. Still, those ruminations were likely to get him morose and melancholy when he was drinking, and it looked like he was going to be, so he tried to think of other things.

Tom saw Grady was sitting on the porch and stopped. He hitched his belt up, touched his hat. "Evenin'."

"Evenin', Tom. Been a while. Where you been?"

"The pen."

"You're spending a lot of time there these days, I hear. Keeping company with our noble savages."

Savages. All Grady saw was farming folk with darker skin and longer hair, wearing expressions pressed on them by hard work. The white man had taken their animals and taken their land and they weren't about to give it back any time soon.

"Noble savages," Tom said, nodding. "Don't see much noble civilized, do we?"

Grady looked Tom over. The last of the light was leaking from the sky but he could see enough in the dusk to know Tom was in a bad way, and drunk with it.

"Got somethin' to talk about," Tom said, showing Grady the bottle he held.

Grady nodded. He got up from his chair with a creak he pretended was the wood and went in for the cups.

⟶

"Alright," said Grady, sitting back in his accustomed chair. There was another beside it, and a small table. They had the whole stretch of planks to themselves. The men inside were sleeping. Grady, though, liked to stay out late, watch the stars.

"It's one of those stories that needs tellin' because it's heavy," Tom said. "Tellin' it makes it easier to carry."

Grady heard a lot of stories like that. Carried a few, too.

"Alright."

He poured them both drinks.

Tom had a story to tell, but he kept quiet a while. That was fine by Grady. He watched the stars do nothing in the sky, and listened to the quiet sounds of men snoring and shifting in their beds behind him. Occasionally a breeze carried the smell of wood smoke and bacon grease from across the yard.

"North wall's goin' be extended," Tom said eventually.

"What for?"

Tom shrugged. "Colonel wants to."

Grady could have asked "what for" again, but didn't like to waste breath he could whistle with.

Tom tipped his cup and took all that was in it, refilling as he swallowed. Grady offered his own cup for more. He didn't want Tom's nerves to soak up all the whiskey. "Slow down, Tom. It's been a while since you and me shared a drink."

Tom acknowledged that with a nod and poured. "Did a round up couple of weeks back," he said. "Mountain flush out."

Grady nodded. Drank. "That a fact?" He knew it was, but this was how it had to start.

"Went into the hills." Tom counted them off on his fingers; "Me. Henry. Cody. Packard. James."

Grady nodded. Five was about right.

"You wanna talk to me about James, Tom?"

"It got messy up there, sir. But I fixed it now."

Tom was paler than the half moon above them, dark rings like smudged soot under his eyes. Tom hadn't been sleeping well, that was how Grady reckoned it. He had questions, but he waited. He'd done his fair share of round ups. Companies went into the mountains looking for Injuns hiding out or just plain missed. There were a lot of them out there still, holed up in caves or just living so remote they were easy to miss first time round, even second and third. Course, the more Injuns they rounded up and persuaded west was best, the more they learnt where others were. Families wanted to go west together. These people had been tribal once and bonds were still strong.

"It was a small place tucked away in the crags," Tom said, "screen of trees round it. Vegetable patch. Chickens. There was a well out front with a low wall."

Tom paused to drink but really he was remembering. He wasn't on the porch with Grady no more. He was somewhere in the mountains.

"The man, he's big. Goliath big. Huge. And he's wearing all this fur that makes him seem bigger. Hair's long and all untied"—Tom gestured with his hands—"down over his face. You seen 'em like that? Real wild looking, but with that look they all got, the one that says he knows they're beat and never had no hope otherwise."

Grady said, "Stamped down like trodden ground."

"Yeah, that's it. That's how he looked. I gave my speech, just like always. Had my ledger, took a record of what they were leaving, told 'em they'd be reimbursed and paid a relocation fee just for going where the land was better anyways."

Grady nodded, but he had his doubts about that last bit. To his mind it was like taking off someone's feet then giving them a pair of boots. Even if they *were* given land, Grady reckoned it wouldn't be long before someone took it back again.

"He wasn't really listenin'," Tom said, "but he started gatherin' things from the yard. Like he'd been expectin' us a while. Two young'ns—"

Tom's voice caught in his throat. He put his cup down and said something to the floor Grady preferred to hear in church.

"A girl and a boy, both dirty 'n' scraped a bit but smiling. They came out to see." He stared at his empty hands as if wondering where his drink had gone.

"The others, they was all in the saddle, same as always. Cody, he had a smoke. James and Packard were talking about Philadelphia. They talked so much about a place they both lived in, I don't know how they managed to say anythin' new. They knew each other all but Biblical." He tried to smile at that but it didn't work. "Then Henry happened."

"Henry?"

"He did what was usual for him. We'd give 'em time to pack and Henry'd use that time to ride round 'n' round their house. Said it put the hurryin' on but really he did it 'cause he liked to rub people wrong. Henry can shoot, salute, 'n' spit a little, but that's about it, so he makes the most of a job like this."

Grady knew the type and said so, but Tom wasn't listening.

"Second time Henry comes round from back he's got a woman followin' him. She's all dressed in deerskin and bird shit, got a cloth tied around her waist held full of eggs. Her hair's long 'n' braided 'n' gathered up a bunch at the back. I remember that 'cause she was shoutin' Injun at him an' shakin' her head and the braids were fallin' loose. Henry just laughed, spurrin' his horse a few steps to turn a circle so as he could laugh back at her face."

"What did she do?" Grady asked, pouring them another drink.

"She threw an egg at him." Tom laughed, but it was a harsh sound. "Got him, too." He slapped his right hand against his left shoulder to show where.

Grady paused, cup hovering at his lips. He knew how a story with a bored young soldier and an angry Injun woman could end after something like that. And Tom had said it was messy. James said the same thing by doing what he did, tasting his own gun and putting a stain of himself on the walls of his bunkhouse.

"What did he do?" Grady asked. "Henry, I mean."

"He crapped in their well."

Tom looked out into the stockade, though there was nothing to see out there but cabins and they was only dark shapes in the gloom. He swallowed his drink down.

"He crapped in their well," Grady said. "Well, sure."

"He did that a lot. If they pissed him off some, or they took too long packin', he'd crap. Got so I wondered if he held back for the occasion. Usually he'd crap front of the house, in the doorway or some place. No reason for it when it's a home they're leavin' anyway, but he knows they don't wanna see that as they leave. It's spittin' in a man's wound. Even Injun knows that."

Grady agreed.

"Henry's got broken egg shell runnin' down his chest, and a face that's fiery fierce. He's dismountin' in a hurry 'n' so am I but my damn boot tangles in the stirrup. Henry's stridin' at this woman, hand on his pistol, and she's ready to throw another one, yellin' at him 'n' all us, and I'm thinkin', shit, my money's on Henry."

Tom was talking in the present sense of things, Grady realized—they were getting to it now.

"I'm too far away to stop anythin', but the big fella, he steps out from the house 'n' grabs his woman's wrist from behind, bursts the egg in her hand. Then he scoops the rest from her apron 'n' lets *them* break as well. He's calm, though. Sayin' soft things to her. Henry calms down too, but not enough to let things be. Not Henry. He strides over to the well they have out front, drops his britches, and takes a crap perched over the edge."

As far as bad stories went, this wasn't one to lose much sleep over, Grady thought. Which only meant it weren't finished yet.

"Henry finds it funny every time he does it, so he's laughin' even as he's droppin' his dirt. James and Packard, they're laughin' too. They've not been out with Henry before so it's new to them, and James is as fresh as tit milk, but even so I reckon they was just easin' down after the tension. Cody don't say nothin', of course."

Grady knew Cody. Everybody did. Cody was likely the oldest in Tom's group and should've been in charge, but for reasons no one talked about he *wasn't* in charge. Those reasons were him leadin' out after Willy Wilson and none but himself coming back. Wilson was a bad man with a greased holster and a fondness for other folk's horses. Just one man, but Cody couldn't put him down clean. That was a long time ago, but people remembered a thing like that.

"Cody keeps out of it," Tom said. "By now the young'ns have come back out because of all the yellin' an' cussin'. The girl's filled a cookin' pot with things to carry out 'n' she hugs it to her stomach, watchin' her mamma stride over to Henry. He's still squatting and straining and she shoves him! Sonofabitch damn near falls in! He makes a wild grab 'n' gets some of the wall 'n' some of her deerskin, and likely he lets another load loose, too, without thinking 'bout it, but then he's laughin'. It's the nervous kind a man has when he's been scared. We all know it, and he knows we know it. So he slaps her across the face."

Grady shifted but couldn't get ready for it. This would be the messy bit.

"Sounded like a bear trap going off," Tom said.

Right now. Blood, most likely.

"Henry's pullin' his pants up, yankin' his belt, but that woman comes right back to push him again, you believe that? He keeps her off with a shove of his own 'n' puts his hand to the grip of his pistol after. I didn't like that, didn't like any of it, but I'm still dancing around with one foot tangled up.

"The big man, all fur 'n' muscle 'n' hangin' hair, he comes over and I think he'll be like before, you know, calm her down some. He puts his basket down and he looks like he's makin' to restrain his squaw cause he puts a hand on her chest to keep her back and he puts another out for Henry. Like he's keepin' them separate. But he shoves Henry hard. Henry backs up a few steps and the well gets him behind the knees and over he goes, topples right in. Gone."

Grady couldn't swallow his drink for a moment. When he did, it choked a single cough from him. Tom didn't notice.

"We don't hear nothin' at first when he falls. He's surprised like us, most likely, and don't scream or nothin'. There's just a sound that's thud and splash.

"We all start yellin'. My foot's finally free but I'm hoppin' round a minute. James dismounts with that flashy kick he has 'n' runs over, Packard right there with him. Cody just turns a tight circle on the spot 'n' says, 'Hey.' Just that. 'Hey.'"

"The Injun fella, though, he ignores everythin' but his wife. Holds her face real gentle with both his big hands, checkin' her. Her cheek's already swellin' and her eye's closin' up. He grunts 'n' kisses her forehead.

"By then James is there with his gun at the Injun's face but looking at the well. He glances down, then back at the Injun, then down the well again. He calls, 'Henry!' but if there's a reply we don't hear it. Maybe because I'm shouting at everyone to shut up and calm the hell down.

"James yells, 'Henry, you down there? I can't see nothin' but dark' and I think, of course he's down there. Packard's yellin' for Henry as well. He's got his gun on the woman. The only people makin' noise is us. Even the young'ns standin' there are quiet, though the girl's got some tears."

Tom stopped and took a ragged breath. He grabbed for the bottle of whiskey but knocked it down. Grady scooped it up quick before anything could spill.

"Only thing that tastes right," Tom said.

Grady agreed. When he thought about it later he realized they weren't talking about it the same way.

"James and Packard got nothin' from the well. Injun fella looks down at James like there's no gun between them. I'm reachin' for 'em, thinkin' I don't know what, when for no reason I can gather other than he's nervous or somethin', James shoots the Injun square in the face."

Grady wasn't surprised, and yet . . . well, he'd hoped different.

Tom nodded as if agreeing with something and wiped at his neck. "A splash of somethin' made a thick noise on my coat and it was on my neck and in my hair. And we're all just starin'. The only noise comes from Cody. This time he's sayin' 'Hold on, hold on' like he needs a minute.

"The Injun, he turns back to his squaw with a hole where his eye used to be, a flap of cheek hangin' down all blistered. He don't seem to know it. Where he's stood, James gets the full effect of that face and whatever he sees up close is enough to make him scared. And James, he lashes out at times like that. So that's what he does."

Grady said, "Christ." Muttered it to clasped hands as he listened, like a prayer.

"Now the wife's screamin'. Forever, seems like. James is beatin' her man who's on his knees now, only still up because of the way James is holdin' 'im, hittin' 'im, scared at what he's done 'n' what he's doin' 'n' but doin' it anyway. Packard's yellin' at the woman to quiet, just quiet, for God's sake quiet."

"And you?"

"Had my gun on James." He looked shamed to say so. "Didn't know 'til I was puttin' it away."

Grady was struck by a memory of Tom: four of them fumbling for a gun at Kathy's, Tom the only one with wits enough to draw clear and clean. There'd been a stupid fight over cards—cards!—and Tom took turns aiming at each of those dumb enough to think a game worth killing over. Drinks were exchanged instead of bullets and Tom got something extra from Kathy, on the house. He'd remind him of that later, when this hellish business was done. Try to put a smile where there was nothing but woe.

"James steps back, blood to the elbow, and the Injun falls down. I can't say *face* down no more on account he's not got one. The woman rips at her own hair. Two whole handfuls come away. She throws it down 'n' jumps on James before any of us can see. She's still screamin' or screamin' again, I'm not sure any more.

"Packard's quicker than me. He gets her round the neck but he can't get her more than a pace back 'n' forth. She's fightin', clawin' his face like a banshee."

Harpy, Grady wanted to say. That would be the usual comparison. But screamin' 'n' all, he supposed banshee would do.

"Packard says, 'Get them damn kids away,' so that's what I do. Took 'em into the trees. They don't resist none. They're confused 'n' cryin', both of 'em, cryin'. I'm sayin' things but I don't know what or if they even understand me but I keep sayin' it anyways. I do that for a long time."

Tom nodded to himself, tracing his thumb back and forth over the rim of his cup. Stayed that way a while.

"What happened while you were gone?" Grady needed an answer but he didn't much want one.

Tom shrugged. "Don't know. Don't *want* to know. All three were bloody when they came back for me and it weren't their blood. Theirs had drained away, making them proper pale-faces." He snorted. It weren't nothing like a laugh but was probably meant to be.

"We said we wouldn't tell. Not ever. But here I am, tellin' it to you."

Grady nodded. He'd heard plenty of bad stories. Probably would for the rest of his days. This one, though, weren't done.

"What about the children?"

"Brought them back here to the holdin' pen."

Something about that didn't sit right, though. It was like wearing a new gun belt—it fit 'n' all, and it held your guns, but until you broke it in it felt all wrong.

Tom picked up on some of that. "I put them with an old squaw who had more blankets than friends. She was happy to take them. Very happy. She didn't ask about parents."

Better, thought Grady. You're breakin' it in some. But that's still not all of it.

⤙⤚

Grady eased back into his chair, the old wood bending and creaking around him. "You want me to report this?"

Tom shook his head.

"I could go to Frazier instead of—"

"No."

"Well shit, Tom, what did you go 'n' tell me a story like that for? I have to do *some*thing."

Murder was murder, be it full-blood, half-blood, Chinaman, whatever. And two murders was two murders, and three was three, which was what it sounded like.

Tom looked away from the empty yard and met Grady's eyes for the first time in a long while. "I ain't done yet."

It didn't seem like he was going to be, neither, for a little while. Grady waited. He listened to the night. Heard its music and thought of dead men.

"We got back," Tom said, "and when we did we swore our secret and went to our bunks. We sold Henry's horse 'n' gear over the river, told people he'd gone to town after a week in the peaks. None of us spent the money." That seemed important to Tom, so Grady nodded.

"That night I dreamt of where Henry *really* went. Saw him fall. Saw the Injun lose his face. Cody 'n' James 'n' Packard dreamt the same but they didn't tell me nothin'."

"You'll have dreams like that a while now," Grady warned him. He had plenty like it himself.

"Every night," Tom agreed. "And worse."

"Worse?"

"The water. It's got blood in it."

Grady said nothing. He looked down into his cup.

"It's true," Tom said. "I can't have nothin' but milk or liquor else I taste it in there."

"What about the others? What about Cody?"

"I can't say because Cody's gone. I'll get to that. James 'n' Packard, *they* taste it." He remembered James. "*Tasted* it. And we *see* them, too."

"See who?"

Tom gave Grady a sideways look and took another drink.

"See who, Tom? Say it loud. Hear how damn foolish it sounds."

"At the window sometimes, in the yard. Once," Tom said in a quick whisper, "Packard woke to see the woman lookin' down at him where he slept. She was standin' on his bed. Her feet left muddy prints on his mattress."

"Y'all talked about this?"

Tom nodded. "Cody gathered us up. Said he was seein' the big man all over the stockade. Said he was going mad, wanted to let us know he was ridin' out before he ruined it for the rest of us 'n' said somethin'. Said he'd let folk down before and it near killed him and he weren't doin' it again. Packard, he saw the squaw. James didn't give details but he said he saw both."

"And *you* see them?"

"Behind every person I speak to. Standin' there. Lookin' at me."

Grady checked around himself, slowly.

"You see them now, Tom?"

Tom turned away and stared out into the darkness of the stockade.

"No. I fixed it."

"Well that's good, Tom. That's good." Grady offered him something to smoke but Tom waved it away so Grady didn't have one either.

"We went back to the place in the mountains. The four of us, drinkin' whiskey for days because we couldn't brew coffee without it havin' the coppery taste of blood, no matter how strong we made it. When we got there it looked just as it did first time. Broken egg shells. Chickens scratchin' around out back. Things were piled up and still there; tools 'n' cookin' gear and the like.

"It took a while to get courage enough to look down the well. When we did it was for nothin' cause we couldn't see. James suggested lowerin' a light, but 'What's the point?' I said. We was there to give the dead proper burial. Mighta been only me willin' to say it, but no one argued. So we rigged a harness 'n' down I went. It was my group and it was my idea and it was me who let things go so bad."

Grady hadn't been there so he couldn't argue, but he thought Tom was probably taking more responsibility than was his. Sounded like there was plenty to go round.

"It stank in that well. You work a ranch or serve as long as we have and you get to know what death smells like, but this was different. This was bad; rank 'n wet and . . . bad. Like . . . Well, I don't know what like. It was a rough well. A shelf of rock down there, too hard to shift, made a ledge next to what looked like a puddle but wasn't. It was much deeper."

He made a shape of it in the air with the drink he held.

"Henry was on this ledge, which explained the thud we'd heard. The other two, the Injuns, were at the watery bottom. They'd been weighted down, so I had to get wet to make sure they were there. I was worried they'd got out, see. And so were the others; Cody, anyways, cause he called, 'They there?' real anxious. Like they might not be.

"I said they were there and then I saw Henry's fingers. They were bloody, and his nails were broken. I held the light up a bit 'n saw where he'd tried to claw his way out. And God Almighty, his son and all the rest of it, that shook me. I looked up at the others, three faces lookin' down at me like I was in my own grave, and that shook me too, so I got the hell out.

"I said nothin' about Henry. I didn't tell them he only had a broken leg 'n a head wound like you'd get in a brawl. Didn't tell them he prob'ly starved down there."

Tom faced Grady. "Do you think if he'd known those two Injuns were down there with him he still would've starved?"

Grady was given plenty of time to answer the question but he chose not to. He wasn't so sure Henry starved, not in that short time. Not with a belt and boots to eat.

"We got them all up 'n' buried, anyhow. If the others saw Henry in pretty good shape, none of 'em said nothin'. We made simple graves, read a bit of God's word, and came back here."

⬦

"Here," Grady echoed, doing away with the cups and passing the bottle. Tom kept it at his mouth for three swallows. He coughed a couple of times, handed it back.

"Quite some story," Grady admitted, taking a pull of his own.

Tom held up his hand. "A bit more. Let me tell it all."

"All right."

Grady was leaning forward in his chair, bottle hanging between his knees. He was looking at Tom who was looking at the past. His features were drawn and weary, his voice heavy.

"I saw the Injuns again as soon as we got back. Saw them playing with their children. All I could do was open my mouth 'n' point. Cody, James, Packard, they all said they saw nothin', 'n' when I looked back they were right. Cody, though, he was lyin'. Saw 'em a few times after, too. Now he's gone. Told someone in his bunkhouse he was off to the same place as Henry. They thought he meant town. I reckon he was bein' more phil'sophical than that."

"What do the others reckon?"

"Well, James shot himself, didn't he."

Grady straightened up. He *knew* that, everyone knew that, and he'd been waiting for it near on an hour now, but he still dropped the whiskey and to hell with it, let it spill. "Shit."

"Yeah." Tom mimed a grim suicide, shot his face with his fingers. "Looked that way, anyway."

"Packard?"

"Locked in his cabin. Right now, even as we sit here. Got furniture at the door 'n' boards on his windows. Won't come out. I told him I'd fixed it. He said if that was true, how come he's lookin' at the biggest scariest fuckin' Injun he's ever seen? Says the two of them are sittin' with him, waitin'."

"Waiting for what?"

Tom shrugged, like he was worn out. "Maybe it takes time. The fixin'. Maybe they're waiting for what I gave 'em."

Tom had told most of his story to the boards at their feet, but now he looked Grady in the eyes for what he had to say.

"I figured it out, see. They're a family lot, these Injuns. You've seen it, sir. Not one of them wants to go west without the rest of 'em."

An idea was fighting through the whiskey. "Oh Tom, what did you do?"

"I went to the old lady and said the parents wanted their kids back." Tom was openly weeping now. "She didn't like that, not once I'd given them her. They were already close, you see. A *new* family. You know how they are."

"Tom . . ."

"I took them from her and I took them to the mountains. Took'm home. Gave them back. We never should have taken them in the first place. None of them. We shouldn't be takin' *any* of them. They were here first. We should give it all back."

"Tom—"

"I made it quick, sir. And I buried them right next to their parents."

He sobbed a while after that and Grady let him. When he fell into a fitful sleep in the chair on his porch, Grady let him do that, too.

◄◆►

In the morning, when Tom woke, Grady asked him to tell the story again. He had Frazier with him.

Frazier was old but an imposing figure, neatly groomed but in a way that said he didn't give a rat's ass if he got dirty. He shrugged his shoulders in a casual gesture that put his coat over the star on his chest, doing his best to be friendly. His moustache was grey-through and thick. It softened his words a little. "It's all right, son. You can tell me."

Tom looked at Grady. Grady looked back. Tom nodded. "Let's do it somewhere else," he said to Frazier, getting up. "This man's heard enough."

I have, Grady thought. And ain't no one can take it back.

Frazier put a hand to his hat, nodded with the gesture, and moved aside so Tom could step down from the porch.

"He's been drinkin' nothin' but whiskey for days," Grady said, "So give him time to straighten his story out. It's got some mighty strange kinks in it."

"Will do, Father."

Frazier was the only one still called Grady that. He took off his hat and ran his hand through his hair. It wasn't quite yet the same colour as his moustache, not entirely, so he grew it long. He put his hat back on and with another nod, this time for Grady, he followed Tom down across the yard.

Grady watched them leave. Frazier's horse was drinking from a trough in the yard and something about that drew Tom's attention.

Then it all went to hell.

Tom screamed and he backed away so fast he fell. He scrambled back to his feet quick but still stumbled some. Frazier's horse reared up, stamping its forelegs in the air, whinnying loud and shrill. Frazier had both his guns drawn but he was pointing them at the trough. Whatever he saw there was enough to stagger *him*, too.

Tom shouted at the water, "I gave 'em back! I'm sorry, y'hear? I gave 'em back!"

What happened next depends on who tells it, but Grady saw it like Tom leapt at the trough. Just dived right in and thrashed about in the water until he drowned. Some say he was pushed in, others that he was yanked forward, but pushed or pulled, nobody could say by who. A few suggested Frazier did it and it made his reputation more fierce than he was used to for a while. Grady, though, he'd seen Frazier at the trough and when that man's hands were in the water he was trying to pull Tom out, not hold him under. Couldn't do it, though. And Grady wouldn't ever say what he saw holding on to Tom to stop him.

Occasionally, when the whiskey was in him, Frazier would add more to the story, but it was a story Grady didn't much like to hear. There's no giving a story back when it's told, so if talk ever went to Tom or James or what Packard did to himself shut up in his cabin, Grady took his old bones elsewhere. He had ghosts enough of his own without adding more.

MY BOY BUILDS COFFINS

GARY MCMAHON

I

Susan found the first one when she was tidying his room.

Chris was at school, and she'd been sprucing up the house before popping off to collect him after the afternoon session. The ground floor was done; the lounge was spick-and-span (as her mother had loved to say) and the kitchen was so clean it belonged in a show home. The downstairs bathroom was clean enough for a royal inspection. The en-suite would do, she supposed, and her and Dan's bedroom was the best it could be considering they both liked to dump their dirty clothes all over the floor and the furniture.

Now it was time to tackle Chris's room, which was about as messy as any eight-year-old could hope to achieve.

She pushed open the door, holding her breath, and walked into the chaos. His blow-up punch bag had been moved into the centre of the room and left there. The floor was littered with books, magazines, Top Trumps playing cards, rogue counters from board games, art supplies, and—oddly—old cardboard toilet roll holders.

"Jesus, Chris . . ." She tiptoed across the room to the window, trying not to step on anything that might break. When she got there, she pushed open the window to let in some fresh air. The room smelled stale, as if it hadn't been lived in for months.

"Okay," she murmured. "Let's get this shit sorted."

First she tackled the floor. Patiently, she picked up everything and put it away where it belonged—or at least where she thought it belonged, or where it looked like it belonged. After twenty minutes the room was already looking much better. At least she could move around without fear of treading on something.

Next she tidied up the top of his desk—where she found old DVDs without cases, more playing cards, flakes of dried modelling clay, small stones from the garden, bits and pieces of magic tricks, and other sundry boy-items.

The desk was almost clear, and she was looking for a drawer into which she could squeeze yet more art supplies, when she found the coffin.

It was in the bottom drawer, where at one time Chris had kept his football shirts—one a year, from birth, because his dad supported Manchester United.

She stood silently and stared into the drawer. It was empty but for the coffin.

It was made out of what looked to be a fine grade timber—pale and with a neat wood grained pattern. The wood was unpainted and untreated; it was bare, nude, but smooth, as if it had been sanded. Attached to the lid of the coffin was a small brass plate with the word "Daddy" engraved across it in a neat, delicate script.

For a moment Susan felt as if someone else had entered the room behind her. She resisted the urge to turn and look, but she felt a presence there. She knew it was nonsense, there was no one there, but all the same she sensed it. Standing right behind her, perhaps even peering over her shoulder. At the coffin.

She moved to her knees and looked closer. The coffin was small. It was probably the right size to hold an Action Man doll ("It isn't a doll," Chris always protested, "It's an action figure!") and she wondered if that was indeed what the casket contained.

Carefully, she reached into the drawer and placed her hands on the sides of the coffin. She lifted the coffin out of the drawer, stood, and carried it over to the bed. She put it down and thought about what she was going to do.

Then, on impulse that wasn't really an impulse because she'd been planning it all along, she reached down and lifted the lid off the coffin.

Inside was a thin layer of dirt. She ran her fingers through the dirt, feeling its gritty reality. It felt soft and slightly damp, like soil from the garden.

"What the hell is this?"

Part of her tensed in anticipation of a reply from that unseen figure: the one that wasn't there, oh no, not really there at all. Because she was all alone in her son's room, wasn't she?

II

She broached the subject over dinner that evening.

Chris was tucking into his chicken, gravy smeared across his lips and his cheeks: the boy couldn't eat anything without wearing it. Dan was reading a computer printout at the table as he nibbled at his own meal, taking small, delicate bites. She was so sick of asking him not to read at the table that she'd stopped saying it over a month ago.

"Chris."

The boy looked up from his meal. He smiled. "Yes, Mummy." His teeth were covered in gravy, too.

"I tidied your room today."

"Sorry, Mummy. I meant to do it, but I forgot."

She sighed. "Yes, I know . . . just like you forget everything, except sweets and comics and DVDs."

He grinned. "Can I watch a DVD tonight?"

"No," said Dan, putting down his printout. "It's a school night. That's a weekend treat."

Chris began to pout. He picked at his chicken with his fork. The tines scraped against the plate, making Susan wince. He'd stopped having the tantrums over a month ago, but there was always the risk that he'd go off on one again.

"Listen, Chris . . . about your room."

"Yeah." He didn't look up—he was sulking.

"I found something. In a drawer."

Dan glanced at her, raising his eyebrows in a question. She shook her head: she would deal with this.

"Mummy found something . . . a little bit strange."

Chris looked up from his food. He was frowning. "What was it?"

"Let me show you." She stood and pushed her chair away from the table. She crossed the room and took the coffin out of the cupboard where she'd put it for safekeeping. She carried it back to the table, cleared the condiments out of the way, and set it down in front of her family. It felt ritualistic, like the beginning of some obscure rite. She pushed the thought away. It wasn't helpful.

"This is what I found."

Dan stared at the coffin. His face wasn't sure what expression to form. Chris smiled at her.

"Do you know what this is, Chris?"

Dan glanced at his son, remaining silent for now.

"Yes. It's a box." The boy reached out for the coffin, but she moved it across the table and out of his way, as if it might infect him or something.

"Where did you get it, darling?" She was trying to keep things light, but a strange mood had begun to descend upon the dining table. It felt as if a shadow had entered the room, dimming the lights, and the temperature had dropped by a few degrees. "Well, Chris. Where did you get this . . . box? Where did it come from?"

"I made it, Mummy. I made it for Daddy." He turned to face Dan, his small face beaming, his eyes large and expectant, as if he'd done something miraculous and was due a large reward. Some sweets, perhaps. Or a new DVD.

"I . . ." Dan looked from her to the boy, and then back again. "Thank you," he said, absurdly. Then he looked at Susan again, searching for help. "Did you make it at school?"

"No. Here. At home." Chris's smile dropped. His small face seemed to crumple inwards. He was clearly making a concerted effort not to lose his temper, despite the odd situation, and she loved him for it.

"Well who taught you how to make it? I mean, *someone* must have helped you?"

The boy shook his head. Refusing to say anything more.

"Well?"

He shook his head again.

Susan intervened before things became more fractious: "Okay, you pop off and get your jim-jams on, and after you've done your teeth I'll read to you for a while before you go to sleep."

Dan walked away, obviously troubled. Chris dragged his feet as he slowly left the room.

III

"So what the hell's going on here?" Dan was pacing the floor and drinking whisky. He looked harried. His hair was a mess from where he'd been running his fingers through it—like he always did when he was stressed. His face was pale and his shirt was hanging out of the waistband of his trousers. "I mean, this isn't . . . normal. It isn't normal behaviour, is it?"

"Just calm down a minute. Let's think this through."

"That's easy for you to say," he said, his shoulders slumping. "He didn't build *you* a coffin."

"He's eight years old, Dan. He doesn't know what he's doing. He probably saw it in a magazine, or something. Or on the telly. I bet he thought he was doing something nice for you."

Dan laughed: a single barking sound. "Fucking hell, Susan." He only ever called her that when he was anxious, usually it was Sue. "Maybe we should call someone. A doctor . . . or a psychiatrist. Get him seen to again. Maybe this is to do with the old trouble."

"Don't be silly. You're overreacting. We don't need anyone. He's over all that anger business. This is . . . different. Something we can cope with ourselves."

Dan did not seem convinced. "You saw the craftsmanship on that thing. Look at it." He strode across the room and picked up the coffin. His mouth twisted into an unconscious grimace, as if he were touching something rotten. "Look at it. The perfectly mitred joints, the smooth finish . . . this is *beautiful* work." The way he said that word, he gave it the opposite effect to what it really meant. "An eight-year-old kid can't do this kind of work . . ." He sat down in the armchair, looking tired and defeated. He still held the coffin, but loosely. He didn't seem to want to let it go.

"I don't pretend to understand this, either, honey, but I think we need to tread carefully . . . just in case it triggers an episode, or something."

He was rubbing the side of the coffin with his thumb. "It's got dirt inside . . . grave dirt."

"Don't be silly."

"*Grave* dirt," he said again, as if repetition might diminish the power of the words. "My grave . . ."

"It's soil from the garden." She got up and walked over to him, snatched away the coffin. She moved over to the fireplace and put the coffin down on the mantelpiece, next to last year's school photo: Chris smiled at her from inside the frame, his hair neatly combed, his shirt collars sticking out from the neck of his grey school sweater, his cheeks shining from the heat of the photographer's lights. He looked like a typical small boy, but underneath it all he'd been a mess of conflicting emotions, a child governed by an inexplicable rage.

"Okay," said Dan, behind her. "So we tread softly." He sounded more relaxed, less wound up.

She turned around. He was still seated and pouring another large shot of whisky into the glass. "Could I have one of those?" She held out her own glass, but made no move to approach him. "I could really use it." She smiled.

He nodded.

She walked over, but instead of waiting for him to pour she knelt down before him and ran her hands across his thighs. "It'll be okay. He's just a kid. He had no idea of the effect something like this might have."

"But the workmanship . . ." Dan's face was pleading. It made him look years younger, almost like a child himself.

"I know . . . it's weird, I'll admit that. But that's all it is—weird and unusual. There's nothing to worry about. I promise. We'll deal with it, as a family. No more pills and doctors."

IV

A few days later she found the second coffin.

This one had been left on her bed. It was a Saturday and Dan was out playing five-a-side football, making cross-field runs and dirty tackles just to relax. She was hanging up some clothes, and when she turned around from the wardrobe to face the room, the coffin was there, on her pillow. The brass plate on this one read "Mummy."

It hadn't been there when she entered the room. She was sure. She would have noticed.

"Chris?"

There was no reply. The house was quiet. Outside, she could hear traffic on the nearby main road, some kids shouting on another street, and the sound of someone mowing their lawn. They were real noises, the sounds that connected you to reality. There was nothing to fear here, in this friendly little neighbourhood.

"Are you there, baby?"

She heard a shuffling sound in the hall. For a moment, she was afraid to cross the room and look through the doorway. Some unreasonable fear held her there, afraid of her own home. Her own son. The noises outside now seemed as if they were miles away, part of some other, safer world.

She recalled the worst of his rages, not that long ago. He'd left her battered and bruised, but the worst pain was in knowing that someone created from her own flesh and blood was capable of losing control to such a startling degree.

But that was over now. He was better. They'd worked things out, with the help of a good child psychologist and some medication. There was no need to go back, to return to any of that. This time was different.

"Chris!" She used the strength of her resolve to fuel her, and moved quickly to the door. When she looked outside, the landing was empty. Sunlight lanced through the landing window, capturing the dust motes in the air like flecks of epidermis suspended in fluid. She went back inside the room and sat down on the bed.

She stared at the coffin on the pillow.

Outside, the sound of the lawn mower cut out. The screaming kids moved away and their din began to fade. The traffic noises seemed to quieten.

Susan reached out and lifted up the lid of the coffin. As she'd expected, inside was a thin layer of soil. She picked up the coffin and shook it, disturbing the loose particles of earth. As she watched, something was uncovered. She reached inside with her forefinger and thumb, pushing aside the soil, and picked out an object. It was her wedding ring. She looked at her hand—at her wedding finger—and saw a pale band of flesh, a tan line where the ring should have been.

This was new. There had been nothing but dirt in Dan's coffin.

Her stomach tightened; her head began to throb dully. She couldn't remember taking off her wedding ring. In fact, she hardly ever did so, not even in the bath or the shower. She was superstitious; she liked to keep it on, so as not to tempt fate. She remembered an old friend who'd lost her wedding ring, and three months later her husband had dropped down dead from a sudden heart attack. Nonsense, she realised, but still . . . you just never could tell.

Things like this were symbolic. Things like wedding rings. And coffins.

She glanced up, looking at the doorway. There was no sound. No movement. Just dead air, empty space.

She put the lid back on the coffin and backed away from the bed, as if it were some kind of ferocious animal that had come into the room. She picked up her mobile phone from the bedside table, and then she wondered who the hell she was thinking of calling anyway. Dan? Her mother? The fucking police?

This was stupid. It was insane.

Her boy built coffins—that was all. There was nothing wrong with that, not really. It was just a bit strange, a little offbeat. No harm done; nobody was getting hurt. At least he was taking an interest in arts and crafts.

Susan stifled a mad giggle.

She put down the phone and left the room, leaving the coffin in there.

Chris's room was just along the hall. She could see from where she was standing that his door was shut. She walked along the landing and stood outside, listening. She couldn't hear a thing from inside his room, not even his television or his music playing.

She reached out and grabbed the door handle, turned it, pushed open the door.

Chris was sitting on his bed reading a book. He glanced up as she stepped inside. He smiled. He looked entirely normal; he was the same as always, her beautiful little boy. He wasn't a monster. He hadn't been taken over by some alien force. He was her boy. He built coffins.

"Everything okay, son?"

He nodded. "I'm reading." He held up his book, cover facing outwards, for her to see. "Moshi Monsters," he said. "I love them." He turned his attention back to the book; his face became serious as he continued to read.

"Chris?"

"Yeah." He was distracted. He didn't want to talk. He wanted to read. He'd always loved books, even when he was being a brat. He was a good little reader—top of the class in English. Maths, too. A clever boy. A good kid. A reader. A builder of coffins.

"Did you put something in Mummy's room earlier? When I was hanging up the clothes. Did you bring me a present?"

"Yes." He nodded. "I built you a box. Just like Daddy's."

She swallowed. Her throat was dry. "Why, baby? Why did you build Mummy a box?" It was the first time the question had been asked. She and Dan had agreed to approach the situation with caution, in case they said the wrong thing or pushed too hard. They'd been monitoring Chris—his moods, his speech, everything they could think of. He'd been just the same as always . . . their bright young son, mended now. Nothing was different. He was acting the same as always.

Apart from this, she thought. *Apart from the coffins.* And the thought made her admit that they were lying to each other. Chris *was* acting different, and they were both too confused and afraid to confront these changes in their boy. His rages might be over, but something else had replaced them. These days he was . . . secretive. He kept things from them. Things like this: the origins of his coffin-making.

"I thought you'd like one." Still, he didn't look up from his book.

"Why's that, baby?" She took another step inside the room, letting the door shut to behind her.

"Dunno. Just thought you would." He looked up, smiling.

"Where did you get the soil, baby? The soil you put in the . . . boxes."

"Out of the hole."

The world seemed to compress around her, threatening to crush her. "What hole?"

"The one outside, in the garden. The magic hole, down beside the back wall."

As if in a dream, she moved across the room and stood at the window. She looked down at the garden to the rear of the house, taking in the expansive lawn, the trees that grew alongside the dividing fence, and the small water feature Dan had put in three summers ago. There was a dry stone wall at the bottom boundary, separating their garden from the field beyond. The grass and bushes there were overgrown; Dan had neglected the area because he said he liked it to look wild, like the countryside.

Wild. Untamed.

"Where's this hole, baby? Tell Mummy where the magic hole is."

He was still on the bed. Still reading. He seemed utterly unconcerned. "Down there . . . at the bottom of the garden. Right next to where we buried Mr. Jump last year."

Mr. Jump was Chris's pet rabbit. He'd frozen to death the previous winter, and they'd conducted a small family funeral involving an old shoe box, a children's bible, and two flimsy wooden lolly sticks glued together in a cruciform pattern to make a grave marker.

"Okay, baby. Thank you. Thanks for making me the box."

She turned away and left the room, walking back along the landing and down the stairs. She counted the stairs as she descended, just to help herself remain calm. She wasn't sure what she was supposed to be frightened of, but she was terrified. It was like being a child again, fearful of the dark but not knowing why: scared of the unknown.

She sat down in the kitchen and waited for the kettle to boil, then she made a pot of tea and waited for Dan to come home, rubbing at her bare wedding finger with the ball of her thumb.

V

They waited until Chris was asleep. They didn't want to disturb him, and if he saw them digging around out there he might start to feed off their fear. They were sure of nothing, but they knew that they didn't want to give their son any cause for further confusion.

It crossed Susan's mind that this is what they did in every horror film she's ever seen: they waited for darkness before making their move. It always ended badly.

"What the hell do you think we're going to find out there?" Dan was standing by the back door, bathed in the light from the kitchen. He was holding a shovel and wearing his gardening clothes—torn jeans, a baggy sweater, and thick leather gloves. Susan held the torch.

"I have no idea, but we have to take a look. Don't we?" She realised that she wanted him to say no. She was desperate for him to put the brakes on the situation and make them both return indoors. She didn't want to make the decisions; she wanted him to step up and take control.

"I suppose you're right."

She waited for a moment, looking up at the sky, searching for inspiration. It was black, the stars were tiny, and the moon was nothing but a pale, undistinguished saucer amid the wispy clouds. "I'm scared," she said.

Dan took a few steps towards her, paused, and then came the rest of the way. He rested the shovel against the wall and put his arms around her, drawing her close. "I know . . . but this is our son we're talking about. We have to find out what's going on. What choice do we have?"

She nodded against his shoulder, saying nothing. This wasn't a horror film; it was real life. Even if things got messy, she and Dan would sort it all out. It's what people did, in real life.

"Who the hell are we meant to turn to for help? We don't even know what's going on." Her voice was strained.

Dan pressed against her. "We'll think about that when we have some facts."

She nodded again, closed her eyes and sniffed at him. She'd always loved how he smelled; his aroma was a comfort. Whenever he was away on business, she slept with his football shirt on her pillow, just so she could smell him in the night.

"Let's go," she whispered.

He pulled away and grabbed the shovel. She followed him across the grass, along the fence line, to the bottom of the garden, pointing the jittery torch beam ahead of them. They kicked at the weeds, looking for anything that might be called a hole. At first they didn't see a thing, but after a short while Susan stumbled, almost twisting her ankle as she stepped on the edge of the hole.

"Here," she whispered. "I've found it." She reached down and rubbed at her ankle.

"Why are you whispering?"

"I have no fucking idea." It was a funny moment, she supposed, but neither of them laughed.

Dan started pulling at the weeds, tearing them out and throwing them against the dry stone wall. She put down the torch and bent down to help him, peering into the hole. It was small—about the same diameter as her soup pan at home—but it looked deep. It was too dark to tell exactly how deep, but she couldn't see the bottom, even when she shone the torch's beam directly into the hole.

Before long they'd cleared away the weeds and the overgrown grass from around the hole. It was remarkably neat and round, as if it had been bored into the ground by a machine. Susan knelt down at the side of the hole and bent over it, trying again to judge its depth.

"Here," said Dan. "Drop this down." He handed her a small, smooth stone.

She dropped the stone down the hole. Waited. Didn't hear it hit bottom. Picking up the torch again, she shone the light down the hole, but it was swallowed by the darkness down there.

"What the fuck?" said Dan.

She turned and looked at him. He was nothing but a dark silhouette standing against the sky; he had no face. He was form without substance.

"Let's just cover it over," she said. "Fill it in and forget about it."

"No," said Dan. "I have to know."

"Have to know what?"

He leaned down towards her. For once, she failed to detect his comforting smell. "I don't know."

Dan started digging. She moved out of the way, staying well back to give him some room. He dug the hole wider, creating a circular pit roughly two feet in diameter. The pit tapered inwards, down towards the original hole, which sat at its centre, black and threatening.

"You can't just keep digging," she said. "What if you never reach the end?"

Dan paused in his labour, wiping the sweat from his brow with the back of his hand. "What else can I do?"

He resumed digging, hunched over the shovel like an old man.

Susan glanced up at Chris's bedroom window. The curtains were closed and the lights were off, but she was certain that she could make out the shape of someone standing there, perhaps watching them. She closed her eyes, wishing it away, but when she opened them again the shape was still there. She stared at it for a long time, and eventually it blended into the background, becoming less clear, a stain on the fabric of night. Perhaps there had been nothing there all along.

"Shit," said Dan.

She looked over at him. He stopped digging, and glanced up at her, looking into her eyes.

Slowly, Dan bent down and moved something around with his fingers in the ditch. He straightened up, holding whatever it was in his hands. He leaned forward, into the light, and held out his hands to show her what he'd found.

Dan was holding what Susan supposed must be some of Mr. Jump's bones. But there was something wrong with them: they were twisted, distorted, as if proximity to the hole had warped them, pulled them out of shape. The skull was elongated, weasel-like; the ribs were fused together, like white armour, and the forelegs were crooked, ending in grasping, claw-like bony paws.

Dan threw away the bones, scattering them into the darkness. A look of intense distaste crossed his face, and then he picked up the shovel and continued with his task.

It wasn't long before the shovel scraped against something solid.

"What is it?"

"I think . . . I think it's a coffin."

"Another one?"

He shook his head. "This one's bigger."

She stood and helped him clear away the earth from the coffin. It looked exactly the same as the others, except it was much larger. It was made from the same fine timber, possessed a similar hand-rubbed finish, and had a brass plate attached to the lid. When Susan shone the torch onto the coffin lid, the word she saw etched onto the plate made her go cold.

It said *Son*.

By the time they'd unearthed the coffin in its entirety, the sun was starting to rise. The sky in the east was smeared with red; the clouds there looked painted on. It took both of them to man-handle the coffin out of the hole, but still it wasn't too heavy.

"Shall we . . ."

"Open it?"

Susan nodded. She knew there would be nothing in there, except perhaps some more dirt. It wasn't heavy enough to have anything more substantial inside. But they had to be sure. They could leave nothing to chance.

Dan used the shovel to wedge open the lid. He slid the sharp end of the shovel's blade into the joint and stepped on the handle. The lid popped open with the sound of splintering wood; it jerked to one side, revealing a glimpse of the interior. Dan bent down and heaved the lid across the coffin, shoving it onto the ground at the side of the hole. The coffin was filled almost to the top with torn scraps of paper, like the cheap packaging that came with items sent through the post.

"I don't want to see." She took a step backwards, away from the coffin.

Dan ignored her. He reached down and began to push the paper out of the way, scattering some of the scraps across the ground.

Susan held her breath. She saw a flash of colour: pale pink, like the petals of the roses in her garden. It was skin. Human skin. Dan kept clearing away the paper, and she knew what she was going to see even before it was uncovered. She tried to deny the sight, but she couldn't. She wished herself blind, but it didn't work.

Son

Lying in repose, with his hands crossed neatly over his chest, was Chris. He was naked. His shallow chest had sunken slightly; his forearms were unbearably thin. His face was narrow, like that of an old man. He looked like he'd been dead for a long time, but not long enough for his body to rot. It was as if something were keeping him that way, cold and lifeless, yet pristine: like the sanctified remains of a saint.

"Dan . . . Oh, Dan. What the hell is it?"

Dan fell down onto his knees and lifted the corpse partially out of the coffin. The body was obviously light; Dan lifted it with ease and stumbled slightly. The arms slid away from the chest, the head tilted to one side, the dark hair falling wispily across the thin white face, the bony legs bent and the knees came up, as if it were trying to stand.

"No," said Dan, as if he couldn't quite accept what he was seeing, what he was holding. "Oh, no . . . fuck no. Not this."

Susan looked up at Chris's bedroom window. The figure was still there, but now the curtains were open. The figure was small—much smaller and thinner than their son. The figure's hands looked unnaturally long and seemed to wriggle too many fingers as they reached up to twitch the curtains further apart. As it flapped limply forward, pressing its dark, smooth face up against the glass, she was reminded of a crudely fashioned doll or a puppet—something animated, but clumsily; a thing that should never have been given life, a hastily assembled imitation of the human form.

She turned back to her husband and sank to the ground. He was sitting on the ground, rocking and wailing as he clasped their pale son to his breast. "He's too light . . . there's nothing left inside him . . ."

Dan looked up and turned their boy's face towards her. It was oddly blank, as if waiting for an expression to be carved there. His body looked light, empty, just as much of a puppet as the thing now capering inside his room. ". . . nothing left inside . . ."

Dazed, afraid, confused to the point of idiocy, Susan rose slowly and awkwardly to her feet and started walking stiffly towards the house. Whatever was in there—whatever had taken the essence of her son; her wonderful son who'd built such fine, fine coffins—she would find it and she would kill it. Before she lost her sanity completely, she would make it pay.

Susan dropped the torch. She would not need light where she was going. It might, in fact, be better to work in darkness.

As she became more surefooted and began to run, she made herself a promise: before this day was done, she would force whatever had replaced Chris into a tiny coffin of its own, and dance upon its grave.

THE WOMAN IN THE HILL

TAMSYN MUIR

D ear Dorothy,
     This is the last time I intend ever to write to you. Though you
     may take this letter as a freak or crank, I ask that you reconsider how
likely it is that I would write such madness—that is, unless I knew it were
the truth. In my need to convince you I will lay out the events using only
fact—what I saw with my own eyes and have subsequently acted upon based
on rational belief—and at the last, pray to God you believe me.

I know you heard the gossip and the insinuation surrounding my young
friend Elizabeth W—. I will emphasise again her workaday nature and good
common sense, not at all given to the morbid or fantastic, the model of a
farmer's wife. This concerns last April, when she had been recently married
and had moved to the property opposite the old Broomfield slip. Regarding
my silence on the scandal that surrounded her afterward, I may only defend
myself by saying I thought it none of my business to relate.

It must have been eleven o'clock one summer's night when I was startled
from sleep by a fearful knocking. It was such a frenetic scraping and hammering that I would have been up and dressing at that alone, and with
Kenneth's gun, even had I not recognised Elizabeth calling for help. Her voice
was so slurred that for a moment I thought her drunk, and when I let her
in I thought worse. She was shivering and febrile in my kitchen for a long

time—so unable to talk and so fearful that I half-convinced myself that the foolish rumours were true and we were under invasion by the Māori. After a strong cup of tea and some whisky she told me this:

An old friend of hers had lived on the Peninsula and her sad story was well-known there. The husband worked in transporting wood down to the estuary and was often away and she left alone. This friend, Alice N—, missed a visit to Elizabeth one day, and the postman found the house empty. Everyone thought she had been called away and thought too little of it, but then the husband came back months later and found his wife gone and being a grim and miserable man made any number of accusations. It was a sad, short scandal. I did not think it unusual in this country, where English brides come to marry and then regret, but Elizabeth found it uncharacteristic and went herself to the Peninsula cottage. The house was shut up by then. The husband had left for Auckland and no trace of Alice remained. But the whole preyed on Elizabeth's mind and she found something so unwholesome about the mystery that she determined to investigate.

It being early in the day, she took to the bush behind the house. I acknowledge that this would be foolish for most, but in Elizabeth's defence it was dry weather, no chance of slips. She had enough bush-sense to know when she had to turn back. She was sufficiently suspicious but not so alarmed as to get assistance. She knew there was no danger in Clifton and certainly not from the local tribes. I cannot blame her for it now. She examined the back of the property and past the Waikopua into the hills. There was nothing of Alice—or it seemed so—and here, Elizabeth quit her story and let out a trill of laughter.

It made me jump; Dorothy, it was the awful laughter of a hysteric. She would not be calmed until I locked the door and lit the fire. When she looked at me her eyes were red as though she had been weeping, but there was not a tear-stain on her face. When more composed she told me that, deep in a hot and untidy part of the valley, she had seen a *door in the hill*—not the remnants of a *pā* or even an old *raupo* hut — but a door.

When I questioned her on this she described a portal—a cave-entrance that had been propped with slabs of stone, one atop two others like a mantel, and that the stone had been crudely worked. The carvings did not resemble native carvings and Elizabeth could not really describe what they *did* resemble, except that they were ugly and looked as though they had been done in violence:

as though someone had taken a chisel and scored cuts to no purpose. I gave her another blanket and I asked if she had gone inside.

Yes, naturally. She had prowled around the outside and found that the earth around did not crumble, and that the doorway was wide and tall and could have easily taken a man twice her breadth and size. I did not chide her for going inside, for I was too appalled and bewildered and she continued in a mutter and did not look up from her tea:

She had gone inside. She had found the passage quite spacious. She had meant to turn back once reaching the end of this corridor, but that it had made a steep turn and she had seen a light at the end: not torchlight, but the sickly radiance one sees in the Aranui grottoes. And it was not a cavern at all, she said, but *made*. I questioned her on this. Elizabeth did not answer. There were many corridors leading off from a main chamber and her assumption at this point was that she had found some horrid smuggling cave or tuckaway. There were things in the alcoves but she said she had not touched them and repeated this as though it was important, that she *had not touched them*.

All this time she had been calling for Alice and not listening, and then she became aware of a sound. It was the incessant lapping of water on stone. She pushed on down until she reached the cathedral-room of this catacomb, very high and square, and here there was a great pool of slow-moving water sloshing up against the rock. Here also there was a stone block she described as being about hip height and an enormous basin. Standing there was Alice, said Elizabeth. And after that she fled.

I was greatly puzzled, Dorothy. When I asked her to explain, Elizabeth began to shake again and would not drink, and she pushed off the blanket as though she were hot. She kept muttering catches of nonsense. She said that Alice was not right. Unwell, I asked, or somehow injured? No; but all the same she was not right. The two had talked, and Alice had claimed—and I confess the word gave me a thrill of strange horror—that she was *imprisoned*. Elizabeth could not say any more. Now indeed I thought that I had unearthed the source of all her misery—that in an uncharacteristic terror she had fled back out into the bush and the upper air, and left her friend behind. Now she was consumed by guilt and shame. I told her that I would fetch the men from Whitford Hall and we would go to the cave at once.

Dorothy, here Elizabeth screamed. Her voice was the idiot squeal of an animal. No! she said, no! It was too late, Alice had gone now. Elizabeth crawled from her chair and kneeled in front of me and clawed at my floorboards beyond reason until I saw her fingernails split, and she cried out again and what she said made me afraid in all the ways it should have made me pity her hysteria:

"But I'm here—tell me I'm here, Caroline—*for the love of God, keep me here!*"

I gave her what comfort I could give a madwoman, put her in the spare bedroom, and sent for her husband at first light. Come morning she was so weary that she was biddable, though also hollow-eyed and stupid, like a dreamer waking in a strange room. Looking back—the madness in me to let her go!—but what choice did I have? It was nonsense. She had experienced a cruel scare for someone else's benefit, or a nightmare of the subconscious, or some other sad and inexplicable reason that would come to light eventually. She needed rest and not pandering. Yet as she was led away my palms were tight and hot, for there was a look in her eyes that is inane to describe, yet I must describe it: it was the dead terror of a man before the Pit.

Time lulled me into an uneasy security. My evenings never recovered. I had even ventured with Elizabeth one hot day to the Peninsula, in order to lay her fears to final rest, though she startled like a white-eyed colt the whole venture. Naturally, there was no door. We re-traced her steps and found the valley she had come to in her story, and there was nothing but dead trunks of the rough tree fern where a door had been in her memory. I even pushed hard at the earth and scrabbled around at the rocks to show there was nothing beneath, but at this she shuddered and pulled at my sleeves to stop.

"Don't! Lord, don't, Caroline," she said lowly. "We'll find nothing."

The next three months I heard from her seldom and after six I heard nothing at all. She had grown increasingly withdrawn and was "out" to callers when neighbours knew perfectly well she was in, and would plead migraines when it came to the monthly church meeting, even though she had been such a pillar of the Christian Women's Society. She returned my letters in a cursory fashion, then stopped altogether, and I felt such a curious admixture of rebuff and relief that I became derelict in my duty and quit all attempts. I had not written for two months before I realised she was gone. Her husband had been too mad with worry and pain to think of singling me out in the scandal. His mare had returned without her on it, rolling its eyes and nearly dead with sweat, and that was all he knew.

How could I voice my suspicions? I could barely voice them to myself. It seemed the saddest and most likely happenstance was that Elizabeth, wasted from months of nerves, had come to grief alone in the Bush; that spectres and nightmares had led to her death, but the sort that were immaterial, borne from anxiety. I told this to myself every evening and morning and scourged my thoughts of that benighted valley—that squatting, phylacteric depression, that mad hallucination of a waiting door—ready for grief to take its rightful place and forgetfulness to come after.

Grief and distance did not mount their rightful thrones. My nights were pitiable, Dorothy, my days worse. I have lived forty years and not let morbidity touch me, I have never maundered nor dwelt on death, yet I could not escape imaginings of a darkened door, Elizabeth struggling down filth-smeared corridors in the dark, Elizabeth as waxen and afraid as she was the day I set to the side of the hill. I was sleeping with the door barred and with Kenneth's gun. I would wait by the window in the most profound darkness and watch for some figure to crest the hill—Elizabeth's, or faceless Alice's, they were all one. Perhaps you are now saying to yourself, "Caroline, you should have sent for the doctor and diagnosed a guilty conscience." But guilt had never troubled me either.

That June, I made for the Peninsula. The hills were grey and wet with drizzle. I had left a note explaining where I had gone, to be picked up by the postman if I did not retrieve it before morning. I had made sensible arrangements. I had supplies. Thus fortified, I went to the valley where I had gone with Elizabeth, to a slanted part of the hill, in a clinging mist—and sunk between the cringing branches of fern was *a door*.

It was made of two slabs of violently worked stone with a third sitting on top. The earth around this stone was churned and grey, with fresh gouges cut out of the hillside. My lamp made little impression on those clouded shadows within, instead bouncing the darkness to and fro. When I looked more closely at the carvings I found them grotesque, forming faces the one minute, then meaningless gibberish the next, somehow aggressively gross and foul. I examined them little. Like Elizabeth before me, I chose to make my way down that long, breathless passage to the bowels of the hill.

The corridor was so steep that I had to hold my lamp at waist height to descend. And it would suddenly zig-zag—break off at an angle, double in on itself, more of a passage laid down by a burrowing creature than one by an architect—so that I scraped myself badly on irregularities in the wall, for I am a bigger woman than Elizabeth. I held out my lamp to them at one point and was repulsed. They seemed like meaningless notches until I pulled back to see them in toto, and there I saw the repeated graffito of a figure in chains. I thought it was a patterned line of yoked animals, each holding the beast ahead's tail in its jaws, but the carving was an undeveloped scribble. The animals continued on and on and down the stairs in their endless march. Their eyes bulged and their manes tangled in their teeth. It was not worth looking at. A final drastic descent forced my eyes away from the carvings and to attend the more urgent business of not breaking my neck.

The bottom level opened up into a narrow room with eight sides. An alcove was set into each, with each alcove pock-marked with niches. An archway led into the dark main artery and a half-arch into two connecting rooms. My lamplight was increasingly sulky despite the fresh oil and wick, and in this light, like Elizabeth had, I took the whole for a smuggler's den. Inside each niche was an irregularly wrapped bundle of rough sacking or crudely pounded flax.

I took my knife and eased out one of the bundles, not liking the greasy sacking or the oily stains it left on my fingers. If there had been filthy remains in there I might have been less disturbed than I was by what I found: an unfamiliar calico dress, with a blouse, jacket and boots. A quick slash of another bundle proved to similarly hold a woman's clothes, neatly folded. The next room was so peppered with niches it looked like a beehive, and each contained more of these effects. Some of the clothes were of an antiquated style. One bundle held a fibrous patterned wrapper such as some Māori still wear. My guttering lamp hinted at more chambers ahead—more chambers, and deeper, that I never visited—alcove upon alcove, and God knows they were all probably full.

I took my lamp away from those miserable artefacts. Trophies, I thought then, pointing to some grotesque kidnapping or slavery spree.

I continued on down the main passage. It sloped down sharply and I had to press on the ice-cold, slippery walls in order not to lose my footing. The final descent took me to an enormous chamber, Dorothy, as Elizabeth had described, only more vast and empty and black than she could ever have communicated. I set my lamp down and it shuddered and spluttered in the face of such enormous shadow. Here I became aware of the hush only a great and quiet body of water can make. My sight slowly adjusted to some dim braziers filled with what looked like greenish coals—flameless and crawling, moving independently of each other somehow—and the light cast weird ripples on a pool of wide, drear, fathomless water. The light also fell upon a great stone slab where the water sloshed down into carved channels and washed about its base, and fell on a basin big enough for a child to curl up inside it, and it fell also on my friend Elizabeth.

But not Elizabeth's miserable corpse: Elizabeth alive and well and living, Elizabeth as fresh as though she had come through the door with me.

"Oh, Caroline, thank God," she said, as naturally as ever. More naturally, even, than she had been of months previous; something like her of old, with that same familiar ease. But it was wrong, Dorothy. I cannot describe, as she could not describe either. It was dim in that room but I could see the stark whites of her eyes and the hairs rose on the back of my neck. "What a relief *you* came."

Of course I asked her if she was all right, if she was hurt in any way; she gave me a brief, almost lipless smile, and this was not an expression I had ever seen her wear. She denied injury. She was fine, she said; she'd tell me all about it later. What was important was that I could let her out.

I asked her why she needed to be *let out* and she said she couldn't get out alone. I couldn't see why not, as it wasn't as though the corridors were so labyrinthine and nothing seemed to bar her. The water washed close to her bare brown feet. I grew impatient. I demanded to know where had she been and by what means was she now *here*, in the very place she had feared most?

"Caroline," she said calmly, "I never left."

Then she walked toward me. I cannot write clearly of how she moved because every time I think of it my head pounds and my nose often bleeds. But yet she moved and the manner in which her bones shifted inside her skin, and in contrast to how you or I would move—

I believe there is a part of the mind that decides upon courses of action without requiring conscious thought. I also believe that these are left over from the antique days when Man was preyed upon, before cities and civilization. I told you I had been sensible, Dorothy; it was a matter of conscious decision that I had brought Kenneth's gun. But it was on this aforementioned instinct that I lifted it, took aim, and shot Elizabeth dead.

I did not wait around to see her fall. I could rely upon my accuracy. I fled into the lapping darkness while all around me the sound of water filled my ears—deafened, driven mad by a sound I did not know if I was conjuring up, desperate to find light as a swimmer to break water. I scrambled up the narrow steps and through the angular shaft, convinced that if I stopped to heave for breath or look over my shoulder I would meet my end.

Did I murder a young woman, or did I avenge her? Did she die there down in the dark, Dorothy, or is the very idea I could have killed her a laughable one? Perhaps it would have been cleverer to search in those insidious bundles until I found the one that had been hers. Certainly everything down there should have been burnt. But not by my hand, Dorothy, not by any hand I have met in this life, I think, nor yours. What is down there should not be sought, not even for purposes of expurgation.

That place showed itself to me in my dreams and did not leave me after waking; it simply widened its window to the very edges of my vision. I have seen the cave and the water and the altar constantly since then. Even if I take the medicine that the doctor prescribed, the one to help me sleep, it never comes to any good. I was never a beauty but I have grown twisted and haggard for lack of peace. It's little wonder that they all think I am ill. At least I have no husband to wonder at my malaise and my megrims, like poor Elizabeth's. I may sit and tremble alone every time I think a door in my house creaks open. I never go anywhere without Kenneth's gun now. It sits next to me as I write.

And yet I know I must go back. I will go back. I have held on this long, but it has been unbearable suffering. I have concluded that the door is a disease and that the act of passing through its foetid dark is enough to invalid one. Perhaps I had nothing to fear from what Elizabeth had become. I am not sure. Maybe you are not meant to go back until the place is ready for you and your own alcove is empty. I am ready now: last night I took all the drugs Dr. Miller had left and I still woke at the end of my garden, digging at a slope there with my bare and bleeding hands. I will not sleep again.

Dorothy, I took that place with me. It is inside me now. Whosoever is its master is well-versed in claiming victims. You are the one to whom I may try to communicate it and therefore, I will warn you before I succumb. You must not come. The only woman you may save now is yourself. You have been a rare friend and correspondent. If you deem me a madwoman I won't care, just so long as you stay in town and never set foot in Turanga. It is too much like you to come and investigate if I disappeared from hearing. If I present you the facts to begin with, it may quell your desire to procure them. Do not come. This is not your mystery.

I do not know my purpose. I do not know what I am to be, nor Elizabeth, nor Alice—those numberless alcoves, Dorothy, where have we gone? Elizabeth was the merest child. The cruelties it could do with you I cannot imagine. When I think of how she moved—this country is so new to us and so old to the world, and its emptiness should have been a warning rather than an invitation—there are terrible things in the darkness and I will not let you become another of them.

My final wish is this: that you respect our long friendship in the face of derangement. Do not come. Do not question. Live a long life and go into the hills as seldom as possible. Remember me kindly and for my sake, remember Elizabeth kindly, and for hers a woman called Alice and hundreds else. We passed through the door. We have been trapped and set loose. I wish to be the last.

If by awful chance you see the door—if it comes to you invidiously in its defiled stone and darkness—the entrance to the water and to the holes where we go, you must think of me within. Then use dynamite.

I remained
Your faithful friend
Caroline B—.

This letter was found concealed in the effects of Auckland resident Dr. Dorothy L—, eight months after her May 1908 disappearance.

THE UNDERGROUND ECONOMY

JOHN LANGAN

That's not what I want to talk about. If you're interested in hearing about the day to day of a stripper, there are plenty of books you can read. Some of them are pretty good. Or you could watch *Showgirls*. No, it's not accurate, but it's the kind of movie most of the girls I danced with would have made about themselves. So there's that.

It's a person—Nicole AuCoeur, the girl who told me I should try out at The Cusp, they were hiring and I could make some serious cash. I want to talk about her, about this thing that happened to her.

We weren't friends. We'd been in a couple of classes together at SUNY Huguenot. Both of us wanted to be writers. Nikki said she was going to be a travel writer. I was planning on writing screenplays. We took the same fiction-writing workshops, and were in the same peer-critique group. I read two or three of her stories. They were pretty good. The teacher was into fantasy, *The Lord of the Rings*, *Game of Thrones*, so Nikki turned in that kind of story. She was that type of student. Figure out what the professor likes and play to it.

I didn't know she was working at The Cusp. She was always late for class, and she always showed up stoned. She drenched herself in some kind of ginger-citrus perfume, to hide the smell, but it clung to her hair. She had long, brown hair that she wore in long bangs, like drapes. If anything, I thought she was some kind of dealer. I remember this one time, in the middle of class, she opened her purse and started to root through it—I mean, frantically, taking stuff out of it and piling it on her desk. The professor asked her if everything was okay. She said, "No, I can't find my stash." The guy didn't know how to respond to that. The rest of us tittered.

Anyway. I ran into her the summer after that class. I was sitting in Dunkin' Donuts, making lunch out of a small coffee and a Boston cream donut. Nikki sat down across from me. I hadn't realized she was still in town. I assumed she'd gone home for the summer. She said she'd stayed in Huguenot to work. I asked her what she was doing. She said dancing at The Cusp.

I blushed. Everyone knew about the club. It was on 299, on the way into town, a flat-roofed cinderblock building. We used to call it The Cusp juice bar, because they couldn't serve alcohol there, on account of the girls dancing fully nude. I hadn't known anyone who worked there—well, not that I was aware of—but I knew people who'd known people. Although what I'd heard from them had concerned the professors who were regulars at the place. There was a story about this one old guy who'd paid for a girl to come to his place and pee on him, so I guess I had an idea of the place as one step up from a brothel.

Nikki ignored my blush. She said the money was fantastic, and the club was hiring. If I was interested, there were auditions the following Wednesday. We made conversation for a couple of minutes, then she left.

To make a short story shorter, I tried out, was offered the job, and took it. Money—yeah, the money was better than I could make anyplace else in town without a college degree, and in a lot of cases with one. I had been working part-time as a cashier at Shop Rite, but I couldn't get enough hours to cover the rent, my car—which was a piece of shit that spent as much time at the mechanic's as it did on the road—and groceries. Not to mention utilities. And going out. My dad had wanted me to come home for the summer, and when I didn't, he got pissed and said if I wanted to stay in Huguenot so bad, I could find a way to pay for it.

So I did. I had to shave my crotch, which was no fun, and keep it shaved, to give the customers a clear view of what I was waving in their faces. The dancing wasn't, not really. It was wriggling around on stage, teasing I was going to undo my top, wriggling some more, removing my top with one hand but keeping my boobs covered with the other, wriggling some more, etcetera, until I was down to my shoes. Oh, and the garter the guys stuffed their dollar bills into. The air stunk of cigarette smoke, mostly from the dancers. All the same, I smiled at everyone. Not because I was enjoying myself, but because it made me more money if the customers thought I was enjoying myself. It intimidated some of them, too, which did please me. I wasn't especially nervous working at The Cusp. Probably, I should have been. But I was sure I could handle any creeps who tried anything with me. My dad had been a marine, and a martial arts nut, and I had grown up knowing how to punch an attacker in the throat, tear off his ears, and gouge out his eyes. Plus, there were always at least two bouncers in close proximity, in case things in the private rooms got seriously out of hand.

That was where the real money was. Private dances. Lap dances, mostly, which were forty dollars for five minutes plus whatever you could convince the guy to tip you. Some girls could keep a customer in there for two or three dances in a row. I didn't, not usually. There was also a room at the back of the club, the Champagne Parlor. Two-fifty for half an hour with the girl of your choice. And a complimentary bottle of non-alcoholic champagne. That was mainly for the guys whose buddies had brought them to The Cusp for their bachelor parties.

Nikki was the queen of the private dances. She had this routine. The DJ would announce her as "Isis," which was the stage name she used. (Mine was Eve. I know: subtle, right?) She would walk out onto the stage in a long, transparent gown that trailed along the floor behind her. She danced to Led Zeppelin, "The Battle of Evermore." I think she'd studied ballet at some point. There were a lot of ballet moves in her routine. She stood on one leg and held the other leg out in front of her, or behind her, or to the side. She skipped across the stage on the tips of her toes. She half-crouched, leapt, and came down in another half-crouch. She twirled, sometimes on her toes, her arms stretched above, sometimes with one leg bent behind, her head thrown back, her arms curved in front. The gown floated after, whipped around her. She let it drift away. Underneath, she was wrapped in scarves, each of which she undid and sent fluttering to the floor. Throughout, she went from customer to customer, bending towards them, giving them a closer look at what lay beneath the remaining scarves.

By the end of the song, all she had left on was a pair of fairy wings. I guess that's what you'd call them. They were like something from a Halloween costume, one for adults. Sexy Tinkerbell or whatever. A pair of clear straps looped them around her shoulders. They weren't that big, and they were made of thick plastic. When the lights played over them, they filled with a rainbow of colors that slid about inside them like oil. Something to do with the plastic. They weren't butterfly wings, which is what most fairy costumes come with. They were long, narrow, shaped like blades. Hornet wings, or an insect from that branch of the family. If I thought about them that way, they almost freaked me out. Nikki danced stoned—she did everything stoned, from what I could tell—and the glaze the pot gave her eyes made them resemble the hard eyes of an insect. Together with the wings, they lent her the appearance of an extra from a grade-z sci-fi flick, *Attack of the Wasp Women* or something.

None of the customers noticed this. Or, if any of them did, he had a kink I don't want to think about. Nikki never danced more than one song. As Zeppelin faded away, she was off the dance floor, followed by one and sometimes two guys. Most of them went for lap dances, which took place in one of a row of booths set up opposite the club's bar. Yeah, the juice bar. The booths were basically large closets with small couches in them. The customer reclined on the couch, and the dancer did her thing. Each booth had a camera mounted high in one of its corners. For the safety of the dancers, supposedly, and to ensure no one went from lap dance to out-and-out hooking. Part of the bouncers' jobs was to keep an eye on the video feed; although I never saw any of them cast more than a glance in the monitors' direction. I don't think Nikki ever unzipped anyone's jeans, but there's a lot you can do before you reach that point. To be sure, as far as tips went, none of the rest of us could keep up with her.

Not that she was stingy with her money. If it was a night the club closed early, a bunch of us would head into one of the bars in town, and Nikki would cover our drinks. If we were working a late night, once the last customer was out and the front door locked, she'd produce a bottle of Stoli for us to mix with the juice bar's juices. Those times—sitting around the club, shooting the shit—were better than being at an actual bar, more relaxed. Most of us changed into our regular clothes, jeans, T-shirts, wiped the makeup off our faces. Not Nikki. She stayed naked as long as she could. Except for her wings. She wandered around the club, a drink in her hand, the wings bouncing up and down with each step, clicking together. She would lean against the bar, where I was sitting with a cup of coffee because I had an 8 a.m. class

I'd decided to stay awake for. We didn't say a lot to one another. Mostly, we traded complaints about the amount of reading we had to do for school. But having her beside me gave me an opportunity to study the tattoo that decorated her back, so I did what I could to keep to keep the conversation going, such as it was.

That tattoo. All of the girls had ink. In most cases, it was in a couple of places, the lower back and the shoulder, say. That's where mine were. I had a pair of coiling snakes on my back, and the Chinese character for "air" on my right arm. There's a story behind each of them, but they're not part of this story. One girl, Sheri, had ink on most of her body, brightly-colored figures that were enacting an enormous drama on her skin. Nikki had a single tattoo, a square panel that covered most of her back. It was difficult to see clearly, warped by the plastic wings lying over it. The artist had executed the image in black and dark blue, with here and there highlights of pale yellow and orange. There was a car in the middle of it, an older model with a narrow grill like the cowcatcher on a train. The headlights perched high on either side of the grill. The car stretched along a foreshortened road, its rear wheels and end dropping behind the horizon. I wasn't sure if the distortion was supposed to represent speed, or just an extra-long car. To the right of the car, a cluster of tall figures filled the scene. There were five or six of them. They were dressed in black suits, and black fedoras. Their faces were the same pale oval, eyes and mouths empty circles. To the left of the car, a steep hill led to a slender house whose wall was set with a half-dozen mismatched windows. Within each frame, there seemed to be a tiny figure, but I couldn't make out what any of them were. A rim of orange moon hung over the scene in a sickly smile. The picture had been done in a style that reminded me of something from *Mad* magazine, exaggerated in a way that was more sinister than comic. It fascinated me. I asked Nikki what it was supposed to be. She said, "Oh, you know, just a picture." Which could have been true, for all I knew. At the same time, that was a lot of investment in a random image.

The customers didn't mind it. Not that I heard, anyway. Most of them were too timid to say anything. They acted as if they were cool, confident, but it was obvious they weren't. It was as if they were tuning forks, and our bare skin was what they'd struck themselves on. They vibrated, made the air surrounding them quiver. There were exceptions, sure. One guy who was a long-haul trucker. Not too big. Kept his hair short, his beard long. Had on a red flannel shirt every time he entered the club, which was about once a month. He was quiet, polite, said, "Yes ma'am," "No ma'am." But there was a stillness to him. It was what you'd expect from a wolf, or one of the big cats, a tiger. The utter focus of a predator. That I know, he hadn't tried anything with any of the girls before I started at The Cusp. He behaved himself while I was there, too. If I'd heard he owned a cabin in the woods, though, whose walls were papered in human skin, I would not have doubted it. I gave him a lap dance, once, and spent the five minutes planning the elbow I'd throw at his temple or throat when he grabbed me. He didn't, and he tipped pretty well. That said, I wouldn't have done it a second time.

The other exception was a group of guys who squeezed into the club one Thursday night. There were five of them, plus a man who said he was their driver. The bouncer who was working the front door said he saw them pull up in a white van. The five guys were huge, the biggest men I'd ever seen in person. I'm going to say seven feet tall, each, three feet and change wide. Three fifty, four hundred pounds. All dressed in the same khaki safari shirts, khaki shorts, and sandals. They had the same style crewcuts that squared the tops of the heads. Their faces were blank, unresponsive. They stared straight ahead, and didn't so much as glance at any of the girls. In the club's mix of white and blue lighting, their skin looked dull, gray. They could have been in their early twenties. They could have been twice that. They stood beyond the front door in a group and did not move. They reminded me of the stone heads on Easter Island. They weren't still—they were inert.

Not their driver, though. He was smaller—average-sized, really. It was standing in front of his passengers that made him appear diminutive. He was wearing a beige, zip-up jacket over a white dress shirt with a huge collar and brown bell-bottom slacks. His hair was black, freshly-cut and gelled, but his skin had the yellow tinge of someone with jaundice. He was younger pretending to be older. I figured he was in charge of the five guys. Actually, what I thought was, the five passengers were residents of one of the local group homes, and the driver had decided to treat them to a night out. I know how it sounds, but things like it happened often enough for it not to seem strange, anymore.

The driver didn't waste any time. He spoke to the front door guy, who pointed him to the bartender. She leaned across the bar to hear what he had to say, then motioned to one of the girls who was killing time with a cranberry spritzer to fetch someone from the dressing room. I read her lips: Isis. Nikki. The driver nodded at the bartender, and passed her a folded bill. I'm pretty sure it was a hundred.

Nikki emerged from the dressing room wearing her assortment of scarves, but without the long gown. She looked across the club to where the driver was standing with his hands in his trouser pockets. Her head jerked, as if she recognized him. When she walked up to him, she kept her expression neutral, which only seemed to confirm that she knew the driver. He tilted forward to speak into her ear. Whatever he had to say didn't take long, but she took a while to respond to it. She stared at the driver, as if trying to bring him into focus, then nodded and said, "Sure."

Apparently, what the driver wanted was a lap dance for each of his five passengers, all of them provided by Nikki. He gestured for the nearest of the huge guys to come forward. Nikki took hold of one enormous hand and led the guy to the middle lap dance booth. He had to stoop to enter it; I wondered if he'd fit inside. He did. His four buddies didn't register his departure in the slightest. The driver stationed himself midway between the rest of his passengers and the booth. He gazed into space, and waited.

I didn't see Nikki emerge from the booth with the first giant in tow, because I'd been called to the dance floor. It took me two songs into my three-song routine to sell a customer a private dance. He was a college student. I almost thought I recognized him from one of the big lecture classes. He was free with his money, and it wasn't difficult to keep him in the booth for two dances. We were to the right of Nikki and whichever of the enormous guys she had with her. The walls of the booths weren't thick. All kinds of sounds leaked through from the adjoining spaces. That center booth, though, was silent. I noticed this, but I don't know if it seemed strange to me or not. I'm not sure. I was busy with the college student. I want to say that there was something off about that lack of sound. It was as if it was a gap in sound, a blank spot in the middle of a song, rather than the end of it.

Nikki and I finished our dances at the same time. I didn't notice anything wrong with her, then, standing naked outside the booths. She was flushed, but she'd been working hard for almost thirty straight minutes. She was sweaty, too, which was odd. The club was air-conditioned, in order to keep the dancers' sweat to a minimum. I wondered if the driver was going to ask for his turn, next. He didn't. He passed Nikki the biggest roll of bills I had and have ever seen, collected his giant cargo, and exited The Cusp without another word. Nikki gathered her scarves from inside the booth and retreated to the dressing room.

She didn't stay there long. She dropped the scarves on the floor, stuffed the roll of money into her purse, and returned to the club. The first customer she approached was a middle-aged guy wearing gray slacks and a white button-down shirt. He was sitting back from the stage, so he could watch the show and not have to pay out too much cash. Nikki straddled him in his chair and ground her pelvis against him. Whatever prudence he'd imagined he possessed flew out the window. He trailed behind her to the lap dance booths.

A minute later, he was screaming. The booth's door flew open, and Nikki stumbled out of it. There was blood all over her legs, her ass. She stopped, found her balance, and walked toward the dressing room. As she did, her customer emerged, still screaming. The front of his slacks was dark with blood. Of course I assumed he'd done something to her. His face, though. He was wide-eyed, horrified. One of the bouncers was already next to him. I went to check on Nikki.

She was bent over one of the makeup tables, attempting to roll a joint. The backs of her legs, the cheeks of her ass, were scarlet. Closer to her, I saw that her skin had been scraped raw. It reminded me of when I'd been a kid and wiped out on my bike, dragging my palms or shins across the blacktop. The air smelled coppery. Blood ran down Nikki's legs and pooled on the floor. Blood flecked the bottoms of the plastic wings, the tattoo. She wasn't having any luck with the joint. Her hands wouldn't do what she wanted them to. I pushed in beside her and rolled the spliff as best I could. I passed it to her with fingers that weren't trembling too much, then held her lighter for her.

I didn't know what to say. Everything that came to mind sounded inane, ridiculous. Are you hurt? Her legs and ass looked like hamburger. Do you need a doctor? Obviously. What happened to you? Something bad. Who were those guys? See the answer to the previous question. I couldn't look away from the ruin of her flesh. When I'd started working at The Cusp, I'd thought that I was entering the world as it really was, a place of lust and money. Now I saw that there was a world underneath that one, a realm of blood and pain. For all I knew, there was somewhere below that, a space whose principles I didn't want to imagine. I mumbled something about taking her to a doctor. Nikki ignored me.

By the time one of the bouncers and the bartender came to check on her, Nikki had located her long gown and tugged it on. She checked her pocketbook to be sure the roll of cash was there, took it in the hand that wasn't holding the joint, and crossed to the fire exit at the opposite end of the dressing room. Without breaking stride, she shoved it open, triggering the fire alarm. She turned left towards the parking lot as the door clunked shut behind her.

The bouncer, the bartender, and I traded looks that asked which of us was going to pursue her. I did. I hurried along the outside of the club and across the parking lot to where Nikki parked her Accord. The car was gone. I ran back towards the building, which everyone was pouring out of. I could hear a distant siren. Most of the customers were scrambling for their cars, hoping to escape the parking lot before the fire engines arrived and boxed them in. I considered making a dash inside for my keys and was brought up short by the realization that I didn't know where Nikki lived. I had an approximate idea—the apartments down by the Svartkill—but nothing more. I could drive around the parking lots, but what if she'd gone to the emergency room, or one of the walk-in care facilities? I didn't even have her cell number, another fact which suddenly struck me as bizarre. Why couldn't I get in touch with her? Why didn't I know her address? The strangest sensation swept over me there in the parking lot, as if Nikki, and everything connected to her, had been unreal. That couldn't have been the case, though, could it? Or how would I have found out about the job at The Cusp?

I didn't see Nikki for the rest of the time I worked at the club. I stayed through the end of the fall semester, when I graduated early and moved, first back in with my dad, then down to Florida. The five enormous guys, their jaundiced driver, didn't return during those months. The customer whose pants had been soaked with Nikki's blood did. Less than a week later, he appeared at the front door, insisting he had to talk to her. His face was red, sweaty, his eyes glazed. He looked as if he had the flu. The bouncer at the door told him that the girl he was looking for no longer danced here, and no, he didn't know where she'd gone. The guy became agitated, said he had to see her, it was important she know about the cards, the hearts. The bouncer placed his hands gently but firmly on the guy's chest and told him the girl wasn't here and he needed to leave. The guy broke the bouncer's nose, his right cheek, and three of his ribs. It took the other two bouncers on duty to subdue him, and they barely managed to do that. The cop who answered the bartender's 911 call took one look at the guy and requested backup. The cop said they would transport the guy across the Hudson, to Penrose Hospital, where there was a secure psych ward. As far as I know, that's what happened. I don't know what became of Nikki's last customer, only that I didn't see him again.

Years went by. I left Florida for Wyoming, big sky and a job managing a bank. I bought a house, a nice car. The district manager was pleased with my performance, and recommended me for a corporate event in Idaho. I took 80 west to Utah, where I picked up 84 and headed north and west into Idaho. Somewhere on the other side of Rock Springs, a white van roared up behind me and barely avoided crashing into the back of my rental. I swore, steered right. The van swung wide to the left, so sharply it rose up on its right wheels. I thought it was going to tip over, roll onto the median. It didn't. It swerved towards me. I should have braked. Instead, I stomped the gas. The rental surged past the van. As it did, I glanced at the vehicle's passengers. Its rear and middle seats were filled by a group of enormous men whose crewcut heads did not turn from the road ahead. In the front seat, a driver with black hair and yellowed skin laughed uproariously along with a woman with long brown hair. Nikki. Together, she and the driver laughed and laughed, as if caught by an emotion too powerful to resist. He wiped tears from his eyes. She pounded on the dashboard.

I pulled onto the shoulder and threw the car into park. My pulse was hammering in my throat. I watched the van speed west down the highway until it was out of sight. I waited another half hour before I shifted into drive and resumed my journey. The remainder of the drive to Idaho, and all of the way home, I didn't see the van. But I was watching for it.

I still am.

For Fiona, and in memory of Joel Lane.

THE ROOMS ARE HIGH

REGGIE OLIVER

A man that looks on glass
On it may stay his eye;
Or if he pleaseth, through it pass
And then the heav'n espy
—George Herbert

"You could always stay at old Ma Carsett's, I suppose," said Lockwood. "Never went there myself, but I heard good things. But of course you must always remember 'the rooms are high.'"

"What do you mean 'the rooms are high'?" Savernake asked. "I thought you said this place was inexpensive. Do you mean the prices are high?"

"No, no. Just 'the rooms are high.'"

"You mean the rooms have high ceilings, or that they're high up? Or what?"

"No. This is just what several chaps who'd been there told me: 'the rooms are high.'"

"Didn't you ask what it meant?"

"There seemed no point since I wasn't going to stay there."

"Then why are you telling me?"

"Just passing it on, old chap, since you *are* going there, or might be. 'The rooms are high.'"

Lockwood gave him what Savernake assumed was meant to be an enigmatic smile. Savernake had known Lockwood since they shared a set of rooms in their first year at Oxford nearly forty years ago and was both amused and irritated by him. They had kept up this rather odd friendship, and at least once a year they would have lunch at Savernake's club and at his expense. Savernake had become a solicitor and Lockwood an actor.

Lockwood was no fool but he had the actor's tendency to vagueness and imprecision where facts and figures were concerned. This inability to impart an exact meaning concerning Mrs. Carsett's rooms at Norgate was a typically annoying example.

It was not long after the death of his wife that Savernake felt the need to get away. None of the familiar reasons seemed quite to correspond with his feelings. His wife's last illness had been too protracted for him to feel anything but relief when she finally went. At the same time, though childless, it had not been an unhappy marriage and Savernake sensed the loss of a valuable part of himself without being able to define precisely what it was. For several years while he had been looking after his wife Savernake had taken no holidays, despite the advice of friends that he must have "a break." Now it was all over the need suddenly asserted itself, so that it became almost an obsession; and the fact that he could not define a precise reason for the need made it no less urgent. All the same this ignorance annoyed him: his solicitor's professional deformity clamoured for unambiguous causes.

Abroad seemed the obvious place to go—a cruise perhaps—but this did not appeal. On a cruise he would be thrown into contact with people whom he neither knew nor wanted to know; abroad and alone he would be too much a stranger. It had to be somewhere in England where his isolation would be unremarked: he wanted a place of stillness and solitude with which he had a modicum of familiarity. Norgate came into his mind, the old resort on the Kent Coast. He had been there as a child; in fact he had gone to a school not far away from Norgate near the North Head, a promontory of chalk cliff that jutted into the English Channel.

Savernake was not nostalgic about any aspect of his past, but he liked the idea that he had existed in another world, before his professional life, his marriage, and all that went with it existed. It was a world without the embarrassments and obligations that he had come to associate with adult life. Now, wifeless and semi-retired, he felt ready to return to another kind of being. It was in search of this rather nebulous ideal that he decided to go to Norgate.

He could have afforded to stay at the Cleveland, the most expensive hotel in Norgate, but that would not have suited him. He liked the idea of being obscure, anonymous, part of the landscape. During the annual lunch with Lockwood at his club, Brummel's, the subject came up, and that was when his friend suggested Happydene, Mrs. Carsett's bed and breakfast establishment. Lockwood had recently been on tour with a thriller and the Victoria Theatre, Norgate had been one of the venues, so he pronounced himself an expert on cheap digs in Norgate.

A brief trawl of the Internet yielded the details of Happydene, which was in a little side street just off the sea front. This too recommended itself to Savernake's reclusive frame of mind. He rang up and booked a room for the following week. Mrs. Carsett, to whom he spoke on the phone, seemed pleasant and businesslike, but not very forthcoming. Perhaps that was just as well; he did not want to explain why he was coming to Norgate for a week in early April.

An ambitious tourist, in search of the stupendous, might have chosen Venice or Samarkand, but Norgate seemed to suit Savernake. He congratulated himself on having chosen the right place. The South Coast of England was enjoying a warm spring and Norgate's modest charms were to be seen at their best. It pleased Savernake to think that the little seaside town fostered tranquil lives—long, featureless, passionless existences—because that was what he craved himself. The slow decline of his wife into sickness and dementia had been, in its sordid way, full of drama, but not of the ennobling kind. It had been relentless: he had felt both grief and anger. Now that final line of Milton's:

". . . and calm of mind, all passion spent."—seemed to him most beautiful.

He arrived by train and took a taxi to Happydene. He had not been back to Norgate for almost half a century and he wondered how much it had changed. The short drive down to the sea front from the station told him that it had not, at all. There was the same air of worn respectability about the houses; the touch of flamboyance in the pier and the Victoria Theatre. There were the ice-cream parlours, the amusement arcades, the beach of coarse sand divided by military rows of breakwaters. The extent to which it had remained the same made him uneasy. He was not suffused by a glow of nostalgia. Had it been a mistake after all? He tried to suppress his disquiet because he could not explain it.

Happydene was a Victorian terraced house in a street of Victorian terraced houses. Nothing distinguished it except for the sign HAPPYDENE in flowing script on a plaque and a small No VACANCIES sign in the window. Savernake thought he should be reassured by its air of respectability, but he was not. Expectation of the unknown robbed him of all comfort. Here he was, at last a free man and the freedom, even in these dainty surroundings, daunted him.

The door was opened by a woman, perhaps in her thirties with mousy, lustreless hair. She wore an overall.

"Mrs. Carsett?" asked Savernake, even though he knew instinctively that it was not she.

"I'm her daughter Alice. Mr. Savernake isn't it? We were expecting you. Come in."

Savernake noted that Alice had the pale, shapeless look of someone who had never married, and was probably under the dominion of her mother. Though he was a widower and approaching sixty, Savernake had not quite rid himself of the habit of assessing every woman he met for their sexual possibilities. Alice had few it would seem, but this very lack gave Savernake an odd frisson. Elderly and judging himself to be no longer very physically appealing, Savernake recognised that he would have to set his sights conventionally low if he ever wanted another woman. Besides, he had heard from Lockwood about the acronym LDO that actors would put in the visitor's books of lodging houses. It stood for *Landlady's Daughter Obliges*. He would inspect that book later.

⟶◦⟵

The room to which he was shown by Alice who insisted, very much against Savernake's gentlemanly instinct, on carrying one of his bags, was on the third floor and faced onto the back of the house. From the window he could make out a band of blue sea across and between the slate roofs of other houses.

"We thought you would like a sea view," said Alice. She was staring at Savernake, awaiting his reaction. He obliged with a nod.

"Is there anyone else staying here?"

"Just Mr. Milson," said Alice. "He's our regular."

"No-one else?"

Alice shook her head and smiled.

"But there's a No Vacancies sign in the window."

"Mum's very particular about who comes to Happydene." There was again that smile, as if Alice wholly approved of her mother's actions and had joined her in a secret conspiracy against the world. For a fleeting moment she looked up at the ceiling and Savernake followed suit. It was not particularly high, but the plaster ceiling rose was of a peculiar design. It was shaped like a classical head of indeterminate sex, surrounded by wavy hair—or were they tiny serpents? From the open mouth came the stem of the chandelier which lit the room.

"Unusual design," said Savernake. Alice suppressed a giggle.

"Will you be having your evening meal here tonight?"

"Yes. Thank you. I think I shall."

"The evening meal is at 6:30. We like to offer our guests a complimentary glass of sherry in the lounge at six beforehand. I'll leave you now to settle in. Here is your front door key and the key to the room." These she handed to him while turning away her face. Savernake thought she was hiding a smile, but why? Had he become, for some reason, an object of mockery? Alice left the room quickly. Savernake thought he heard a choke of repressed laughter outside his door.

Unpacking restored, to some extent, his poise and self-regard. The air in his room was cool and refreshing in an unaccustomed way. Savernake realised that it was a contrast to the stale, overheated atmosphere of his home during his wife's last illness, and the sterile warmth of the hospice where she died. The air would do him good, he told himself, but without much conviction.

Having settled himself, Savernake found that there was over an hour before he could enjoy his "complimentary glass of sherry" in the lounge. *Probably some awful supermarket "pale cream,"* thought Savernake, who could be a wine snob. He would go out to explore the town.

Once out of Happydene, Savernake turned to his left and walked the hundred or so yards to the sea front. It was a clear evening. Clouds were scarce, high and tinged with yellow. A cool wind fumbled with him and made him tighten the scarf about his neck. The houses along the front were white stucco, the sea pale blue; the whole suggested the delicate, light tones and meticulous detail of a Victorian watercolour. Little or nothing seemed to have changed in half a century.

Savernake expected to be invaded by a flood of memories, but it was not so. It was curiously like the first time he had seen the dead body of his wife. She had died in the night at the hospice and he was summoned over the following morning. It was expected of him that he should want to see the body and be alone with it, and he complied with the expectation, but it was not a significant experience. He looked at the familiar features, now robbed of all sense and meaning. He held his breath, half believing that a movement from her would return all to normality, but no movement came and he felt shamefully relieved that it was so. Now here he was in Norgate, enduring a pale reflection of that event. It was all familiar; it was all meaningless.

Nevertheless Norgate was a pleasant place, and in April free of the noisy crowds he would have detested. Savernake was beginning to find the wind that buffeted him, with its faint, sticky smell of sea, bracing. Or that was what he told himself: such a hearty, old-fashioned, private-school word, "bracing." He turned left again along the broad sea front esplanade and made towards the North Head promontory, behind which and a little further inland had been his old school, Stone Court.

Walking ahead of him was an elderly man in a grey tweed overcoat, his back to him, slightly hunched so that only the very top of his white head was visible. He used a walking stick and his manner of walking, though brisk, was curiously jerky, as if one leg were shorter than the other. It was a characteristic movement, and suddenly, unpleasantly, familiar.

Good God, could it be Hoppy?

Hoppy, as he had been universally known, in fact a Mr. Twells, had been a master at Stone Court. Already then, half a century ago, Hoppy had seemed to Savernake's admittedly young eyes to have lapsed into a tweedy, seedy middle age. He was unmarried and taught geography, French, and, to a select few, Greek. The strange hopping movement as he walked, which had earned him the sobriquet, had been acquired in the war when he had lost his right foot and had it replaced with an artificial extremity. Heroic reasons had been attributed, and not denied by Hoppy himself, but it was subsequently found to have been caused by a fragment of falling masonry in the London Blitz where Hoppy had been fire watching.

But this man on the esplanade couldn't be Hoppy, could he? He would have to be at least ninety, and he seemed, despite the limp, to be so spry.

Savernake did not want to find out, so he turned round and began to walk in the opposite direction towards the pier. It was all nonsense; it was a coincidence. Nevertheless, Savernake found himself trembling uncontrollably.

Shortly after six Savernake entered the lounge of Happydene. A short stout man, whom Savernake guessed to be in his seventies, was seated in the corner of the room. He wore fawn slacks, a beige cardigan, a check shirt, and a striped tie, all of them crisp and clean. Savernake thought he detected the drab, unfashionable neatness of a former military man: the tie looked regimental.

"Ah, you must be Savernake," he said. "Jack Milson." Milson rose and they shook hands. "Help yourself to a sherry. Ma Carsett always likes us to help ourselves."

He indicated a sideboard on which stood a small sherry glass and a half empty bottle of supermarket Pale Cream Sherry. Savernake poured himself an exiguous mouthful.

"First time here, isn't it? How did you find out about us?"

Savernake explained that he had been recommended Happydene by an actor.

"The actors, eh? I don't go in for all that theatre stuff. Not an actor yourself, are you?" Savernake shook his head. "Don't go in for all that argy bargy and bum tickling nonsense. I like to keep regular. I expect you've gathered, I'm a permanent fixture here. Not a bad sort of billet, Happydene. The grub's okay. Keeps you regular. That's the secret, you know. I have a good big breakfast; go out for a constitutional. Lunchtime, I might have a pint or two in the local, have a read of the paper. I don't socialise much; don't go in for all these clubs and things. To me it's a waste of time, all these cliques and talking shops. Keep yourself to yourself and keep regular. People ask me: 'Jack, what's your secret?' They ask me, you see. I tell them. I say: 'strong drink, weak women and regular bowel movements.' That always gets them!"

Milson laughed heartily at his maxim and Savernake felt it impolite not to join in.

"I could tell you a thing or two about life. I've seen it all. I was at Dunkirk, you know, Normandy Landings, the lot. Sergeant in the Fusiliers. Became a fitness instructor after the war."

"You were in the war? But you must be—?"

"Want to know how old I am? Have a guess. Go on, have a guess."

"Well, I suppose you must be—"

"Ninety-three! That's what I am! Ninety-three! And I'll tell you something for nothing: I've a few good years yet before I hand my papers in. Oh, yes! If you want to know a thing or two about life, Jack Milson's your man. I can tell them." There was a faint clanging sound. "Hold your horses! That's the gong for grub. Mustn't keep Ma Carsett waiting. This way. Follow me!"

Two separate tables for one were laid out in the dining room. The tablecloths and napery were white and crisp. Milson sat down and tucked his napkin neatly into the top of his shirt. Alice brought in two plates of greyish coloured soup. She was wearing a frilly white blouse and a tight black skirt which seemed only to accentuate her dowdiness.

The soup was followed by some sort of fish in bread crumbs with vegetables. Like the soup it was bland but edible. During the meal Milson appeared to concentrate all his energies on eating, barely looking up from his food. Towards the end of the main course Savernake asked him if Mrs. Carsett was likely to put in an appearance.

"Don't see her much, to tell the truth," said Milson briskly. "She likes to keep herself in the background, if you know what I mean." And he winked at him.

Before Savernake could ask Milson what he did mean, Alice entered to clear the plates. She carried a leather-bound book under her arm.

"I wonder if you could sign our register," she said, addressing Savernake and placing it open on the table where the remains of his fish had been a moment before. "Just put your name and address," she added, as if Savernake might otherwise have included a résumé of his life, or a short poem. Savernake complied, noting that there was a column in the register headed "Remarks." There were some entries in this section made by previous guests, but all had been heavily blacked out with a marker pen. He flipped back through previous pages, guiltily searching for the acronym LDO. All the entries under "Remarks" had been crossed out, some more effectively than others. On one page Savernake thought he could detect the initial letters LD, but the third letter was not clearly decipherable: a K perhaps or an N? Just then the book was snatched from him and in its place was put a bowl of apple crumble and custard.

"Thank you, Mr. Savernake." He looked up at her. Alice's usually pale, indeterminate features had a harder look to them. A hint of menace and sexual allure showed itself and then vanished. Alice was best seen from below: it suited her.

When the meal was over Milson rose, folding his napkin as he did so.

"Well, I'm off to the lounge to watch the news. Never miss the news. Care to join me?"

"Not tonight," said Savernake. "I think I'll go to my room and read."

"Ah, yes," said Milson. "I like a good book myself, but none of this fiction malarkey. I like a good book of facts. *Guinness Book of World Records*, that sort of thing."

Savernake said goodnight and went upstairs to his room. On the landing he met Alice. She seemed a little agitated.

"I've just been turning down your bed, Mr. Savernake," she said. "Is there anything further you wanted?"

Savernake shook his head and thanked her.

"All right. Sleep well, then, Mr. Savernake." She seemed to take pleasure in uttering his name. She was about to go, then halted. "Oh, Mr. Savernake, do you like a Continental or a Full English in the morning?"

For a moment Savernake was utterly baffled by her question. Then his brain began to work once more.

"Ah. Breakfast, you mean?"

Alice's pale lips were visited by the suggestion of a smile. "That's right, Mr. Savernake."

"Er . . . Full English, then."

"Full English it is, Mr. Savernake. Good night, Mr. Savernake." As she passed him to go down stairs she brushed her body against his which she needn't have done, or so it seemed to Savernake. It was strange that during the whole of his wife's illness the thought of sex never entered his head, now he couldn't stop thinking of it. And Alice Carsett was not an attractive woman.

In his room Savernake went to the window and looked out. It was dark now and he could see fragments of the necklace of lights threaded along the promenade. He opened the window. Norgate was quiet. There was no sound except the gentle rush of the sea, but it was bitter cold. He shut the window and stared out again, but his eyes could not focus on anything beyond the glass. They stubbornly refused to see anything but the grey ghost of his own reflection on the window. A semi-transparent old man stared back at him, a stranger and afraid.

For a while he sat in the armchair in his room and tried to read the poems of George Herbert, a writer he and his wife had once enjoyed, but he could not concentrate enough. He tried a novel, but that failed too. Eventually he gave up and went to bed. Suddenly he was very tired.

As so often when Savernake went to bed thoroughly exhausted, he slept heavily for three or four hours and then woke up abruptly. It was shortly after midnight when he was aroused. Because the window was closed and the heating, as so often in small hotels, could not be turned off, he found himself in a stuffy atmosphere with a headache. The heaviness of his limbs made him reluctant to get up and fetch himself a glass of water and an aspirin. He lay on his back, hoping that his headache would disappear if he kept himself as still as possible. He stared at the ceiling in the dim light that filtered in from the window whose curtains he had forgotten to draw. It did look higher than he had remembered it, though, curiously, the Gorgon's head ceiling rose had expanded to cover almost the whole space above him. Savernake felt giddy and blinked several times to rid himself of these unpleasant impressions, but they had not adjusted themselves to normality when he looked again.

A cool part of Savernake's mind understood that he was suffering from some kind of hallucination. He looked at the head which appeared to him at once vast and extremely far away. The curved metal tendrils of the chandelier vomited from the Gorgon's mouth had elongated themselves into tentacles, at the end of which bristled tiny and insignificant light bulbs like buds. He should get out of bed and turn on the light but now he found he could not move.

The head appeared to quiver although he knew it could not, like the head of his wife after she had died. The spaces above him remained grey but stretched further into the distance and the little buds at the ends of the chandelier fittings seemed to shiver for a moment before they formed themselves into hands. The hands stretched down towards him and he felt them smoothing their cold hard fingers against his thighs and torso. Once more he jerked himself convulsively awake and lay there staring at an infinitely high grey ceiling.

In the dining room the following morning, Savernake was the only breakfaster. Mr. Milson was not only absent, but no place had been laid for him. Savernake made enquiries about this when Alice came in with his eggs and bacon.

"I'm afraid Mr. Milson was taken poorly in the night," Said Alice.

"What happened? I didn't hear anything. Where is he?"

"He was taken away in an ambulance, for treatment."

"I'm very sorry to hear that. Perhaps I should visit him in hospital."

"There's no need for that, Mr. Savernake. Mum's calling in on him."

"I have yet to meet your mother."

"Oh, she's out at the moment, seeing Mr. Milson. Tea or coffee, Mr. Savernake?"

Further questions when Alice brought Savernake's tea yielded no more information. Alice was unsure of what had ailed Milson, how he was doing, or even quite where he was at the moment. Savernake lost interest in Milson, but was intrigued by Alice's obscurantism. He decided to put it from his mind and go for what Milson would have called a "constitutional": it was a fine day.

Norgate was livelier than it had been the previous afternoon. A few cloudlets were high in the sun's blue dungeon. Savernake thought he would walk as far as the North Head and see what had become of his old school. Research on the Internet told him it had been sold and transformed into an exclusive housing estate. Curling avenues of carefully individualised dwellings now covered the former playing fields, while the old school building—a Regency house of white stucco—had been divided into luxury apartments. Savernake had vague thoughts of moving down here into one of them, perhaps to make something neat and circular out of his existence.

Savernake was striding along the promenade with the North Head in sight when he saw the man with the distinctive walk again. Could it be Hoppy? Since his encounter with Milson the night before, it had become a possibility, even a probability. He was coming towards Savernake.

The features were undoubtedly those of Hoppy but ancient and in ruins. White stubble frosted his cheeks and the pendulous jowls that fell from his face and made it gaunt. The eyes were rheumy but alive with anger and, despite his impediment, he moved rapidly with the aid of a stick. He wore a heavy dark overcoat over the back of which curled locks of yellowish white hair; a grimy black and white check scarf was knotted around his neck. Savernake was quite sure that the man would not recognise him, but he felt somehow obliged to make the encounter.

"It's Hoppy, isn't it?"

Hoppy halted and struck a pose, as an actor might have done in similar circumstances.

"Good God! I haven't been called that in many a long year. And who might you be? A former alumnus of Stone Court, perchance?" The flowery mode of address was familiar to Savernake: it brought back memories. In Stone Court days it had been much imitated, and sometimes admired.

"Savernake," he said.

Hoppy came up and peered at him, so close that Savernake could smell the Guinness and old age on his breath. "Ah, yes. Savernake *minor*, unless I am much mistaken. Savernake *major* was the good looking one." It gave Savernake a shock to have his older brother mentioned. "How do you do?" Hoppy held out his hand and Savernake reluctantly shook it. It felt remarkably like the hand he had known long ago only too well, smooth and hard and cold, a polished marble hand.

"And what brings you to this well-nightingaled vicinity?" said Hoppy.

Savernake muttered something vague about needing a break. There was a pause, awkward and full of stifled recollections, then Savernake on impulse said: "Would you care for a coffee or something?"

"Thank you, Savernake. I know of an establishment on the pier which serves a very passable cup of coffee and a not entirely contemptible toasted teacake. Let us repair thither."

They walked to the pier without exchanging many words. Savernake noticed that Hoppy was breathing hard and devoting all his attention to movement. The burst of florid language, he guessed, had been something of an act and had, temporarily, exhausted his mental faculties.

When they were settled in the pier café, Hoppy ordered from the young waitress not only coffee and teacake but, as he put it, "a slice of your very excellent chocolate gateau." If he was attempting to charm the girl in question he signally failed. When she was gone Hoppy turned his attention to Savernake.

"And now, Savernake Minor, tell me all about your beautiful and extraordinary life."

Savernake gave him the curtest possible résumé of his career that was consistent with politeness. As he had expected, Hoppy was not particularly interested. When the coffee and cake came his attention became almost exclusively devoted to the victuals. Once he had devoured a slice of teacake, he said:

"And what of your brother, Savernake *ma?*"

Savernake told him that he had died four years ago. He did not inform him that his brother had, for no known reason, committed suicide. That would have been to open an old wound, and with Hoppy of all people. He did not even know what he was doing here, feeding cake to this dreadful old man.

"Have you been living here all the time?" Savernake asked.

"More or less. Shortly after you left Stone Court I was—what is the euphemism?—'asked to leave.' Some nonsense over one of the boys. He wrote to his parents about me. Such rubbish. Sorry. One has to be very politically correct these days and take all that cant about 'abuse' seriously, doesn't one?"

He looked at Savernake, searching for some kind of approval. None was given.

"It was a difficult time for me. The worst of it was I became so short of cash I had to sell the old Alvis. Do you remember the Alvis? A thing of beauty, but not, as it turned out, a joy forever?"

Savernake remembered the Alvis, the raffish second-hand sports coupé in which Hoppy would take out groups of boys for a drive round the North Head. There was fierce competition over who would *not* get to sit in the front seat beside him. Savernake had once lost out. He shivered at the memory.

"Somehow I stayed on in Norgate. It caused great irksomeness to that worthy old hypocrite Beresford, the head master. Perhaps that's why I did it. Got a job clettering dishes at a greasy spoon down by the beach. Then I started pulling pints at the Captain Digby: you remember, the pub where all the Stone Court masters used to drink. That caused much alarm and despondency, I'm happy to say. And so I have lived on. Now I am a venerable burden on the State, and I still get my little war pension for the old foot. All I asked for was occasionally to put my hand inside your little short trousers, or to get you to put your soft hand inside my not so short ones. Perhaps a little more than that on occasion. The Greeks would have thought nothing of it, you know. After all, it was part of their education. Am I shocking you? I do hope so."

Savernake looked into those ancient rheumy eyes and saw a glimmer of malice. He himself felt nothing; he was frozen.

"Nowadays, I and a few like-minded companions have to make do with the technical wizardry of what they call 'The Inter Net.' It's wax fruit after the real thing, you know."

Hoppy leaned forward, once more hoping for a reaction. Savernake found himself paralysed, unable to move either physically or emotionally. He was remembering something his brother had said to him shortly before he died.

"And so I have gone on. I thought I would be dead long before this, and so, no doubt would you, had you given it any thought, but, as you see, I didn't die. Somehow I have failed in that endeavour. It must be this bracing Norgate air. Or perhaps simply the thing I am has made me live. Now I am an ancient, a *struldbrugg*; I sometimes wonder if I shall ever die. I often long for it, but I am consoled by the thought that at least I have outlived all my persecutors. It is my revenge."

"Or your punishment."

Hoppy stared at him through narrowed eyes. "Fuck off, Savernake Minor," he said quietly. "And now, I must be on my wicked way. Thank you for the sustenance. You won't try a little of this gateau? I can't finish it, I'm afraid, but it really is 'to die for,' as the modern *argot* has it. Where are you staying, incidentally?"

"Happydene."

"Ah, Happydene! Spent a night there with a rent boy once in earlier, more carefree days. Latvian, if I remember rightly. The rent boy, that is. Couldn't understand a word he said, but pneumatic bliss. Happydene: I remember it well. The rooms are high."

"What the hell does that mean?"

"Mean? If you don't know now, you'll never understand. Farewell, Savernake Minor. You wouldn't like to lend me a tenner, would you?"

"No, Hoppy."

"I thought not. Adieu. Parting is such sweet sorrow." He lurched up from his seat and hobbled off.

That evening Savernake felt somehow obliged to dine in at Happydene. He would be dining alone anyway and might as well be doing it here. When Alice entered with the greyish soup Savernake asked after Milson.

"He'll be right as rain soon," said Alice. "They're treating him at the moment."

"Will he be coming back here?"

"Oh, I expect so."

"Is your mother here at the moment?"

"She's just gone out."

As Alice bent over to put the soup before him, almost involuntarily Savernake stroked her behind. She was once more wearing the tight black skirt, but Alice did not recognise the action by so much as a flicker. When she had left the room he was amazed at himself and guilty. It had been a moment's aberration, but he could not explain it. The malign influence of his meeting with Hoppy was a poor excuse. Alice's next entrance (with steak and kidney pudding) found him rather rigidly holding a book in both hands and pretending to read.

After supper he sat in the lounge watching the news on television, but the events of the outside world meant nothing to him. Bombs had exploded; aircraft had been torn from the skies; yet another popular television personality had been found guilty of sexual molestation: not even the last item aroused him. Very soon he tired of it all and made his way up to his bedroom. On the landing, in the same place as the night before, he met Alice.

"I've just been turning down your bed, Mr. Savernake," she said. "Is it the Full English you wanted in the morning?"

"That's right, Alice. Good night."

"Good night, Mr. Savernake. I hope you sleep well."

As she passed him to go down stairs she once again brushed her body against his. Savernake watched her ample retreating form with increasing bewilderment. For a moment he was almost overwhelmed with desire; he wanted to rush down the stairs after her and seize her, but the madness abated. He went to his room.

It was unbearably stuffy there. Had Alice deliberately turned up the heating? He opened the window, but it was raining heavily outside and the rain blew in at him venomously. He shut the window and stared at it. A thousand evanescent droplets dashed themselves against the window pane, obscuring all vision of Norgate beyond. Savernake propped his door open to cool the room a little, then turned off the light and lay on his bed fully clothed.

He closed his eyes, trying to organise his thoughts around the day's proceedings but he could not concentrate. Even straightforward moral censure seemed meaningless. He heard a roll of thunder. It was coming from directly above his head. He did not open his eyes; he wanted only to sleep, but the thunder persisted. It sounded almost as if someone was clambering about on the roof above him, and the sound of the rain was no longer a rattle, but more like stertorous breathing. He opened his eyes and was sickened to find himself in the world of the night before.

Above him a great grey expanse stretched up into infinity from which little silver droplets fell occasionally, stinging his face. There was the white Gorgon's head from which came the budded metal tendrils which became hands as they stretched downwards. Now the hands, cold, smooth, and hard, were touching him and he knew them from memory. He closed his eyes to shut it out, to struggle from nightmare into the light, but a huge weight was holding him down.

He managed to open his eyes, heavy though they were, and saw the white face again, but it was not the Gorgon in the ceiling rose but the face of Alice towering above him. Her mouth was open and her face full of madness. She was straddling Savernake, her black skirt tucked up around her bulbous waist, great expanses of soft white thigh on either side of him. Her white blouse was torn open and his hands were grasping at her pendulous breasts. He heard her breath come and go in frenzied gasps, and her spittle stung his cheeks, as she rode him. Above all he felt her weight bearing down on his loins, his stomach, his chest. Beyond her the infinitely high room went black.

◂◦▸

As they wheeled him out of Happydene and into the waiting ambulance Savernake opened his eyes again. It was morning. The sky was a cloudless icy blue, faultless and infinite, washed clean after the rain. He feared it might fall on him; he would be glad of another death.

ALL THE DAY YOU'LL HAVE GOOD LUCK

KATE JONEZ

The sun sinks down behind a bank of puffy lavender clouds that are much prettier than dusty old broke-down Frederick, Oklahoma, deserves. The carnival lights come on all at once like a mad scientist flipped one of those old-timey switches. This is the part of day I like best. Not too early; not too late.

There's something about the way the yellow, red, and white lights stand out against the sky that makes the scene feel more special than it is. Like this is a moment captured for a postcard that's going to be sold at the newsstand up at the rest stop by the highway.

Dear whoever: Wish you were here. Wrote no one ever who passed through Frederick.

From up on the little swell behind the closed-down Ace Hardware where I'm watching for my cue, I catch sight of my mom leaning over the railing and waving to Lainey on the Dumbo ride. Even with Baby June, who obviously is not a real baby, on her hip she's still the best looking woman in the town. She takes a lot of care with her hair and makeup and wears stylish clothes that stand out from everybody else's. In Dallas, my mom says, nobody even notices. They know how to dress in Dallas. I wouldn't know. We stick to the small towns in Texas, Oklahoma, and sometimes Arkansas.

I wouldn't want to bother with fixing my hair and makeup I don't think. Seems to me it's better just to blend in. Better to see than be seen.

The women in town say they hate my mom because she's not a good Christian. They don't even try to keep their feelings to themselves. They speak right up in line at Piggly Wiggly or when they're talking to each other at the Laund-O-Rama. Maybe it's true and Christians only like each other, but it's so completely obvious that they're jealous. The fact that Mom moved us in with the sheriff, Paul Ray Pearson, who up until recently was the most eligible man in town doesn't help either. My mom knows all this and doesn't even care.

This whole situation, pretending we're the family of the sheriff; I can take it or leave it. It's not like it's a permanent thing. My mom isn't really going to marry Paul Ray likes he thinks she is. We aren't ever going to be his kids, no matter what. That's just not who we are. My mom tries and tries, but she's no good at the long game.

I like living in Paul Ray's house, I guess. I like having my own room even if it did used to belong to Paul Ray's son Calvin and it's not really clear if I have to sleep on the couch when he comes back to visit. So far he hasn't come home which makes me think he didn't move out of his own free will. The room especially the closet and bed smells like a cross between farm animals and bleach. It still has his football trophies on a shelf and posters of women in bikinis on the wall. I can't guess what it was that he did to get kicked out, but it must have been bad because football players are loved more than Jesus in Frederick.

I found a box he must have hidden under his bed and forgotten about. It's got letters he wrote to a girl he was in love with. He's not much of a writer, but the feelings still come through. He loved her a lot. From the words he used you could tell he would have done anything to be with her. There's a picture of her that must be from when she was a little kid because she looks way too young to be anyone's girlfriend. He's even got a lock of her hair. She must have loved him a lot too because it's really thick. I wouldn't cut that much of my hair off for anyone. And a fingernail. A full fingernail, not a clipping. I feel like I know Calvin when I look in that box.

I see Calvin sometimes before or after school in the seniors' parking lot. He sits on the hood of his truck and calls out to the senior girls as they walk by. They don't usually answer back. They hurry past him in fact. Guys from the football team hang out with him sometimes. I think he brings beer. Calvin looks a lot like Paul Ray except he doesn't have a pot belly. He's got muscles in his stomach that show when he lifts up his shirt, which he does a lot. It must be a nervous tic. Unlike Paul Ray, Calvin has lots of really nice long brown hair. I walk past him sometimes and wonder if he knows I sleep in his bed. He called out to me once, but I kept walking. I'm supposed to be invisible. It was weird being seen like that. I'm not from the town and I'm only thirteen. I could feel his eyes on me as I walked to class by myself. I thought about going back to sit with him on the hood of his truck. I thought about asking if I could have a beer, but I didn't even though I always wanted to try drinking beer and cutting class.

I'm pretty sure Calvin doesn't go to school anymore. If I could, I'd get out of it too. I'm not doing good in school. At all. But living in a house means I have to go to school even though that's just asking for trouble.

When I take a step, my flip-flops make a sticky noise on the black-top like a Band-Aid being pulled off. I walk fast, but keep it casual like I'm supposed to do. I like the sound of the ground kissing my feet. It's still hot in Frederick, Oklahoma, in spite of it being the end of September. The parking lot at the empty Ace Hardware is host to what is probably going to be the last carnival to come through town this year.

It's okay that carnival season is over. Frederick has high school football. That's even better than this lame-o carnival that's only got kiddie rides and hardly any good games. High school football games are packed and everyone is screaming and jumping around. That's perfect for me.

My mom thinks things in Frederick are grand. I think it's just a matter of time before someone catches on to us. She does the best that she can. That's what she says anyway. Seems like a grownup would be able to look at the past and be able to see what's going to happen in the future. Seems like a grownup would be able to make a new plan and not just do the same thing over and over and hope things will turn out different. Maybe my mom is lying to herself. Maybe she's lying to us. I have to believe her, though. Who else am I going to believe?

My shadow spreads out before me long and lanky as a willow tree. I wish I was my shadow and I could change shape as the sun goes down. Just at that moment, just as I am thinking that thought my flip-flop almost lands on a penny stuck in the tar. It's a good one too. Heads up.

"Find a penny. Pick it up." I whisper as I squat down to get it. There's some more to the rhyme but I'm not sure what it is. I don't usually go to school, so there are a few holes in my education. The penny is stuck pretty good. I try to get my thumbnail under it and pry it up, but it won't budge. I would like my wish to come true.

"Pits," I say. It's my new favorite swear word. I like it because it sounds like a combination of *piss* and *shit* which are both pretty good swears. But *pits* is way better. When teachers get mad about cursing there's not one single thing they can do about a word that isn't officially on the list of bad words. It's catching on around school. I even heard Calvin say it.

Lainey's first wail rolls across the parking lot. I jump up and leave the penny behind. I'm not in position. My mom is going to be seriously mad. I jog across the distance between me and my crying sister. The music from speakers that are supposed to be for tornado warnings sounds like the a.m. radio in our camper. The song might be saying something about love from spring to autumn, but the words are too muddy to tell for sure. It sounds different from the twangy guitar and slick voices that play in every store and restaurant in Frederick. It sounds like it's from some faraway place where people dress nice and speak with fancy language. Dallas maybe.

I'm moving faster than I should but chances are that nobody is going to notice me anyway. I'm not the kind of girl who gets noticed.

People are starting to gather around the pink elephant ride. The ride operator who seems like he's on the bad end of a hangover is looking at my mom with an expression that's melting from annoyed into scared.

Lainey is our screamer. She my nine-year-old sister and she's got a natural talent for it. Even if we didn't have a use for her screaming she'd still do it, I'm pretty sure.

She's sitting on the ground inside the gate, clutching her ankle. Her face is tear-stained and the smear of dirt across her cheek is convincing. The look on her face says she may never walk again. My mom, still holding baby June, is cooing over her, pretending she's trying to get her to be quiet.

People are gathering around, trying to help. One thing I'll say for Oklahomans, they don't walk by people in trouble like they do in some other places.

I should be up there already. I jog a little faster. Just as I slide into place at the edge of the crowd, my Mom makes eye contact. Her look is stern.

It's a crack in the mask she wears when she's working. She reaches her arm out to help Lainey to her feet. Baby June clings to my mom like a trained circus monkey.

Just like she's supposed to, Lainey goes off like a siren. My mom adds her own hysterical voice to the din.

A man in the crowd flails his arms around. "Call an ambulance," he yells.

His words work like a magic spell to turn the pandemonium up a level. Perfect.

I snake through the crowd like I'm doing a ballet dance and slide my fingers into a wallet on this one, a purse on that. My mom says to only take cash because we have to live in this town and there's no way we're able to use cards. I get one anyway. Never know.

"Stand back!" a man calls out. "Let me take a look."

I glance in the direction of the voice. Dr. Olney looks like every other old guy in town with his starched plaid shirt and shiny cowboy boots except he's got droopy eyes and extra saggy cheeks that make him look like a long-eared dog. He's the same doctor who checked Lainey out when the Summer Fun Fair came through Frederick back in July. Pits, this isn't good.

I snag two twenties with the tips of my fingers. They don't slide out like they should and for a moment I'm exposed with my fingers wedged in the back pocket of a pair of black and white checked pants. The guy is squeezed into them as tight as a pork sausage in casing. I feel a little flutter in my chest but I'm not really scared. I'm like a shadow. No one ever catches me. With a little tug the bills come free. The fat guy moves his arms like he's going to reach back, but he doesn't. I stuff the cash in my bra before I squeeze through the crowd to see what the doctor is doing. My mom can have the rest. This forty bucks is mine. I earned it.

Lainey's cute red curls are bouncing and her big blue eyes are blinking and bleary but still incredibly china doll pretty. She's howling and putting on her very best show for the doctor who kneels down beside her and waves someone over from the crowd.

I could keep on working, but it's not such a good idea since we aren't moving along to the next town. Even in Oklahoma, only so many crimes can get blamed on brown people. It's got to suck to be an honest person and have dark skin and always get blamed for everything whether you did it or not.

Don't crap where you eat, as Paul Ray says. He's always got something wise and insightful to say. Seems like someone so smart would be able to figure out what's going on right under his nose. Especially since he's a sheriff and all. Men get all weird and dopey in the presence of a woman. My mom says that's the biggest advantage we have as females of the species. She's always telling me I should learn to work it more. I don't see myself doing that anytime soon.

The doctor presses his fingers up and down Lainey's leg. He doesn't even look at my mom like most guys do when they are supposed to be paying attention to us kids. He's intent and serious. "Broken," he says and casts a glance designed to induce shame at the ride operator. "She's got to come in to the office so I can set it."

What the pits? Lainey's leg is not broken. What's happening? This is not good. This is not good at all.

We need a distraction. It's obviously time to hit the road. We're not far at all from the patch of mesquite scrub where we hid our camper. I could probably see it from here if I was a couple of inches taller. I remember the first thing we saw when we got to Frederick was the back of the closed down Ace Hardware. We could start the camper up before anyone even noticed. We could finally be on our way again. If ever there was a time for screaming, this would be it, but Lainey doesn't make a sound. I think about doing some screaming of my own. But I don't.

I see my mom looking into the crowd. Looking for me. I hunker down. I don't want to be part of this. That doctor must know Lainey's leg isn't broken. What are we supposed to do now? He's flushing us into the open like the hound dog he looks like. This isn't going to end well. A lump grows in my stomach like somebody kicked me.

"Move along, now. Nothing more to see." Dr. Olney hoists Lainey up and holds onto her without touching her leg.

The crowd disburses and I lose my cover.

"Take care of June while I see to Lainey." My mom sets Baby June on the ground.

I search my mom's face for some clue about what I'm supposed to do. She's got on her working mask. It's smooth and calm. I can't detect a crack.

Baby June runs over to me. A few people glance at her sideways because she runs like the seven-year-old kid that she really is. It's a weird thing to see. She's supposed to take tottering baby steps whenever she walks. My mom makes her practice it all the time and yells at her when she walks normal. Today she doesn't even notice June is walking wrong. This must be really serious.

Even though every one of the kids in my family has a different dad, we're the same because of how far away we are from ordinary people. Only with Baby June it shows.

June is supposed to act like a baby just like Lainey is supposed to scream and I'm supposed to move through a crowd like a shadow. Even if we wanted to, there's no way to change who we are. It's just a fact. Baby June hates it though. She hates that she's never going to grow even one inch taller. I feel bad for her. How can she hate herself? That's just as bad as hating air or water.

My mom turns and walks along next to the doctor. The carnival lights flicker on them like lights from the sheriff's car.

Paul Ray Pearson will have to put my mom in jail when he finds out who she really is. He'll have to do it even if he loves her with all of his heart. He's a sheriff. That's what they do. Just like my mom is who she is. It seems kind of sad. We're all on a train headed for a cliff and nobody can do anything about it no matter how much they might want to. I know my mom is trying to love Paul Ray Pearson back. It just isn't in her nature.

I'll have to take Lainey and Baby June and run away before they catch us and lock us up too. I could do it, but it won't be easy. I sure won't get caught and leave little kids all alone to take care of themselves. It wouldn't hurt my mom to try a little harder. It's one thing to be who you are. It's another thing entirely to be lazy about it.

The music coming from the tornado speakers has horns and saxophones. It sounds slippery like a fancy nightclub on TV. It's big city music. Maybe I'll get as far away from Frederick and the stupid carnival circuit as I can and go see Dallas for myself. Baby June would like that. I can't say for sure about Lainey.

"Give me some money." June tugs on the hem of my shorts. "I want to play a game." With her other hand she rips out the ribbon that holds her hair in a ponytail on top of her head. Her fine black hair floats down around her shoulders.

"You know you're not supposed to do that."

June looks up at me with an anger in eyes that is more than any seven-year-old should have. "What difference does it make?"

She's right. What does it matter if anyone knows she's not a baby? It's just a matter of time before they figure all of us out anyway.

I reach down my shirt and take out the twenties. I give one to June. "Stay close by though. I'm supposed to be watching you."

"Whoa." She looks at the money. "I can play a million games. Thanks." June spins around so fast her little dress flairs out.

I like making June happy. She's so mad most of the time that she hardly notices little things. A twenty-dollar bill is big enough to get her attention.

"I saw what you done."

My head snaps around at the sound of the voice.

Calvin's face hovers a foot over my head. His eyes are intense and serious just like his dad Paul Ray's are when he's telling us a story he thinks we're going to learn from. Something about that look makes me feel good. I'm mostly invisible, but with him looking at me like that, I feel seen. Calvin is half smiling and holding onto the hem of his shirt like he's about to lift it up. I kind of wish he would at the same time I hope he doesn't.

A weird feeling grabs my stomach like the knot from before came untied.

His smile flashes in his eyes. He looks happy, excited like a kid on his birthday who's just been handed a package. I catch a whiff of soap and that slight doggy smell that lingers in his bedroom. It smells good enough that I'm tempted to step a little closer to him.

"I saw what you done." He tilts his chin at the twenty I've still got in my hand.

I fold the money in half and stuff it in my pocket a little too fast. I feel off balance, like I'm getting caught in a lie. Something I *never* do. "There's nothing to tell," I say. My voice wavers. I sound like a liar. Pits!

"Saw you do it. Saw you reach in that guy's pocket."

I'm pretty sure I'm going to puke. How I'm feeling on the inside must show on my face.

"Don't worry." He puts his hand on my shoulder. "I'm not going to tell."

My instinct is to shake his hand off. I stop myself because that will make me look even guiltier. His big fingers grab onto me not tight but not too loose either. The pukey feeling shifts into something different. Kind of like the feeling when a roller coaster is tick, tick, ticking up the track. Is he telling the truth? Will he really not tell even though his dad is the sheriff? His grin grows wider and shinier somehow. "You want to get a Coke or something?" he asks really nice, like he cares if I say yes or no.

"I don't know," I say. His hand grows heavier. It's slightly damp. I want to go with him, I think I do, but I've never met someone from outside my family who knows so much about me. I like that he knows, but also I don't like it. It's exciting and scary at the same time. I guess I believe him. What other choice do I have?

I glance over at June. She's convinced someone to lift her up on a stool and she's leaning over the counter of the ring toss. She's going to win something. The carny will take all her money but he won't let her leave without a prize. She's too cute and too small. And hopefully she remembers a thing or two about the power of little girl tears.

"Come on." Calvin's hand is still on my shoulder. "I'm buying." His voice is deeper than other boys. It's a rumbling voice but soft and slow too because he's from Oklahoma. Maybe he's not exactly a boy. But he's Paul Ray's son, so he can't be a man. I decide he must be something in between.

The way he says he's buying like we're going to the bar at the racetrack makes me feel grown up. I'm not beautiful like my mom or pretty like Lainey, but when he says that I feel like I am.

We walk over to the concession stand and the hand he has on me slides easily down and we're walking together with his arm around me like we're boyfriend and girlfriend. It's weird but nice. The soapy, doggy smell is all around me like a blanket.

There are two girls I recognize from school up at the counter ahead of us. When they turn around, big sodas and chocolate-covered pretzels in their hands, they look surprised to see us behind them. They look afraid actually, but that doesn't make sense. One of them, the girl with the slightly blonder hair, Gayla or Gay Anne, opens her mouth to say something to me which she has never done before.

"Go on. Get along," Calvin says to her before she has a chance to speak.

The girl looks like she might cry.

Her friend, Maitlin or Caitlin, bumps her hard. "Go, go!"

The first girl looks me hard in the eyes like she's trying to tell me something, then both of them run away.

What is their problem? Townies are so odd.

Calvin gives me a big paper cup filled with the good kind of slushy ice and some sort of reddish liquid. "I got you a Suicide."

"What's that?" I wonder if this is another one of those things that everybody but me knows.

"You'll like it. It's all the flavors in one cup. Drink it down a little so I can put in the good stuff."

I take a big drink. It's extra sweet and tastes mostly like Dr. Pepper. It's not my favorite but it's okay. Brain freeze tickles around the top of my head, but doesn't take hold.

We drift away from the concession stand.

Calvin takes a silver flask out of his back pocket. He rests his cup on a ledge while he unscrews the top and pours clear liquid into his cup.

"Give it here." He indicates my cup and holds the flask out to me.

"What is it?"

"Part of the Suicide."

I know what it is. I've been around enough to know liquor when I see it. I'm not sure why I asked. Something to say, I guess. I always did want to try drinking. I hold out my cup.

He fills up my cup to the rim. "Stir it up real good." He grabs my straw and swishes it around. "If you stir it up, it don't taste so bad."

I take a taste. It's kind of like gasoline with a little sweetness mixed in but I pretend I like it anyway. This makes Calvin happier than it seems like it should. He's standing still but his body is moving in the way a puppy does when it's trying hard to hold its energy in.

Baby June has moved on from the ring toss. She's shooting rubber balls from an air gun at crazy-looking clown heads. She did okay at the last game. She's got a stuffed donkey sitting at her feet.

"I've got to go check on my sister."

"You coming back?" There's a tremble in his voice like he really and truly wants me to say yes.

I shrug out from under his arm as though I just might have somewhere better to be, but before I can take even one step toward my sister Paul Ray dressed up in his sheriff's uniform steps up to the game June is playing and snatches her up. Baby June squeals and kicks. "I was winning motherfucker!"

I glance over at Calvin. He's ducked out of sight around the side of a tent. He holds his finger up to let me know he doesn't want me to say anything about him to his dad.

Paul Ray clamps his hand over June's mouth which doesn't do a thing to settle her down. The opposite in fact.

Paul Ray doesn't quite get Baby June. He treats her like she's a baby even though he's heard her talk and seen her walk like herself. He seems to be holding two truths in his head at the same time. Can people even do that?

"Jessup, what's your sister doing out her by her lone self?" He raises his voice to be heard over the drone of the music, the bubble of the crowd and the calls of the carnies.

"I'm watching her, Paul Ray," I call back. I don't rush over to them. I probably should but I don't. I cast my eyes sideways. Calvin is still squatting down beside the tent with his finger to his lips. Something is weird in his eyes. He's scared of something.

Paul Ray hitches June up on his shoulder and takes several strides toward me. "Don't look like it to me." He's trying to sound gruff and mean, but it isn't working. I like Paul Ray's big face with the mustache as prickly as a toothbrush. And his wide, happy smile that makes me feel the way eating eggs sunny side up with crispy bacon does on cold mornings when all the windows are frosty.

June is still kicking and squirming but not so hard anymore.

Calvin hunkers down like he's trying to make himself invisible.

"Where's your mama anyhow?" Paul Ray asks.

Pits, pits, pits. What am I supposed to say to that? My mind races to find a good answer. He doesn't know? Nobody called him to take my mom to jail yet.

"She's with Lainey." I say. That's the truth. The absolute truth.

That seems good enough for Paul Ray which is something I didn't expect.

"I'm going to take this girl on home. Past her bedtime. You coming?"

My insides knot up. I take a big drink of my Suicide. This time it tastes more like gasoline mixed with cherry Coke. I don't feel anything. I already know what I'm going to say, so why do I have this feeling like I'm standing on the high dive at the pool at the Howard Johnson's? I know I'm going to jump, but if I want to I can still climb back down the ladder.

"I'm going to stay for a while," I say. "If that's okay," I add just to show him the respect he's due.

June's eyes are as mad as I've ever seen them. "Don't you leave me." Tears dribble down her face. She hardly ever cries. Never did, even when she really was a baby. "Don't you leave me."

Paul Ray scrunches his mustache over to one side like he's thinking it over. "Alrighty, can't see no harm in you staying a while. You got some money?" He props June on his shoulder and grabs his wallet with his other hand. He holds it open. "Get you one of them twenties."

I almost say no because nobody should be that nice to a shadow like me. I would have stolen that twenty and more if opportunity had ever presented itself.

"Thanks," I say. I feel like maybe I might cry too. I can't figure out why.

Paul Ray turns away and lumbers toward the parking lot.

June looks over his shoulder at me. "Don't leave me. Dontleaveme-donleavemedonleaveme." Her words blur together and become a single sound like a train blowing its horn as it passes out of town.

Baby June will understand one day. How am I supposed to take care of a kid like her? She'll be better off with someone who isn't a shadow.

I tuck Paul Ray's money into my pocket with the other twenty I stashed there. I catch a glimpse of Gayla or Gay Anne walking fast toward the parking lot. She's with a woman who is every bit as blond as she is. Her mother. Has to be. The mother whips her head from side to side like she's a mouse with a cat on her tail. She breaks into a full run dragging her daughter with her when she spies Paul Ray.

I walk back over to where Calvin is beside the tent. He's on his feet.

"Why were you hiding from your dad?"

"Me and him don't get along."

"Oh." Paul Ray seems easy enough to get along with, but what do I know. Maybe he's different with his own kids.

"You want to ride the Ferris wheel?"

I turn my head up to look. Red and yellow lights wink in the blue velvet sky. A big, full moon makes the night brighter than it needs to be. At the top, three seniors I recognize from school are rocking their basket. One boy, with a red rash of pimples across his nose, is doing the rocking. The other has his arms around a curvy red-haired girl who's pretending to be afraid. The top of the Ferris wheel looks like it would be a great place to be, but I can't picture myself up there. It's not a place a shadow would go.

"Do you think we could walk around a while first?"

"I guess. If that's what you want to do." He reaches out and grabs my hand. He's trembling a little which makes me feel powerful. I've never made anyone nervous before.

We embark on our stroll down the midway. The salty-oil of popcorn, the sticky pink of cotton candy and the corny-sweet of hushpuppies mingle in a cloud of carnival perfume.

"You want another drink?" Calvin asks making his cup gurgle. We've walked to the edge of the midway, almost to where the mesquite scrub and brambles start.

"No thanks."

"You want me to make that one stronger?"

The alcohol doesn't seem to be doing anything and I would like to know what all the fuss is about. "Okay."

He tosses his empty out into the dark tangle just beyond where we're standing and takes my cup from me. He pours more liquor from his flask into my cup, and then takes a swig. As he swishes my cup around to mix things up, I let my eyes wander out into the field. I try as hard as I can to remember exactly what I saw on that very first night we got to Frederick.

"You want to walk back?" he asks.

"Let's walk around the edge instead."

Calvin's smile looks just like that bacon-and-egg smile of his dad's. He wraps his hands around my arms and pulls me up against him. He leans down and presses his mouth against mine. He pushes his tongue in my mouth.

I'm still holding my cup and the sweaty wax paper is squishing up against him. I'm not sure what to do with my other hand so I let is settle on his hip. He feels hard. Muscle hard. So different from anyone I've ever touched before. His tongue is in my mouth and I wonder what he thinks of my teeth. No one has ever been on the inside of my mouth before. Not even my mom.

"I like you," he says in a gasping-for-air breathy voice.

I like him too, but I'm not so sure I like kissing. I know better than to say that. I like that he wants to kiss me even if I'm not all that thrilled with the actual activity. Maybe I'll get used to it. Having another person's tongue in my mouth is the weirdest thing I've ever experienced. "Umm hmmm." I murmur.

When it's over and he pulls back I'm relieved.

"Let's walk some more," I say. I take his hand and squeeze it.

"Awright," he says. "You want to go somewhere? You know, more private."

I nod like that's exactly the thing I want most. I've got a pretty good idea what he's got on his mind, but I'm absolutely sure. I don't have the first clue about how to do what he wants. He's going to think I'm really stupid. I wish I was more sexy.

As we're walking around the outside edge, I look for the white shell of our camper. I know it's not far away. Calvin drapes his arm around my shoulder and lets his hand rest on my boob. Not that it's much of a boob but it's all I've got. It feels weird when he rubs his pinky finger over my nipple. It's like he doesn't even notice I'm only wearing a training bra instead of a real one.

"Do you know I sleep in your bed?" I say. My voice sounds kind of gravelly. I wanted it to sound grown up and sexy but instead it sounds like I need to clear my throat.

"Yup. I knew that."

"Did your dad tell you?"

"Me and him don't talk."

The music from the carnival sounds far away, like the sound has traveled across a lake. A pump jack thump, thumps in the distance. I can't see it cranking around and around pulling the oil from the ground but I hear it louder than my own heartbeat. Seems odd Calvin doesn't talk to his own father, the person he's spent all his life with. How could he possibly know what goes on in the house if his dad didn't say?

Calvin pulls me in closer against his body. Walking feels a little awkward. We aren't exactly in sync as we wind our way through the trailers at the edge of the carnival. I still like having his arm around me even though it would be easier to walk without it. Nobody is around. The carnival seems to be winding down for the night. Sometimes we step out into the overgrowth until it gets too thick and we tromp through the plant life and back onto the black top. I still haven't spotted the camper but we're close. We must be.

"Why don't you talk to your dad?" I ask.

"He don't like some of the things I done. He says they ain't right and I can't be his son unless I change my ways."

"What kind of things?"

"Don't matter. Ain't like nothing is gonna change. I'm different from other folks. There's nothing I can do about it." He flips his long, brown hair over his collar. It falls on his shoulder in a nice soft-looking way. I have the urge to pet it. "It's just how I am."

"I know exactly what you mean," I say. I get an excited feeling. I *do* know exactly what he means. I've never met anyone outside of my family who was an outsider like us. Pity wells up in my chest. I think it might choke me. It must be even harder to be different without even one other person to understand.

I understand him though.

"You want to be my girlfriend?"

I never thought I wanted a boyfriend before. My mom has them all the time and it never works out all that good, but for some reason this seems like a good idea. Like something I could be better at than my mom.

"Yeah." I feel like I know Calvin better than anyone. It's like there's a new member of my family. I can tell him anything. Everything. I don't know where to start.

We stop walking again and Calvin leans down. I get the feeling he's going to kiss me again but he doesn't. He puts his hands on my head and tangles his fingers in my hair. He's holding onto my hair kind of tight, but it doesn't hurt. Not really.

"Can I lop of a piece of your hair?"

"For your box?" The words spill out before I even think about them.

Calvin's eyes flash and all the muscles in his face tighten up.

"What box is that?"

It's probably private. Guilt churns in my stomach. I shouldn't have looked at Calvin's personal stuff.

With one hand he grips my hair, with the other he reaches into his pocket and pulls out a folding knife. He flicks it open with his thumb.

The way he's holding my hair makes my head tilt to the side. Everything looks just a little off kilter from this perspective. The back of the Ace Hardware looks exactly the same as the first night I saw it.

It must be pretty late by now. The doctor has probably figured out that Lainey's leg isn't broken and my mom is probably on the way to jail in the back of Paul Ray's sheriff car.

The pump jack thump thumps only this time my heart is thumping louder.

"I'm just going to cut off a little chunk. Only because I like you so much."

"Okay." I say, but it doesn't feel like it's okay. I'm not so worried about what I want to tell Calvin anymore. He doesn't seem in the mood to hear about me. I shouldn't have listened to my mom and practiced my feminine wiles. I think I might have used too much.

I remember that one complete fingernail, not a clipping, that Calvin keeps in that box. How would someone come by something like that?

Calvin holds my hair so tight tears are welling in my eyes. He saws with his knife. It's a relief when he cuts through and my head is free again. I'm tempted to touch my hair and see how much is gone. I'm feeling mad about this now that it's sunk in some, but this isn't the type of situation where getting mad is going to do any good. He did it because he likes me after all. Even if it is a messed up thing to do. Pits. This is not going how I thought it would.

Calvin wraps his arms around me and pushes his mouth against mine. His tongue feels like a big chunk of meat. I want to breathe more than I can with him on me like this. His leg keeps wrapping around me like he's trying to knock me down. I don't want to fall. Not now. Not here on the blacktop behind the dirty carnival vans.

The top of the camper, the part that fits over the cab where me, Lainey, and June watch what goes on after my mom sends us to bed, peeks out from a tangle of trees not much taller than me. I feel like I just saw Thanksgiving dinner laid out in all its glory. That camper is the best home I ever had. Our old pickup might have a flat tire or even two and probably not too much gas but I know exactly where the screwdriver is that starts the ignition. I can make it go. I'm sure of it. I can get that old truck out of this field and out of Frederick. I bet the forty dollars I've got will get me most of the way to Dallas. In a flash the memory comes back to me: I never gave my mom the take. I've got plenty of money. I can go anywhere.

"Wait," I say, pushing Calvin away and untangling myself from his octopus grip. "I got a better idea."

"What's that?"

Before he even gets out the whole question, I leap away and plow into the overgrown field. I crash through the weeds and branches. I don't even care how bad I'm getting scratched. Now I'm the mouse with a cat on my tail. I've just got to get to the camper.

Breathless, I finally make it. I jerk open the door. The smell of my mom's Opium perfume and the liniment we rub on Baby June's knees splashes in my face. I glance back.

"You got a camper?" Calvin grins and stomps down a bunch of weeds. He reaches out for me.

As hard as I'd run I only managed to keep two steps ahead of him. I dive for the screwdriver but he grabs me around the waist and lifts me up before I can get it.

Now I know how Baby June feels when people pick her up. I kick and thrash but it doesn't do any good. I scream and he clamps his hand over my mouth.

I can't get enough air in. I can barely hear the thump, thump of the pump jack over the sound of my heart. I can barely hear the whoop, whoop of the sheriff's siren.

Calvin opens the door to the camper and lugs me inside. He drops me on the floor and falls on top of me.

I wriggle and writhe but can't get out from under him. The button on my shirt tears off. He's heavy on my chest and his hand is clamped down hard on my mouth. The air won't come no matter how hard I try to get it.

"Hey, look!" I say gasping. It's a good one. Heads up."

Maybe it's my words or maybe it's the whoop, whoop of the sheriff's siren and the crunch of men pushing through the mesquite brush that catches his attention and makes him look up.

It's too late for us. We're always going to be different and they're coming to lock us up.

I push and scramble just enough. I lunge for the penny. My shadow spreads out before me long and lanky as a willow. My hand wraps around the copper. I melt into its warm chocolaty embrace.

As the siren whoops grow insistent and the sheriff's men shout to each other how they found the camper, poor Calvin finds himself holding what's left of the girl I used to be like a scarecrow husk.

It's a trick, but a good one. Or maybe it's not.

I am a shadow.

LORD OF THE SAND

STEPHEN BACON

Without Facebook, it never would have happened. We'd have all just continued living our lives, content to let the past remain the past. All of the bad feelings would have stayed deeply buried.

But Facebook allows you to assemble a ribbon of detritus from your life—a place where current friends mingle with barely remembered school chums, former work colleagues mass like mementos from all the shit jobs you've ever had. I've even acquired a couple of ex-girlfriends on mine, just for old times' sake. What I'm saying is that I *realise* the past is a different country—and it certainly *was* in our case because we'd fought in it. So when the invitation to attend the reunion arrived, I should've just walked away. I should have let bygones be bygones. Looked forward instead of back. My God, how I wish I'd done just that.

By this time my army career felt like it had happened to someone else. Don't get me wrong—I'm grateful I experienced the things I did, grateful too for the training and qualifications I attained; achievements which—once my decade serving Queen and Country had ended—became the launch-pad into my new career as a telecommunications engineer. But as I'd grown older my political stance had shifted marginally. Operation Desert Storm had seemed an absolute necessity at the time. However, things had changed; I now felt uneasy about the way the West was dealing with the Middle East. Twenty-five years had made one hell of a difference.

Christ, I'm starting to sound like my dad.

Anyway, the reunion of the Royal Regiment of Fusiliers 3rd Battalion was arranged for December 2nd in the function room of the Golden Plover, four miles outside Hastings. It had been chosen largely due to its accessibility from London and its close proximity to the home of the organiser, Shaun Adams.

I hadn't seen Shaun—or Beaky as we'd called him—since Fallujah in 1991. But his Facebook photos told me he'd barely changed other than a receding hairline and a few wrinkles. I was curious to catch up, to see what had happened to everyone during the intervening years. I'd initially joined the army with no clear idea of where I was going. Those qualifications that I mentioned earlier—they meant that I was now quite proud of what I'd ended up doing. The group messages suggested there would be quite an attendance if all those invited turned up.

I'd booked into a Travelodge that lay within walking distance of the pub. At the appointed time I nervously strolled into the function room, trying my best to look as slim as I'd been in the early nineties. The DJ was working overtime in recapturing the era—all Chesney Hawkes and Color Me Badd and Jesus Jones. I allowed myself to be swept up into the slightly surreal experience of meeting people from my distant past; people I'd once entrusted with my life, but who now just looked vaguely familiar. The beer-bellies and slap-heads were in attendance everywhere. Within ten minutes I'd sunk three pints, all the better to steady my nerves. I'd been introduced to several wives (and managed to promptly forget their names), reminded of a dozen hilarious memories (which time had subsequently wiped), and raised sombre toasts to a couple of fallen comrades. And then, shortly before nine o'clock, Beaky made his entrance.

At this point I probably need to mention that Beaky had occupied a rather special position in our regiment. He'd been a thin, nervous lad; twitchy and unprepared for the horrors that awaited us in Iraq. Unfortunately he hadn't fared well. There were times when he'd skirted close to cracking. He'd been the butt of many of the pranks that had been played, borne the brunt of the majority of teasing. Not *bullying*, you understand, although I had felt a slight nervousness at seeing him again; a twinge of guilt that had manifested over the intervening years.

But I needn't have worried. Beaky was welcomed like a returning hero, his slight frame embraced by drunken ex-squaddies and surprised girlfriends. As organiser of the reunion, he was also congratulated as to its success, with slurred pledges to make it an annual event. Very soon he found himself at my table, occupying the empty seat beside me.

We made small talk for a while. I offered to buy him a drink, but he advised me he was driving—something that puzzled me, given how close to the Plover he lived—surely he could afford the cost of a taxi. Nevertheless I returned from the bar with his Coke and another pint for me.

I tried discreetly to make light of his experience in the forces, quizzing him enthusiastically about his current life, overcompensating with the positives. Despite his Facebook pictures indicating otherwise, he appeared rather vacant; brittle and broken. There was a sallow, haunted sheen to his skin. His eyes constantly watched the door, restless and anxious. He admitted that he'd been prescribed powerful drugs for his insomnia. It seemed like he harboured the same debilitating lack of self-worth he'd displayed back then. I felt dreadfully sorry for him. At that point he excused himself and went to the toilet.

Beaky was obviously edgy as hell. And deep inside I knew why.

Brad Hoggard was conspicuous by his absence. Six-foot-five, blond-haired Brad had served as our sergeant. He could handle himself, and by God, did he know it. His biceps were so thick it must have used a gallon of ink just to tattoo the Celtic bands that encircled them. I was relieved that he hadn't shown up, even if it meant the central character from our regiment was missing. We all understood that it was Hoggard's mean streak which had fuelled the campaign of victimisation that Beaky had been forced to endure. He'd mentally bullied the kid as much as inflicting the physical damage on him. And I took no consolation in the fact that Hoggard had been the instigator of the bullying—every time I'd looked away or pretended not to hear, another part of my insides had withered. If I'm honest I suspect that most of us had just felt relieved that the victim—Beaky, always Beaky—had been someone else instead of us.

Anyway, about half-nine I was chatting to a bloke who'd been airlifted out of Iraq early into our tour, when he swore under his breath and nodded towards the door. I glanced up and felt my heart sink.

The disco lights strobed against an imposing figure that was striding into the room. The silhouette was unmistakable. As he crossed the dance floor I caught sight of Hoggard for the first time in decades. It seemed like nature had played a cruel hand; unlike the rest of us—all beer bellies, wrinkles, bald heads, jowls—Hoggard had apparently taken good care of himself. His hair was fashionably cut, the tight shirt accentuating his flat stomach and defined muscles. I noticed quite a few wives and girlfriends watching his progress as he strode over to our table. His skin looked like he'd been fucking airbrushed.

I stood and tried to spot Beaky at the bar. Several lads cautiously greeted Hoggard and he seemed to bask in the attention. I headed to the bar to distract Beaky, maybe even prepare him for the appearance of his nemesis. Someone turned and I heard him mutter, "Why the fuck has he been invited?" and someone replied, "Which dickhead invited him anyway?" I shrugged and in that moment decided to take on the role of peacemaker. But in the end it was all needless anyway.

The evening progressed not at all in the way I expected. Hoggard actually proved to be, whilst not exactly *likeable*, extremely more amiable than he'd been as our sergeant. His career hadn't progressed further than sergeant however (that may have had more to do with his overt sociopathic tendencies than any lack of ambition). And I was heartened to see that Beaky had let bygones be bygones. At one point I even saw them laughing together.

By the time last orders were called at the bar, the whole place had slipped into a merry state of inebriation. We'd all had a bloody good time. My ears were ringing with the music and I glanced about, intending to get in a final round of drinks. It was then that I spotted Hoggard slumped forward across a table nearby. I made some comment about how the big man obviously wasn't able to hold his beer any more. Beaky laughed and we went over to see if he was okay.

Hoggard was absolutely paralytic. We attempted to lift him up, his eyes rolling in their sockets. Someone suggested calling an ambulance, but that idea was quickly dismissed. I was just about to volunteer to let him stay in my room at the Travelodge, when Beaky piped up about how he knew Hoggard's address and—as he'd not been drinking—he'd drive him home. That was quickly agreed, and it took three of us to help him out to Beaky's Vectra and see them off, pleas to stay in touch echoing round the car park.

By the time I returned to the bar, the bell had gone so I missed the last drink. As a result, I began to sober up slightly. That fact proved to be important later.

The crowd had thinned. People were drifting away, swapping phone numbers and drunkenly telling each other how much they'd enjoyed the evening. I felt a satisfied glow at how it had turned out. And then a passing comment tore my cosy world to shreds.

I remarked about how unfounded my concerns for Beaky had been; that Hoggard's appearance had failed to spoil the party. I received a puzzled glance, and was told that Beaky had *made contact* with Hoggard through Facebook and pretty much begged him to attend the reunion.

To clear my head, I went out to the car park. I looked thoughtfully at the space that the Vectra had recently vacated, suddenly noticing the overflowing bin nearby, its top filled with discarded cigarette ends. There was an empty packet of tablets stuffed in among the rubbish, the prescription sticker torn off. I had to use my iPhone to google the word—Flunitrazepam—recognising the name Rohypnol, a powerful muscle relaxant commonly prescribed for chronic insomnia.

The cogs were clicking in my brain. I ran back inside, babbling at the DJ that I needed to know Beaky's address. His blank face masked the concern he must have felt. I demanded to know the contact details of the bloke that had organised the evening. His reluctance crumbled when I told him I'd found Beaky's house keys in the car park. He looked it up in his notepad, and I wrote it down and called a taxi.

I was there in half an hour. There was a light burning in every window of Beaky's house. It was a rather shabby semi-detached property, with thin trees casting a shadow onto the bay window. I paid the taxi and fought to compose myself as I crept up the drive.

He took ages to come to the door. He looked surprised when he saw me, but then I detected something shift in his eyes, and he held the door open and invited me in.

The house was silent. It looked like it hadn't been redecorated since John Major had been in power. He led me into the lounge and I sat down on a sagging sofa as its springs wheezed beneath me in protest.

"Drink?"

I shook my head. I'd had enough. Besides, I felt sick. "Where's Hog?"

He shrugged. "Sleeping like a baby, I imagine."

I felt relieved at his relaxed manner. Perhaps I was blowing this situation out of all proportion.

"He's still got his looks, hasn't he?" Beaky took a seat in the armchair opposite me. "Looked after himself."

I nodded. His house was cramped and cluttered. Bric-a-brac and cheap ornamental tat lined the shelves, entirely covering the surface of a scratched sideboard.

"Yeah, he looked well. How's life been since the army, Beak-err, Shaun?"

He shrugged. "Not bad, I suppose." He looked up sharply. "I enjoyed my time in the forces, you know—despite what happened."

"Good."

"Do you think about them days much?"

I shook my head. "Feels like it happened to someone else." The silence that descended then was bloated and dense. To break it, I said, "Do you?"

A thin smile played around his lips. Then he said quietly, "I try not to."

To change the subject, I glanced around. "You've got a nice pad here."

He raised his eyebrows. "Suits me well enough. I've got everything I need here. I don't have many friends."

I nodded slowly. Something on a wooden cabinet in the corner caught my eye. "What's that?"

"Ah. My boys, my boys."

I stood and approached. It was a large glass tank. There was a metal lid on top, housing a heater. The interior of the container was dark, deliberately steeped in shadow. A stack of rocks lay half buried in a deep layer of sand. I bent and peered into the far recesses of the tank. "What you got in here?"

Beaky moved behind me. "I suppose they're my mementos from our time in Iraq. Did you bring anything back with you?—Any . . . *trinkets*?"

I looked at him sharply, studying his face. I was thinking of what I had hidden in my loft wrapped in a plastic bag—an automatic handgun, its serial number filed blank. I turned back to the tank. "My God—what is it?"

"Lords of the Sand." He moved his face close to the glass. "My two little babies." His voice had taken on a detached, dreamlike quality.

I stared into the tank, my eyes picking out the nest of threads that lined the shallow burrows of sand. I could make out the desiccated husks of several large crickets tucked into the niche. Slowly, expectantly, something scuttled out of the darkness. I could discern the fine hairs that coated the spider's pale legs. Its grotesque chelicerae twitched, lending it a monstrous image.

Camel spiders—or wind scorpions as they're sometimes called—are universally feared in the Middle East. Whilst not dangerously toxic, they possess powerful jaws which can inflect great damage on larger mammals. Some of the African lads referred to them as *beard-cutters* due to their reputation for clipping hair from sleeping men in order to line their burrows. I thought that was a load of old bollocks—but out in Iraq I *had* once seen one kill and devour a huge lizard. It was brutal and unforgettable. It was said their bite released an anaesthetic toxin which allowed it to chew away at its prey's numb flesh without detection. Several years ago I'd watched a documentary on the National Geographic channel where a camel spider had eaten the leg of a sleeping cat, stripping the flesh down to the bone. They were known as the Lords of the Sand.

"Christ, mate—why'd you want theses fuckers as pets?" I was caught halfway between repulsion and fascination.

Beaky smiled then, and I noticed his lidded eyes were cast low. "I became obsessed with them out in Fallujah. They seemed to represent something which struck a chord with me—they *can* actually attack camels, you know. I imported this pair a few years ago."

My eyes searched for the other one, the unseen partner. I was only vaguely aware of what Beaky was saying.

"I find them fascinating—how something of this size can be unafraid of taking on something as large as a camel . . . it's admirable, don't you think? The bigger they are, the harder they fall."

Something clicked in my brain. I turned to him. "Beaky, where's the other one? I can only see one here."

He laughed sharply. His face now looked reptilian, unreal. I felt the hairs on my forearms bristle.

"The other one's feeding."

I peered closely at the tank. "Where?"

"I've kept the other one isolated for a week or so." He turned away. "Just to get him nice and hungry."

In a second I was pushing past him, moving out of the lounge. The dining room was in darkness, but I could see the light spilling from the stairs. I bounded up them two at once.

"Hoggard!" My voice sounded deafening in the silence.

I reached the top of the stairs, feeling disorientated by the doors that faced me. Instinctively I moved to the left, barging the door with my shoulder.

It was the spare bedroom. A lamp illuminated the room from its place on the bedside cabinet. The next few seconds were difficult to comprehend because I experienced everything at once.

A shape was rising from the bed, sluggish and leaden. As I took in the sight of the figure, I stepped backwards. Vaguely I recognised Hoggard from his clothing, although at first I had the impression that he was wearing a mask.

The lower half of his face was a ruined mess. There was a gaping red hole where his nose should have been, pale strands of gristle protruding through the bloodstained remnants of his nasal cavity. His teeth were exposed in a fearsome grin. The skin around his lips was gone, revealing a slender jawbone. There was very little blood. His eyes blinked mechanically, betraying the fact that he was alive. *How could he be, when the lower half of his face had been stripped away, consumed?* His legs wobbled, and he stumbled back against the bed. I had a feeling the drug was wearing off. His wrecked face was rendering the cries unintelligible.

And then I spotted the huge spider on the duvet. It looked bloated and satisfied. Its legs trembled horribly. I flicked the material of the duvet and it fell to the floor, trying to scuttle away. My boot stamped quickly, squashing it against the carpet. Pale legs twitched. I swear I heard a sickening crunch.

I tried to grab my phone as Hoggard rolled around on the bed, shrieking frantically, fingering his destroyed face. He was mad with terror. It was a nightmarish scene.

And above the sound of his screams I could hear Beaky's unhinged laughter from downstairs.

WILDERNESS

LETITIA TRENT

The airport was small, squat like a compound, its walls interrupted in regular intervals by tall, shaded windows. When Krista looked out the windows, the sky seemed slate-gray and heavy, but when the front doors opened, she remembered that it was really blue and cloudless outside.

She was early for her flight back to New Haven. She liked to arrive at the very earliest time the flight website recommended. She was prepared to wait, liked it even. It was calming to have nothing to do and nowhere she had to be. She had brought a book about the history of wilderness and America, something left over from college that she had never read. She liked the cover, a picture of a Pilgrim family, small and sickly, their clothes black and heavy on their bony bodies, facing an expanse of trees so tall and green you could see nothing beyond them. She underlined phrases in the book out of old college habit: *Wilderness remained a place of evil and spiritual catharsis. Any place in which a person feels stripped, lost, or perplexed, might be called a wilderness.*

She shared a red plush armrest with a large woman who had almost incandescent butter-blonde hair. Her skin was so tan that it reminded Krista of a stain. Coffee on blonde wood.

The blonde had apparently just come from a trip to Maine. She told an older woman next to her—an even larger woman with tight pin-curls and wire-rimmed glasses, wearing those boxy, pleated shorts that middle-aged women often wear on holidays—about her trip. The blonde had stayed in *the cutest hotel.* Her entire room had been *done up all nautical.* The other woman nodded in agreement with everything the blonde said, as if she had had an identical experience.

Krista watched the airport attendants and one airport policeman patrol the area. They sometimes stepped into the waiting room and observed the crowd with what appeared to be either worry or constipation (they pressed their lips together, their hands on their hips, and blew the air from their mouths as if making silent raspberries). They had a vague air of agitation. She watched them carefully for signs of what might be wrong, but they revealed nothing in their pacing. Nobody else seemed to notice.

On Krista's left, opposite the blonde, was a family, a mother and two children separated from her by one seat. The mother was thin and loud and wore shorts with many utilitarian pockets and a simple tank shirt without a bra. She seemed infinitely capable, as if she ran her own business or perhaps even managed some kind of sports team. Krista admired thin, efficient women like this, women who wore comfortable, rubber-soled sandals and clothing with enough functional pockets. The woman and her children all spoke on their individual cell phones, all telling somebody variations on the news that they would arrive soon, that it was only thirty minutes until boarding.

An announcement crackled over the loudspeakers, the sound delivered in one chunk of indiscernible static.

Krista looked around the room, hoping for the scraps of somebody else's conversation to explain what had just been said.

Plane's delayed for an hour, the blonde said to her husband, who had also missed it. Storms down in Boston.

A general grumble rose. People shifted in their seats and took out their recently stowed cell phones. The blonde woman called her husband's name, which Krista immediately forgot.

Phone me up a pizza, she told him. I won't eat that shit from the vending machine.

⊸⊶

As it grew darker in the waiting room, Krista struggled to make out the print of her book. The primary row of fluorescent lights hadn't been turned on, but nobody else had complained about the dark yet. She wouldn't be the first. She read until she had to squint in the darkness at the small, cramped words.

As she tried to concentrate on the increasingly turgid prose of her book (pages and pages about national forests, conservationists, things that Krista wasn't particularly interested in, though she knew that she should be), the blonde woman spoke energetically about her two dachshunds, Buckeye and Alexis. They liked to eat the carpet, she said, so she had soaked the edges of the carpet in Tabasco sauce, which was, incidentally, the same color as the carpet. The pin-curled woman asked how they managed to walk on the carpet if it was soaked with Tabasco sauce. The blonde shrugged, as if this were a mystery to her as well, though a boring one that she had no interest in pursuing.

Krista gave up on her book.

The mother and her children slept on the carpet below their chairs, their bookbags slung up on the seats above them, the fabric of their bulky Plymouth Rock sweatshirts bunched under their heads as pillows.

Krista wished that she could step outside and occupy herself with a cell phone, as many others did, but she didn't have a cell phone (she had canceled it when she'd left her job) and had nobody to call. Nobody was waiting to meet her in New Haven, and nobody was worried that her flight was late. She stood up and let the cheese cracker crumbs gathered in the folds of her t-shirt fall to the carpet.

◄◦►

Krista stood in the fluorescent lights of the bathroom, listening for shuffling feet, a toilet paper roll spinning. She was alone. Her stall door wouldn't shut completely (how did doors come unlined from their frames? She didn't understand what would cause it, other than a fundamental shifting of the floor), so she kept one hand on the door as she pulled down her underwear. A bumper sticker on the inside of the door said REPUBLICANS FOR VOLDEMORT. She had never seen a Harry Potter movie or read one of the books, but she vaguely knew who Voldemort was. She was in on the joke.

She put her hand on the sticker and tried to keep the door closed as she eased her jeans and underwear down. It was just as she'd thought—in the middle of the bone-colored strip of fabric, a slight red stain. She peeked out her door into the empty bathroom: no machines.

Krista stuffed a ball of toilet paper between her legs and pulled her pants back up, letting the door open slightly, as she needed both hands. As she did this, just as the door swung open and she saw a middle-aged woman in the bathroom mirror carefully applying liquid eyeliner, the bathroom lights cut out. Nothing hummed or whirred and she could hear people in the hallway shuffling and speaking.

She buttoned her pants in the darkness and stepped into the bathroom, lit only by the dusky light seeping through the high, small window above the sinks. The woman applying eyeliner hissed *shit* and left, slamming her purse or hip into the plastic trash barrel as she left.

Before Krista even had time to panic or feel anything but mild interest, the electricity came back on again. The fluorescents above her buzzed with the effort and her blue-lit face appeared in the mirror. She was alone again. She washed her hands and pressed her wet palms over her face.

-◦-

Ladies and gentlemen, a police officer said, shaking the flashlight in his hand in time with the syllables, sorry for the inconvenience. He and one of the nervous attendants stood before the check-in desk.

It's only a temporary outage, the officer assured them. Nothing serious.

Krista made her way back to the waiting room, stepping over legs and bookbags.

The news drifted into the main room, where Krista's jacket was twisted around one leg of her chair, her carry-on bag placed on her seat to save it. The blonde next to her watched the progress of her bag as she removed it and sat down again. She knew that she shouldn't leave her bags unattended—signs on every wall said so in bold red letters. All she had in the bag were dirty clothes, a brochure about Maine blueberries that her mother had given her, and a business card from her father's company with a telephone number scrawled on the back. Nothing she was afraid of losing.

Her parents wanted her to come back home to Maine. She hadn't told them yet that she wouldn't. She was jobless now, that was true, but it wasn't as they feared—she wasn't beyond help. She had skills. She imagined herself combing through the classifieds in a coffee shop, circling job after job, making cheerful telephone inquiries, putting more action words in her resume (*implemented, facilitated, utilized*). The idea didn't scare her. It seemed liberating. Fun, even. She remembered several cheerful montages from romantic comedies that included these very scenes. They had to have happened to somebody.

Did you hear what he said back there? the blonde demanded. It was a rhetorical question, since she obviously knew. Krista nodded and told her anyway.

So what's the problem? the blonde asked. She was suspicious, if not of Krista, then at least of the policeman's words.

Storms. Storms are the problem, Krista repeated.

The woman sniffed and shook her head, kicking off her pink flip-flops. Storms. I bet.

◄◦►

It was completely dark out now. Somebody had put the lights on in the main room, so Krista could no longer see the parking lot and tree-heavy outskirts from the window. The pizza delivery car had taken forty-five minutes to reach the airport. He had reported heavy wind and rain somewhere close and coming toward them. The woman and her husband ate an entire large pizza all by themselves. Krista didn't want any of their pizza, but she found it rude for people to eat in the presence of others who were not eating.

She couldn't concentrate on her book. She put it away and tucked her luggage under her seat. She stood up, feeling the blood rush back into her legs. She'd go outside—the air in here was stuffy, full of the smells of powdered cheese and industrial cleaning liquid.

The glass doors folded away instantly for her, as if she had bid them to do so.

Outside it was still, but the streets were slick, as if it had recently rained, though she had seen no rain. A group of men stood by the doorway, talking about a sports team that she didn't know.

He could really fucking get that ball across the field, he said. That boy was something else. This was from an airport attendant, one she had not seen before, a young man with a slightly fat, womanish body—large hips and a round ass. The other men nodded in unison. They made brief eye contact with Krista and nodded in turn, as if she were a visiting dignitary, somebody who needed at least a modicum of acknowledgement. She smiled and looked down, the proper response.

The streetlights reflected back against the cloud-covered sky, giving it a uniform orangey, sick tinge. Shallow puddles of water collected at the edges of the lot. The entire parking lot was lit by rows and rows of light.

Out beyond the parking lot, Krista saw a paved footpath from the airport to a big, empty industrial complex next door. The flight, according to her blonde neighbor, was delayed for another hour. She had time for a walk.

She set off across the lot, hoping that the men on the steps were watching. She didn't want to be stranded if the plane happened to arrive early and everybody boarded without her. She imagined coming back to find the waiting room empty, her piece of luggage the only sign left that the place had once been inhabited.

The air was humid but cool. A cold sweat gathered on her bare throat and forehead as she pumped her arms and walked fast to reach the walkway. She wanted to be far away from the airport, to be able to see it from a distance. As a child, she had often fantasized about opening the car door and just running into the woods that lined the highways in Maine, disappearing from her parents and never arriving at whatever place they'd intended to take her. She often had a desire for literal distance from places, to see them in perspective to the sky or horizon. It calmed her to see something that made her afraid or unhappy small against a forest or cloudbank.

She crossed the wooded median and broke through to the parking lot of the complex. She turned around. The airport looked small in comparison to the huge building next to her, which had at least a dozen stories and was completely made of glass.

A light swiveled continually from the airport's roof. From a distance, she could see the people inside the building below the fluorescent lights. The blonde chewed a piece of crust. One of the men outside lit a cigarette. The match flamed in his hands and then disappeared. She sat down on a bench facing the airport, and then rested her head on the slats. She was tired, she realized, and the swampy air increased the feeling. She would only close her eyes for a while.

—◇—

Ma'am. Ma'am! The voice woke Krista immediately. A flashlight bobbed around her face. She tried to speak, but only a low moan came out.

Are you hurt? Are you all right, ma'am? The policeman (Krista could see his badge and recognized his slick black hair from the airport) flashed his light into her eyes. She sneezed, then sat up, wiping her nose on the back of her hand.

I'm fine, she said. Is something the matter?

The policeman stood up from his crouching position. He towered over her as she sat, stood too close. Her nose was level with the brass button on his pants. She stood up.

I'm supposed to get everybody back to the airport. Storm coming. The flight is delayed for another hour. He jerked his head toward the airport. The men over there said you'd walked out thisaway and I came to get you. The policeman turned and started back toward the airport, so Krista followed.

I'm sorry to trouble you, she said to his back. She hadn't imagined somebody would come to get her—why would he do that? Had he been watching her?

His shoulders were very broad. She liked how every policeman called every woman ma'am, even if the woman was clearly younger than he was.

The policemen shook his head. No trouble. He didn't turn to look at her.

Krista wondered when the storm would come. The sky was still a strange, flat, orange-black.

◄◦►

When Krista entered the room, the blonde woman and her husband looked away.

Found the last one, the policeman announced to the airport attendant.

Go ahead and take a seat, he told her.

It seemed to her that the whole room watched as she walked to her seat, removed her luggage, and sat down. Some of them didn't take their eyes from her even as the airport attendant began to speak. She looked at the floor.

It looks like we'll be keeping you for another hour, ladies and gentlemen, he said. The airport attendant looked around the room nervously, his hand resting on the top of his walkie-talkie. He wanted to leave, Krista could tell. He placed one foot behind him, ready to pivot him away. The flight is having minor technical difficulties, which should be resolved within the hour. He took a breath. But we got one request from the local authorities—you all must stay inside until the airplane lands.

At the word *authorities*, the room's temperature changed. The blonde's husband sat up straight in his seat and began to protest, as did several other men. The children looked at their mothers. The mothers pulled their children close.

What *authorities*, exactly? a few voices asked, stepping closer to the front counter.

Krista watched the airport attendant's face. He put his hand up and grimaced. I don't have any information beyond what I have given you.

Safe from what? What kind of danger, exactly, might we be in? A balding man in khaki pants stepped forward. He stood with two children—a boy and a girl of seemingly equal age, both thin and uncannily poised, their hair long and neat and pulled away from their faces. They looked just like him, tall and thin with large, bony elbows and hands.

The attendant shook his head. Sir, I only know what I've been told. All I know is that you are not in any immediate danger, as long as you stay in the airport.

Krista felt her stomach pang. She'd been outside. Was she in danger? Or was it only right now that the outdoors was dangerous? She turned and tried to see outside the windows, but she could only see the reflection of the group on the glass.

Listen, another man said, we need to know—but the attendant's walkie-talkie crackled and he held his hand up, pressing it against his face. He spoke into it, a series of yeses and nos. The attendant held up one finger to the crowd, indicating *just a minute,* and returned to the gated doors that separated the waiting room from the security check.

When he left, people looked around, dazed. Some began to speak to each other, to people they would not otherwise speak to. Fear, Krista saw, made them trust each other with their own fear. They turned to each other and said plainly *I am afraid.* Not in those words, but in other words and in the angles of their bodies, in how much closer they leaned, how much more quickly they spoke.

The skinny mother with many-pocketed pants called *hey, hey* in Krista's direction, and she gradually realized that the woman was speaking to her.

Did you see anything while you were outside?

Krista felt the attention of the room turned to her.

She shook her head. Nothing. I didn't see anything. It was completely calm.

The blonde's husband snorted. Calm, he repeated. Krista looked at him, not sure what he meant. Did he think she was lying?

Did you see any people out there? the woman asked, her eyes darting around Krista's head.

No, nobody but the policeman. Krista didn't like the way they watched her. Their eyes narrowed as if they couldn't quite get her into focus.

◄◦►

The police arrived thirty minutes later. She could see their squad cars' headlights momentarily illuminate the otherwise black parking lot. They did not have their sirens on, but when they emerged from the squad cars, they were wearing masks. It was difficult to see exactly what kind of masks (she had only the light from their headlights to see by), but they seemed to be gas masks—a thick tube like an elephant tusk hung down from each policeman's mouth and nose.

One of the children said *His mask is scary*. He pointed, and they all looked out the window, some running up to press their hands and faces to the glass. The entire window was covered with people trying to see through it. Krista remained seated. She'd seen the masks and didn't know how it would help to see more. She could also feel that she was bleeding and was afraid to stand up.

Fuck this, said a young man, one of the people pressed against the glass. He was handsome in a slim, well-groomed way that made Krista nervous. Men like this didn't notice her unless she was doing something for them—putting their call through at her office, for instance (her *former* office, she reminded herself), or reminding them to sign a form. They might reply *thank you*, while looking right through her. This man was dark-haired and wore a t-shirt of a solid, rich color—a brownish brick. He looked as if he'd stepped from an Eddie Bauer catalog. Krista's mother got an Eddie Bauer catalog every month. She remembered admiring those outdoorsy people, thirtysomething, financially stable, wearing primary colors and sturdy shoes. They had formed her idea of what it meant to be a happy adult.

I'm going to see what's going on here, he told the room. People around him nodded, even the mothers, who Krista thought might be offended by the fact that he had just said *fuck,* but maybe they excused the language in an emergency situation.

The man walked up to the glass accordion doors. Before, they had immediately opened when anyone stepped close to them. Now, they didn't open. They must have cut the power to the doors. For the first time that night, she began to understand why everybody else was so frightened. It had taken her longer, she thought, because she only had herself to be afraid for.

The Eddie Bauer man pounded lightly on the glass doors, which shook under his fists. They were not very solid. He could have broken them if he wanted to.

Give us some fucking information! he screamed at the plastic seal in the middle of the door. Krista had an urge to laugh, but she turned it into a cough. She didn't want to offend the man, who had done nothing to warrant unkindness.

It must be chemicals. Some kind of chemicals outside, the blonde said. Then she repeated it, looking around the room for somebody to tell. It must be chemicals. We've been attacked with chemicals and we're stuck here. Her husband nodded.

Some of the men, older ones with children, went to look for the airport attendant and the policeman, who had all disappeared during the half hour before the police in gas masks had arrived.

Did you smell any gas out there? The blonde turned to Krista. This is important. Did you smell anything?

She wanted to help the woman. She tried to remember smells. The hedges smelled like pine. The bed of flowers around the industrial complex smelled like fresh manure and maple syrup.

No, I didn't smell anything unusual. Krista shifted in her seat and felt her stomach heave and salt at the back of her throat. She was going to be sick. But she couldn't be sick here, not with then all looking at her, thinking she'd been poisoned.

The blonde shook her head and turned from Krista, done with her. I don't want to die in the goddamn place. I don't want to die. Her husband gathered her in his arms and pulled her away from Krista. He shot her a look of mild anger, as if it were her fault that the woman was upset.

Krista stood up, hoping to leave the room for a while, to go to the bathroom and rest her cheek against the cool stall door and be away from the constant noise, the questions.

Mommy! A girl raced down the hallway, almost colliding with Krista as she ran. Mommy, the water hurt me! The little girl's mouth was red with blood. It smeared her lips like lipstick. At first Krista thought it *was* lipstick, but it was wet on her hands, too, which she held out before her.

What did you do, baby? What happened? This wasn't the many-pocketed mother, but a more frantic mother, one who wore a jumper and a headband. She was as upset as the child.

What hurt you, baby?

Krista stood in the hallway watching, like everyone else, waiting to hear what was wrong. She stood perfectly still, afraid that moving would collide her with whatever had hurt the child. The child sniffled and hiccupped, but eventually, she managed to get something out. She had only taken a drink from the water fountain. It had cut her, and she had come back here to tell her mother about it.

As the mother wiped the child's mouth clean with a napkin from her purse, they heard a rustle from the front of the room—the security door opened and the attendant stepped out, his walkie-talkie crackling.

Good, you're all here, the airport attendant said, surveying the group. He did not seem to notice that they were gathered together strangely, turned toward the mother and child in the middle.

You might have noticed the police presence, he said. They are here to secure the airport. He held up his hand when somebody spoke, the tone angry, though they were not able to get out a word. The plane is scheduled to leave in thirty minutes, it has just landed. We've put a plastic tunnel from the door to the plane so you don't have to go outside when you board, just as a precaution—understand? He paused and looked at the bulky, digital face of his watch.

The blonde jumped in, ignoring his still-raised hand. What's going on? Have we been attacked? She held a paper towel to her eyes and dabbed beneath them where her eyeliner bled.

The attendant shook his head. No ma'am, no evidence of that. The FBI determines that. You'll know as soon as I know. The man nodded at them all, and, as the questions began, as the mother with the bloody-mouthed child tried to bring the child forward, a paper-towel held against the girl's still lips, the man walked fast—almost jogged—back to the gated security area, slid through the smallest possible sliver of open door, and then locked the door behind him.

The crowd was still for what seemed like a very long time to Krista, though she knew it was probably only a few seconds. Then, the Eddie Bauer man ran up the slight slope to the locked entrance and shook the gate like somebody in a prison movie or a primate behind old-fashioned zoo bars.

We've got a kid bleeding in here. We want to speak to somebody in charge. His voice echoed in the empty security area and bounced back down to the crowd.

The mother held her daughter and began to cry. The child was dry-eyed. Everyone was speaking but Krista. Unlike the others, she was uncoupled, without a child or a traveling companion. In Victorian novels, women always went with traveling companions, maiden aunts or cousins to keep them safe from the influence of crowds and sinister men. They also served another purpose, one which Krista had not thought of before—they were for company, somebody to be with, a buffer against loneliness beyond the everyday loneliness of being in one's own head. She usually enjoyed her own company, but her aloneness oppressed her here. Even now, people did not usually travel alone, at least not the way she was, aimlessly and with nowhere to go, no one to care if she arrived or not.

She imagined that the others sometimes looked at her sideways, never directly. Krista wasn't sure if she was exaggerating their glances—her mother said that she tended to suspect dislike where it wasn't present. *You were always a fussy, fearful child,* she'd said during her latest visit, after Krista had explained what had happened at her job, with her boss, how she had been shamed into leaving, how he had never called her again. *I'm sure it would have blown over if you'd just waited. If you'd just been a little more goddamn calm about it.*

Being fearful makes people want to hurt you, her mother had said. *When you shrink away, people want to give you a reason to shrink.*

Krista tried to breathe deeply to calm herself. She opened her bag and took out her book. She had read only one half-sentence (*Wild animals added danger to the American wilderness and here, too, the element of the unknown intensified feelings*) before she felt her stomach tighten. She had the urge to stretch out on the floor until the sickness passed, but she couldn't. She put her book away and rose. As she stood up, the blonde, now sitting with her head between her hands, the empty pizza box occupying the seat next to her, turned to watch.

Are you sick or something? The woman looked at Krista, though she kept her head in her hands.

I'm OK, Krista said. Just had too much water.

Her mother had always called her period her *monthly friend,* and Krista had been encouraged to adopt similar euphemisms for bodily functions. *Going number two. Making water. Making wind.* She couldn't imagine answering the woman's question truthfully.

The woman pursed her lips and nodded, but turned to Krista again, her face still blank. Sure you didn't pick up something from outside? You went farther out than any of us. As she said this, the woman weeping on her bleeding child's blonde head looked up.

Did you drink out of the water fountain? Did you get something from outside on the fountain?

Krista shook her head, rising again. No, no. I have my own water. I swear, there's nothing wrong with me. Nothing was wrong outside when I was out there. She looked at the two women, both staring at her, their mouths hardened, their teeth not showing.

Excuse me, she told them, as if ducking away from a dinner party. I have to use the restroom.

-◦-

In the bathroom, Krista leaned her warm forehead against the bathroom stall, then thought better of it and pulled away. She didn't know it was safe to touch. Maybe she was getting poison on everything she touched. The woman's fear was convincing.

In the stall, she knelt and rested her head in her hands. Her head ached dully. She couldn't take one of the Tylenol she'd brought in her carry-on bags—she didn't have any water left in her bottle. She knelt until the sickness passed. But she had to go back. She couldn't hide.

Before she left the bathroom, she caught a flash of light in the small window above her eye level. They were just outside, the men in masks. Krista wondered if she could see anything—maybe something she could tell the others about, gain their favor with—through the small, rectangular window in the bathroom. She turned over the bathroom's metal trash can and climbed on it, holding the wall for balance, until she could see outside.

The window looked out into the front lawn of the airport. She saw three figures in jumpsuits gliding their flashlights along the lawn. One seemed to be examining the grass. Another seemed to be looking at the edge of the building, where the foundation met the ground. Another was farther off, sweeping his light in the little stand of trees between the airport and the industrial complex. Their motions seemed cursory, almost mocking, as if they were only putting on a show of searching, and not even a very convincing one.

Looking for someone you know? A man's voice surprised her, and Krista turned on the trash can, almost falling. It was the blonde's husband. He wasn't wearing his baseball cap and his reddish, curly hair was flat and greasy against his head like a stack of smashed bread.

You scared me, she said, not sure how to understand the man's presence in the women's room. Is something wrong with the men's room?

The man shook his head. I just came to make sure you were all right. You were taking so long. His voice was wrong; it didn't match his words. He smiled at Krista and motioned for her to join him.

Come on back out here. We've all got some questions.

Krista nodded, though she didn't understand what he was saying. Questions for her? When she entered the waiting room, she saw that her baggage had been opened. The Eddie Bauer man had her book in his hands. He wore rubber gloves (Krista wondered where he had gotten them—did he pack rubber gloves whenever he traveled?).

What are you doing?

The people around him looked up at her. They had all let him do this, she could see. They all approved.

We found this, the blonde said, pointing at Krista's seat. The red seat was stained black in a neat, tea saucer-sized circle. You're bleeding. Why didn't you tell us?

They think I'm sick, she thought. It isn't— she began, but the woman with the many pockets interrupted her.

You haven't spoken, and you're traveling here alone, he said. You go outside right before the attack. You visit the restroom five or six times after. You don't call anyone to let them know what happened. You don't ask any questions, and you don't seem to be fazed by what's happening here. The woman held her hands up, palms to the sky. What are we supposed to think?

Listening to the woman, Krista almost felt convinced of her own suspicious behavior. She was vaguely afraid that they would find her out. But there's nothing to find, she soothed herself, there's nothing wrong with me. I'm only alone. There's nothing wrong with that.

You can't do this to me, she said instead, the words surprising her. How dare you do this to me? The words seemed familiar, like something she had seen on television, and they made her feel powerful. She wanted to hit the Eddie Bauer man and take back her book back. She wanted to make the blonde stop smiling or smirking or whatever she was doing with her mouth.

What, do you think you are some kind of important person? That you're better than the rest of us? This was from the blonde. She crossed her arms over her chest. Krista imagined that this was the way she stood when scolding her children.

I am important, she told them, not sure what she was trying to say. *Tell them about your monthly friend*, she told herself and almost laughed out loud. I'm as important as—

She stopped when the lights went out. A few of the children screamed and the mothers hissed words of comfort. Krista didn't move. It seemed safer to stay where she was. No need to drag it out. No need to make things harder on everyone. Though it was dark, she could hear the rustle of someone moving toward her.

FABULOUS BEASTS

PRIYA SHARMA

"Eliza, tell me your secret."

Sometimes I'm cornered at parties by someone who's been watching me from across the room as they drain their glass. They think I don't know what's been said about me.

Eliza's odd looking but she has something, don't you think? Une jolie laide. A French term meaning ugly-beautiful. Only the intelligentsia can insult you with panache.

I always know when they're about to come over. It's in the pause before they walk, as though they're ordering their thoughts. Then they stride over, purposeful, through the throng of actors, journalists, and politicians, ignoring anyone who tries to engage them for fear of losing their nerve.

"Eliza, tell me your secret."

"I'm a princess."

Such a ridiculous thing to say and I surprise myself by using Kenny's term for us, even though I am now forty-something and Kenny was twenty-four years ago. I edge past, scanning the crowd for Georgia, so I can tell her that I've had enough and am going home. Maybe she'll come with me.

My interrogator doesn't look convinced. Nor should they be. I'm not even called Eliza. My real name is Lola and I'm no princess. I'm a monster.

⬧

We, Kenny's princesses, lived in a tower.

Kath, my mum, had a flat on the thirteenth floor of Laird Tower, in a northern town long past its prime. Two hundred and seventeen miles from London and twenty-four years ago. A whole world away, or it might as well be.

Ami, Kath's younger sister, lived two floors down. Kath and I went round to see her the day that she came home from hospital. She answered the door wearing a black velour tracksuit, the bottoms slung low on her hips. The top rose up to reveal the wrinkled skin that had been taut over her baby bump the day before.

"Hiya," she opened the door wide to let us in.

Ami only spoke to Kath, never to me. She had a way of ignoring people that fascinated men and infuriated women.

Kath and I leant over the Moses basket.

"What a diamond," Kath cooed.

She was right. Some new babies are wizened, but not Tallulah. She looked like something from the front of one of Kath's knitting patterns. Perfect. I knew, even at that age, that I didn't look like everyone else; flat nose with too much nostril exposed, small eyelids and small ears that were squashed against my skull. I felt a pang of jealousy.

"What's her name, Ami?"

"Tallulah Rose." Ami laid her head on Kath's shoulder. "I wish you'd been there."

"I wanted to be there too. I'm sorry, darling. There was nobody to mind Lola. And Mikey was with you." Kath must have been genuinely sorry because normally she said Mikey's name like she was sniffing sour milk. "Where is he now?"

"Out, wetting the baby's head."

Kath's expression suggested that she thought he was doing more than toasting his newborn. He was always hanging around Ami. *Just looking after you, like Kenny wants*, he'd say, as if he was only doing his duty. Except now that there were shitty nappies to change and formula milk to prepare he was off, getting his end away.

Ami wasn't quite ready to let Kath's absence go.

"You could've left Lola with one of my friends."

Ami knew better. Kath never let anyone look after me, not even her.

"Let's not fight now, pet. You're tired."

Ami's gaze was like being doused in ice water. It contained everything she couldn't say to me. *Fucking ugly, little runt. You're always in the way.*

"You must be starvin'. Let me get you a cuppa and a sandwich and then you can get some sleep."

We stood and looked at the baby when Ami had gone to bed.

"Don't get any ideas. You don't want to be like your aunt, with a baby at sixteen. You don't want to be like either of us."

Kathy always spoke to me like I was twenty-four, not four.

Tallulah stirred and stretched, arms jerking outwards as if she was in freefall. She opened her eyes. There was no squinting or screaming.

"The little scrap's going to need our help."

Kath lifted her out and laid her on her knee for inspection. I put my nose against the soft spot on her skull. I fell in love with her right then.

"What do you wish for her?" Kath asked, smiling.

Chocolate. Barbies. A bike. A pet snake. Everything my childish heart could bestow.

◄◦►

Saturdays were for shopping. Kathy and I walked down Cathcart Street towards town. We'd pass a row of grimy Victorian mansions on our way that served as a reminder of once great wealth, now carved up into flats for social housing or filled with squatters who lay in their damp dens with needles in their arms.

After these were the terraces, joined by a network of alleyways that made for easy assaults and getaways. This model of housing was for the civic minded when everyone here had a trade, due to our proximity to the city of Liverpool. The shipbuilding yards lay empty, and the 1980s brought container ships that did away with the demand for dockers. The life inside spilled out into the sun; women sat on their steps in pyjama bottoms and vest tops, even though it was lunchtime. Fags in hand, they'd whisper to one another as Kathy passed, afraid to meet her gaze. A man wore just shorts, his pale beer belly pinking up in the sun. He saluted when he saw Kathy. She ignored him.

I followed Kathy, her trolley wheels squeaking. The sound got worse as it was filled with vegetables, cheap meat shrink-wrapped on Styrofoam trays, and bags of broken biscuits.

Kathy stopped to talk to a woman with rotten, tea-stained teeth. I was bored. We were at the outskirts of town, where the shops were most shabby. House clearance stores and a refurbished washing machine outlet. I wandered along the pavement a way until something stopped me. The peeling sign over the shop window read "Ricky's Reptiles." The display was full of tanks. Most were empty, but the one at the front contained a pile of terrapins struggling to climb over one another in a dish of water.

The shop door was open, revealing the lino floor that curled up at the corners. It was a shade of blue that verged on grey, or maybe it was just dirty. I could see the lights from the tanks. The fish were darting flashes of wild colour or else they drifted on gossamer fins. I was drawn in. The man behind the counter looked up and smiled, but to his credit he didn't try and talk to me, otherwise I would've run.

Then I saw it, a long tank along the back wall. I went closer. The snake was magnificent, from the pale skin on her belly to the brown scales on her back.

She slithered closer, eyeing me, and then raised her head and the front third of her body lifted up as if suspended on invisible thread. I put my forehead against the glass.

"She likes you," the man murmured.

She moved up the side of the tank. I realised that I was swaying in time with her, feeling unity in the motion. I was aware of her body, each muscle moving beneath her skin, her very skeleton. I looked into the snake's black eyes and could see out of them into my own. The world was on the tip of her forked tongue; my curiosity, the shopkeeper's sweat and kindness, the soft flavour of the mice in the tank behind the counter.

A hand gripped my shoulder, hard, jerking me back to myself. It was Kathy.

"Get away from that thing." Her fingers were digging into me. "Don't you ever come in here again, understand?"

She looked at the snake, shuddering. "God, it's disgusting. What's wrong with you?"

She shouted at me all the way home, for putting the wind up her, letting her think some pervert had taken me. I didn't realise just how afraid she was. That she was looking at me like she didn't know what she'd birthed.

⤙⚬⤚

The novelty of motherhood soon wore off. Ami sat in the armchair of our flat, her toenails painted in the same tangerine shade as her maxi dress. She was sunbed fresh and her lips were demarcated in an unflatteringly pale shade of pink. Her hair was in fat rollers ready for her evening out.

"Guess where I went today?" she asked, her voice bright and brittle.

"Where, doll?" Kath puffed on her cigarette, blowing a stream of smoke away from us.

If Ami was slim, Kath was scrawny. The skin on her neck and chest was wrinkled from the lack of padding and twenty-five cigarettes a day. She wore a series of gold chains and her hands were rough and red from perpetual cleaning. Her face was unbalanced: nose too small and large ears that stuck out. Round eyes that never saw make-up. I forget sometimes, that she was only twenty-four then.

"To see Kenny."

Tallulah got up and I thought she was leaving me for Ami but she was just fetching her teddy. When she sat back down next to me, she wriggled against me to get comfortable. Ami bought Tallulah's clothes. Ridiculous, expensive things to dress a toddler in, old fashioned and frilly.

"Kenny always asks after you." Ami filled the silence.

"Does he?" Kath tipped the ash from her cigarette into the empty packet. God love her, she didn't have many vices.

"He never says but he's hurt. It's all over his face when I walk in and you're not with me. You're not showing him much respect or loyalty. All he wants to do is look after you and Lola, like he looks after me and Tallulah."

"I don't want Kenny's money. He's not Robin Hood. He beat a man to death."

"He's our *brother*."

Which was funny, because I didn't know that I had an uncle.

Kath's face was a shutter slamming shut.

"He loves to see pictures of Lola."

"Photos? You showed him photos?" Kath was blowing herself for a fight.

"I only showed him some pictures. He wanted to see her. What's up with you?"

"Lola's *my* business. No one else's."

"Well, I'm taking Tallulah for him to see next time."

"No, you're not. Not to a prison."

"She's mine. I'll take her where the fuck I want."

"You've done well to remember you've got a daughter."

"What's that mean?"

"You're always out with your bloody mates. You treat me like an unpaid baby sitter. She spends more time here than with you and then you've got the cheek to tell me to mind my own."

"So it's about money?"

"No," Kath threw up her hands, "it's about you being a selfish, spoilt brat. I'm your *sister,* not your mum. And it's about how you treat Tallulah."

"At least I know who her dad is."

Kath slapped her face. A sudden bolt that silenced them both. It left a red flush on Ami's cheek. Whenever I asked about my dad, Kath told me that she'd found me in a skip.

"I'm sorry, Ami . . ." Kath put out her hands. "I didn't mean to. I mean . . ."

"Tallulah," Ami snapped, holding out her hand.

Tallulah looked from me to Kath, her eyes wide. Ami pulled her up by the arm. She screamed.

"Be careful with her."

"Or what, Kath?" Ami lifted Tallulah up, putting her under one arm like she was a parcel. "Are you going to call Social Services? Fuck off."

Calling Social Services was a crime akin to calling the police.

Tallulah was in a full-on tantrum by then, back arched and legs kicking. Fierce for her size, she proved too much for Ami, who threw her down on the sofa. She lay there, tear stained and rigid. Ami had started to cry too. "Stay here then, see if I sodding care."

◄◦►

There are times when I feel lost, even to myself, and that what looks out from behind my eyes isn't human.

I'm reminded of it each day as I go to work at the School of Tropical Medicine.

Peter, one of the biochemists from the lab downstairs, has come up for a batch of venom. He watches me milk the snakes when he can overcome his revulsion.

Michael, my assistant, tips the green mamba out of her box. I pin her down with a forked metal stick, while Michael does the same, further along her body. I clamp a hand just beneath her neck, thanking her silently for enduring the indignity of this charade. If it were just the two of us, she'd come to me without all this manhandling. I'll make it up to her later with mice and kisses. She's gorgeous in an intense shade of green, her head pointed.

"You have to stop that work when you get too old," says Peter, "you know, reflexes getting slow and all that."

The deaths of herpetologists are as fabled as snakes are touchy. There's no room for lax habits or slowness. Handled safely for years, a snake can turn on you, resulting in a blackened, withered limb, blood pouring from every orifice, paralysis and blindness, if not death.

Peter's a predator. He's been a swine to me since I knocked him back. I turn to him with the snake still in my hand. She hisses at him and he shrinks away.

I hook the mamba's mouth over the edge of the glass and apply gentle pressure. The venom runs down the side and collects in a pool.

What Peter doesn't know is that when my darlings and I are alone I hold them in my arms and let them wind around my neck. Our adoration is mutual. They're the easy part of my job.

"They like Eliza." Michael is offended on my behalf. There's not been a bite since I've been here.

"Concentrate," I snap at him as he brings the mamba's box to me. I regret my churlishness straight away. Michael is always pleasant with me. He never takes offence at my lack of social graces but someday he will.

Snakes are easy. It's people that I don't know how to charm.

◄◦►

Tallulah trailed along beside me. She looked like a doll in her school uniform; pleated skirt and leather buckled shoes. I didn't begrudge her the lovely clothes that Ami bought her. She jumped, a kittenish leap, and then she took my hand. We swung arms as we walked.

We turned onto Cathcart Street. Laird Tower was ahead of us, dwarfing the bungalows opposite. Those used by the elderly or infirm were marked out by white grab handles and key safes.

A pair of girls sat on a wall. They jumped down when they saw us. School celebrities, these playground queens, who knew how to bruise you with a word. They'd hurt you for not being like them, or not wanting to be like them.

"Is she your sister?" Jade, the shorter one, asked Tallulah.

"No," Tallulah began, "she's . . ."

"Of course not," Jade cut across her, keen to get out the rehearsed speech. Jade didn't like my prowess in lessons. I tried to hide it, but it occasionally burst out of me. I liked the teacher. I liked homework. I even liked the school, built in red brick, that managed to still look like a Victorian poorhouse.

Jade was sly enough not to goad me for that, going for my weakness, not my strength. "You're too pretty to be Lola's sister. Look at her ugly mug."

It was true. I remained resolutely strange; my features had failed to rearrange themselves into something that would pass for normal. Also, my sight had rapidly deteriorated in the last few months and my thick lenses magnified my eyes

"Be careful." Jade leant down into Tallulah's face. "You'll catch her ugliness."

Tallulah pushed her, hard, both of her small hands on her chest. Jade fell backwards a few steps, surprised by the attack. She raised a fist to hit Tallulah.

My blood was set alight, venom rising. Water brash filled my mouth as if I were about to be sick. I snatched at Jade's hand and sunk my teeth into her meaty forearm, drawing blood. I could taste her shock and fear. If she was screaming, I couldn't hear her. I only let go when her friend punched me on the ear.

◄►►

After I'd apologised I sat in the corner of the room while Kath and Pauline, Jade's mum, talked.

"I thought it would be good if we sorted it out between us, like grown ups," Pauline said.

Social Services had already been round to confirm that I was the culprit.

Has she ever done anything like this before?

No, Kathy was calm and firm, *Lola wasn't brought up that way.*

"I'm so sorry about what happened." Pauline lifted her mug of tea, her hand trembling a fraction. She took a sip and set it down, not picking it up again.

"Why?" Kath sat up straighter. "Lola bit Jade. *I'm* sorry and I'll make sure that she is too by the time I'm done with her."

"Yes, but Jade was picking on her."

"That's no excuse for what Lola did. She should've just walked away."

"It's time that someone cut Jade down to size."

"My daughter *bit* yours." Exasperation raised Kathy's voice a full octave.

"She was asking for it."

Kathy shook her head. Then, "How is she?"

Jade had lain on the pavement, twitching. Red marks streaked up her arm, marking the veins.

"She's doing okay," Pauline swallowed. "She's on antibiotics. She's a bit off colour, that's all."

"The police and Social Services came round earlier."

"I've not complained. I'm not a nark. I'd never do that."

"I didn't say you had."

"You'll tell Kenny, won't you? We're not grasses. We won't cause you any bother. I'll skin Jade if she comes near your girls again." We were known as Kathy's girls.

"Kenny?" Kathy repeated dully.

"Please. Will you talk to him?"

Kath was about to say something but then deflated in the chair.

"Ami's says she's visiting him soon, so I'll make sure he gets the message."

◄◦►

Kathy closed the door after Pauline had gone.

"What did you do to her?" It was the first time she'd looked at me properly since it had happened.

"It wasn't her fault." Tallulah stood between us. "She was going to hit me."

"What did you do to her?" Kathy pushed her aside. "Her arm swelled up and she's got blood poisoning."

"I don't know," I stammered. "It just happened."

She slapped me. I put my hands out to stop her but she carried on, backing me into the bedroom. She pushed me down on the floor. I curled my hands over my head.

"I didn't bring you up to be like that." Her strength now was focused in a fist. Kathy had hit me before, but never like that. "I swear I'll kill you if you ever do anything like that again. You fucking little monster."

She was sobbing and shrieking. Tallulah was crying and trying to pull her off. Kathy continued to punch me until her arm grew tired. "You're a monster, just like your father."

◄◦►

We stayed in our bedroom that night, Tallulah and I. We could hear Kathy banging about the flat. First, the vacuum hitting the skirting boards as she pulled it around. A neighbour thumped on the wall and she shouted back, but turned it off and took to the bathroom. She'd be at it all night, until her hands were raw. The smell of bleach was a signal of her distress. There were times when I thought I'd choke on the stench.

The skin on my face felt tight and sore, as if shrunken by tears. Tallulah rolled up my t-shirt to inspect the bruises on my back. There was a change coming, fast, as the shock of Kathy's onslaught wore off.

It hurt when Tallulah touched me. It wasn't just the skin on my face that felt wrong. It was all over. I rubbed my head against the carpet, an instinctual movement as I felt I'd got a cowl covering my face. The skin ripped.

"I'll get Kathy."

"No, wait." I grabbed her wrist. "Stay with me."

My skin had become a fibrous sheath, my very bones remoulding. My ribs shrank and my slim pelvis and limbs became vestigial. My paired organs rearranged themselves, one pushed below the other except my lungs. I gasped as one of those collapsed. I could feel my diaphragm tearing; the wrenching of it doubled me over.

I writhed on the floor. There was no blood. What came away in the harsh lamplight was translucent. Tallulah held me as I sloughed off my skin which fell away to reveal scales. She gathered the coils of me into her lap. We lay down and I curled around her.

I couldn't move. I could barely breathe. When I put out my forked tongue I could taste Tallulah's every molecule in the air.

◄◦►

The morning light came through the thin curtain. Tallulah was beside me. I had legs again. I put a hand to my mouth. My tongue was whole. My flesh felt new. More than that, I could see. When I put my glasses on the world became blurred. I didn't need them anymore. The very surface of my eyes had been reborn.

My shed skin felt fibrous and hard. I bundled it up into a plastic bag and stuffed it in my wardrobe. Tallulah stretched as she watched me, her hands and feet splayed.

"Tallulah, what am I? Am I a monster?"

She sat up and leant against me, her chin on my shoulder.

"Yes, you're *my* monster."

◄◦►

I ache for the splendid shabbiness of my former life, when it was just Kath, Tallulah, and me in the flat, the curtains drawn against the world and the telly droning on in the background. Tallulah and I would dance around Kath, while she swatted us away. The smell of bleach and furniture polish is forever home. Kath complaining when I kept turning the heating up. Being cold made me sluggish.

Endless, innocuous days and nights that I should've savoured more.

"How was your test?"

"Crap." Tallulah threw down her bag. "Hi, Kath."

"Hi, love," Kathy shouted back from the kitchen.

Tallulah, school uniformed, big diva hair so blonde that it was almost white, a flick of kohl expertly applied at the corner of her eyes.

"I'm thick, not like you." She kicked off her shoes.

"You're not thick. Just lazy."

She laughed and lay on her belly beside me, in front of the TV. She smelt of candy floss scent that she'd stolen from her mum. Tallulah was the sweetest thing.

There was the sound of the key in the door. I looked at Tallulah. Only her mum had a key. We could hear Ami's voice, followed by a man's laugh. A foreign sound in the flat. Kathy came out of the kitchen, tea towel in hand.

Ami stood in the doorway, flushed and excited, as if she was about to present a visiting dignitary.

"Kath, there's someone here to see you."

She stood aside. I didn't recognise the man. He was bald and scarred. Kathy sat down on the sofa arm, looking the colour of a dirty dishrag.

"Oh, God," he said, "aren't you a bunch of princesses?"

"Kenny, when did you get out?" Kath asked.

"A little while ago." He took off his jacket and threw it down. A snake tattoo coiled up his arm and disappeared under the sleeve of his t-shirt. It wasn't the kind of body art I was used to. This hadn't been driven into the skin in a fit of self loathing or by a ham-fisted amateur. It was faded but beautiful. It rippled as Kenny moved, invigorated by his muscles.

"Come and hug me, Kath."

She got up, robotic, and went to him, tolerating his embrace, her arms stiff by her sides.

"I've brought us something to celebrate."

He handed her a plastic bag and she pulled out a bottle of vodka and a packet of Jammy Dodgers.

"Just like when we were kids, eh?" he grinned.

"See, Kenny's got no hard feelings about you staying away." Ami was keen to be involved. "He's just glad to be home."

They both ignored her.

"Now, girls, come and kiss your uncle. You first, Tallulah."

"Well, go on." Ami gave her a shove.

She pecked his cheek and then shot away, which seemed to amuse him. Then it was my turn. Kath stood close to us while Kenny held me at arm's length.

"How old are you now, girl?"

"Eighteen."

"You were born after I went inside." He sighed. "You've got the family's ugly gene like me and your mum but you'll do."

For what? I thought.

Kenny put his fleshy hand around Kath's neck and pressed his forehead against hers. Kathy, who didn't like kisses or cuddles from anyone, flinched. I'd never seen her touched so much.

"I'm home now. We'll not talk about these past, dark years. It'll be how it was before. Better. You'll see. Us taking care of each other."

◄◦►

Georgia's unusual for a photographer in that she's more beautiful than her models. They're gap-toothed, gawky things that only find luminosity through the lens. Georgia's arresting in the flesh.

I hover beside our host who's introducing me to everyone as though I'm a curio. We approach a group who talk too loudly, as if they're the epicentre of the party.

"I find Georgia distant. And ambitious."

"She lives on Martin's Heath. In one of the old houses."

"Bloody hell, is that family money?"

"Rosie, you've modelled for Georgia. Have you been there?"

"No."

Rosie sounds so quiet and reflective that the pain of her unrequited love is palpable. At least I hope it's unrequited.

"Have you seen her girlfriend?"

"Everyone, meet Eliza," our host steps in before they have a chance to pronounce judgement on me within my earshot, "Georgia's partner."

I shake hands with each of them.

"Georgia's last shoot made waves. And I didn't realise that she was such a stunner."

We all look over at Georgia. Among all the overdressed butterflies, she wears black trousers, a white shirt, and oxblood brogues.

"Don't tell her that," I smile. "She doesn't like it."

"Why? Doesn't every woman want that?" The man falters, as if he's just remembered that I'm a woman too.

These people with their interminable words. I came from a place where a slap sufficed.

"Don't be dull," I put him down. "She's much more than her face."

"What do you do, Eliza?" another one of them asks, unperturbed by my rudeness.

"I'm a herpetologist."

They shudder with delicious revulsion.

I glance back to Georgia. A man with long blond hair reaches out to touch her forearm and he shows her something on his tablet.

I'm a pretender in my own life, in this relationship. I know how my jealousy will play out when we get home. I'll struggle to circumnavigate all the gentility and civility that makes me want to scream.

Eventually Georgia will say, *What's the matter? Just tell me instead of trying to pick a fight.*

She'll never be provoked, this gracious woman, to display any savagery of feeling. I should know better than to try and measure the breadth and depth of love by its noise and dramas but there are times that I crave it, as if it's proof that love is alive.

—◊—

Ami took Tallulah away with her the first night that Kenny came to the flat.

"But it's a school night. And all my stuff's here."

"You're not going to school tomorrow." Ami picked up her handbag. "We're going out with Kenny."

Tallulah didn't move.

"Mind your mum, there's a good girl." Kenny didn't even look up.

After the front door closed, Kathy locked and chained it.

"Get your rucksack. Put some clothes in a bag. Don't pack anything you don't need."

"Why?" I followed her into her bedroom.

"We're leaving."

"Why?"

"Just get your stuff."

"What about college?"

Kathy tipped out drawers, rifling through the untidy piles that she'd made on the floor.

"What about Tallulah?"

She sank down on the bed.

"There's always someone that I have to stay for. Mum. Ami. Tallulah." She slammed her fist down on the duvet. "If it had been just us, we'd have been gone long ago."

"Stay?"

She wasn't listening to me anymore.

"I waited too long. I should've run when I had the chance. Fuck everyone."

She lay down, her face to the wall. I tried to put my arms around her but she shrank from me, which she always did when I touched her and which never failed to hurt me.

⟶

If we were his princesses then Kenny considered himself king.

"Kath, stop fussing and come and sit down. It's good to be back among women. Without women, men are uncivilised creatures." He winked at me. "Tell me about Ma's funeral again, Kath."

Ami sat beside him, looking up at him.

"There were black horses with plumes and brasses. Her casket was in a glass carriage." Kath's delivery was wooden.

"And all the boys were there?"

"Yes, Kenny. All the men, in their suits, gold sovereign rings, and tattoos."

"Good," he said, "I would've been offended otherwise. Those boys owe me and they know it. I did time for them. Do you know the story?"

"Bits," Tallulah said.

"I told her, Kenny." Ami was keen to show her allegiance.

"You were what, twelve?" He snorted. "You remember nothing. We did a job in Liverpool. A jeweller who lived in one of those massive houses around Sefton Park. We heard he was dealing in stolen diamonds. I went in first," he thumped his chest. "At twenty-three I was much thinner back then, could get into all sorts of tight spots. I let the others in afterwards. We found his money but he kept insisting the diamonds were hidden in the fireplace, but his hidey hole was empty. He kept acting all surprised. He wouldn't tell, no matter what." Kenny shrugged. "Someone grassed. A copper picked me up near home. Under my coat, my shirt was covered in his blood. I kept my trap shut and did the time. The others were safe. Eighteen years inside. My only regret is what happened to Ma. And missing her funeral."

"There were white flowers, everywhere, spelling out her name." Ami said. He patted her arm in an absent way, like she was a cat mithering for strokes.

"I wish they'd let me out for it. Ma was a proper princess, girls. She was touched, God bless her, but she was a princess."

Kath sat with her hands folded on her knees.

"Do you remember what Dad said when he was dying?"

Kath stayed quiet.

"He said, *You're the man of the house, Kenny. And you're the mother, Kathy. Kenny, you have to look after these girls.* Poor Ma, so fragile. When I heard about her stroke, I was beside myself. It was the shock of me being sent down that did it. Whoever grassed me up has to pay for that, too. I should've been here, taking care of you all."

"I managed," Kathy squeezed the words out.

"I know. I hate to think of you, nursing Ma when you also had a baby to look after. You were meant for better things. We didn't always live in this shithole, girls. We grew up in a big rambling house. You won't remember much of it, Ami. Dad bred snakes. He was a specialist. And Ma, she was a real lady. They were educated people, not like 'round here."

The words stuck in my gut. 'Round here was all I knew.

"Happy days, weren't they, Mouse?" Kenny looked directly at Kathy, waiting.

"Mouse," Ami laughed like she'd only just noticed Kathy's big eyes and protruding ears, "I'd forgotten that."

Mouse. A nickname that diminished her.

"What's *my* pet name?" Ami pouted.

"You're just Ami." He said it like she was something flat and dead, not shifting his gaze from Kathy.

There it was. Even then, I could see that Kathy was at the centre of everything and Ami was just the means to reach her.

⬦

There's a photograph in our bedroom that Georgia took of me while we were travelling around South America. It embarrasses me because of its dimensions and scares me, because Georgia has managed to make me look like some kind of modern Eve, desirable in a way that I'll never be again. My hair is loose and uncombed and the python around my shoulders is handsome in dappled, autumnal shades. My expression is of unguarded pleasure.

"Let's stay here, forever," I said to her when she put the lens cap back on, "It's paradise."

What I was really thinking was, *What would it be like to change, forever, and have the whole jungle as my domain?*

"Do you love it that much?" Georgia replied in a way that suggested she didn't. "And put him down. Poor thing. If he's caught he'll end up as a handbag."

So it is that serpents are reviled when it's man that is repulsive.

⬦

I got off the bus at the end of Argyll Street and walked towards home. Kenny was sat on a plastic chair outside The Saddle pub, drinking a pint. He was waiting for me.

"What have you been doing today?" He abandoned his drink and followed me.

"Biology." I was at college, in town.

"Clever girl. That's from your grandparents. I used to be smart like that. You wouldn't think it to look at me."

There was an odd, puppyish eagerness to Kenny as he bounced along beside me. I darted across the road when there was a gap in the traffic. The railway line was on the other side of the fence, down a steep bank. Part way down the embankment was a rolled-up carpet, wet and rotted, and the shopping trolley that it had been transported in.

"Let me carry your bag. It looks heavy."

"I can manage."

"I wasn't always like this. I had to change for us to survive. Fighting and stealing," he shook his head, embarrassed. "I only became brutal to stop us being brutalised. Do you understand?"

The sky had darkened. Rain was on its way.

"We lost everything when Dad died. The house. The money. Your grandma lost her mind. It was the shock of having to live here. We were posh and we paid for that. On our first day at school a lad was picking on Kathy. Do you know what I did? I bit him, Lola. Right on the face. He swelled up like a red balloon. He nearly choked. Nobody picks on my princesses."

Nobody except him.

"Are you special, Lola?"

"I don't know what you mean."

I dodged him as he tried to block my path. Tallulah wouldn't have told him anything. Ami though, she had told him to prevent Pauline and Jade getting a battering.

"I can wait." He didn't pursue me, just stood there in the drizzle. "We have lots of time now."

◄◦►

"We're going for a ride today." Kenny followed Kath into the kitchen. He'd started turning up at the flat every day.

"I can't, Kenny, I've got loads to do."

"It can all wait."

Kenny had the last word.

"Where are we going?" Tallulah asked.

"You're not going anywhere except to Ami's. She needs to get her house in order. A girl needs her mum. She's sorting your bedroom, so you're going to live with her. Properly."

"I don't want to."

"Want's not in it."

Kathy stood between them. He pushed her aside.

"I live *here*." Tallulah wouldn't be moved.

"You live where I tell you." He had this way of standing close to you, to make himself seem more imposing, and lowering his voice. "You act like you're something with that pretty little face of yours. Well, I'm here to tell you that you're not special. You're fucking Mikey Flynn's daughter. And he's a piece of dead scum."

Poor Mikey Flynn, rumoured to have done a runner. I wondered where Kenny had him buried.

"Go home, Tallulah." Kathy raised her chin. "Kenny's right. You're not my girl. You should be with your own mother."

Tallulah's eyes widened. I could see the tears starting to pool there.

"Go on, then," Kathy carried on, "you don't belong here."

"Mum," I opened my mouth.

"Shut it." Kathy turned on me. "I've been soft on you pair for too long. Now help Tallulah take her stuff to Ami's."

"No," Kenny put a hand on my arm, "Lola stays with us."

⋅◦⋅

As Kenny drove, the terraces changed to semis and then detached houses. Finally there were open fields. It felt like he'd taken us hours away but it wasn't more than thirty minutes. We turned up an overgrown drive. Branches whipped the windscreen as Kenny drove.

"Kenny." Kath's voice was ripped from her throat. He patted her hand.

The drive ended at a large house, dark bricked with tall windows. It might as well have been a castle for all its unfamiliar grandeur. Overgrown rhododendrons crowded around it, shedding pink and red blossoms that were long past their best.

"Come on."

Kenny got out, not looking back to see if we were following.

Kath stood at the bottom of the steps, looking up at the open front door. There were plenty of window bars and metal shutters where I grew up, but the windows here were protected by wrought iron foliage in which metal snakes were entwined. The interior was dim. I could hear Kenny's footsteps as he walked inside.

"This is where we used to live." Kathy's face was blank. She went in, a sleep walker in her own life. I followed her.

"Welcome home." Kenny was behind the door. He locked it and put the key on a chain around his neck.

—◦—

Kenny showed us from room to room as if we were prospective buyers, not prisoners. Every door had a lock and every window was decorated in the same metal lattice work.

I stopped at a set of double doors but Kenny steered me away from it. "Later. Look through here, Kathy. Do you remember the old Aga? Shame they ripped it out. I thought we could get a new one."

He led us on to the lounge, waving his arm with a flourish.

"I couldn't bring you here without buying *some* new furniture." He kept glancing at Kathy. "What do you think?"

The room smelt of new carpet. It was a dusky pink, to match the sofa, and the curtains were heavy cream with rose buds on them. Things an old woman might have picked.

"Lovely, Kenny."

"I bought it for us." He slung his arm around her neck. It looked like a noose. "You and me, here again, no interference." His face was soft. "I've plenty of money. I can get more."

"Go and play," Kath said to me.

It'll shame me forever that I was angry at her for talking to me like I was a child when all she was trying to do was get me out of his way.

I went, then crawled back on my belly to watch them through the gap in the door.

Kath broke away from him and sat down. Kenny followed her, sinking down to lay his head on her knee. Her hand hovered over him, the muscles in her throat moving as she swallowed hard. Then she stroked his head. He buried his face in her lap, moaning.

"What happened to us, Mouse?"

Mouse. He'd swallow her whole. He'd crush her.

"You said you can get more money. Do you mean the money from the job in Liverpool?"

He moved quickly, sitting beside Kathy with his thigh wedged against the length of hers.

"Yes." He interlaced their fingers, making their hands a single fist. "I want you to know that I didn't kill anyone."

"You didn't? You were covered in blood."

"It was Barry's son, Carl. He always had a screw loose. The man wouldn't tell us where the diamonds were and Carl just freaked. He kept on beating him."

"But you admitted it."

"Who would believe me if I denied it? I did the time. Barry was very grateful. I knew it would set us up for life. I hated waiting for you. I imagined slipping out between the bars to come to you. I was tempted so many times. I hated the parole board. There *were* diamonds, Kath. I took them before I let the others in. I stopped here and buried them under the wall at the bottom of the garden. I nearly got caught doing it. Then the police picked me up, on my way back to you. That's why I had to do the stretch, so nobody would suspect. They're safe, now. Shankly's looking after what's left of them." He laughed at his own cryptic comment. Every Merseysider knew the deceased Bill Shankly, iconic once-manager of Liverpool Football Club. "Did I do right, Kath?"

Then she did something surprising. She kissed him. He writhed under her touch.

"Mouse, was there anyone else while I was inside?"

"No, Kenny. There's never been anybody else."

He basked in that.

"It'll be just like I said."

I sensed her hesitation, so did he.

"What's wrong?"

"It won't be like we said though, will it?"

"Why?"

"It should be just us two." She leant closer to him. "Lola's grown up now. She can look after herself."

"Lola's just a kid."

"I was a mother at her age." She put her hand on his arm.

"No, she stays."

Her hand dropped.

"Lola," Kenny called out. "Never let me catch you eavesdropping again. Understand?"

-◦-

"I'll just say goodnight to Lola." Kath stood in the doorway to my new bedroom, as if this game of fucked-up families was natural.

"Don't be long."

I sat on the bed. The new quilt cover and pillow case smelt funny. Kenny had put them on straight out of the packaging without washing them first. They still bore the sharp creases of their confinement.

"Lola." Kathy pulled me up and whispered to me. "He said to me, when we were kids, 'I'm going to put a baby in you and it's going to be special, like me and Dad,' as if I had nothing to do with it. I can't stand him touching me. When I felt you moving inside me, I was terrified you'd be a squirming snake, but you were *mine*. I'd do anything to get him away from us and Ami. I was the one who told the police."

Uncle. Father. Any wonder that I'm monstrous?

"Kenny's always been wrong. He thought it was from Dad, although he never saw him do it. It's from Mum. It drove her mad, holding it in. She nearly turned when she had her stroke. I have to know, can you do it too?"

"What?"

"We can't waste time. Can you turn into"—she hesitated—"a snake?"

"Yes." I couldn't meet her gaze.

"Good. Do it as soon as I leave." She opened the window. "Go out through the bars. Will you fit?"

"I don't know if I can. I'm not sure that I can do it at will."

"Try. Get out of here."

Panic rose in my chest. "What about you?"

"I'm going to do what I should've done a long time ago." She showed me the paring knife in her back pocket and then pulled her baggy sweater back over it. It must've been all she had time to grab. "I won't be far behind you."

"What if you're not?"

"Don't ask stupid questions." She paused. "I'm sorry for not being stronger. I'm sorry for not getting you away from here."

"Kathy," Kenny's voice boomed from the corridor, "time for bed."

After she left I heard the key turn in the lock.

-◦-

I went through the drawers and wardrobe. Kenny had filled them with clothes. I didn't want to touch anything that had come from him. There was nothing that I could use as a weapon or to help me escape.

I'd not changed since the time I'd bitten Jade. I lay down, trying to slow my breathing and concentrate. Nothing happened. The silence filled my mind along with all the things he would be doing to Kathy.

I dozed, somewhere towards early morning, wakening frequently in the unfamiliar room. I missed Tallulah beside me in the bed we'd shared since childhood. I missed her warmth and tangle of hair.

When Kenny let me out it was late afternoon.

"Where's my mum?"

"Down here."

There was a chest freezer in the basement. Kenny lifted the lid. Kathy was inside, frozen in a slumped position, arms crossed over her middle. Frozen blood glittered on the gash in her head and frosted one side of her face.

Kenny put his hand on my shoulder like we were mourners at a wake. I should've been kicking and screaming, but I was as frozen as she was.

One of Kathy's wrists was contorted at an unnatural angle.

"She betrayed me. I always knew it, in my heart." He shut the lid. "Now it's just you and me, kid."

He took me up through the house, to the room at the back with the double doors. There were dozens of tanks that cast a glow. Some contained a single serpent, others several that were coiled together like heaps of intestines.

"My beauties. I'll start breeding them."

There were corn snakes, ball pythons, ribbon snakes, though I had no names for them back then, all of which make good pets. I stopped at one tank. He had a broad head with a blunted snout.

"Ah, meet Shankly." Kenny put his hand against the glass. "He was hard to come by. They're called cottonmouths because they open their mouths so wide to show their fangs that you see all the white lining inside."

The cottonmouth must have been young. I remember his olive green colour and the clear banded pattern on his back, which he would lose as he got older.

"Are you special, Kathy?"

"I'm Lola."

"Yes, of course you are. Are you like me?"

"I'm nothing like you. Leave me alone."

"I'll look after you. Like you're a princess. You'll want for nothing. And you'll look after me because that's how it works."

"Don't fucking touch me."

Kenny pressed my face against the tank. Shankly showed me his pale underbelly as he slid towards me.

"Be afraid of him," Kenny nodded at the snake, "he still has his fangs. I'll make a mint from his venom."

Shankly climbed up a branch in his tank and settled there.

Kenny pushed me down with one hand and undid his belt buckle with the other.

"I'm your daughter." It was my last defence.

"I know."

Then he put his forked tongue in my mouth.

-◦-

I couldn't move. The place between my legs was numb. I'd already tried sex with a boy from college. I knew what it was about. We'd fumbled and fallen in a heap in the bushes by the old boating lake one afternoon. It wasn't an experience to set the world alight but it was satisfactory enough.

This wasn't just a sex crime, it was a power crime. Kenny wanted my fear. I shrunk into the distant corners of myself trying to retreat where he couldn't follow. His orgasm was grudging, delivered with a short, gratified moan.

Afterwards he sat with his trousers open, watching me like he was waiting for me to do something. I was frozen. I'm not sure I even blinked. That was how Kathy must have felt, forever stuck in that single moment of inertia and shock that kept her in the same spot for a lifetime. She was right. She should have run while she had the chance. Fuck her mother. And Ami, for all the good she'd done her.

Kenny stood up. I thought, *It's going to happen again and then he's going to dump me in the freezer.* Instead, he went upstairs, his tread heavy with disappointment.

"Don't stay up too late, pet."

I think I was waiting for something too, when I should've been searching for something sharp to stick between his ribs. I couldn't summon anything; I was still too deep inside myself.

I was colder than I'd ever been before, even though the summer night was stifling. The room felt airless despite the window being wide open and butting up against the grille. Sometimes, when Georgia's away, I feel that cold.

Get up, get up before he remembers you and comes back down for more.

"Lola." A voice carried through the window.

It was Tallulah, a pale ghost beyond the glass. Her mouth was moving as she clutched at the bars.

I turned my face away, in the childish way of *if I can't see her, then she can't see me.* I didn't want her to see me like this. It occurred to me that she might have been a witness to the whole thing. I turned back but she'd gone, so I closed my eyes.

I should've known that Tallulah would never leave me. The snakes swayed in their tanks, enraptured. Tallulah was long and white, with pale yellow markings. Slender and magnificent. She glided over me and lay on my chest, rearing up. I couldn't breathe because she took my breath away. I could feel her muscles contracting and her smooth belly scales against my bare chest.

Get up, get up, or he'll come down and find her like this.

Are you special?

Her tongue flicked out and touched my lips. I had no choice. I had to do it, for her. There was the rush of lubricant that loosened the top layer of my skin. The change was fast, my boyish body, with its flat chest and narrow hips perfectly suited to the transformation.

I crawled out of my human mantle. Moulting was good. I shed every cell of myself that Kenny had touched.

⬥

Both Tallulah and I are unidentifiable among my extensive research of snakes, bearing properties of several species at once. We made a perfect pair for hunting. The pits on my face were heat sensitive, able to detect a variation of a thousandth of a degree, feeding information into my optic nerves. I saw the world in thermal. Kenny's heart was luminous in the dark. I slid up the side of his bed and hovered over his pillow. Tallulah lay beside him on the mattress, waiting.

Look at your princesses, Kenny. See how special we are.

Kenny snored, a gentle, almost purring noise.

It's a myth that snakes dislocate their jaws.

I opened my mouth as wide as I could, stretching the flexible ligament that joined my lower jaw to my skull. I covered his crown in slow increments. He snorted and twitched. I slipped down over his eyes, his lashes tickling the inside of my throat. He reached up to touch his head.

Tallulah struck him, sinking her fangs into his neck. He started and tried to sit up, limbs flailing, which was a mistake as his accelerating heartbeat sent the venom further around his circulation.

Trying to cover his nose was the hardest part, despite my reconfigured mouth. I thought my head would split open. I wasn't sure how much more I could stomach. Not that it mattered. I wasn't trying to swallow him whole. A fraction more and I was over his nostrils completely.

There was only one way to save himself. I recognised the undulations he was making. I could feel the change on my tongue, his skin becoming fibrous. I had to stop him. I couldn't imagine what he'd become.

He was weakening with Tallulah's neurotoxins, slumping back on the bed, shaking in an exquisite fit. He'd wet himself. I stretched my flesh further and covered his mouth and waited until long after he was still.

◄◦►

I woke up on the floor beside Tallulah. We were naked. My throat and neck were sore. The corners of my mouth were crusted with dried blood. We lay on our sides, looking at one another without speaking. We were the same, after all.

"How did you find me?" I was hoarse.

"I had to wait until Ami went out. I found the house details in her bedroom drawer. I didn't have any money so I had to get a bus and walk the rest of the way. I'm sorry that I didn't get here sooner."

"It doesn't matter now."

Tallulah picked up our clothes and then our skins which lay like shrouds. It was disconcerting to see how they were moulds of us, even down to the contours of our faces.

"I'll take these with us. We can burn them later."

I went upstairs. I edged into the darkened room as if Kenny might sit up at any moment. He was a purple, bloated corpse with fang marks in his neck. I fumbled with the chain around his neck, not wanting to touch him.

"Where's Kathy?" Tallulah asked.

I told her.

"Show me."

"No, I don't want you to remember her like that." I seized Tallulah's face in my hands. "You do know that she didn't mean what she said, about you not belonging with us? She was trying to protect you."

Tallulah nodded, her mouth a line. She didn't cry.

"We have to bury her."

"We can't. Tallulah, we have to get out of here. Do you understand? Ami will come for you when she realises you've gone. There's something else."

I put my hand in the cottonmouth's tank. It curled up my arm and I lifted it out, holding it up to my cheek. He nudged my face.

"Lift out the bottom."

Tallulah pulled out bits of twisted branch and foliage, then pulled up the false base. She gasped. Out came bundles of notes and cloth bags. She tipped the contents out on her palm. More diamonds than I could hold in my cupped hands.

We loaded the money into Kenny's rucksack and tucked the diamonds in our pockets.

"What about the snakes?"

We opened the tanks and carried them outside. I watched them disappear into the undergrowth. Except for Shankly. I put him in a carrier bag and took him with us.

→o←

There are days when I wake and I can't remember who I am, like a disorientated traveller who can't recall which hotel room of which country they're in.

I'm hurt that Georgia didn't want me to collect her from the airport.

There's been a delay. I won't get in until late. Go to bed, I'll get a cab.

I wished now that I'd ignored her and gone anyway instead of lying here in the dark. The harsh fluorescent lights and the near-empty corridors of the airport are preferable to the vast darkness of our empty bed.

Not going is a stupid test with which I've only hurt myself. I've resolutely taken her consideration for indifference. I want her to be upset that I wasn't there, as if she secretly wanted me there all along.

See, I confuse even myself.

The front door opens and closes. I should get up and go to her. She comes in, marked by the unzipping of her boots and the soft sound of her shedding clothes.

Love isn't just what you feel for someone when you look at them. It's how they make you feel about yourself when they look back at you.

Georgia is the coolest, most poised woman that I know. We're older now and our hearts and flesh aren't so easily moved but I still wonder what she sees when she looks at me.

"Do you love me?" It's easier to ask it with the lights off and my head turned away from her.

Everything about us is wrong. We're lovers, sisters, freaks.

She answers in a way that I have to respond to. I glide across the floor towards her and we become a writhing knot. We hunt mice in our grandiose pile and in the morning we are back here in our bed, entwined together in our nest.

When we wake again as human beings she says, "Of course I love you, monster."

When we shed the disguises that are Georgia and Eliza, and then the skins that are Lola and Tallulah, we *are* monsters. Fabulous beasts.

DESCENT

CARMEN MARIA MACHADO

We gathered for the last time in October, under the pretense of discussing a novel that was currently bobbing along in the zeitgeist like a rubber duck at sea. It was unusually cold for October—the summer season had lasted long and hard and then dropped precipitously in a matter of days. Now we came bundled to Luna's house, sweaters beneath jackets and dishes in chapped hands and the novel tucked into our armpits.

Luna's house was oddly tall and narrow, set back from the street in a way that seemed appropriate for Luna herself. Reserved. As the sun had already dropped away, the entire house was swallowed in shadow, and could only be identified by a pre-arranged marker—a red balloon tied to a wrought-iron railing, whipping around in the breeze like an angry dog tied to a tree, straining and strangling in its collar. The street, though I knew it to be residential, and full of families, seemed deserted, except for a car door that opened halfway down the block.

Diane and I both came to the base of the stone steps at the same time. Approaching, she had appeared to be a tall, slender man, but now I recognized her. She gestured with her casserole dish, which steamed in the gloaming.

"After you," she said, and we mounted the steps into the darkness.

◄o►

Luna's girlfriend, whose name I did not know, answered the door. She was rosy-cheeked with good cheer, and the house glowed with contentment behind her. She invited us in. We were the last to arrive; the others were already in their cups, in their chairs, and arguing about the novel's finale.

"It dangles," Janet was saying. "I can't abide endings that dangle."

Luna laughed stiffly. Irritation snaked through her low, musical voice like a virus. "You can pick the next book," she said. She opened the novel, shuffled through the pages as though searching for something, and then shut the back cover. She reached her hand out and her girlfriend placed a glass of red wine into it before heading to the kitchen.

The living room was gorgeous, an eclectic blend of dark wood and strange artifacts: religious iconography, taxidermied animals, art deco prints, needle-point. The whole place looked like a tastefully decorated curio shop. Piano notes drifted hazily from a small set of speakers. A preserved crocodile head, no larger than my hand, rested on a bookshelf. I pressed my finger into the teeth of its open mouth.

"Welcome!" Luna said, and I jerked away.

Diane and I set our contributions on the table and poured ourselves drinks. The tumbler of bourbon was weighty in my hand, and I sat and scratched their cocker spaniel behind his soft ears as the day's events blurred. In the kitchen, Diane spoke to Luna's girlfriend, and I heard snatches of words— "sleep," "nothing," and "cold"—through the softness.

After a while they joined us, and there we were, in our circle, white ceramic plates balanced on our knees and the novel unopened at our feet. There was Luna, hostess and teacher at a local private girls' high school; her girlfriend, whose name I had not yet caught but it was now too late to inquire without embarrassment; Diane, whose gamine features contrasted oddly with the wine cooler in her hand; Janet, the youngest of the group at thirty-five, and apparently a neighbor from around the corner; and myself. The cocker spaniel walked into the middle of our circle, worried his paw over an invisible spot on the floor, and then curled up in a ball.

Janet picked up her copy of the novel and gestured toward its cover, with its red and black and white, its serif text. "Shall we begin?" she asked.

No one answered. We squeaked forks across their plates. Throats rippled with long sips. The wind had that late-autumn quality that, if you closed your eyes, suggested a great, stripped tundra in the furthest reaches of the world, and not a Philadelphia suburb at all. The branches of the trees that surrounded the house rustled and tapped on the windows.

"I'm so glad that you all made it tonight. I had a very strange week," Luna said. She drank deeply of her glass, and her girlfriend refilled it. "An awful week, actually."

I finished my bourbon—I don't remember how many glasses I'd consumed by then—and gestured toward her with the tumbler. "Tell," I said. "Tell."

"Very well," she said, setting down her fork.

◄◦►

And here is what Luna told us:

"As you all know, after the shooting at Brandywine, they temporarily shut down the school and transferred the students to other high schools, including ours. I was against it from the start. I told the principal and anyone else who would listen that you can't just unload traumatized kids into a new school like that. I told him he was inviting trouble. His reasoning was that a private girls' school might be the kind of calm environment the survivors needed in the middle of the media blitz. I'm sure the fact that he's about to throw a large fundraiser probably helped his charity along, but in any case: there we were, a month-and-a-half into the semester, and suddenly there was an influx of new students. I had two in my AP English class—a small, slender girl named Salma and a tall, quiet one named Nicki.

"I didn't know what to expect, but I figured they'd want to be near one another, so I arranged the desks so there were two empty ones together. But when they came in on Monday—I don't know if you saw the news, but it was the same day they found the shooter's manifesto in that weird hovel in the woods, do you remember?—they went to opposite sides of the room. I told the rest of the class that we had two new students. The girls didn't speak. Salma opened a notebook in front of her and placed a pencil in the concave of the binding but didn't move once to make a note. Nicki just stared out the window, drawing a figure eight with her finger on the fabric of her skirt.

"After class was over, I walked down to the principal's office to talk to him about the girls. Did they have a file? Doctor's notes? Anything I should know? But his admin told me he was out, and to come back later.

"It was free period, so I walked outside and hiked down to the amphitheater. There's something about its geometry—those concentric circles, down and down into the center—that I've always found soothing. It looks like one of those collapsible camping cups pushed into the ground, you know? I used to have one of those in Girl Scouts. It leaked something terrible, but it was really—anyway.

"When I got down to the bottom, I found Salma sitting in the grass.

"'Hello,' I said to her. 'Salma?'

"She did not move for a long while, but then turned her head slowly toward me, as if my voice was coming to her from underwater.

"'Are you all right?' I asked.

"She looked down at her palms as if she saw something on them, and then wiped them against her skirt. 'I'm supposed to be in a class,' she said. Her voice was high and soft.

"'Which class?'

"'I don't know.'

"'I can write you a pass,' I said. 'It's okay, really.' I sat down next to her. 'Did you come out here for some air?'

"She shook her head. Then she twisted around and looked out of the amphitheater, toward the school.

"'These rings,' she said, gesturing around. 'Arcs of stone. Like steps for giants.'

"'Yeah,' I said, smiling. 'I guess they are.'

"'Like we're at the bottom of a bowl,' she said. 'Like we're food.' Then her face closed off, an invisible door slammed on her private whimsy.

"I wanted to say something to her, but what could I say? I'm sorry a crazy person shot up your school? I'm sorry he killed dozens of your classmates for no discernible reason? The randomness of it, the entropy, came over me suddenly and I felt like I was going to drown. I suggested to her that we walk back and we could find out which class she's in. I wanted to take her by the hand; I wanted to just hold her.

"I've never wanted kids—we've never wanted kids—but I wanted to protect her. I'd never felt more maternal than at that moment. I reached out to touch her on the shoulder, but she pulled away and began to run up the levels of stone and grass until she was out of sight.

⟶⟨◦⟩⟵

"So of course, then I had to know. I had to know if these girls were just other students from a now shut-down high school, or if they'd *seen* something, you know? I figured there was no way to be an effective teacher without having a sense of your students. Like, I know that Bea's parents are getting divorced and that was why every paper she turns in chews over themes of betrayal whether the text contains it or not. I know that Lily is a hypochondriac and constantly presses her index and middle finger to her throat to check her own pulse. I know that Tia is having romantic troubles, and so on. It helps to know these things.

"When I got to the office, the admin eyed me uneasily.

"'He's still out,' she said, before I said anything.

"'Well, I need to see the files of my new students,' I said.

"'I can't show those to you without his permission,' she said, primly. She was wearing glasses that were only stylish because she'd had them so long. I tapped my fingers on the counter.

"'I can't teach these kids if I don't know what's going on with them,' I said.

"'Come back later,' she said, and went back to her typing.

"So I went back to my classroom and dug through some articles about the shooting. A long time ago, when they were less common, the coverage would have already been extravagant. But it's not the first school shooting this year. It's not even the first in the state this year. There were the expected articles, the timeline of events as pieced together by journalists, op-eds about gun control. Like every shooting, this one had its own gruesome signature: that the shooter had spent a significant portion of the day killing off individual students quietly and stashing their bodies around the school. When he finally opened fire, the number of students who'd come running out of the building was abnormally small. It was only after he killed himself and they combed the building that they found the two dozen dead propped up in broom closets and on toilets in the bathrooms.

"It was awful to read. I felt sick. I swigged the antacid I kept in the desk. When my next set of students came in, I put in a movie and sat there in the darkness, tipping my head back so the tears that kept welling up wouldn't fall.

◄o►

"On Wednesday, I put my students into discussion pairs. 'Go to it,' I said, once they'd all turned their desks toward one another.

"For the first time all week, Nicki spoke.

"'What about Jessica?' she said. She gestured toward an empty desk in the corner.

"'What?' I said.

"'Who is Jessica paired with? You don't have an even number.'

"I pretended to look down at the attendance list in front of me, like I was looking for a Jessica, but no such student existed in this class. I didn't know what to say.

"'I—' I began. 'I don't—'

"Salma stood up and backed away from away from the empty desk. She began to scream, and then tripped. When she landed, I could hear her wrist breaking even through her howling. A student ran and got the nurse, who came and hustled her away as fast as possible. The whole class was shaken, except for Nicki, who remained in the corner, seemingly unperturbed by the entire event. She crossed her arms over her chest and chewed on her lip, like nothing had happened.

"I went to the nurse's office when class was over. Salma was lying down on those uncomfortable plastic beds with a cold pack over her eyes and her wrist in a splint. The nurse said that she'd been sleeping for the whole period. She told me that she'd called Salma's parents, but neither of them had answered their phones.

"I sat down on the chair next to the bed and took the cold pack off her eyes. They were wide open. She blinked. 'Salma,' I said, 'You need to tell me what's going on. I can't help you if I don't know.'

"She didn't move, but a tear slid down her temple and into her hairline.

"'Is it the shooting?' I asked her. 'Did you see something?'

"She shook her head, and then began to weep. She wept raw, like she hadn't cried since birth. I'd never heard anything like it. The nurse stuck her head in, but I just reached out and rubbed Salma's arm. She cried like that for a few minutes, like something had to come out of her. Eventually, it receded into a gentle sob. When she started breathing normally again, she began to speak."

◄◦►

And here is what Salma said:

"We just moved here this year. We used to live in the city, but then Dad got a new job.

"My grandmother lives with us. She's been sick for a long time, and she doesn't walk very well. One morning after we got here, I had to take her to the bathroom. When she sat on the toilet, she started to mumble and look past me, and shake her head like something was on it. I thought she was having a stroke, and I kept saying to her, 'Abuela, what's wrong?' Then she grabbed my arm and squeezed it hard and began talking to me in this horrible, loud voice, like it was the last thing she'd ever say to me."

◄◦►

And here is what Salma's grandmother told her:

"Arrogance. Arrogance is what makes you think you can't see Death. You think Death wears dark clothes and walks around with a stick in its hand? It doesn't. It can look like anyone. It can be anyone. One day you find out you got one fewer children than you think you got. Or that you're the only one who can see the new neighbor. Or that the woman next to you on the train doesn't have any breath in her. And then once you think it, you look at them and they've changed. You can see what's underneath. You can see the emptiness that's below all of our feet. It's a face but there's nothing behind it. It's the worst thing you can see.

"And once you see it, it knows. And it comes for you, at its leisure. You think you see Death because it's your time? If you see Death, it becomes your time."

◄◦►

Outside, the wind knocked over the grill and sent its lid crashing into the patio door. We all jumped. Luna's girlfriend laughed uneasily and stood, opening the patio door with a muted *whoosh*. We heard the crash and bang as she righted it. The room chilled with the influx of cold air. Janet put on her cardigan.

"Keep going, Luna," Diane said.

◄◦►

Here is what Salma said next:

"That day—the shooting. I was one of the students who hid instead of running. I was at lunch. I grabbed the hand of the girl sitting next to me and dragged her into a broom closet in the hallway. I heard more shots but he didn't see us go in.

"We sat there in the dark. The closet smelled like metal and chlorine. We heard his footsteps approach, and he even opened the door slightly. I saw him, but he didn't see me. He looked like he'd once been scared, and angry, but then something had lanced him open, and all that came out was calm. There was a sound at the other end of the hall. He closed the door as casually as he opened it and walked away. There was more gunfire. One of them was the shot that killed him, but I didn't know that. I stepped backwards and my foot slipped in something. I began to cry softly.

"'It's going to be all right,' the girl said. 'Don't be afraid.'

"That's when I realized I couldn't hear her breathing.

⟶

"When the police opened the door, light cut across the closet. I was there. There were bodies rolled underneath the shelves, cooling. And the girl next to me—she was—

"She wasn't. She wasn't her. I'd been sitting next to Death the whole time. Her face—her face was just—

"I screamed. I screamed 'Get the fuck away from me,' and they pulled me out. I kicked and clawed. They had to stick me with a needle, to drug me. They told me I was in shock, because of the bodies in the closet. But it wasn't that. I'd sleep forever in a room full of bodies to have never seen that face.

"And now I'm just—I'm just waiting. Just waiting for it to end."

⟶

When Luna stopped speaking, we realized we'd all been leaning forward in our chairs. She took a long sip of wine and tapped the drained glass on the side table. Her shaking hand knocked it over and it shattered on the floor. We all instinctively drew our socked feet up from the hardwood. Diane went into the kitchen for a broom, and swept up the pieces.

"Jesus," said Janet.

"I'm so sorry, Luna," I said.

She shrugged. Her chin dimpled and trembled, but then steadied. "It's not even my suffering," she said. "That's the worst part. It's not even my suffering. Why am I so upset? That girl went through something I can't even imagine."

"But still," said Diane.

"Her parents came for her, eventually. She hasn't been to school in a few days. I'm just—what did she think she saw?"

She closed her eyes and pressed her fingers into them. "And now I feel like—I don't know. I have the heebie-jeebies. Like something's going to happen. Another shooting, or—I don't know. We have to do all of this emergency training. All I can think is, what would I do if someone tried to kill my students? Would I be the hero who threw herself in front of the bullet? Would I have just run? I just don't know. I don't even know what kind of person I am. I've always thought of myself as basically good, but—" Her voice drifted away.

Diane touched Luna's hand. "Why don't we change the subject?" she said. We all looked down at the novel at our feet, but talking about it seemed impossible, irritating.

"Your place is gorgeous, Luna," I said. "The interior design in here—I'm jealous." The cocker spaniel pressed its cold nose into my leg, and I scratched its head. "And the floors. You must spend a fortune buffing out the scratches."

Luna looked up from her lap, where she'd been linking her fingers together. "Scratches? From all of the glasses I break?" She lifted her sleeve to her eye and decorously wiped it.

"From the dog's claws."

Luna frowned. "We don't have a dog."

My fingers froze deep in the lush fur of the cocker spaniel, tips resting against the smooth bowl of its skull. The wind skittered the tree branches against the house. I breathed deeply and pulled my spine straighter. I closed my eyes and then opened them again. The other women were staring at me strangely, drinks cocked in their hands.

I looked down.

HIPPOCAMPUS

ADAM NEVILL

Walls of water as slow as lava, black as coal, push the freighter up mountainsides, over frothing peaks, and into plunging descents. Across the rolling backs of vast waves the vessel ploughs ungainly, conjuring galaxies of bubbles around its passage and in its wake; vast cosmos appear for moments in the immensity of onyx water, forged and then sucked beneath the hull, or are sacrificed fizzing to the freezing night air.

On and on the great steel vessel wallops, staggering as if up from soiled knees before another nauseating drop into a trough. There is no rest and there is no choice but to rear, dizzy, near breathless, over and over again to brace the next great wave.

On board, lighted portholes and square windows offer tiny, yellow squares of reassurance amidst the lightless, roaring ocean that stretches all around and so far below. Reminiscent of a warm home offering a welcome on a winter night, the cabin lights are complemented by the two metal doorways that gape in the rear house. Their spilled light glosses portions of the slick deck.

All of the surfaces on board are steel, painted white. Riveted and welded tight to the deck and each other, these metal cubes of the superstructure are necklaced by yellow rails intended for those who must slip and reel about the flooded decks. Here and there, white ladders rise, and seem by their very presence to evoke a *kang kang kang* sound of feet going up and down quickly. Small lifeboat cases resembling plastic barrels are fixed at the sides of the upper deck, all of them intact and locked shut. The occasional crane peers out to sea with inappropriate nonchalance, or at the expectation of a purpose that has not come. Up above the distant bridge, from which no faces peer out, the aerials, satellite dishes and navigation masts appear to totter in panic, or to whip their poles, wires, and struts from side to side as if engaged in a frantic search of the ever-changing landscape of water below.

The vast steel door of the hold's first hatch is raised and still attached to the crane by chains. This large square section of the hull is filled with white sacks, stacked upon each other in tight columns that fill the entire space. Those at the top of the pile are now dark and sopping with rain and sea water. In the centre, scores of the heavy bags have been removed from around a scuffed and dented metal container, painted black. Until its recent discovery, the container appears to have been deliberately hidden among the tiers of fibre sacks. One side of the double doors at the front of the old container has been jammed open.

Somewhere on deck, a small brass bell clangs its lonesome, undirected cry; a traditional affectation as there are speakers thrusting their silent horns out from the metallic walls and masts. But though the tiny, urgent sound of the bell is occasionally answered by a gull in better weather, out here tonight the bell is answered by nothing save the black, shrieking chaos of the wind and the water it ploughs.

There is a lane between the freighter's rear house and the crane above the open hatch. The lane is unpeopled, wet, and lit by six lights in metal cages. Muster Station: Lifeboat 2 is stencilled on the white wall in red lettering. Passing through the lane, the noise of the engine intake fans fills the space hotly and the diesel heat creates the apprehension of being close to moving machine parts. As if functioning as evidence of the ship's purpose and life, and rumbling across every surface like electric current in each part of the vessel, the continuous vibration of the engine's exhaust thrums.

Above the open hatch, and beside the lifeboat assembly point, from out of one of the doors that has been left gaping in the rear house, drifts a thick warmth, as if to engulf wind-seared faces in the way the summer sun cups cheeks.

Once across the metal threshold the engine fibrillations deepen as if muted underground. The bronchial roar of the intake fans dull. Inside, the salty-spittle scour of the night air, and the noxious mechanical odours, are replaced by the scent of old emulsion and the stale chemicals of exhausted air fresheners. A staircase leads down.

But so above so below. As on deck, no one walks here. All is still, lit bright and faintly rumbled by the bass strumming of the exhaust. The communal area appears calm and indifferent to the intense, black energies of the hurricane outside.

A long, narrow corridor runs through the rear house. Square lenses in the steel ceiling illuminate the plain passageway. The floor is covered in linoleum, the walls are matte yellow, the doors to the cabins trimmed with wood laminate. Half way down, two opposing doors hang open before lit rooms.

The first room was intended for recreation to ease a crew's passage on a long voyage, but no one seeks leisure now. Coloured balls roll across the pool table with the swell that shimmies the ship. Two cues lie amongst the balls and move back and forth like flotsam on the tide. At rest upon the table tennis table are two worn paddles. The television screen remains as empty and black as the rain-thrashed canopy of sky above the freighter. One of the brown leatherette sofas is split in two places and masking tape suppresses the spongy eruptions of cushion entrails.

Across the corridor, a long bank of washing machines and dryers stand idle in the crew's laundry room. Strung across the ceiling are washing line cords that loop like skipping ropes from the weight of the clothing that is pegged in rows: jeans, socks, shirts, towels. One basket has been dropped upon the floor and has spilled its contents towards the door.

Up one flight of stairs, the bridge is empty too; monitor screens glow green, consoles flash and flicker. One stool lies on its side and the cushioned seat rolls back and forth. A solitary black handgun skitters this way and that too, across the floor. The weapon adds a touch of tension to the otherwise tranquil area of operations, as if a drama has recently passed, been interrupted, or even abandoned.

Back down and deeper inside the ship, and further along the crew's communal corridor, the stainless steel galley glimmers dully in white light. A thin skein of steam drifts over the work surfaces and clouds against the ceiling above the oven. Two large and unwashed pots have boiled dry upon bright red cooker rings. From around the oven door, wisps of black smoke puff.

Inside the oven, a tray of potatoes has baked to carbon and now resembles the fossils of ancient reptile guano.

Across the great chopping board on the central table lies a scattering of chopped vegetables, cast wide by the freighter's lurching and twisting. The ceiling above the work station is railed with steel and festooned with swaying kitchen wear. Six large steaks, encrusted with crushed salt, await the abandoned spatula and the griddle that is now hissing black and dry. A large refrigerator door, resembling the gate of a bank vault, hangs open to reveal crowded shelves that gleam in a vanilla light.

Inside a metal sink the size of a bathtub lies a human scalp.

Lopped roughly from the top of a head and left to drain beside the plughole, the gingery mess looks absurdly artificial. But the clod of hair was once plumbed into a circulatory system because the hair is matted dark and wet at the fringes and surrounded by flecks of ochre. The implement that removed the scalp lies upon the draining board: a long knife, the edge serrated for sawing. Above the adjacent work station, at the end of the rack that holds the cook's knives, several items are missing.

Some dripping *thing* was taken from the sink area and out of the galley and along the corridor, and down one flight of stairs to the crew's quarters. Red droplets that have splashed as round as rose petals lead a trail into the first cabin that is situated in an identical corridor to the communal passage on the deck above. The door to this cabin is open. Inside, the trail of scarlet is immediately lost within the engulfing borders of a far bigger stain.

A fluorescent jacket and cap hang upon a peg just inside the door of the cabin. All is neat and orderly upon the bookshelf holding volumes that brush the low white ceiling. A chest of drawers doubles as a desk. The articles on the desk top are weighed down by a glass paperweight and are overlooked by silver-framed photographs of wives and children at the rear of the desk. Upon the top of the wardrobe, life jackets and hardhats are stowed. Two twin beds, arranged close together, are unoccupied. Beneath the bed frames, orange survival suits remain neatly folded and tightly packed.

The bedclothes of the berth on the right-hand side are tidy and undisturbed. But the white top sheet and the yellow blanket of the adjacent berth droop to the linoleum floor like idle sails. There is a suggestion that an occupant departed this bed hurriedly, or was removed swiftly. The bed linen has been yanked from the bed and only remains tucked under the mattress in one corner. A body was also ruined in that bed: the middle of the mattress is blood-sodden and the cabin now reeks of salt and rust. Crimson gouts from a bedside frenzy have flecked and speckled the wall beside the bed, and part of the ceiling.

Attached to the room is a small en suite bathroom that just manages to hold a shower cubicle and small steel sink. The bathroom is pristine, the taps, shower head, and towel rail sparkle. All that is amiss is a single slip-on shoe, dropped to the floor just in front of the sink. A foot remains inside the shoe with part of a hairy ankle extending from the uppers.

From the cabin more than just a trail of droplets can be followed down the passage and to the neighbouring berths. A long intermittent streak of red has been smeared along the length of the corridor and past the four doors that all hang open and drift back and forth as the ship lists. From each of these cabins, other collections have been made.

What occupants there once were in the crew's quarters all appear to have arisen from their beds before stumbling towards the doors as if cause for alarm had been announced nearby. Just before the doorways of their berths, they seem to have met their ends quickly. Wide, lumpy puddles, like spilled stew made with red wine, are splashed across the floors. One crew member sought refuge inside the shower cubicle of the last cabin because the bathroom door is broken open, and the basin of the shower is drenched near black from a sudden and conclusive emptying. Livestock hung above the cement of a slaughterhouse and emptied from the throat, leave similar stains.

Turning left at the end of the passage, the open door of the captain's cabin is visible. Inside, the sofa beside the coffee table and the two easy chairs sit expectant but empty. The office furniture and shelves reveal no disarray. But set upon the broad desk are three long wooden crates. The tops have been levered off, and the packing straw that was once inside is now littered about the table's surface and the carpeted floor below. Intermingled with the straw is a plethora of dried flower petals.

Upon a tablecloth spread on the floor before the captain's desk, two small forms have been laid out, side by side, in profile. They are the size of five year old children and black in colour. Not dissimilar to the preserved forms of ancient peoples, protected behind glass in museums for antiquities, they appear to be shrivelled and contorted with age. Vestiges of a fibrous binding have fused with their petrified flesh and obscured their arms, if they are in possession of such limbs. The two small figures are primarily distinguished by the irregular shape and silhouettes of their skulls. Their heads appear oversized, and the swollen dimension of the crania contributes to the leathery ghastliness of the grimacing faces. The rear of each head is fanned by an incomplete mane of spikes, while the front of each head elongates and protrudes into a snout. The desiccated figures have also had their lower limbs bound tightly together to suggest long and curling tails.

Inside the second crate is a large black stone, crudely hollowed out in the middle. The dull and chipped character of the block also suggests a great age. A modern addition has been made, or offered, to the hollow within the stone. A single human foot. The shoe around the disarticulated foot matches the footwear inside the shower cubicle of the crew member's cabin.

The contents of the third crate have barely been disturbed. In there lie several artefacts that resemble jagged flints, or the surviving blades of old weapons or knives to which the handles are missing. The implements are hand-forged from a stone as black as that of the basin that has become a receptacle for a human foot.

Pictures of a ship and framed maps have been removed from the widest wall, and upon this wall a marker pen has been used to depict the outlines of two snouted or trumpeting figures that are attached by what appears to be long and entwined tails. The imagery is crude and childlike, but the silhouettes are not dissimilar to the embalmed remains laid out upon the tablecloth.

Below the two figures are imprecise sticklike forms that appear to cavort in emulation of the much larger and snouted characters. Set atop some kind of uneven pyramid shape, another group of human shapes have been excitedly and messily drawn with spikes protruding from their heads or headdresses, and between these groups another plainer individual has been held aloft and bleeds from the torso into a waiting receptacle. Detail has been included to indicate that the sacrificed victim's feet have been removed and its legs bound.

The mess of human leavings that led here departs the captain's cabin and rises up a staircase to the deck above and into an unlit canteen. Light falls into this room from the corridor, and in the half-light two long tables, and one smaller table for the officers, is revealed. Upon the two larger crew tables long reddish shapes are stretched out and glisten: some twelve bodies dwindling into darkness as they stretch away from the door. As if unzipped across the front, what was once inside each of the men has now been gathered and piled upon chairs where the same men once sat and ate. Their feet, some bare, some still inside shoes, have been amputated and are set in a messy pile at the head of the two tables.

At the far end of the cafeteria that is barely touched by the residual light, and to no living audience, perversely, inappropriately and yet grimly touching, two misshapen shadows flicker and leap upon the dim wall as if in a joyous reunion, and then wheel and wheel about each other, ferociously, but not without grace, while attached, it seems, by two long and spiny tails.

Back outside and on deck, it can be seen that the ship continues to meander, inebriated with desolation and weariness, or perhaps it has even been punched drunk from the shock of what has occurred below deck.

The bow momentarily rises up the small hillside of a wave and, just once, near expectantly, looks toward the distant harbour the vessel has slowly drifted toward overnight since changing its course. On shore and across the surrounding basin of treeless land, the lights of a small harbour town glow in white pinpricks as if desperate to be counted in this black storm. Here and there, the harbour lights define the uneven silhouettes of small buildings, suggesting stone facades in which glass shimmers to form an unwitting beacon for what exists out here upon these waves.

Oblivious to anything but its own lurching and clanking, the ship rolls on the swell, inexorably drifting on the current that picked up its great steel bulk the day before and now slowly propels the hull, fizzing and crashing, but perhaps not so purposelessly as was first assumed, towards the shore.

At the prow, having first bound himself tight to the railing with rope, a solitary and unclothed figure nods a bowed head towards the land. The pale flesh of the rotund torso is whipped and occasionally drenched by sea spray, but still bears the ruddy impressions of bestial deeds that were both boisterous and thorough. From navel to sternum the curious, temporary figurehead is open, or has been opened blackly to the elements, and the implement used to carve such crude entrances to the heart is now long gone, perhaps dropped from stained and curling fingers into that far-below obsidian whirling and clashing of a monumental ocean.

As if to emulate the status of a king, where the scalp has been carved away, a crude series of spikes, fashioned from nails, have been hammered into a pattern resembling a spine or fin across the top of the dead man's skull. Both of his feet are missing and his legs have been bound with twine into one, single, gruesome tail.

BLACK DOG

NEIL GAIMAN

There were ten tongues within one head
And one went out to fetch some bread,
To feed the living and the dead.

—Old Riddle

I: The Bar Guest

Outside the pub it was raining cats and dogs.

Shadow was still not entirely convinced that he was in a pub. True, there was a tiny bar at the back of the room, with bottles behind it and a couple of the huge taps you pulled, and there were several high tables and people were drinking at the tables, but it all felt like a room in somebody's house. The dogs helped reinforce that impression. It seemed to Shadow that everybody in the pub had a dog except for him.

"What kind of dogs are they?" Shadow asked, curious. The dogs reminded him of greyhounds, but they were smaller and seemed saner, more placid and less high-strung than the greyhounds he had encountered over the years.

"Lurchers," said the pub's landlord, coming out from behind the bar. He was carrying a pint of beer that he had poured for himself. "Best dogs. Poacher's dogs. Fast, smart, lethal." He bent down, scratched a chestnut-and-white brindled dog behind the ears. The dog stretched and luxuriated in the ear-scratching. It did not look particularly lethal, and Shadow said so.

The landlord, his hair a mop of gray and orange, scratched at his beard reflectively. "That's where you'd be wrong," he said. "I walked with his brother last week, down Cumpsy Lane. There's a fox, a big red reynard, pokes his head out of a hedge, no more than twenty meters down the road, then, plain as day, saunters out onto the track. Well, Needles sees it, and he's off after it like the clappers. Next thing you know, Needles has his teeth in reynard's neck, and one bite, one hard shake, and it's all over."

Shadow inspected Needles, a gray dog sleeping by the little fireplace. He looked harmless too. "So what sort of a breed is a lurcher? It's an English breed, yes?"

"It's not actually a breed," said a white-haired woman without a dog who had been leaning on a nearby table. "They're crossbred for speed, stamina. Sighthound, greyhound, collie."

The man next to her held up a finger. "You must understand," he said, cheerfully, "that there used to be laws about who could own purebred dogs. The local folk couldn't, but they could own mongrels. And lurchers are better and faster than pedigree dogs." He pushed his spectacles up his nose with the tip of his forefinger. He had a muttonchop beard, brown flecked with white.

"Ask me, all mongrels are better than pedigree anything," said the woman. "It's why America is such an interesting country. Filled with mongrels." Shadow was not certain how old she was. Her hair was white, but she seemed younger than her hair.

"Actually, darling," said the man with the muttonchops, in his gentle voice, "I think you'll find that the Americans are keener on pedigree dogs than the British. I met a woman from the American Kennel Club, and honestly, she scared me. I was scared."

"I wasn't talking about dogs, Ollie," said the woman. "I was talking about . . . Oh, never mind."

"What are you drinking?" asked the landlord.

There was a handwritten piece of paper taped to the wall by the bar telling customers not to order a lager "as a punch in the face often offends."

"What's good and local?" asked Shadow, who had learned that this was mostly the wisest thing to say.

The landlord and the woman had various suggestions as to which of the various local beers and ciders were good. The little muttonchopped man interrupted them to point out that in his opinion *good* was not the avoidance of evil, but something more positive than that: it was making the world a better place. Then he chuckled, to show that he was only joking and that he knew that the conversation was really only about what to drink.

The beer the landlord poured for Shadow was dark and very bitter. He was not certain that he liked it. "What is it?"

"It's called Black Dog," said the woman. "I've heard people say it was named after the way you feel after you've had one too many."

"Like Churchill's moods," said the little man.

"Actually, the beer is named after a local dog," said a younger woman. She was wearing an olive-green sweater, and standing against the wall. "But not a real one. Semi-imaginary."

Shadow looked down at Needles, then hesitated. "Is it safe to scratch his head?" he asked, remembering the fate of the fox.

"Course it is," said the white-haired woman. "He loves it. Don't you?"

"Well. He practically had that tosser from Glossop's finger off," said the landlord. There was admiration mixed with warning in his voice.

"I think he was something in local government," said the woman. "And I've always thought that there's nothing wrong with dogs biting *them*. Or VAT inspectors."

The woman in the green sweater moved over to Shadow. She was not holding a drink. She had dark, short hair, and a crop of freckles that spattered her nose and cheeks. She looked at Shadow. "You aren't in local government, are you?"

Shadow shook his head. He said, "I'm kind of a tourist." It was not actually untrue. He was traveling, anyway.

"You're Canadian?" said the muttonchop man.

"American," said Shadow. "But I've been on the road for a while now."

"Then," said the white-haired woman, "you aren't actually a tourist. Tourists turn up, see the sights and leave."

Shadow shrugged, smiled, and leaned down. He scratched the landlord's lurcher on the back of its head.

"You're not a dog person, are you?" asked the dark-haired woman.

"I'm not a dog person," said Shadow.

Had he been someone else, someone who talked about what was happening inside his head, Shadow might have told her that his wife had owned dogs when she was younger, and sometimes called Shadow *puppy* because she wanted a dog she could not have. But Shadow kept things on the inside. It was one of the things he liked about the British: even when they wanted to know what was happening on the inside, they did not ask. The world on the inside remained the world on the inside. His wife had been dead for three years now.

"If you ask me," said the man with the muttonchops, "people are either dog people or cat people. So would you then consider yourself a cat person?"

Shadow reflected. "I don't know. We never had pets when I was a kid, we were always on the move. But—"

"I mention this," the man continued, "because our host also has a cat, which you might wish to see."

"Used to be out here, but we moved it to the back room," said the landlord, from behind the bar.

Shadow wondered how the man could follow the conversation so easily while also taking people's meal orders and serving their drinks. "Did the cat upset the dogs?" he asked.

Outside, the rain redoubled. The wind moaned, and whistled, and then howled. The log fire burning in the little fireplace coughed and spat.

"Not in the way you're thinking," said the landlord. "We found it when we knocked through into the room next door, when we needed to extend the bar." The man grinned. "Come and look."

Shadow followed the man into the room next door. The muttonchop man and the white-haired woman came with them, walking a little behind Shadow.

Shadow glanced back into the bar. The dark-haired woman was watching him, and she smiled warmly when he caught her eye.

The room next door was better lit, larger, and it felt a little less like somebody's front room. People were sitting at tables, eating. The food looked good and smelled better. The landlord led Shadow to the back of the room, to a dusty glass case.

"There she is," said the landlord, proudly.

The cat was brown, and it looked, at first glance, as if it had been constructed out of tendons and agony. The holes that were its eyes were filled with anger and with pain; the mouth was wide open, as if the creature had been yowling when she was turned to leather.

"The practice of placing animals in the walls of buildings is similar to the practice of walling up children alive in the foundations of a house you want to stay up," explained the muttonchop man, from behind him. "Although mummified cats always make me think of the mummified cats they found around the temple of Bast in Bubastis in Egypt. So many tons of mummified cats that they sent them to England to be ground up as cheap fertilizer and dumped on the fields. The Victorians also made paint out of mummies. A sort of brown, I believe."

"It looks miserable," said Shadow. "How old is it?"

The landlord scratched his cheek. "We reckon that the wall she was in went up somewhere between 1300 and 1600. That's from parish records. There's nothing here in 1300, and there's a house in 1600. The stuff in the middle was lost."

The dead cat in the glass case, furless and leathery, seemed to be watching them, from its empty black-hole eyes.

I got eyes wherever my folk walk, breathed a voice in the back of Shadow's mind. He thought, momentarily, about the fields fertilized with the ground mummies of cats, and what strange crops they must have grown.

"*They put him into an old house side*," said the man called Ollie. "*And there he lived and there he died. And nobody either laughed or cried.* All sorts of things were walled up, to make sure that things were guarded and safe. Children, sometimes. Animals. They did it in churches as a matter of course."

The rain beat an arrhythmic rattle on the windowpane. Shadow thanked the landlord for showing him the cat. They went back into the taproom. The dark-haired woman had gone, which gave Shadow a moment of regret. She had looked so friendly. Shadow bought a round of drinks for the muttonchop man, the white-haired woman, and one for the landlord.

The landlord ducked behind the bar. "They call me Shadow," Shadow told them. "Shadow Moon."

The muttonchop man pressed his hands together in delight. "Oh! How wonderful. I had an Alsatian named Shadow, when I was a boy. Is it your real name?"

"It's what they call me," said Shadow.

"I'm Moira Callanish," said the white-haired woman. "This is my partner, Oliver Bierce. He knows a lot, and he will, during the course of our acquaintance, undoubtedly tell you everything he knows."

They shook hands. When the landlord returned with their drinks, Shadow asked if the pub had a room to rent. He had intended to walk further that night, but the rain sounded like it had no intention of giving up. He had stout walking shoes, and weather-resistant outer clothes, but he did not want to walk in the rain.

"I used to, but then my son moved back in. I'll encourage people to sleep it off in the barn, on occasion, but that's as far as I'll go these days."

"Anywhere in the village I could get a room?"

The landlord shook his head. "It's a foul night. But Porsett is only a few miles down the road, and they've got a proper hotel there. I can call Sandra, tell her that you're coming. What's your name?"

"Shadow," said Shadow again. "Shadow Moon."

Moira looked at Oliver, and said something that sounded like "waifs and strays?" and Oliver chewed his lip for a moment, and then he nodded enthusiastically. "Would you fancy spending the night with us? The spare room's a bit of a box room, but it does have a bed in it. And it's warm there. And dry."

"I'd like that very much," said Shadow. "I can pay."

"Don't be silly," said Moira. "It will be nice to have a guest."

II: The Gibbet

Oliver and Moira both had umbrellas. Oliver insisted that Shadow carry his umbrella, pointing out that Shadow towered over him, and thus was ideally suited to keep the rain off both of them.

The couple also carried little flashlights, which they called torches. The word put Shadow in mind of villagers in a horror movie storming the castle on the hill, and the lightning and thunder added to the vision. *Tonight, my creature,* he thought, *I will give you life!* It should have been hokey but instead it was disturbing. The dead cat had put him into a strange set of mind.

The narrow roads between fields were running with rainwater.

"On a nice night," said Moira, raising her voice to be heard over the rain, "we would just walk over the fields. But they'll be all soggy and boggy, so we're going down by Shuck's Lane. Now, that tree was a gibbet tree, once upon a time." She pointed to a massive-trunked sycamore at the crossroads. It had only a few branches left, sticking up into the night like afterthoughts.

"Moira's lived here since she was in her twenties," said Oliver. "I came up from London, about eight years ago. From Turnham Green. I'd come up here on holiday originally when I was fourteen and I never forgot it. You don't."

"The land gets into your blood," said Moira. "Sort of."

"And the blood gets into the land," said Oliver. "One way or another. You take that gibbet tree, for example. They would leave people in the gibbet until there was nothing left. Hair gone to make bird's nests, flesh all eaten by ravens, bones picked clean. Or until they had another corpse to display anyway."

Shadow was fairly sure he knew what a gibbet was, but he asked anyway. There was never any harm in asking, and Oliver was definitely the kind of person who took pleasure in knowing peculiar things and in passing his knowledge on.

"Like a huge iron birdcage. They used them to display the bodies of executed criminals, after justice had been served. The gibbets were locked, so the family and friends couldn't steal the body back and give it a good Christian burial. Keeping passersby on the straight and the narrow, although I doubt it actually deterred anyone from anything."

"Who were they executing?"

"Anyone who got unlucky. Three hundred years ago, there were over two hundred crimes punishable by death. Including traveling with Gypsies for more than a month, stealing sheep—and, for that matter, anything over twelve pence in value—and writing a threatening letter."

He might have been about to begin a lengthy list, but Moira broke in. "Oliver's right about the death sentence, but they only gibbeted murderers, up these parts. And they'd leave corpses in the gibbet for twenty years, sometimes. We didn't get a lot of murders." And then, as if trying to change the subject to something lighter, she said, "We are now walking down Shuck's Lane. The locals say that on a clear night, which tonight certainly is not, you can find yourself being followed by Black Shuck. He's a sort of a fairy dog."

"We've never seen him, not even on clear nights," said Oliver.

"Which is a very good thing," said Moira. "Because if you see him—you die."

"Except Sandra Wilberforce said she saw him, and she's healthy as a horse."

Shadow smiled. "What does Black Shuck do?"

"He doesn't do anything," said Oliver.

"He does. He follows you home," corrected Moira. "And then, a bit later, you die."

"Doesn't sound very scary," said Shadow. "Except for the dying bit."

They reached the bottom of the road. Rainwater was running like a stream over Shadow's thick hiking boots.

Shadow said, "So how did you two meet?" It was normally a safe question, when you were with couples.

Oliver said, "In the pub. I was up here on holiday, really."

Moira said, "I was with someone when I met Oliver. We had a very brief, torrid affair, then we ran off together. Most unlike both of us."

They did not seem like the kind of people who ran off together, thought Shadow. But then, all people were strange. He knew he should say something.

"I was married. My wife was killed in a car crash."

"I'm so sorry," said Moira.

"It happened," said Shadow.

"When we get home," said Moira, "I'm making us all whisky macs. That's whisky and ginger wine and hot water. And I'm having a hot bath. Otherwise I'll catch my death."

Shadow imagined reaching out his hand and catching death in it, like a baseball, and he shivered.

The rain redoubled, and a sudden flash of lightning burned the world into existence all around them: every gray rock in the drystone wall, every blade of grass, every puddle and every tree was perfectly illuminated, and then swallowed by a deeper darkness, leaving afterimages on Shadow's night-blinded eyes.

"Did you see that?" asked Oliver. "Damnedest thing." The thunder rolled and rumbled, and Shadow waited until it was done before he tried to speak.

"I didn't see anything," said Shadow. Another flash, less bright, and Shadow thought he saw something moving away from them in a distant field. "That?" he asked.

"It's a donkey," said Moira. "Only a donkey."

Oliver stopped. He said, "This was the wrong way to come home. We should have got a taxi. This was a mistake."

"Ollie," said Moira. "It's not far now. And it's just a spot of rain. You aren't made of sugar, darling."

Another flash of lightning, so bright as to be almost blinding. There was nothing to be seen in the fields. Darkness. Shadow turned back to Oliver, but the little man was no longer standing beside him. Oliver's flashlight was on the ground. Shadow blinked his eyes, hoping to force his night vision to return. The man had collapsed, crumpled onto the wet grass on the side of the lane.

"Ollie?" Moira crouched beside him, her umbrella by her side. She shone her flashlight onto his face. Then she looked at Shadow. "He can't just sit here," she said, sounding confused and concerned. "It's pouring."

Shadow pocketed Oliver's flashlight, handed his umbrella to Moira, then picked Oliver up. The man did not seem to weigh much, and Shadow was a big man.

"Is it far?"

"Not far," she said. "Not really. We're almost home."

They walked in silence, across a churchyard on the edge of a village green, and into a village. Shadow could see lights on in the gray stone houses that edged the one street. Moira turned off, into a house set back from the road, and Shadow followed her. She held the back door open for him.

The kitchen was large and warm, and there was a sofa, half-covered with magazines, against one wall. There were low beams in the kitchen, and Shadow needed to duck his head. Shadow removed Oliver's raincoat and dropped it. It puddled on the wooden floor. Then he put the man down on the sofa.

Moira filled the kettle.

"Do we call an ambulance?"

She shook her head.

"This is just something that happens? He falls down and passes out?"

Moira busied herself getting mugs from a shelf. "It's happened before. Just not for a long time. He's narcoleptic, and if something surprises or scares him he can just go down like that. He'll come round soon. He'll want tea. No whisky mac tonight, not for him. Sometimes he's a bit dazed and doesn't know where he is, sometimes he's been following everything that happened while he was out. And he hates it if you make a fuss. Put your backpack down by the Aga."

The kettle boiled. Moira poured the steaming water into a teapot. "He'll have a cup of real tea. I'll have chamomile, I think, or I won't sleep tonight. Calm my nerves. You?"

"I'll drink tea, sure," said Shadow. He had walked more than twenty miles that day, and sleep would be easy in the finding. He wondered at Moira. She appeared perfectly self-possessed in the face of her partner's incapacity, and he wondered how much of it was not wanting to show weakness in front of a stranger. He admired her, although he found it peculiar. The English were strange. But he understood hating "making a fuss." Yes.

Oliver stirred on the couch. Moira was at his side with a cup of tea, helped him into a sitting position. He sipped the tea, in a slightly dazed fashion.

"It followed me home," he said, conversationally.

"What followed you, Ollie, darling?" Her voice was steady, but there was concern in it.

"The dog," said the man on the sofa, and he took another sip of his tea. "The black dog."

III: The Cuts

These were the things Shadow learned that night, sitting around the kitchen table with Moira and Oliver:

He learned that Oliver had not been happy or fulfilled in his London advertising agency job. He had moved up to the village and taken an extremely early medical retirement. Now, initially for recreation and increasingly for money, he repaired and rebuilt drystone walls. There was, he explained, an art and a skill to wall building, it was excellent exercise, and, when done correctly, a meditative practice.

"There used to be hundreds of drystone-wall people around here. Now there's barely a dozen who know what they're doing. You see walls repaired with concrete, or with breeze blocks. It's a dying art. I'd love to show you how I do it. Useful skill to have. Picking the rock, sometimes, you have to let the rock tell you where it goes. And then it's immovable. You couldn't knock it down with a tank. Remarkable."

He learned that Oliver had been very depressed several years earlier, shortly after Moira and he got together, but that for the last few years he had been doing very well. Or, he amended, relatively well.

He learned that Moira was independently wealthy, that her family trust fund had meant that she and her sisters had not needed to work, but that, in her late twenties, she had gone for teacher training. That she no longer taught, but that she was extremely active in local affairs, and had campaigned successfully to keep the local bus routes in service.

Shadow learned, from what Oliver didn't say, that Oliver was scared of something, very scared, and that when Oliver was asked what had frightened him so badly, and what he had meant by saying that the black dog had followed him home, his response was to stammer and to sway. He learned not to ask Oliver any more questions.

This is what Oliver and Moira had learned about Shadow sitting around that kitchen table:

Nothing much.

Shadow liked them. He was not a stupid man; he had trusted people in the past who had betrayed him. But he liked this couple, and he liked the way their home smelled—like bread-making and jam and walnut wood-polish—and he went to sleep that night in his box-room bedroom worrying about the little man with the muttonchop beard. What if the thing Shadow had glimpsed in the field had *not* been a donkey? What if it *had* been an enormous dog? What then?

The rain had stopped when Shadow woke. He made himself toast in the empty kitchen. Moira came in from the garden, letting a gust of chilly air in through the kitchen door. "Sleep well?" she asked.

"Yes. Very well." He had dreamed of being at the zoo. He had been surrounded by animals he could not see, that snuffled and snorted in their pens. He was a child, walking with his mother, and he was safe and he was loved. He had stopped in front of a lion's cage, but what had been in the cage was a sphinx, half lion and half woman, her tail swishing. She had smiled at him, and her smile had been his mother's smile. He heard her voice, accented and warm and feline.

It said, *Know thyself.*

I know who I am, said Shadow in his dream, holding the bars of the cage. Behind the bars was the desert. He could see pyramids. He could see shadows on the sand.

Then who are you, Shadow? What are you running from? Where are you running to?

Who are you?

And he had woken, wondering why he was asking himself that question, and missing his mother, who had died twenty years before, when he was a teenager. He still felt oddly comforted, remembering the feel of his hand in his mother's hand.

"I'm afraid Ollie's a bit under the weather this morning."

"Sorry to hear that."

"Yes. Well, can't be helped."

"I'm really grateful for the room. I guess I'll be on my way."

Moira said, "Will you look at something for me?"

Shadow nodded, then followed her outside, and round the side of the house. She pointed to the rose bed. "What does that look like to you?"

Shadow bent down. "*The footprint of an enormous hound*," he said. "To quote Dr. Watson."

"Yes," she said. "It really does."

"If there's a spectral ghost-hound out there," said Shadow, "it shouldn't leave footprints. Should it?"

"I'm not actually an authority on these matters," said Moira. "I had a friend once who could have told us all about it. But she . . ." She trailed off. Then, more brightly, "You know, Mrs. Camberley two doors down has a Doberman pinscher. Ridiculous thing." Shadow was not certain whether the ridiculous thing was Mrs. Camberley or her dog.

He found the events of the previous night less troubling and odd, more explicable. What did it matter if a strange dog had followed them home? Oliver had been frightened or startled, and had collapsed, from narcolepsy, from shock.

"Well, I'll pack you some lunch before you go," said Moira. "Boiled eggs. That sort of thing. You'll be glad of them on the way."

They went into the house. Moira went to put something away, and returned looking shaken.

"Oliver's locked himself in the bathroom," she said.

Shadow was not certain what to say.

"You know what I wish?" she continued.

"I don't."

"I wish you would talk to him. I wish he would open the door. I wish he'd talk to me. I can hear him in there. I can hear him."

And then, "I hope he isn't cutting himself again."

Shadow walked back into the hall, stood by the bathroom door, called Oliver's name. "Can you hear me? Are you okay?"

Nothing. No sound from inside.

Shadow looked at the door. It was solid wood. The house was old, and they built them strong and well back then. When Shadow had used the bathroom that morning he'd seen the lock was a hook and eye. He leaned on the handle of the door, pushing it down, then rammed his shoulder against the door. It opened with a noise of splintering wood.

He had watched a man die in prison, stabbed in a pointless argument. He remembered the way that the blood had puddled about the man's body, lying in the back corner of the exercise yard. The sight had troubled Shadow, but he had forced himself to look, and to keep looking. To look away would somehow have felt disrespectful.

Oliver was naked on the floor of the bathroom. His body was pale, and his chest and groin were covered with thick, dark hair. He held the blade from an ancient safety razor in his hands. He had sliced his arms with it, his chest above the nipples, his inner thighs and his penis. Blood was smeared on his body, on the black and white linoleum floor, on the white enamel of the bathtub. Oliver's eyes were round and wide, like the eyes of a bird. He was looking directly at Shadow, but Shadow was not certain that he was being seen.

"Ollie?" said Moira's voice, from the hall. Shadow realized that he was blocking the doorway and he hesitated, unsure whether to let her see what was on the floor or not.

Shadow took a pink towel from the towel rail and wrapped it around Oliver. That got the little man's attention. He blinked, as if seeing Shadow for the first time, and said, "The dog. It's for the dog. It must be fed, you see. We're making friends."

Moira said, "Oh my dear sweet god."

"I'll call the emergency services."

"Please don't," she said. "He'll be fine at home with me. I don't know what I'll . . . please?"

Shadow picked up Oliver, swaddled in the towel; carried him into the bedroom as if he were a child; and then placed him on the bed. Moira followed. She picked up an iPad by the bed, touched the screen, and music began to play. "Breathe, Ollie," she said. "Remember. Breathe. It's going to be fine. You're going to be fine."

"I can't really breathe," said Oliver, in a small voice. "Not really. I can feel my heart, though. I can feel my heart beating."

Moira squeezed his hand and sat down on the bed, and Shadow left them alone.

When Moira entered the kitchen, her sleeves rolled up, and her hands smelling of antiseptic cream, Shadow was sitting on the sofa, reading a guide to local walks.

"How's he doing?"

She shrugged.

"You have to get him help."

"Yes." She stood in the middle of the kitchen and looked about her, as if unable to decide which way to turn. "Do you . . . I mean, do you have to leave today? Are you on a schedule?"

"Nobody's waiting for me. Anywhere."

She looked at him with a face that had grown haggard in an hour. "When this happened before, it took a few days, but then he was right as rain. The depression doesn't stay long. So, just wondering, would you just, well, stick around? I phoned my sister but she's in the middle of moving. And I can't cope on my own. I really can't. Not again. But I can't ask you to stay, not if anyone is waiting for you."

"Nobody's waiting," repeated Shadow. "And I'll stick around. But I think Oliver needs specialist help."

"Yes," agreed Moira. "He does."

Dr. Scathelocke came over late that afternoon. He was a friend of Oliver and Moira's. Shadow was not entirely certain whether rural British doctors still made house calls, or whether this was a socially justified visit. The doctor went into the bedroom, and came out twenty minutes later.

He sat at the kitchen table with Moira, and he said, "It's all very shallow. Cry-for-help stuff. Honestly, there's not a lot we can do for him in hospital that you can't do for him here, what with the cuts. We used to have a dozen nurses in that wing. Now they're trying to close it down completely. Get it all back to the community." Dr. Scathelocke had sandy hair, was as tall as Shadow but lankier. He reminded Shadow of the landlord in the pub, and he wondered idly if the two men were related. The doctor scribbled several prescriptions, and Moira handed them to Shadow, along with the keys to an old white Range Rover.

Shadow drove to the next village, found the little chemists' and waited for the prescriptions to be filled. He stood awkwardly in the overlit aisle, staring at a display of suntan lotions and creams, sadly redundant in this cold wet summer.

"You're Mr. American," said a woman's voice from behind him. He turned. She had short dark hair and was wearing the same olive-green sweater she had been wearing in the pub.

"I guess I am," he said.

"Local gossip says that you are helping out while Ollie's under the weather."

"That was fast."

"Local gossip travels faster than light. I'm Cassie Burglass."

"Shadow Moon."

"Good name," she said. "Gives me chills." She smiled. "If you're still rambling while you're here, I suggest you check out the hill just past the village. Follow the track up until it forks, and then go left. It takes you up Wod's Hill. Spectacular views. Public right of way. Just keep going left and up, you can't miss it."

She smiled at him. Perhaps she was just being friendly to a stranger.

"I'm not surprised you're still here though," Cassie continued. "It's hard to leave this place once it gets its claws into you." She smiled again, a warm smile, and she looked directly into his eyes, as if trying to make up her mind. "I think Mrs. Patel has your prescriptions ready. Nice talking to you, Mr. American."

IV: THE KISS

Shadow helped Moira. He walked down to the village shop and bought the items on her shopping list while she stayed in the house, writing at the kitchen table or hovering in the hallway outside the bedroom door. Moira barely talked. He ran errands in the white Range Rover, and saw Oliver mostly in the hall, shuffling to the bathroom and back. The man did not speak to him.

Everything was quiet in the house: Shadow imagined the black dog squatting on the roof, cutting out all sunlight, all emotion, all feeling and truth. Something had turned down the volume in that house, pushed all the colors into black and white. He wished he was somewhere else, but could not run out on them. He sat on his bed, and stared out of the window at the rain puddling its way down the windowpane, and felt the seconds of his life counting off, never to come back.

It had been wet and cold, but on the third day the sun came out. The world did not warm up, but Shadow tried to pull himself out of the gray haze, and decided to see some of the local sights. He walked to the next village, through fields, up paths and along the side of a long drystone wall. There was a bridge over a narrow stream that was little more than a plank, and Shadow jumped the water in one easy bound. Up the hill: there were trees, oak and hawthorn, sycamore and beech at the bottom of the hill, and then the trees became sparser. He followed the winding trail, sometimes obvious, sometimes not, until he reached a natural resting place, like a tiny meadow, high on the hill, and there he turned away from the hill and saw the valleys and the peaks arranged all about him in greens and grays like illustrations from a children's book.

He was not alone up there. A woman with short dark hair was sitting and sketching on the hill's side, perched comfortably on a gray boulder. There was a tree behind her, which acted as a windbreak. She wore a green sweater and blue jeans, and he recognized Cassie Burglass before he saw her face.

As he got close, she turned. "What do you think?" she asked, holding her sketchbook up for his inspection. It was an assured pencil drawing of the hillside.

"You're very good. Are you a professional artist?"

"I dabble," she said.

Shadow had spent enough time talking to the English to know that this meant either that she dabbled, or that her work was regularly hung in the National Gallery or the Tate Modern.

"You must be cold," he said. "You're only wearing a sweater."

"I'm cold," she said. "But, up here, I'm used to it. It doesn't really bother me. How's Ollie doing?"

"He's still under the weather," Shadow told her.

"Poor old sod," she said, looking from her paper to the hillside and back. "It's hard for me to feel properly sorry for him, though."

"Why's that? Did he bore you to death with interesting facts?"

She laughed, a small huff of air at the back of her throat. "You really ought to listen to more village gossip. When Ollie and Moira met, they were both with other people."

"I know that. They told me that." Shadow thought a moment. "So he was with you first?"

"No. *She* was. We'd been together since college." There was a pause. She shaded something, her pencil scraping the paper. "Are you going to try and kiss me?" she asked.

"I, uh. I, um," he said. Then, honestly, "It hadn't occurred to me."

"Well," she said, turning to smile at him, "it bloody well should. I mean, I asked you up here, and you came, up to Wod's Hill, just to see me." She went back to the paper and the drawing of the hill. "They say there's dark doings been done on this hill. Dirty dark doings. And I was thinking of doing something dirty myself. To Moira's lodger."

"Is this some kind of revenge plot?"

"It's not an anything plot. I just like you. And there's no one around here who wants me any longer. Not as a woman."

The last woman that Shadow had kissed had been in Scotland. He thought of her, and what she had become, in the end. "You *are* real, aren't you?" he asked. "I mean . . . you're a real person. I mean . . ."

She put the pad of paper down on the boulder and she stood up. "Kiss me and find out," she said.

He hesitated. She sighed, and she kissed him.

It was cold on that hillside, and Cassie's lips were cold. Her mouth was very soft. As her tongue touched his, Shadow pulled back.

"I don't actually know you," Shadow said.

She leaned away from him, looked up into his face. "You know," she said, "all I dream of these days is somebody who will look my way and see the real me. I had given up until you came along, Mr. American, with your funny name. But you looked at me, and I knew you saw me. And that's all that matters."

Shadow's hands held her, feeling the softness of her sweater.

"How much longer are you going to be here? In the district?" she asked.

"A few more days. Until Oliver's feeling better."

"Pity. Can't you stay forever?"

"I'm sorry?"

"You have nothing to be sorry for, sweet man. You see that opening over there?"

He glanced over to the hillside, but could not see what she was pointing at. The hillside was a tangle of weeds and low trees and half-tumbled drystone walls. She pointed to her drawing, where she had drawn a dark shape, like an archway, in the middle of clump of gorse bushes on the side of the hill. "There. Look." He stared, and this time he saw it immediately.

"What is it?" Shadow asked.

"The Gateway to Hell," she told him, impressively.

"Uh-huh."

She grinned. "That's what they call it round here. It was originally a Roman temple, I think, or something even older. But that's all that remains. You should check it out, if you like that sort of thing. Although it's a bit disappointing: just a little passageway going back into the hill. I keep expecting some archaeologists will come out this way, dig it up, catalog what they find, but they never do."

Shadow examined her drawing. "So what do you know about big black dogs?" he asked.

"The one in Shuck's Lane?" she said. He nodded. "They say the barghest used to wander all around here. But now it's just in Shuck's Lane. Dr. Scathelocke once told me it was folk memory. The Wish Hounds are all that are left of the Wild Hunt, which was based around the idea of Odin's hunting wolves, Freki and Geri. I think it's even older than that. Cave memory. Druids. The thing that prowls in the darkness beyond the fire circle, waiting to tear you apart if you edge too far out alone."

"Have you ever seen it, then?"

She shook her head. "No. I researched it, but never saw it. My semi-imaginary local beast. Have you?"

"I don't think so. Maybe."

"Perhaps you woke it up when you came here. You woke me up, after all."

She reached up, pulled his head down towards her and kissed him again. She took his left hand, so much bigger than hers, and placed it beneath her sweater.

"Cassie, my hands are cold," he warned her.

"Well, my everything is cold. There's nothing *but* cold up here. Just smile and look like you know what you're doing," she told him. She pushed

Shadow's left hand higher, until it was cupping the lace of her bra, and he could feel, beneath the lace, the hardness of her nipple and the soft swell of her breast.

He began to surrender to the moment, his hesitation a mixture of awkwardness and uncertainty. He was not sure how he felt about this woman: she had history with his benefactors, after all. Shadow never liked feeling that he was being used; it had happened too many times before. But his left hand was touching her breast and his right hand was cradling the nape of her neck, and he was leaning down and now her mouth was on his, and she was clinging to him as tightly as if, he thought, she wanted to occupy the very same space that he was in. Her mouth tasted like mint and stone and grass and the chilly afternoon breeze. He closed his eyes, and let himself enjoy the kiss and the way their bodies moved together.

Cassie froze. Somewhere close to them, a cat mewed. Shadow opened his eyes.

"Jesus," he said.

They were surrounded by cats. White cats and tabbies, brown and ginger and black cats, long-haired and short. Well-fed cats with collars and disreputable ragged-eared cats that looked as if they had been living in barns and on the edges of the wild. They stared at Shadow and Cassie with green eyes and blue eyes and golden eyes, and they did not move. Only the occasional swish of a tail or the blinking of a pair of feline eyes told Shadow that they were alive.

"This is weird," said Shadow.

Cassie took a step back. He was no longer touching her now. "Are they with you?" she asked.

"I don't think they're with anyone. They're cats."

"I think they're jealous," said Cassie. "Look at them. They don't like me."

"That's . . ." Shadow was going to say "nonsense," but no, it was sense, of a kind. There had been a woman who was a goddess, a continent away and years in his past, who had cared about him, in her own way. He remembered the needle-sharpness of her nails and the catlike roughness of her tongue.

Cassie looked at Shadow dispassionately. "I don't know who you are, Mr. American," she told him. "Not really. I don't know why you can look at me and see the real me, or why I can talk to you when I find it so hard to talk to other people. But I can. And you know, you seem all normal and quiet on the surface, but you are so much weirder than I am. And I'm extremely fucking weird."

Shadow said, "Don't go."

"Tell Ollie and Moira you saw me," she said. "Tell them I'll be waiting where we last spoke, if they have anything they want to say to me." She picked up her sketchpad and pencils, and she walked off briskly, stepping carefully through the cats, who did not even glance at her, just kept their gazes fixed on Shadow, as she moved away through the swaying grasses and the blowing twigs.

Shadow wanted to call after her, but instead he crouched down and looked back at the cats. "What's going on?" he asked. "Bast? Are you doing this? You're a long way from home. And why would you still care who I kiss?"

The spell was broken when he spoke. The cats began to move, to look away, to stand, to wash themselves intently.

A tortoiseshell cat pushed her head against his hand, insistently, needing attention. Shadow stroked her absently, rubbing his knuckles against her forehead.

She swiped blinding-fast with claws like tiny scimitars, and drew blood from his forearm. Then she purred, and turned, and within moments the whole kit and caboodle of them had vanished into the hillside, slipping behind rocks and into the undergrowth, and were gone.

V: The Living and the Dead

Oliver was out of his room when Shadow got back to the house, sitting in the warm kitchen, a mug of tea by his side, reading a book on Roman architecture. He was dressed, and he had shaved his chin and trimmed his beard. He was wearing pajamas, with a plaid bathrobe over them.

"I'm feeling a bit better," he said, when he saw Shadow. Then, "Have you ever had this? Been depressed?"

"Looking back on it, I guess I did. When my wife died," said Shadow. "Everything went flat. Nothing meant anything for a long time."

Oliver nodded. "It's hard. Sometimes I think the black dog is a real thing. I lie in bed thinking about the painting of Fuseli's nightmare on a sleeper's chest. Like Anubis. Or do I mean Set? Big black thing. What was Set anyway? Some kind of donkey?"

"I never ran into Set," said Shadow. "He was before my time."

Oliver laughed. "Very dry. And they say you Americans don't do irony." He paused. "Anyway. All done now. Back on my feet. Ready to face the world." He sipped his tea. "Feeling a bit embarrassed. All that Hound of the Baskervilles nonsense behind me now."

"You really have nothing to be embarrassed about," said Shadow, reflecting that the English found embarrassment wherever they looked for it.

"Well. All a bit silly, one way or another. And I really am feeling much perkier."

Shadow nodded. "If you're feeling better, I guess I should start heading south."

"No hurry," said Oliver. "It's always nice to have company. Moira and I don't really get out as much as we'd like. It's mostly just a walk up to the pub. Not much excitement here, I'm afraid."

Moira came in from the garden. "Anyone seen the secateurs? I know I had them. Forget my own head next."

Shadow shook his head, uncertain what secateurs were. He thought of telling the couple about the cats on the hill, and how they had behaved, but could not think of a way to describe it that would explain how odd it was. So, instead, without thinking, he said, "I ran into Cassie Burglass on Wod's Hill. She pointed out the Gateway to Hell."

They were staring at him. The kitchen had become awkwardly quiet. He said, "She was drawing it."

Oliver looked at him and said, "I don't understand."

"I've run into her a couple of times since I got here," said Shadow.

"What?" Moira's face was flushed. "What are you saying?" And then, "Who the, who the *fuck* are you to come in here and say things like that?"

"I'm, I'm nobody," said Shadow. "She just started talking to me. She said that you and she used to be together."

Moira looked as if she were going to hit him. Then she just said, "She moved away after we broke up. It wasn't a good breakup. She was very hurt. She behaved appallingly. Then she just up and left the village in the night. Never came back."

"I don't want to talk about that woman," said Oliver, quietly. "Not now. Not ever."

"Look. She was in the pub with us," pointed out Shadow. "That first night. You guys didn't seem to have a problem with her then."

Moira just stared at him and did not respond, as if he had said something in a tongue she did not speak. Oliver rubbed his forehead with his hand. "I didn't see her," was all he said.

"Well, she said to say hi when I saw her today," said Shadow. "She said she'd be waiting, if either of you had anything you wanted to say to her."

"We have nothing to say to her. Nothing at all." Moira's eyes were wet, but she was not crying. "I can't believe that, that *fucking* woman has come back into our lives, after all she put us through." Moira swore like someone who was not very good at it.

Oliver put down his book. "I'm sorry," he said. "I don't feel very well." He walked out, back to the bedroom, and closed the door behind him.

Moira picked up Oliver's mug, almost automatically, and took it over to the sink, emptied it out and began to wash it.

"I hope you're pleased with yourself," she said, rubbing the mug with a white plastic scrubbing brush as if she were trying to scrub the picture of Beatrix Potter's cottage from the china. "He was coming back to himself again."

"I didn't know it would upset him like that," said Shadow. He felt guilty as he said it. He had known there was history between Cassie and his hosts. He could have said nothing, after all. Silence was always safer.

Moira dried the mug with a green and white tea towel. The white patches of the towel were comical sheep, the green were grass. She bit her lower lip, and the tears that had been brimming in her eyes now ran down her cheeks. Then, "Did she say anything about me?"

"Just that you two used to be an item."

Moira nodded, and wiped the tears from her young-old face with the comical tea towel. "She couldn't bear it when Ollie and I got together. After I moved out, she just hung up her paintbrushes and locked the flat and went to London." She blew her nose vigorously. "Still. Mustn't grumble. We make our own beds. And Ollie's a *good* man. There's just a black dog in his mind. My mother had depression. It's hard."

Shadow said, "I've made everything worse. I should go."

"Don't leave until tomorrow. I'm not throwing you out, dear. It's not your fault you ran into that woman, is it?" Her shoulders were slumped. "There they are. On top of the fridge." She picked up something that looked like a very small pair of garden shears. "Secateurs," she explained. "For the rosebushes, mostly."

"Are you going to talk to him?"

"No," she said. "Conversations with Ollie about Cassie never end well. And in this state, it could plunge him even further back into a bad place. I'll just let him get over it."

Shadow ate alone in the pub that night, while the cat in the glass case glowered at him. He saw no one he knew. He had a brief conversation with the landlord about how he was enjoying his time in the village. He walked back to Moira's house after the pub, past the old sycamore, the gibbet tree, down Shuck's Lane. He saw nothing moving in the fields in the moonlight: no dog, no donkey.

All the lights in the house were out. He went to his bedroom as quietly as he could, packed the last of his possessions into his backpack before he went to sleep. He would leave early, he knew.

He lay in bed, watching the moonlight in the box room. He remembered standing in the pub, and Cassie Burglass standing beside him. He thought about his conversation with the landlord, and the conversation that first night, and the cat in the glass box, and, as he pondered, any desire to sleep evaporated. He was perfectly wide awake in the small bed.

Shadow could move quietly when he needed to. He slipped out of bed, pulled on his clothes and then, carrying his boots, he opened the window, reached over the sill and let himself tumble silently into the soil of the flower bed beneath. He got to his feet and put on the boots, lacing them up in the half dark. The moon was several days from full, bright enough to cast shadows.

Shadow stepped into a patch of darkness beside a wall, and he waited there.

He wondered how sane his actions were. It seemed very probable that he was wrong, that his memory had played tricks on him, or other people's had. It was all so very unlikely, but then, he had experienced the unlikely before, and if he was wrong he would be out, what? A few hours' sleep?

He watched a fox hurry across the lawn, watched a proud white cat stalk and kill a small rodent, and watched several other cats pad their way along the top of the garden wall. He watched a weasel slink from shadow to shadow in the flower bed. The constellations moved in slow procession across the sky.

The front door opened, and a figure came out. Shadow had half-expected to see Moira, but it was Oliver, wearing his pajamas and, over them, a thick tartan dressing gown. He had Wellington boots on his feet, and he looked faintly ridiculous, like an invalid from a black and white movie, or someone in a play. There was no color in the moonlit world.

Oliver pulled the front door closed until it clicked, then he walked towards the street, but walking on the grass, instead of crunching down the gravel path. He did not glance back, or even look around. He set off up the lane, and Shadow waited until Oliver was almost out of sight before he began to follow. He knew where Oliver was going, had to be going.

Shadow did not question himself, not any longer. He knew where they were both headed, with the certainty of a person in a dream. He was not even surprised when, halfway up Wod's Hill, he found Oliver sitting on a tree stump, waiting for him. The sky was lightening, just a little, in the east.

"The Gateway to Hell," said the little man. "As far as I can tell, they've always called it that. Goes back years and years."

The two men walked up the winding path together. There was something gloriously comical about Oliver in his robe, in his striped pajamas and his oversized black rubber boots. Shadow's heart pumped in his chest.

"How did you bring her up here?" asked Shadow.

"Cassie? I didn't. It was her idea to meet up here on the hill. She loved coming up here to paint. You can see so far. And it's holy, this hill, and she always loved that. Not holy to Christians, of course. Quite the obverse. The old religion."

"Druids?" asked Shadow. He was uncertain what other old religions there were, in England.

"Could be. Definitely could be. But I think it predates the druids. Doesn't have much of a name. It's just what people in these parts practice, beneath whatever else they believe. Druids, Norse, Catholics, Protestants, doesn't matter. That's what people pay lip service to. The old religion is what gets the crops up and keeps your cock hard and makes sure that nobody builds a bloody great motorway through an area of outstanding natural beauty. The Gateway stands, and the hill stands, and the place stands. It's well, well over two thousand years old. You don't go mucking about with anything that powerful."

Shadow said, "Moira doesn't know, does she? She thinks Cassie moved away." The sky was continuing to lighten in the east, but it was still night, spangled with a glitter of stars, in the purple-black sky to the west.

"That was what she *needed* to think. I mean, what else was she going to think? It might have been different if the police had been interested . . . but it wasn't like . . . Well. It protects itself. The hill. The gate."

They were coming up to the little meadow on the side of the hill. They passed the boulder where Shadow had seen Cassie drawing. They walked toward the hill.

"The black dog in Shuck's Lane," said Oliver. "I don't actually think it is a dog. But it's been there so long." He pulled out a small LED flashlight from the pocket of his bathrobe. "You really talked to Cassie?"

"We talked, I even kissed her."

"Strange."

"I first saw her in the pub, the night I met you and Moira. That was what made me start to figure it out. Earlier tonight, Moira was talking as if she hadn't seen Cassie in years. She was baffled when I asked. But Cassie was standing just behind me that first night, and she spoke to us. Tonight, I asked at the pub if Cassie had been in, and nobody knew who I was talking about. You people all know each other. It was the only thing that made sense of it all. It made sense of what she said. Everything."

Oliver was almost at the place Cassie had called the Gateway to Hell. "I thought that it would be so simple. I would give her to the hill, and she would leave us both alone. Leave Moira alone. How could she have kissed you?"

Shadow said nothing.

"This is it," said Oliver. It was a hollow in the side of the hill, like a short hallway that went back. Perhaps, once, long ago, there had been a structure, but the hill had weathered, and the stones had returned to the hill from which they had been taken.

"There are those who think it's devil worship," said Oliver. "And I think they are wrong. But then, one man's god is another's devil. Eh?"

He walked into the passageway, and Shadow followed him.

"Such bullshit," said a woman's voice. "But you always were a bullshitter, Ollie, you pusillanimous little cock-stain."

Oliver did not move or react. He said, "She's here. In the wall. That's where I left her." He shone the flashlight at the wall, in the short passageway into the side of the hill. He inspected the drystone wall carefully, as if he were looking for a place he recognized, then he made a little grunting noise of recognition. Oliver took out a compact metal tool from his pocket, reached as high as he could and levered out one little rock with it. Then he began to pull rocks out from the wall, in a set sequence, each rock opening a space to allow another to be removed, alternating large rocks and small.

"Give me a hand. Come on."

Shadow knew what he was going to see behind the wall, but he pulled out the rocks, placed them down on the ground, one by one.

There was a smell, which intensified as the hole grew bigger, a stink of old rot and mold. It smelled like meat sandwiches gone bad. Shadow saw her face first, and he barely knew it as a face: the cheeks were sunken, the eyes gone, the skin now dark and leathery, and if there were freckles they were impossible to make out; but the hair was Cassie Burglass's hair, short and black, and in the LED light, he could see that the dead thing wore an olive-green sweater, and the blue jeans were her blue jeans.

"It's funny. I knew she was still here," said Oliver. "But I still had to see her. With all your talk. I had to see it. To prove she was still here."

"Kill him," said the woman's voice. "Hit him with a rock, Shadow. He killed me. Now he's going to kill you."

"Are you going to kill me?" Shadow asked.

"Well, yes, obviously," said the little man, in his sensible voice. "I mean, you know about Cassie. And once you're gone, I can just finally forget about the whole thing, once and for all."

"Forget?"

"Forgive *and* forget. But it's hard. It's not easy to forgive myself, but I'm sure I can forget. There. I think there's enough room for you to get in there now, if you squeeze."

Shadow looked down at the little man. "Out of interest," he said, curious, "how are you going to make me get in there? You don't have a gun on you. And, Ollie, I'm twice your size. You know, I could just break your neck."

"I'm not a stupid man," said Oliver. "I'm not a bad man, either. I'm not a terribly well man, but that's neither here nor there, really. I mean, I did what I did because I was jealous, not because I was ill. But I wouldn't have come up here alone. You see, this is the temple of the Black Dog. These places were the first temples. Before the stone henges and the standing stones, they were waiting and they were worshipped, and sacrificed to, and feared, and placated. The black shucks and the barghests, the padfoots and the wish hounds. They were here and they remain on guard."

"Hit him with a rock," said Cassie's voice. "Hit him now, Shadow, *please*."

The passage they stood in went a little way into the hillside, a man-made cave with drystone walls. It did not look like an ancient temple. It did not look like a gateway to hell. The predawn sky framed Oliver. In his gentle, unfailingly polite voice, he said, "He is in me. And I am in him."

The black dog filled the doorway, blocking the way to the world outside, and, Shadow knew, whatever it was, it was no true dog. Its eyes actually glowed, with a luminescence that reminded Shadow of rotting sea-creatures. It was to a wolf, in scale and in menace, what a tiger is to a lynx: pure carnivore, a creature made of danger and threat. It stood taller than Oliver and it stared at Shadow, and it growled, a rumbling deep in its chest. Then it sprang.

Shadow raised his arm to protect his throat, and the creature sank its teeth into his flesh, just below the elbow. The pain was excruciating. He knew he should fight back, but he was falling to his knees, and he was screaming, unable to think clearly, unable to focus on anything except his fear that the creature was going to use him for food, fear it was crushing the bone of his forearm.

On some deep level he suspected that the fear was being created by the dog: that he, Shadow, was not cripplingly afraid like that. Not really. But it did not matter. When the creature released Shadow's arm, he was weeping and his whole body was shaking.

Oliver said, "Get in there, Shadow. Through the gap in the wall. Quickly, now. Or I'll have him chew off your face."

Shadow's arm was bleeding, but he got up and squeezed through the gap into the darkness without arguing. If he stayed out there, with the beast, he would die soon, and die in pain. He knew that with as much certainty as he knew that the sun would rise tomorrow.

"Well, yes," said Cassie's voice in his head. "It's going to rise. But unless you get your shit together you are never going to see it."

There was barely space for him and Cassie's body in the cavity behind the wall. He had seen the expression of pain and fury on her face, like the face of the cat in the glass box, and then he knew she, too, had been entombed here while alive.

Oliver picked up a rock from the ground, and placed it onto the wall, in the gap. "My own theory," he said, hefting a second rock and putting it into position, "is that it is the prehistoric dire wolf. But it is bigger than ever the dire wolf was. Perhaps it is the monster of our dreams, when we huddled in caves. Perhaps it was simply a wolf, but we were smaller, little hominids, who could never run fast enough to get away."

Shadow leaned against the rock face behind him. He squeezed his left arm with his right hand to try to stop the bleeding. "This is Wod's Hill," said Shadow. "And that's Wod's dog. I wouldn't put it past him."

"It doesn't matter." More stones were placed on stones.

"Ollie," said Shadow. "The beast is going to kill you. It's already inside you. It's not a good thing."

"Old Shuck's not going to hurt me. Old Shuck loves me. Cassie's in the wall," said Oliver, and he dropped a rock on top of the others with a crash. "Now you are in the wall with her. Nobody's waiting for you. Nobody's going to come looking for you. Nobody is going to cry for you. Nobody's going to miss you."

There were, Shadow knew, although he could never have told a soul how he knew, three of them, not two, in that tiny space. There was Cassie Burglass, there in body (rotted and dried and still stinking of decay) and there in soul, and there was also something else, something that twined about his legs, and then butted gently at his injured hand. A voice spoke to him, from somewhere close. He knew that voice, although the accent was unfamiliar.

It was the voice that a cat would speak in, if a cat were a woman: expressive, dark, musical. The voice said, *You should not be here, Shadow. You have to stop, and you must take action. You are letting the rest of the world make your decisions for you.*

Shadow said aloud, "That's not entirely fair, Bast."

"You have to be quiet," said Oliver, gently. "I mean it." The stones of the wall were being replaced rapidly and efficiently. Already they were up to Shadow's chest.

Mrr. No? Sweet thing, you really have no idea. No idea who you are or what you are or what that means. If he walls you up in here to die in this hill, this temple will stand forever—and whatever hodgepodge of belief these locals have will work for them and will make magic. But the sun will still go down on them, and all the skies will be gray. All things will mourn, and they will not know what they are mourning for. The world will be worse—for people, for cats, for the remembered, for the forgotten. You have died and you have returned. You matter, Shadow, and you must not meet your death here, a sad sacrifice hidden in a hillside.

"So what are you suggesting I do?" he whispered.

Fight. The Beast is a thing of mind. It's taking its power from you, Shadow. You are near, and so it's become more real. Real enough to own Oliver. Real enough to hurt you.

"Me?"

"You think ghosts can talk to everyone?" asked Cassie Burglass's voice in the darkness, urgently. "We are moths. And you are the flame."

"What should I do?" asked Shadow. "It hurt my arm. It damn near ripped out my throat."

Oh, sweet man. It's just a shadow-thing. It's a night-dog. It's just an overgrown jackal.

"It's real," Shadow said. The last of the stones was being banged into place.

"Are you truly scared of your father's dog?" said a woman's voice. Goddess or ghost, Shadow did not know.

But he knew the answer. Yes. Yes, he was scared.

His left arm was only pain, and unusable, and his right hand was slick and sticky with his blood. He was entombed in a cavity between a wall and rock. But he was, for now, alive.

"Get your shit together," said Cassie. "I've done everything I can. Do it."

He braced himself against the rocks behind the wall, and he raised his feet. Then he kicked both his booted feet out together, as hard as he could. He had walked so many miles in the last few months. He was a big man, and he was stronger than most. He put everything he had behind that kick.

The wall exploded.

The Beast was on him, the black dog of despair, but this time Shadow was prepared for it. This time he was the aggressor. He grabbed at it.

I will not be my father's dog.

With his right hand he held the beast's jaw closed. He stared into its green eyes. He did not believe the beast was a dog at all, not really.

It's daylight, said Shadow to the dog, with his mind, not with his voice. *Run away. Whatever you are, run away. Run back to your gibbet, run back to your grave, little wish hound. All you can do is depress us, fill the world with shadows and illusions. The age when you ran with the Wild Hunt, or hunted terrified humans, it's over. I don't know if you're my father's dog or not. But you know what? I don't care.*

With that, Shadow took a deep breath and let go of the dog's muzzle.

It did not attack. It made a noise, a baffled whine deep in its throat that was almost a whimper.

"Go home," said Shadow, aloud.

The dog hesitated. Shadow thought for a moment then that he had won, that he was safe, that the dog would simply go away. But then the creature lowered its head, raised the ruff around its neck, and bared its teeth. It would not leave, Shadow knew, until he was dead.

The corridor in the hillside was filling with light: the rising sun shone directly into it. Shadow wondered if the people who had built it, so long ago, had aligned their temple to the sunrise. He took a step to the side, stumbled on something, and fell awkwardly to the ground.

Beside Shadow on the ground was Oliver, sprawled and unconscious. Shadow had tripped over his leg. The man's eyes were closed; he made a growling sound in the back of his throat, and Shadow heard the same sound, magnified and triumphant, from the dark beast that filled the mouth of the temple.

Shadow was down, and hurt, and was, he knew, a dead man.

Something soft touched his face, gently.

Something else brushed his hand. Shadow glanced to his side, and he understood. He understood why Bast had been with him in this place, and he understood who had brought her.

They had been ground up and sprinkled on these fields more than a hundred years before, stolen from the earth around the temple of Bastet and Beni Hasan. Tons upon tons of them, mummified cats in their thousands, each cat a tiny representation of the deity, each cat an act of worship preserved for an eternity.

They were there, in that space, beside him: brown and sand-colored and shadowy gray, cats with leopard spots and cats with tiger stripes, wild, lithe and ancient. These were not the local cats Bast had sent to watch him the previous day. These were the ancestors of those cats, of all our modern cats, from Egypt, from the Nile Delta, from thousands of years ago, brought here to make things grow.

They trilled and chirruped, they did not meow.

The black dog growled louder but now it made no move to attack. Shadow forced himself into a sitting position. "I thought I told you to go home, Shuck," he said.

The dog did not move. Shadow opened his right hand, and gestured. It was a gesture of dismissal, of impatience. *Finish this.*

The cats sprang, with ease, as if choreographed. They landed on the beast, each of them a coiled spring of fangs and claws, both as sharp as they had ever been in life. Pin-sharp claws sank into the black flanks of the huge beast, tore at its eyes. It snapped at them, angrily, and pushed itself against the wall, toppling more rocks, in an attempt to shake them off, but without success. Angry teeth sank into its ears, its muzzle, its tail, its paws.

The beast yelped and growled, and then it made a noise which, Shadow thought, would, had it come from any human throat, have been a scream.

Shadow was never certain what happened then. He watched the black dog put its muzzle down to Oliver's mouth, and push, hard. He could have sworn that the creature stepped *into* Oliver, like a bear stepping into a river.

Oliver shook, violently, on the sand.

The scream faded, and the beast was gone, and sunlight filled the space on the hill.

Shadow felt himself shivering. He felt like he had just woken up from a waking sleep; emotions flooded through him, like sunlight: fear and revulsion and grief and hurt, deep hurt.

There was anger in there, too. Oliver had tried to kill him, he knew, and he was thinking clearly for the first time in days.

A man's voice shouted, "Hold up! Everyone all right over there?"

A high bark, and a lurcher ran in, sniffed at Shadow, his back against the wall, sniffed at Oliver Bierce, unconscious on the ground, and at the remains of Cassie Burglass.

A man's silhouette filled the opening to the outside world, a gray paper cutout against the rising sun.

"Needles! Leave it!" he said. The dog returned to the man's side. The man said, "I heard someone screaming. Leastways, I wouldn't swear to it being a someone. But I heard it. Was that you?"

And then he saw the body, and he stopped. "Holy fucking mother of all fucking bastards," he said.

"Her name was Cassie Burglass," said Shadow.

"Moira's old girlfriend?" said the man. Shadow knew him as the landlord of the pub, could not remember whether he had ever known the man's name. "Bloody Nora. I thought she went to London."

Shadow felt sick.

The landlord was kneeling beside Oliver. "His heart's still beating," he said. "What happened to him?"

"I'm not sure," said Shadow. "He screamed when he saw the body—you must have heard him. Then he just went down. And your dog came in."

The man looked at Shadow, worried. "And you? Look at you! What happened to you, man?"

"Oliver asked me to come up here with him. Said he had something awful he had to get off his chest." Shadow looked at the wall on each side of the corridor. There were other bricked-in nooks there. Shadow had a good idea of what would be found behind them if any of them were opened. "He asked me to help him open the wall. I did. He knocked me over as he went down. Took me by surprise."

"Did he tell you why he had done it?"

"Jealousy," said Shadow. "Just jealous of Moira and Cassie, even after Moira had left Cassie for him."

The man exhaled, shook his head. "Bloody hell," he said. "Last bugger I'd expect to do anything like this. Needles! Leave it!" He pulled a cell phone from his pocket, and called the police. Then he excused himself. "I've got a bag of game to put aside until the police have cleared out," he explained.

Shadow got to his feet, and inspected his arms. His sweater and coat were both ripped in the left arm, as if by huge teeth, but his skin was unbroken beneath it. There was no blood on his clothes, no blood on his hands.

He wondered what his corpse would have looked like, if the black dog had killed him.

Cassie's ghost stood beside him, and looked down at her body, half-fallen from the hole in the wall. The corpse's fingertips and the fingernails were wrecked, Shadow observed, as if she had tried, in the hours or the days before she died, to dislodge the rocks of the wall.

"Look at that," she said, staring at herself. "Poor thing. Like a cat in a glass box." Then she turned to Shadow. "I didn't actually fancy you," she said. "Not even a little bit. I'm not sorry. I just needed to get your attention."

"I know," said Shadow. "I just wish I'd met you when you were alive. We could have been friends."

"I bet we would have been. It was hard in there. It's good to be done with all of this. And I'm sorry, Mr. American. Try not to hate me."

Shadow's eyes were watering. He wiped his eyes on his shirt. When he looked again, he was alone in the passageway.

"I don't hate you," he told her.

He felt a hand squeeze his hand. He walked outside, into the morning sunlight, and he breathed and shivered, and listened to the distant sirens.

Two men arrived and carried Oliver off on a stretcher, down the hill to the road, where an ambulance took him away, siren screaming to alert any sheep on the lanes that they should shuffle back to the grass verge.

A female police officer turned up as the ambulance disappeared, accompanied by a younger male officer. They knew the landlord, whom Shadow was not surprised to learn was also a Scathelocke, and were both impressed by Cassie's remains, to the point that the young male officer left the passageway and vomited into the ferns.

If it occurred to either of them to inspect the other bricked-in cavities in the corridor, for evidence of centuries-old crimes, they managed to suppress the idea, and Shadow was not going to suggest it.

He gave them a brief statement, then rode with them to the local police station, where he gave a fuller statement to a large police officer with a serious beard. The officer appeared mostly concerned that Shadow was provided with a mug of instant coffee, and that Shadow, as an American tourist, would form a mistaken impression of rural England. "It's not like this up here normally. It's really quiet. Lovely place. I wouldn't want you to think we were all like this."

Shadow assured him that he didn't think that at all.

VI: THE RIDDLE

Moira was waiting for him when he came out of the police station. She was standing with a woman in her early sixties, who looked comfortable and reassuring, the sort of person you would want at your side in a crisis.

"Shadow, this is Doreen. My sister."

Doreen shook hands, explaining she was sorry she hadn't been able to be there during the last week, but she had been moving house.

"Doreen's a county court judge," explained Moira.

Shadow could not easily imagine this woman as a judge.

"They are waiting for Ollie to come around," said Moira. "Then they are going to charge him with murder." She said it thoughtfully, but in the same way she would have asked Shadow where he thought she ought to plant some snapdragons.

"And what are you going to do?"

She scratched her nose. "I'm in shock. I have no idea what I'm doing anymore. I keep thinking about the last few years. Poor, poor Cassie. She never thought there was any malice in him."

"I never liked him," said Doreen, and she sniffed. "Too full of facts for my liking, and he never knew when to stop talking. Just kept wittering on. Like he was trying to cover something up."

"Your backpack and your laundry are in Doreen's car," said Moira. "I thought we could give you a lift somewhere, if you needed one. Or if you want to get back to rambling, you can walk."

"Thank you," said Shadow. He knew he would never be welcome in Moira's little house, not anymore.

Moira said, urgently, angrily, as if it was all she wanted to know, "You said you saw Cassie. You *told* us, yesterday. That was what sent Ollie off the deep end. It hurt me so much. Why did you say you'd seen her, if she was dead? You *couldn't* have seen her."

Shadow had been wondering about that, while he had been giving his police statement. "Beats me," he said. "I don't believe in ghosts. Probably a local, playing some kind of game with the Yankee tourist."

Moira looked at him with fierce hazel eyes, as if she was trying to believe him but was unable to make the final leap of faith. Her sister reached down and held her hand. "More things in heaven and earth, Horatio. I think we should just leave it at that."

Moira looked at Shadow, unbelieving, angered, for a long time, before she took a deep breath and said, "Yes. Yes, I suppose we should."

There was silence in the car. Shadow wanted to apologize to Moira, to say something that would make things better.

They drove past the gibbet tree.

"*There were ten tongues within one head,*" recited Doreen, in a voice slightly higher and more formal than the one in which she had previously spoken. "*And one went out to fetch some bread, to feed the living and the dead.* That was a riddle written about this corner, and that tree."

"What does it mean?"

"A wren made a nest inside the skull of a gibbeted corpse, flying in and out of the jaw to feed its young. In the midst of death, as it were, life just keeps on happening."

Shadow thought about the matter for a little while, and told her that he guessed that it probably did.

THE 21ST CENTURY SHADOW

STEPHANIE M. WYTOVICH

I was just a boy, an orphan, and there used to be an old woman who lived at the end of my street, who never left her house, who never spoke, who just sat on her porch in her rocking chair, sipping whiskey out of a coffee cup while she hacked and spit in the flower pots on the steps. She wore her gray hair in knots and her nails grew sharp, curved like silver fish hooks, and when she laughed, the air turned salty, cold like a brisk ocean spray. And I don't know what made me talk to her, curiosity, maybe fear, but I think it was the screaming, the screaming that leaked out her basement window, the pleading that lured me to her house. I stopped at the bottom of her porch, my sneakers worn and covered in mud, and I asked her if she needed help, if something was wrong, and she smiled and she smiled, and then she reached into a plastic bucket and pulled out a handful of shells, told me I could hear my mother's voice inside, that the dead lived in the echoes, that they were the voices of the sea.

—◦—

And I prayed that I would hear her,
prayed that she was there,
but all I heard was the old woman laughing,
laughing as the air grew cold
as the world around me turned black.

◄◦►

And it was the ocean that woke me, that reached out and shook me with frigid hands that waved back and forth beckoning me as they cleaned the blood off my hands, but the red kept coming, kept rolling down my neck and there were two slits, two rigid cuts underneath my ears and all I wanted was water, the salt and the sand, but the woman dug shells into my ears, glued starfish to my legs and they itched and they hurt as they dug beneath my skin, as they became new flesh to my soon-to-corpse, and I screamed but the woman ignored me. She chanted words I couldn't understand, words that weren't even real, words that sounded like gibberish, like the fairytale language that mother used to read, that she'd cry out in her sleep when it started to rain. But then I didn't hear anything. I was floating, floating out to sea, and it seemed like years until I heard the voice, the voice within the shells that wasn't my dead mother's but something different, something else, and it pulled me under, tugged me down into the blue. These Gods called me son, and they told me I would be the shadow, the shadow that would cross towns, that would steal children so they could rebuild, so they could resurrect, and they gave me new life, for I was their sweet baby boy.

◄◦►

So when I woke up in this town,
in this century that was not mine,
I smiled at the strange faces with my barbed teeth,
and my coral skin, and I walked until I found her,
drinking her coffee, drinking her whiskey
and I knew I was ready to collect, ready to plunder, for I spoke
her language now and it was my turn to deliver a corpse.

THIS STAGNANT BREATH OF CHANGE

BRIAN HODGE

Beasley had died three times within the last month alone. Each time, they'd brought him back, and each time, it got harder.

The first was a simple heart attack, which they'd fought off by jump-starting him with the defibrillator; later, balloon angioplasty.

That opened the door to human error. Beasley's vitals were normal, until, without warning, he flatlined. They'd traced that to a bag of potassium solution with too high a concentration, and got his pulse going again by shooting him up with insulin and glucose, along with intravenous calcium and inhalations of albuterol.

This last scare was the worst, a line infection that would've begun small, as they always did, then swamped him with tidal waves of bacteria before anyone realized what was happening. That was the insidious thing about line infections. Once one line was compromised, it was all but guaranteed to spread to the rest. And he was hooked up to so many.

They got him through the worst of it, and once it looked as if Donald Beasley would survive another day, they stood down. By now, his room here at Good Sam was an ICU unto itself.

And by now, the routine was familiar enough that Bethany knew what to expect once it was over: *Hello, adrenaline crash, my old friend. Hello, relief, you seductive lie.*

As she always did, once the crisis was averted, the inevitable pushed back a little farther, she retreated to the hall in her green scrubs to shake out the stress and peer out the nearest window to search the sky for signs. Retreating storm clouds, maybe, or a fading giant wisp of faces from years of bad dreams. There was no rational reason it had to be the sky, only that it seemed as good a source as any to unleash . . .

Well, whatever was going to happen the day they *couldn't* bring him back.

"How long can we keep this up?" Bethany asked the attending physician, who was prone to de-stressing in his own way.

Cavendish, his name, but most here just called him Doctor Richard. He puffed at a cigarette as if it were the only thing keeping him upright. He was one of those doctors who continued to smoke in spite of knowing every reason not to. It would never catch up with him. That was the problem. His, hers, and everyone else's.

"How much more can that withered old body of his take?"

"As much as we can force on it," Dr. Richard said. "I'll crack his chest open and crawl in there and stay if I have to."

"Heroics aside," she said. "Just be honest."

He'd been on staff here long enough to have treated her the summer she was eight, after she and her bicycle lost a minor altercation with a car. Today, he looked every year of it.

"If we're having this same conversation a month from now, I'll consider that a miracle." Richard chained another cig off the first. "Honest enough for you?"

A few hours later, when her shift was over, she dropped by Donald Beasley's room to reassure herself that she could leave with a clear conscience. Another post-crisis habit. Like driving past a leaky dam to make sure the cracks hadn't widened. One of the off-duty nurses was sitting in a chair by the bed, watching him. Somebody was always watching him.

The cycles of death and restoration had taken their toll. According to Beasley's charts, he was seventy-six now, but he looked at least a hundred.

He was still unconscious, but would come around again eventually, and she didn't want to be here when that happened. She'd done her time.

Beasley might talk jabbering nonsense. Then again, he might be cognizant of everything, and resume begging for them to let him die. Either option was its own brand of unnervingly awful. He would tug at the restraints holding his wrists to the bed rails, feeble and mewling, and somehow, his desiccated body would find enough moisture for tears. They lived in fear of him thinking to bite through his tongue in an effort to drown in his own blood.

The watch-nurse glanced back over one heavy, rounded shoulder and nodded a dead-eyed hello. They'd gone to high school together, sort of. Janet Swain had been a senior when Bethany had come in as an undersized freshman, no boobs to speak of, and invisible.

They'd all gone to high school together here in Tanner Falls.

"If we can't save him, and we know it, say he's got a little time left, just not long, what would you want to do?" Janet said. "Would you give him what he deserves?"

Bethany squeezed her eyes closed. "Don't ask me something like that."

"I would. I mean, why not? Last chance, why waste the opportunity? It's only what everybody in the whole town has wanted to do to him for years. If we announced it, there'd be a line ten thousand people long. We should raffle off chances while we still can."

"Is that really what you'd want to be thinking of at the end?"

"I'd start with his eyes. Somebody going for your eyes, that's some scary business, right there. I'd leave him one, though, so he could see what I do to the rest of him."

Talk. Bethany tried to dismiss it as empty talk, no risk. They all needed to vent sometimes.

"Even old men are still attached to their ding-dongs." Janet smacked her hand on the bed rail and addressed Beasley directly. "You think that catheter was painful going in, you old buzzard? You have no idea."

If they got it out of their systems this way, maybe it would be enough, and they wouldn't lose control over the urge to act.

"And yeah, that *is* what I'll be thinking of at the end." Janet said this with a glare, almost an accusation. "That's the kind of thing you get to think of when you don't have anybody, and know you never will."

She made companionship sound like a comfort she was denied, but really, was it? Maybe Janet was the lucky one here, and would see it that way when the time came. When not dying alone meant having to watch someone you love die next to you, who really wanted that?

They could all die alone, together.

–◦–

Bethany walked home after her shift, because she could. All the first-stringers on the Beasley team lived close enough for a shoe leather commute. Call it hospital policy, and plain old good sense. They wanted to be able to assemble the top tier crash team in minutes, any time of day or night, regardless of how much rain or snow or wind or ice might get in the way.

The plan had gone into effect years ago, before the old man's health started to decline. It had begun early, as soon as the first of the city fathers from a generation ago died. They would all be sick old men one day. Some of them were already old. Others were already sick middle-aged men. Over time, they'd all done what sick old men do, eventually overcoming each and every extraordinary measure to prolong their selfish lives, until Donald Beasley was the last man standing, however unsteadily.

Children used to sing about him, years ago, and maybe still would, if only there were enough kids around to pass the song down to, the way these things used to work. But after a generation, birth rates had fallen so low, by choice, that children were now a rarity in Tanner Falls. Even they knew something was wrong, in this place where their future had been taken from them before they were born.

"Old Mad Donald had a town,
iä iä oh!
And in that town he had a goat,
iä iä oh!"

Horrible little song. You had to marvel at how jubilantly children could sing of terrible things without appreciating what they were actually about. Yet she still missed the sound of it.

There was a time when Tanner Falls had been a great place to grow up. That was how she'd experienced it. You could roam all day here, under the radar of adults. Even within town, there were pockets of woodland that felt so much farther from civilization than they really were, centuries of trees grown up around ponds and laced together by streams and paths worn smooth by bicycle tires. There were fish to catch and frogs to race. There were railroad tracks to explore, wondering where they led, hunting for treasures that might have fallen from passing trains, and if you couldn't find anything, at least there were plenty of targets daring you to throw rocks at them.

And in the city park, the concrete bandshell always seemed to smell faintly of pee—a phenomenon explained by the shards of brown glass that always seemed to reappear—but it projected your voice in a most wonderful way, especially when you bunched together with your friends to see how loudly all of you could shriek together, so that even the old people who lived by the park came out on their porches to scowl.

And when you grew old enough for four wheels instead of two, you had the drive-in theater on the edge of town, and the A&W, where carhops on skates brought trays to hang on your door, loaded with burgers and onion rings and frosted mugs of root beer. And that was good for a while, as well, until it all started to seem too small, and boredom became an enemy that could only be outrun by going anywhere else but here.

Bethany didn't have to work to remember the town that way. Because it was still the same. It was all exactly the same, as immutably fixed as the old spoke-wheeled cannon on the courthouse lawn, commemorating a war no one alive had even fought in.

Like the shop on the corner over there, Stewart Drug & Sundries. *Sundries*—who even used the word anymore? Here, they did. Across the street and down the block? Where would you even expect to find something called Franklin's Dime Store today, in this, the post-Reagan years of George Bush? But here it was, unchanged from the pictures she'd seen when her parents were children. In any direction you looked where houses stood, you would see a skyline bristling with towering TV aerials, as if no one had heard of cable. They had . . . but it had never come here.

Bethany knew enough of the world beyond to realize you were meant to remember such things fondly because they were no longer around. That was how nostalgia was supposed to work—mourning defunct businesses and outmoded ways and untamed land lost to bulldozers sent by developers who called it progress. Recalling them with a golden luster because they had meant enough to your heart once to crowd out memories of all the uglier things better off forgotten.

Like that sign painted on the huge brick side of the Tanner Hotel, smack in the heart of downtown:

NIGGER, DON'T LET THE SUN SET ON YOU HERE

Nobody wanted it. Nobody liked what it had to say, or what it said now about the town. They could scarcely bring themselves to look at it. It repelled the eye, yet resisted all efforts to erase its existence. Whitewash it, paint over it, paper over it, hang a banner across it from the roof—whatever went up wouldn't last the night. Sandblasting just made a gritty mess. Even attempts at demolition were plagued by mechanical failure.

It had been more than fifteen years since they'd given up trying.

And Tanner Falls stayed just as it was in 1969.

The hotel's insistence on cleaving to the status quo was one of the first bits of evidence that something was wrong here, early proof that someone had done a terrible thing to them all.

People change. People grow. Those who can't, die off, and with luck their worst notions die with them. Nobody wanted that hateful sign anything other than gone.

Except, maybe, for Donald Beasley and the fellow town fathers from a generation ago who had beat him to the grave.

There was a time when Tanner Falls had seemed like a great place to grow up.

What an unlikely thing to have doomed it.

⟨⟩

Matt was already home when she got there, his back-support belt hanging from its peg by the side door. His shift had an hour to go yet, and by the look of things he'd been home long enough for three cans of Iron City already. Matt was the first person she was aware of who'd figured out that once you had a job in Tanner Falls, it was impossible to lose it, a fact of life he exploited with heedless impunity. Termination was change, and hey, they couldn't have that.

So there he was, still moving the same furniture in the same warehouse that had paid him for fifteen hours a week after school in 1969, so he could save up to buy his first real guitar.

He didn't notice her, such was his focus, so for a while she watched him play. Watched him go somewhere else, the only way left to him.

He was a leftie, and so was his Les Paul. Even Bethany, who had assisted while surgeons' hands worked wonders, could never figure out how Matt could be so dexterous as to play three parts at once: rhythms on the bottom two strings, melodies on the top two, and harmony and counterpoint in the middle. The effects pedals between the guitar and amp made it even more expansive, a swirling, psychedelic storm front of thunder and squalls that climbed and plunged, that promised hope and delivered heartache.

Every generation in every town had its Matt Meadows: the guy who could've really done something, gone places, if only he'd left.

He noticed her, finally, and brought the spaceship in for a landing, the last ripple of arpeggios echoing into the sonic horizon, until the only sound left in the hush of the house was the hum of his amp.

And in every town, every girl had her own potential Matt: the guy she ended up marrying because she hadn't left either.

"That good a day, huh?" he said.

Later, they went for a walk, meandering through the neighborhood, then straying west, as she sensed he might, through neighborhoods where the houses got bigger and farther apart. He had a homing instinct, and Bethany knew where they were going to end up long before they did: a pocket of undeveloped woodland tucked alongside a tributary upstream of the falls that gave the town its name. Matt had a need to torture himself with this place, and all it had taken from them.

She regarded this the way she regarded the beer he brought with him, even on a stroll: didn't like it, but didn't object. Let Matt be Matt. Let him have what he needs to get by, because without it, it could be so much worse. Everything would be worse soon enough.

The trees were not packed tightly here, except for a few small, compact groves. It was mostly an open field, with thickets enclosing the sides like walls, and a stream ran through it. Matt and his friends used to put on safety goggles and thick sweatshirts and have BB gun fights here. Nobody had ever lost an eye, a tooth. Welts were as bad as it got. No wonder they'd gotten the idea they were blessed.

They were boys and, for a time, invincible.

In some other life, in some other town, she might have had a son just like that. She would've welcomed the prospect of fretting over every little injury and wound that, in the puzzling way of boys, grounded him with pride and meaning. She would've welcomed a daughter like this just the same.

Only once had the Ortho-Novum failed. She'd kept the procedure quiet, kept Matt in the dark altogether. Nothing good could have come of him knowing. It wasn't that he would have disagreed with her decision; more that she didn't want to give him one more thing to regret.

The hoofprints. Once here, Matt always went for the hoofprints.

It was what people called them, anyway—a row of inches-deep depressions striding along the broadest clearing in the field. They hadn't filled in during the twenty-two years they'd been there, as if something about their creation had seared them in place for all time. Life shunned them. Not even the most opportunistic weeds grew in them, or anywhere close.

Honestly, Bethany didn't know if they were hoof prints or not. They were the right shape, cloven, like mirrored images of half-moons. Then again, each one was as big around as a truck tire.

She'd been a child when the event had happened, not yet ten, and although she hadn't witnessed it, she'd heard so many stories that it felt as if she had. Not that the stories were necessarily trustworthy. People were liars, even if they didn't mean to be. By now the strands of folklore had wound so inextricably around fact that it was impossible to twist them apart and get to the truth of things.

Under the black watch of a springtime new moon, the town had been lit for an instant by a flash of light. It wasn't lightning, though—no account ever mentioned a storm. It was more like reports describing the bright death of a meteorite. Nor was it white. Blue, some said. Others insisted it was green, while still others couldn't pin down a color at all, only that they didn't find it natural.

A fearsome wind had kicked up, too, and that lasted longer. Residents in the north of town swore it blew south, while those in the south swore it blew north. On the east side, they said it swept in toward the west, and here on the west side, the direction depended on how far out people were. They couldn't all be right, unless something had punched a hole in the night, like knocking out a window in an airliner that sucked the air in from everywhere at once.

Maybe it had.

People said that something appeared through the trees that night, big enough to have appeared above even the tallest ones. Some reported a churning cloud, while others swore they witnessed vast legs striding through the woods, coarse with bristling black hair and cloven hooves. A cloud with legs? Oh, why not. Something had changed the fundamentals of reality here.

She couldn't recall the first time she heard someone, in a low voice, speak of the Black Goat of the Woods with a Thousand Young. It was just one of those things you grew up with, like Santa Claus and the Tooth Fairy.

"You think it'll come back, right here?" Matt said. "Is that the way it's supposed to happen?"

"I don't know," she said.

"Beasley, any of them, they've never said anything about what to expect? Not even at the end, or when they were doped out on the good meds?"

"No."

He looked at her in a way that made it feel like they were strangers. He was just thirty-two, and already his face was too lined. "You'd tell me, wouldn't you? You wouldn't keep it to yourself just to spare me?"

Briefly, she wondered if he knew about the abortion after all, how she'd suctioned out the life they'd created rather than see it born into a short, cruel existence as chattel.

"Most of those guys," she said, "I think they were in denial about what they did. They wouldn't admit they'd done anything at all, much less speculate about what the consequences were going to be like. Not to us, anyway. Why would they? They knew by the time it happened, they weren't going to be around to worry about it."

"Yeah, but . . . they had kids, grandkids."

"Denial can cover a lot of ground when you're determined."

They walked and he drank and they pondered issues whose understanding would forever be denied them.

"How does something like that even get started in a town like this?" Matt said. "I bet they didn't even mean it."

"I don't know about that. Whatever happened here, it didn't happen because they were half-assed about it."

"At first, I mean, when they first started. I'll bet it was like some small town, good old boy version of the Hellfire Clubs."

"Hellfire Clubs?" This was a new one. "That sounds ominous enough to me."

"It wasn't. They were just something a bunch of upper crust English and Irish politicians and other outwardly pious types did for a lark. An excuse for them to get together to frolic with whores and feel like bad boys." Matt looked at her, and couldn't have missed her puzzled expression, how this was in his storehouse of knowledge. "I used to read up on stuff like that. When I was a kid, once I got to a certain point, all my favorite bands and musicians, they seemed like there was something dangerous about them. You'd hear how they were *into* things. Secret things. It seemed like maybe they knew stuff nobody else did. It seemed like it should be true. How else could they be so good at what they did? But eventually you realize it's just an image."

"That must've been disappointing," she said.

"I don't know what was worse." He threw his empty can to the ground, because who cared anymore. "Deciding it's all bullshit? Or realizing there's something to it after all, and these goobers here were the ones who figured it out."

⟶⟵

Beasley remained stable over the days to come, but word of his condition had spread. There was no way of keeping a thing like that quiet. Everyone in Tanner Falls had a vested interest in his health, and its insistence on declining set off a fresh wave of subdued panic.

One would think they'd gotten it out of their systems years ago. But no.

At the sound of a daybreak ruckus on her day off, Bethany looked out to see the Hendersons, across the street and three houses down, stuffing their sedan with as much as it could hold. Middle-aged husband, middle-aged wife, twenty-something son still living with them because job prospects were dim. They loaded and argued, squabbled and hurried, and then, in a streak of taillights, they were gone.

As if nobody had ever thought of this before.

If it was happening on their block, she assumed that fear had pushed others across town into trying it, too, hopes bolstered by the mantra of the desperate: *Maybe this time will be different.*

Yeah, good luck with that.

Nearly everyone able-bodied enough to do it had attempted at least once over the last two decades to get away. Failed efforts, all. The early, unsuspecting ones were those who simply had normal, greener-pastures reasons to move along. The later refugees fled in terror, compelled by the very inability of others to leave, and the rumors that had started to spread about why the town shrugged off every attempt at modernity and change.

They'd tried everything from moving vans to impulse exits with little more than the clothes on their backs. They'd driven cars, taken buses, ridden motorcycles. The more adventurous ones had attempted it on foot, as if to steal away with no more noise than what their shoes made would let them pass beneath the notice of what waited and watched, ready to corral them like straying livestock.

Everyone, it seemed, had to prove it for themselves, and often more than once.

They would be back.

The Hendersons would be back.

⋅◦⋅

While Matt slept, she made coffee and set up watch from the porch that night, all cool air and the creaking of crickets. How more normal a night could anyone ask for? Except for the first aid kit by her chair, just in case.

The moon had arced halfway across the sky before things started to happen, when the streetlights flickered and dimmed. However these entities moved, it seemed to create electromagnetic disturbances. It seemed more than a simple factor of visibility. Dimensions, some speculated. They moved in and out of different dimensions.

Bethany had no recollection of the experience herself.

One moment they weren't there, and the next they were, like full-grown trees sprouted on the Hendersons' lawn. But trees didn't scuttle from one place to another, or wield their branches like arms. They were visible only for a few moments, more shadows than details. Far too tall to fit in the house, the three of them simply smashed a pair of second-story windows with their crowns of appendages and jammed their cargo through, then scuttled away from the house and faded from view as if they'd never been there at all.

Had they been aware of her watching them? One seemed to pause and turn her way, but nothing about them remotely suggested that they had faces, much less eyes.

Surprisingly few people had seen them, even though most had been carried by them. These, the general consensus went, were but a few of the Thousand Young, left behind to enforce the pact.

She grabbed her bag and hurried for the Hendersons' house. She wondered how far they'd gotten, and where the car was, if they'd ever see it again, or the possessions they'd deemed important enough to carry. If they would even care. In maintaining the status quo, vehicles didn't seem to matter. People were paramount.

They'd locked their front door when they left this morning, but had overlooked the back, so she let herself into the house that way. It was as silent as it was dark, until she blindly slapped a light switch in the kitchen, then heard them overhead as they started to awaken. They got louder as she made her way up the stairs—the weeping, the sounds on the verge of screams, as if they hadn't yet processed what had happened. These were not cries of physical pain. She was intimately familiar with those. These were worse, in a way. Pain could be managed. Hopelessness and despair came from a deeper place than nerve endings.

She found them lying huddled in the shards of their windows. Cuts, bruises, scrapes—that was the worst of it. She could treat those. The trauma might take a lot longer to get over.

More likely, Old Mad Donald would be dead before they had a chance.

◂◦▸

As went the Hendersons, so went the rest of Tanner Falls.

Few things were more contagious than panic, and few people were in a better position to gauge it than hospital staff. The accident rate spiked again, the way it did whenever fresh fears arose over Donald Beasley's mortality, and those prone to dulling their fears with drink did what drunks often do.

Had Beasley and the others foreseen *this*, in their selfishness?

The suicide rate spiked, too . . . or rather, attempted suicides. It never worked. They were brought in by paramedics and frantic families, and occasionally they came in under their own ghastly power—people who should've been dead, bodies broken, veins opened, brains exposed, yet somehow life had been refused exit. There was nothing worse to treat than screaming people who should've been in the morgue, and knew it; who wanted to be there, and were denied it.

Had Beasley and the rest meant for *this* to happen, in trying to preserve the town they'd claimed to love?

All along, townsfolk had continued to die of natural causes, but cheating was not allowed. Which didn't keep the desperate from trying anyway. They learned the folly of it no better than those who tried to flee, but at least the runners weren't shattering their bodies in the process. In trying to kill themselves, they had instead been slowly killing her sense of compassion, which made it all the easier for Bethany to hate them for it.

The adults, anyway.

It wasn't in her—not yet—to hate today's casualty. Allison, the girl's name. She'd hung from her back yard noose all night, and by the time her father discovered her this morning, her slim neck was stretched by inches. This soon, it was impossible to say if she would ever hold her head upright again. She was fifteen years old.

You did what you could. You made them comfortable. You tried not to contract their despair.

This was no way to live. For anyone.

And as she needed to do more and more, once a crisis was over, Bethany retreated into the hospital hall to shake it out. Soon there followed the smell of cigarette smoke. She'd come to welcome the stink of it, for these little moments of decompression with Dr. Richard.

"There's no meaning in this anymore," said the man who, two weeks ago, vowed to crawl inside Beasley's chest before letting him die.

For the first time in her life, she wished she smoked too, because if she did, that was exactly what she would be doing now. She pointed to the fuming stick between his fingers. "Those things'll kill you, you know."

"If only." He seemed to contemplate snuffing it out, then didn't. "That's been the idea. But I don't think cancer likes me."

"The ones who die naturally . . . do you really think they've escaped what's coming?" she asked. "Or did they just get scooped up earlier than the rest of us?"

He shrugged. "A moot point for me. It was worth a try."

The hallway windows overlooked a stretch of parking lot, and beyond that stood a neighborhood of grand old houses, and beyond that the buildings of downtown, most prominently the Tanner Hotel, with that hateful sign they could never be rid of. It was the tallest thing around. They all lived under it, no matter where their homes were.

"You know, I've never believed in life at all costs. I've been called a heretic for it. Just not by anybody whose good opinion of me mattered," Richard told her. "I could never see the value of using extraordinary measures to squeeze day after day of life out of a patient when the only thing we're accomplishing is prolonging suffering. Quality of life always seemed the better benchmark to me. Somehow I got away from that."

As they stared out the window, from somewhere beyond view came the sound of another siren.

"Is this *really* quality of life?"

"Matt, my husband, says we should go out to Route Fifteen and repaint the *Welcome to Tanner Falls* sign to read *Death Row*," she said. "But of course, that would be change."

"Can't have that." Richard clucked disapproval. "Don't most patients, when it's terminal, want to be the ones to choose when they die? I think they do."

"It's the last decision they can control. At least, it should be."

"Exactly," he said. "I think I'll have a word with the mayor."

She felt the weight of responsibility bearing down from above, from Donald Beasley's room on the second floor. How nice to be rid of it.

"Are you getting at what I think you are?" she asked.

"Probably."

So it had come to this. After a moment's shock, she was surprisingly at peace with it. Then thought of her fellow nurse, Janet, sitting watch over the most hated man in the town's history. *I'd start with his eyes . . .*

"You need to offer people more than just a choice." She couldn't believe the words coming out of her. But it had come to this. "You need to offer them participation."

◄◦►

On the day of the special election, she took another turn as watch-nurse, sitting at Donald Beasley's bedside, listening to the reassuring beep of the cardiac monitor, watching the rise and fall of his chest. Machines hummed and puffed. His face and arms were a topography of wrinkles and tubes.

He was awake, even cognizant. He studiously avoided her, preferring instead to look straight ahead at the far wall, until, after an hour of being ignored, Bethany scooted her chair close enough to lean on the bed rail, and to smell the dry musty odor of him, so he couldn't pretend her away any more.

"I get it," she told him. "I really do. How scared you all must have been. That's the last word any of you would've used with each other, or with yourselves, but that's exactly what you were. Scared. Grown men as scared as little boys when the bully shows up to take a toy truck away."

The more she had to say, the more he creaked his head away from her, toward the window and its view of the town that despised him.

"No, I get it. The whole world must've looked like it was changing all at once back then, and none of it into a place you wanted to go. Guys like my husband, they grew their hair out and started playing music you couldn't understand. Girls like me, they got birth control pills and started realizing there could be a life beyond the kitchen and the crib. We discovered drugs you shot-and-a-beer types never dreamed of."

Now that she'd started, she couldn't turn it off.

"And black people, there was no keeping them to the back of the bus anymore, was there? It didn't matter how many of their leaders bigots like you shot, or how many dogs or firehoses you turned on them, they were going to keep coming no matter what, and that must've scared you most of all."

Under his sheet, Beasley quivered with what she hoped was impotent rage.

"You armchair patriots, you had a war the country was turning against, and deep down, maybe you even suspected that the men who wanted to keep it going were lying to you whenever it fit their agenda, only you were too dug in to admit it."

She wanted tears from him. Maybe he was finally too dried out to weep.

"The world was leaving you behind. You cowards. Everything was slipping away from you. You were probably afraid someone like Charles Manson was going to show up any day, if you didn't do something. *I get it.* So if you couldn't stop the rest of the world from moving on, you wanted to stay hunkered down here in Mayberry while it did. And I can't blame you for that, for being cowards, because that's what cowards do. It's the nature of the beast to cringe."

Under the sheet, his shallow breath had visibly quickened, and the cardiac monitor pulsed more rapidly.

"But how do you go from that to sacrificing everybody else's lives just to sustain your own illusions a little longer? That's a whole different level of greed. A bunch of goddamn sociopaths, the lot of you."

If he had a massive heart attack now, that would be the most merciful thing for him. But he didn't. Good.

"How much could you all *really* have loved your town when you bargained it away to something that shouldn't even exist? Just to keep it the way it was, until the last of your little group was dead, and then to hell with the rest of us, because we were only . . . what, bargaining chips?"

At last, with effort, Beasley rolled his head back to face her.

"The Goat," he whispered, slowly, with a sound like dry reeds. "The Black Goat . . . we never thought she would answer."

Maybe Matt was right. Maybe this whole unconscionable situation began as a stupid lark. Sad little men, still frolicking with whores and pretending to be bad boys, desperate to hold onto what was theirs a little longer, a little longer.

"Here's something else you never thought of." She shouldn't have been telling him, but it seemed important that he experience dread, the same as the rest of them. "Ever since people started to figure this out, the only thing that's kept you alive and whole is their fear of what will happen when you die. But even something like that runs its course. So you may not get off as easily as you thought. You know what's happening right now? The entire town is voting on what to do with you. To see if they're willing to trade these last few days, weeks, whatever we have . . . whatever *you* have . . . for the satisfaction of making you suffer."

And there—there it was. The terror in his eyes. It was what they all needed.

"I already voted before I came to work," she said. "I voted in favor of it."

◂o▸

To the surprise of few, the special ballot initiative passed: 3,658 in favor, 2,077 against, and another 5,100 or so who didn't bother turning out one way or another.

Judgment Day, people were calling it, and preachers argued against it with all the effectiveness of street corner lunatics. The town wanted blood now. There was no divine intervention coming, so they would take what they could get.

It happened in the town square. Thousands filled the streets, while thousands more stayed home. On the courthouse lawn, they erected the platform used for speeches on Veterans Day, Memorial Day, a half-dozen different kinds of parade days.

The mayor was there to officiate, and police officers to keep order, and when Donald Beasley was brought in an ambulance, the crowd parted like water to let it through. His care team was down to just two: one physician, Dr. Richard, and one nurse, her colleague, Janet Swain. Even though they were overseeing his death, their job was still the same: to keep him alive as long as possible.

And Janet got her wish. She drew first blood, taking Beasley's left eye. He'd been strapped to a gurney that was propped upright, so the crowd could see it happen, and a roaring cheer went up at the sight of the emptied socket.

He may have been seventy-six years old, and looked at least a hundred, but he squealed like a feeble child.

Out in the crowd, a few rows away, Bethany averted her gaze to the ground and squirmed her hand into Matt's, to hold tight for as long as they had remaining.

"Do you want to leave?" he asked.

She shook her head. "If you vote for something like this, you should be prepared to see it through."

Anyone who wished it got to take a turn, ushered into a line that filed up the steps on one side of the platform, descended on the other, and as far as what happened in the middle, that was up to them. Some were content to curse Beasley, others to spit on him. The rest were not so easily sated. They slapped him, sliced him, pried off nails with pliers. They took his ears. They knocked out teeth. They ground cigarettes into his forehead, and drizzled trenches into his skin with droppers full of acid.

The cheering quit long before the line was through.

People stayed, people left, people sobbed with a thousand different sorrows. Some were sick. Others wanted to get back in the line again. A few started laughing and never stopped.

Bethany reminded herself that there was a time when Tanner Falls had been a great place to grow up. Scrape the veneer away, though, and this was what you got.

The line kept advancing even after Beasley was pronounced dead, and why not. He may have cheated them out of tomorrow, but they weren't about to let him cheat them out of one last chance to take it out on his corpse.

They had an hour, give or take, before the sky pulsed with a single flash of light—green, perhaps, or blue, or maybe it was no color in the known spectrum. A fearsome wind kicked up, blowing west, pulled toward the source of the flash. They had felt this wind before.

She clutched Matt's hand so hard it had to hurt him. Had to.

All around them, their neighbors shrieked and scattered by the hundreds, and though they were buffeted from all sides, she and Matt decided not to bother. When had running *ever* worked?

"I had this dream last night," he told her, his voice starting to shake. "It felt so real. As real as life. I dreamed I was given some sort of pipe to play for God in the chaos at the heart of the universe."

Soon it became visible over distant trees and rooftops, dark and boiling, as mercurial in appearance as a storm cloud. So this was what they had summoned, called up, bargained with . . . this, the Black Goat of the Woods with a Thousand Young. It was a deity from nightmares still seeking its hold in the world, and in the east, the north, the south, wherever people had fled, they all soon found reason to shriek there, as well. Tanner Falls resounded with it. A thousand young could round up a lot of stragglers.

"So maybe we'll be okay," Matt said.

Closer, and closer still, it rent the air with a screech as if lightning could speak. It churned with mouths that opened and closed and reappeared elsewhere in the anarchy of its form.

"Why," she said, "would you ever think that?"

Three blocks away, it detoured toward the hospital, passing by it, passing *through* it, this warehouse of failed suicides, and timeless moments later the sky disgorged a furious rain of meat and blood.

"What if it could've had us all along?" Matt said. "But waited anyway?"

It was coming.

"Why would it have done that?"

Coming for the town square.

"Maybe it was curious. Maybe it wanted to see what we would do."

It was coming, as ground and pavement alike steamed beneath its pile-driver hooves.

"And maybe now, here, today," Matt said, "some of us finally became . . . worthy."

Bethany shut her eyes as tightly as her hand held Matt's, as it bore down on them with the sound and fury of a cyclone.

At last. At last. At long, elusive last . . .

It was time to leave home.

HONORABLE MENTIONS

Aickman, Robert, "The Strangers" (novella), *The Strangers*.

Ballingrud, Nathan, "The Visible Filth" (novella), This is Horror! Chapbook.

Bartlett, Matthew M., "Rangel," *Dim Shores*, July.

Braunbeck, Gary A., "Paper Cuts," *Seize the Night*.

Bruce, Sadie, "Little Girls in Bone Museums," *F&SF*, March/April.

Bulkin, Nadia, "Seven Minutes in Heaven," *Aickman's Heirs*.

Bulkin, Nadia, "Violet is the Color of Your Energy," *She Walks in Shadows*.

Cadigan, Pat, "Chilling," *Horrorology*.

Campbell, Ramsey, "Her Face," *The Burning Maiden 2*.

Chizmar, Richard, "Last Words," *The Burning Maiden 2*.

Clark, Stephen, "Lithe Tenant," *Soliloquy for Pan*.

Connelly, John, "Razorshins," *Black Static #47/Night Music*.

Devenport, Emily, "Dr. Polingyouma's Machine," *Uncanny #3*.

Duffy, Steve, "Even Clean Hands Can Do Damage," *Supernatural Ta*, 30, Autumn.

Files, Gemma, "Hairwork," *She Walks in Shadows*.

Ford, Jeffrey, "Word Doll," *The Doll Collection*.

Halsall, Rachel, "Hunting," *Wild Things*.

Hodge, Brian, "Eternal, Ever Since Wednesday," *Better Weird*.

Hodge, Brian, "One Possible Shape of Things to Come," *Eulogies III*.

Johnstone, Tom, "What I found in the Shed," *Supernatural Tales 31*.

Jones, Stephen Graham, "Daniel's Theory About Dolls," *The Doll Collection*.

Kadrey, Richard, "Ambitious Boys Like You," *The Doll Collection*.

Kim, Alice Sola, "A Residence for Friendless Ladies," *F&SF*, March/April.

Langan, John, "Corpsemouth," *The Monstrous*.

Lebbon, Tim, "Skin and Bone," *The Doll Collection*.

McAllister, Bruce, "Dog," Tor.com, March 25.

McGroarty, David, "McBIRDY," *Strange Tales V*.

McMahon, Gary, "Unicorn Meat," *SQ Magazine* #20.

Miéville, China, "Listen the Birds," *Conjunctions* #64.

Muir, Tamsyn, "The Deepwater Bride," *F&SF*, July/August.

Newman, Kim, "Guignol" (novella), *Horrorology*.

Oates, Joyce Carol, "The Doll-Master," *The Doll Collection*.

Padgett, Jon, "The Secret of Ventriloquism" *Lovecraft Ezine* #35.

Palahniuk, Chuck, "Red Sultan's Big Boy." *Make Something Up*.

Rabinowitz, Rosanne, "The Lady in the Yard," *Soliloquy for Pan*.

Schliewe, Jeremy, "Distance," *Supernatural Tales 29*, Spring.

Schweitzer, Darrell, "Were-?" *Flesh Like Smoke*.

Shearman, Robert, "Blood," *Seize the Night*.

Tanzer, Molly, "Do Not Loiter in the Glen," *The Burning Maiden 2*.

Taylor, Lucy, "In the Cave of the Delicate Singers," Tor.com, July 27.

Tremblay, Paul, "The Ice Tower," *The Burning Maiden 2*.

Vernon, Ursula, "Wooden Feathers," *Uncanny 7*.

Volk, Stephen, "The Shug Monkey," *Professor Challenger: New Worlds, Lost Places*.

Wagner, Wendy, "Three Small Pieces of Pumpkin Pie," *Farrago's Wainscott* #15, July.

Warren, Kaaron, "Mine Intercom," *The Review of Australian Fiction*, #6 vol 13.

Wehunt, Michael, "The Devil Under the Maison Blue," *The Dark* #10.

Wong, Alyssa, "Hungry Daughters of Starving Mothers," *Queers Destroy Horror*.

Youers, Rio, "Separator," *Seize the Night*.

ABOUT THE AUTHORS

Kelley Armstrong is the author of the Cainsville modern gothic series and the Age of Legends YA fantasy trilogy. Past works include the Otherworld urban fantasy series, the Darkest Powers & Darkness Rising teen paranormal trilogies, the Nadia Stafford crime trilogy, and the co-written Blackwell Pages middle-grade fantasy trilogy.

Armstrong lives in southwestern Ontario with her family.

"We Are All Monsters Here" was originally published in *Seize the Night: News Tales of Vampiric Terror*, edited by Christopher Golden.

—◦—

Stephen Bacon's fiction has been published in *Black Static, Cemetery Dance, Shadows & Tall Trees, Postscripts, Crimewave, Terror Tales of Yorkshire,* and many other magazines and anthologies. His debut collection, *Peel Back the Sky*, was published in 2012 by Gray Friar Press, and was nominated for a British Fantasy Society award.

He lives in South Yorkshire, UK, with his wife and two sons. His website is www.stephenbacon.co.uk.

His novella, *Laudanum Nights*, is due to be published by Hersham Horror Books in 2016.

"Lord of the Sand" was originally published in *The Eleventh Black Book of Horror*, edited by Charles Black.

—◦—

Dale Bailey's new collection, *The End of the End of Everything: Stories*, came out in the spring. A novel, *The Subterranean Season*, will follow this fall. He has published three previous novels, *The Fallen, House of Bones*, and *Sleeping Policemen* (with Jack Slay Jr.), and one previous collection of short fiction, *The Resurrection Man's Legacy: And Other Stories*.

His work has been a finalist for the Shirley Jackson Award and the Nebula Award, among others, and he won the International Horror Guild Award for his novelette "Death and Suffrage," later adapted for Showtime under the title *Masters of Horror*.

He lives in North Carolina with his family.

"Snow" was originally published in *Nightmare*, #33, June.

⤙ο►

Laird Barron is the author of several books, including *The Croning, Occultation*, and *The Beautiful Thing That Awaits Us All*. His work has also appeared in many magazines and anthologies. An expatriate Alaskan, Barron currently resides in upstate New York.

"In a Cavern, in a Canyon" was originally published in *Seize the Night: News Tales of Vampiric Terror*, edited by Christopher Golden.

⤙ο►

Ray Cluley's work has appeared in various magazines and anthologies. It has been reprinted in Ellen Datlow's *Best Horror of the Year*, as well as Steve Berman's *Wilde Stories 2013: The Year's Best Gay Speculative Fiction*, and his work has been translated into French and Polish. He won the British Fantasy Award for Best Short Story in 2013 and was nominated for Best Novella in 2015. His collection, *Probably Monsters*, is available now from ChiZine Press.

"Indian Giver" was originally published in *Probably Monsters*.

⤙ο►

Neil Gaiman is the best-selling author of novels for both children and adults, including *American Gods, The Ocean at the End of the Lane*, and *The Graveyard Book* (the only book to win both the Newbery and Carnegie Medals). Several of his books, including *Coraline* and *Stardust*, have been made into major motion pictures, and future screen adaptations of his work include a television series of *American Gods* and an adaptation of his short stories, *Neil Gaiman's Likely Stories*.

Neil is also the writer of the groundbreaking *Sandman* comic series, which he recently revisited for the first time in many years with *The Sandman Overture*, the *New York Times* bestselling prequel. His newest book is a collection of his non-fiction, *The View from the Cheap Seats*.

His hobbies include singing obscure English nursery rhymes and changing diapers.

"Black Dog" was originally published in his collection *Trigger Warning: Short Fiction and Disturbances*.

◄◦►

Brian Hodge is one of those people who always has to be making something. So far, he's made ten novels, with number eleven due out in late 2016. He's also authored over 120 shorter works and four full-length collections. His first collection, *The Convulsion Factory*, was ranked by critic Stanley Wiater among the 113 best books of modern horror.

Other upcoming works for 2016 include "The Weight of the Dead," slated for June from *Tor.com*, and "The Burning Times v2.0," in *2113: Stories Inspired by the Music of Rush*.

He lives in Colorado, where he also likes to make music and photographs; loves everything about organic gardening except the thieving squirrels; and trains in Krav Maga and kickboxing, which are of no use at all against the squirrels.

Connect through his web site (www.brianhodge.net) or Facebook (www.facebook.com/brianhodgewriter).

"This Stagnant Breath of Change" was originally published in *Shadows over Main Street*, edited by Doug Murano and D. Alexander Ward.

◄◦►

Tom Johnstone's fiction has appeared in various anthologies and magazines, including the *Ninth, Tenth* and *Eleventh Black Books of Horror, Brighton—The Graphic Novel*, and *Wicked Women*, as well as *Strange Tales V, Supernatural Tales*, and *Shroud Magazine*.

In addition, he co-edited the British Fantasy Award-nominated austerity-themed anthology *Horror Uncut: Tales of Social Insecurity and Economic Unease* with the late Joel Lane.

He lives with his partner and two children in Brighton, where he works as a gardener for the local authority. Find out more about Johnstone's fiction at: tomjohnstone.wordpress.com.

"Slaughtered Lamb" was originally published in *The Eleventh Black Book of Horror*, edited by Charles Black.

◂◦▸

Stephen Graham Jones is the author of sixteen novels and six story collections. His most recent is *Mongrels*, from William Morrow. Stephen lives in Boulder, Colorado.

"Universal Horror" was originally published in *October Dreams II: A Celebration of Halloween*, edited by Richard Chizmar and Robert Morrish.

◂◦▸

Kate Jonez is the Shirley Jackson and Bram Stoker Award-nominated author of *Candy House* and *Ceremony of Flies*. Stories of hers have appeared in *Black Static*, *Pseudopod*, and several other anthologies.

She is also the chief editor at Omnium Gatherum, a multiple award-nominated press dedicated to publishing unique dark fantasy, weird fiction, and horror. Jonez is a student of all things scary and when she isn't writing she loves to collect objects for her cabinet of curiosities and research obscure and strange historical figures. She lives in Los Angeles with a very nice man and two little dogs who are also very nice but could behave a little bit better.

"All the Day You'll Have Good Luck" was originally published in *Black Static* #47.

◂◦▸

John Langan is the author of three collections, *Sefira and Other Betrayals* (Hippocampus 2016), *The Wide, Carnivorous Sky and Other Monstrous Geographies*, and *Mr. Gaunt and Other Uneasy Encounters*.

He has written a novel, *House of Windows*, and with Paul Tremblay, co-edited an anthology, *Creatures: Thirty Years of Monsters*.

He's one of the founders of the Shirley Jackson Award and served as a juror during its first three years.

He lives in New York's Hudson Valley with his wife, younger son, and a growing collection of swords.

"Underground Economy" was originally published in *Aickman's Heirs*, edited by Simon Strantzas.

◄◦►

Carmen Maria Machado's debut short story collection, *Her Body and Other Parties*, is forthcoming from Graywolf Press in Fall 2017. She is a fiction writer, critic, and essayist whose work has appeared in *The New Yorker*, *Granta*, *The Paris Review*, *AGNI*, NPR, *Los Angeles Review of Books*, *VICE*, and elsewhere. Her stories have been reprinted or are forthcoming in several anthologies, including *Best American Science Fiction & Fantasy 2015* and *Year's Best Weird Fiction*.

She has been the recipient of many fellowships, including the Elizabeth George Foundation Fellowship and the Michener-Copernicus Fellowship, and has been nominated for both a Nebula Award and a Shirley Jackson Award. She is a graduate of the Iowa Writers' Workshop and the Clarion Science Fiction & Fantasy Writers' Workshop, and lives in Philadelphia with her partner.

"Descent" was originally published in *Nightmare* February #29.

◄◦►

Gary McMahon is the award-winning author of nine novels and several short story collections and novellas. His latest novel releases are *The End* and *The Bones of You*. His acclaimed short fiction has been reprinted in various *Year's Best* volumes.

Gary lives with his family in West Yorkshire, where he trains in Shotokan karate and cycles up and down the Yorkshire hills, screaming and laughing at the rain-swept landscape as he chases down new story ideas. His website is www.garymcmahon.com.

"My Boy Builds Coffins" was originally published in *Black Static* #46.

◄◦►

Tamsyn Muir is a writer from Auckland, New Zealand. Her short-form fiction has appeared in such publications as *Nightmare* magazine, *Weird Tales*, *The Magazine of Fantasy & Science Fiction*, and *Clarkesworld*.

"The Woman in the Hill" was originally published in *Dreams from the Witch House: Female Voices of Lovecraftian Horror*, edited by Lynne Jamneck.

⟶

Adam Nevill was born in Birmingham, England, in 1969 and grew up in England and New Zealand. He is the author of the supernatural horror novels *Banquet for the Damned, Apartment 16, The Ritual, Last Days, House of Small Shadows, No One Gets Out Alive,* and *Lost Girl.* In 2012, 2013, and 2015 his novels were the winners of the August Derleth Award for Best Horror Novel. *The Ritual* and *Last Days* were also awarded Best in Category: Horror, by R.U.S.A.

Adam lives in Devon and can be contacted through www.adamlgnevill.com.

"Hippocampus" was originally published in *Terror Tales of the Ocean,* edited by Paul Finch.

⟶

Reggie Oliver is an actor, director, playwright, and author of fiction. His published work includes six plays, two novels, six volumes of short stories, including *Mrs Midnight* (2012 winner of Children of the Night Award for best work of supernatural fiction), and the biography of Stella Gibbons, *Out of the Woodshed.*

His stories have appeared in over fifty anthologies. *The Sea of Blood,* selected stories including some new, was published in 2015. To be published in 2016: *The Boke of the Divill* (a novel from Dark Renaissance), *Holidays from Hell* (new collection of stories, Tartarus), and *The Hauntings at Tankerton Park and How They Got Rid of Them* (children's book with illustrations by the author, Zagava Press).

"The Rooms Are High" was originally published in Oliver's collection, *The Sea of Blood.*

⟶

Priya Sharma is a doctor who works in the UK. Her short stories have appeared in various places including *Black Static, Interzone,* and on *Tor. com.* She's been reprinted in many "Best of" anthologies. She is terrified of snakes, but while researching this story came to understand that they really are fabulous beasts.

She has a story about crows ("The Crow Palace") out early 2017 in Ellen Datlow's anthology *Black Feathers.*

More about her writing can be found at www.priyasharmafiction.wordpress. com.

"Fabulous Beasts" was originally published on *Tor.com* (July 27, 2015).

⤙⚬⤚

Steve Rasnic Tem's latest collection is *Out of the Dark: A Storybook of Horrors* from Centipede, presenting the best of his uncollected horror. In January 2016, Solaris will bring out his dark SF novel *Ubo*, a meditation on violence as seen through the eyes of some of history's most violent figures.

"Between the Pilings" was originally published in *Innsmouth Nightmares*, edited by Lois Gresh.

⤙⚬⤚

Letitia Trent's most recent novel is *Almost Dark*. Her previous books include the novel *Echo Lake*, the poetry collection *One Perfect Bird*, and the chapbooks *The Women in Charge* and *You aren't in this movie*. Her fiction, poetry, and nonfiction have appeared in publications such as *Fence*, *Pantheon*, *The Journal*, *Menacing Hedge*, and the *Daily Beast*. Trent lives with her husband, son, and three black cats.

"Wilderness" was originally published in first published in *Exigencies*, edited by Richard Thomas.

⤙⚬⤚

Stephanie M. Wytovich is an instructor of English by day and a horror writer by night. She is the Poetry Editor for Raw Dog Screaming Press, a book reviewer for *Nameless Magazine*, and the assistant to Carlow University's MFA program for Creative Writing. She is a graduate of Seton Hill University's MFA program for Writing Popular Fiction.

Wytovich's three poetry collections, *Hysteria: A Collection of Madness*, *Mourning Jewelry, and An Exorcism of Angels*, were all Stoker Award nominees.

Her debut novel, *The Eighth*, will be out in 2016 from Dark Regions Press. Follow Wytovich at stephaniewytovich.blogspot.com and on twitter @JustAfterSunset.

"The 21st Century Shadow" was originally published in *Shadows over Main Street*, edited by Doug Murano and D. Alexander Ward.

ACKNOWLEDGMENT OF COPYRIGHT

ABOUT THE EDITOR

Ellen Datlow has been editing science fiction, fantasy, and horror short fiction for over thirty years. She currently acquires short fiction for Tor.com. In addition, she has edited more than sixty science fiction, fantasy, and horror anthologies, including *Lovecraft's Monsters*, *Fearful Symmetries*, *The Monstrous*, and *The Doll Collection*.

She's won multiple World Fantasy Awards, Locus Awards, Hugo Awards, Stoker Awards, International Horror Guild Awards, Shirley Jackson Awards, and the 2012 Il Posto Nero Black Spot Award for Excellence as Best Foreign Editor. Datlow was named recipient of the 2007 Karl Edward Wagner Award, given at the British Fantasy Convention for "outstanding contribution to the genre," was honored with the Life Achievement Award given by the Horror Writers Association, in acknowledgment of superior achievement over an entire career, and has been honored with the Life Achievement Award by the World Fantasy Convention.

She lives in New York and co-hosts the monthly Fantastic Fiction Reading Series at KGB Bar. More information can be found at www.datlow.com, on Facebook, and on twitter as @EllenDatlow.